BENEATH A PALE SKY

"The stories in Beneath a Pale Sky are elegant, unsettling, and beautifully wrought. One of the best collections I've read in a long while."

CHRISTOPHER GOLDEN

"Highlights the author's skill at capturing disasters, gore, and cosmic horror."

PUBLISHERS WEEKLY

also by Philip Fracassi

Behold the Void
Sacculina
Shiloh
Commodore

BENEATH A PALE SKY

PHILIP FRACASSI

LETHE
PRESS

For Laird Barron

"...there is a certain place in any discussion of any one thing in existence where knowledge ends and the Great Vacuum extends on out into infinity."

Ray Bradbury

INTRODUCTION

THE SCARIEST HORROR story is the one told by a stranger on the front porch of a house party, plastic cup in hand, the two of you crossing paths circumstantially, both out to get some air, the music loud inside. He asks what you do. For people like me and Philip Fracassi, the subject of horror stories is never more than a few exchanged pleasantries away. But even if you don't live in the genre, the subject comes up. Often, the stranger tells you his ghost story. It's never more than a few sentences. He was gathering laundry from the basement. Saw his dead aunt peer around the furnace. She winked at him.

You say wow.

He says yeah.

Then he's off, back inside, leaving you alone to fill in the gaps.

You can almost see the bar graph, can't you? Dependent lines: the briefer the story, the more room to imagine horrors of your own. Some might say the horror story works best the smaller it is. Our stranger on the porch has given us more story than he knows: he's the main character, after all, and speaking so suddenly about ghosts sets the mood. Yet, us readers, we long for more. At least a little more. Sometimes a lot. We want to spend time, as much time as we can, inside that scary story. Yet, we want that front porch mood to remain...

Where to look?

For a lot of us, the novel is home. The horror novel. And if the author fails at maintaining the menace for more than 300 pages? That's alright, we give him or her a pass, it's not an easy thing to do. But still, we jones, we fiend, we start to explore avenues where the scare is less diluted, less cluttered, less buried. The novella, we say. The novella! Without the full diversions of the novel, and with less expectation of things being neatly summed up, we find in the novella something closer to the experience we might find outside a house party.

Yet… even a hundred pages starts to feel too long. The brevity of the stranger's story is never entirely out of our minds. Neither is the feeling it gave us.

His dead aunt.

Peering.

Winking.

Give us *that!* we say. Without all the build-up, without all the plot! Give us the smallest thing you got.

But it still has to scare us apart.

So, we turn, at last, to the short story.

And it's here where we unearth horror at its most potent.

If you've spent a lifetime in books, you've no doubt read more than a handful of short story collections. Some readers explore this world exclusively, but most of us spend our time in Novel Land, with vacations to where the short stuff lives. Yet, every time we go, we ask ourselves why we don't just move there. Buy a bungalow. Make a friend. Become a regular at the short story bars.

I have a theory about this.

I can easily remember reading Ray Bradbury's *The October Country* in various settings in Michigan, each of those places fading into nothingness as Bradbury delivered unbelievable punch after punch. I started to get excited, in the nervy way, nearly manic: here wasn't just a *book*, but a series of ideas so fierce, the electricity of the first story hadn't worn off by the second. Bradbury simply didn't let up. The same thing happened, the same state achieved, with Penguin's *American Supernatural Tales*. I made notes after each entry, bullet-point ideas of my own. That single collection inspired a dozen novel ideas to come. M.R. James's *Collected Ghost Stories* was another. Algernon Blackwood, too. The unforgettable fire of Edgar Allan Poe.

I learned from these books and others: the short story collection was where the real writers told tales. And anybody who could pull off a complete collection, cover to cover, without a dip on the way, was someone to applaud.

Applaud, then, for Philip Fracassi.

Beneath a Pale Sky belongs in that fantastic club.

Prepare yourself for this book. It won't come at you with a sledgehammer, it's not that kind of horror, but you'd be nuts to call what happens in these pages *quiet*. And while I'm not going to go through the book story by story, I'll try my best to express how it's going to make you feel.

Is it possible Fracassi grouped these particular stories together because he discovered in them a similar sound, a similar depth? It feels that way. It feels like he recognized the intoxicating combination that occurs in each: small scenario, enormous repercussions. In these pages we've got friends who ought to be lovers, earthquakes and drunk pilots, all the passion of life balancing atop the Ferris Wheel. Herein lies friends of the Devil and greedy scientists, mental homes and the music of Hell.

Was Fracassi aware of the *collection* as he pieced this together? Was Bradbury ever aware of his? Because the best collections are the ones where the stories work in tandem, the stories play as a team. This is not to say Fracassi left easter eggs of one story in another, but rather, *Beneath a Pale Sky* rolls out like music. Suggestions of early themes grow-up by the end, and the echoes of the those we began with never entirely go away.

I realized early on that this was a book for the ages. I tweeted as much and I privately wrote some friends. I wrote Philip Fracassi, too, story by story, as I finished reading them, unable to stop myself, not wanting to stop myself, aware that I was in rare hands. Like the collections that electrified me in the past, *Beneath a Pale Sky* doesn't let up, and it's not difficult to imagine these stories populating an entire season of an anthology television show on their own.

You're probably at the point where you want to read these for yourself. Great. I'll step aside here. But first, a prediction:

You will read these stories, and you will think of them the next time you find yourself on the front porch of a party, a stranger two-sheets to the wind, suggesting he saw his deceased aunt winking from behind a furnace. But this time you will stop the stranger as he heads back into the house. You will think of Philip Fracassi's stories and you will say, *Wait a minute. Hold on. I've got one for you, too...*

Josh Malerman
Michigan

HARVEST

THE BLUE SKY was vast. Cornstalks reached to the heavens, unfurled green leaves turned upward like praying hands with crispy brown fingertips. Late September heat simmered and circled.

The antlers of the male flower pushed through the top of the stalks. Pollen lifted from the knobby stems in the autumnal breeze, clung to the feet of hungry insects, found the silky threads of female hair in a five-hundred-acre mating dance. The semi-sheathed beards took it in, the shy ladies fertilized, ready to birth budding shafts of sweet corn. A joyous miracle that would be plowed, harvested, and repeated. The time for reaping was near. Winter was still far off, but summer had been long left behind.

At the edge of the harvest rested a white church, its broad plank siding bright and clean. The tall arched windows marched along its sides were stretched shadows tinged with midnight blue where hazy sunlight caught the glass. Out front, an ancient gnarled oak craned up past the steeple, thick leafy arms stretched outward in every direction. Its massive trunk stood near the entrance, where it had endured for more than 150 years; settled firmly on its roots, stealing life from the soil, its weathered bark far older than

5

the church and even the immense crop surrounding it. But age and frailty are close friends, and a poison ran through the great tree. Dehydration and decay festered in its veins. Leaves, most the size of an adult hand, lay strewn along its base, browned and weathered. The arching branches still clung tightly to an assortment of summer holdovers, the clingers-on dangling lifelessly as ancient Chinese fans, adorning the dying tree with a ghastly dystopic headdress, the entire milieu a symbol for the end of all things, or at the very least a season. And yet the great tree stood, stubborn, clinging to life and pride like a dying giant in a fairy tale.

And on this autumnal day it watched, wearily, as a broken line of cars approached from the distance, each chased by a cloud of dust. A spattering of parishioners en route for the ceremony to come.

CARRIE WORE WHITE and stared dazedly through a church window at the seemingly infinite army of marching green stalks. At the edge of the crop she observed a clay-colored cottontail slip briefly onto the perimeter of shorn grass, sniff the air, then shoot back into the folds of the cornfield. Mother sipped coffee in the corner, a napkin between palm and cup ready to catch any wayward drop that might infect her best yellow dress. Carrie's bridesmaids wore cauliflower blue silk with a lace top and only one shoulder exposed, a concession she'd made in exchange for serving liquor at the reception. Beth and Trish took turns pouting lips into the vestry's lone mirror, smoothing eyebrows, tucking loose hairs. They were chatting enthusiastically, but it was white noise to Carrie. Static.

Trish had flown in from school. She was sweet and harmless, fat and plain. Beth was pretty but petulant, liked to mouth-off to impress whoever was within earshot. She'd slept with the groom once, before he and Carrie had been serious, and both girls had been forced to swallow resentment like sin-eaters in order to remain friends. The three women had known each other since preschool but were not as close as some might believe. Deep down, Carrie had secretly hoped they wouldn't come at all but… well, here they were.

The vestry was small, and after a few hours pacing its confines, primping and filling the enclosed air with banal gossip, Carrie had begun to feel claustrophobic. Staring out the window at the navy-blue sky and bushy green field eased her mind and settled her nerves. She noticed clouds plotting in the far distance, rubbing shoulders like hazy mountaintops...

Navy blue? Carrie thought, distracted from her inner musings. Had the sky really turned a shade darker than it was only minutes before?

Carrie closed her eyes and cursed under her breath. She prayed for a beautiful day. A perfect day. She also prayed for peace, and perhaps a little quiet, as the constant attention from her attendants wore thin. Thankfully her overly-fretful nana, the most vocal and challenging of the small group, had left to secure arrangements in the sanctuary. Carrie figured she had Pastor Willard's elbow by now, pacing him through his well-worn Book of Common Prayer to steel his resolve against adding any modern flourishes to the traditional ceremony language.

"Carrie, darling." Mother. "You should eat something."

"I've had a sip of wine, and Nana brought lemon cookies. I've had three." Carrie patted the taut tummy of her embroidered wedding gown. "Besides, I'm too nervous. I'll eat at the reception."

"If you don't faint first. Such a humid autumn, my god," her mother said, patting her throat and chin with a tissue. "Girls, go find a pitcher of water. Some iced tea." They laughed and ignored her.

It was warm, especially for the season, but Carrie thought *stifling* the more appropriate adjective. Thankfully, the church had brought a fan into the vestry which pushed the heavy flower-scented air around enough to keep any dew drops of perspiration bursting from her pores. Despite her gown being full-sleeved and high-necked, the fabric along the arms and shoulders was light – a semi-opaque lace – that allowed her tanned skin to breathe. And despite what she told her mother, she wasn't nervous in the slightest.

Anxious, perhaps.

Parker was a good man. Handsome. He would run his father's (quite profitable) wheat mill one day – the largest in Gehenna County – securing their financial future. Her anxiety stemmed not from her future husband, or her tedious mother, but from a nagging, damnable black string which tugged at the back of her mind. A black string that wore overalls socially and knew all of her most private thoughts. Her secrets. A six-foot problem with blue eyes and haystack-colored hair.

Eli.

Carrie's heart beat faster at the thought of him, and she clenched a tight fist, shut her eyes, said another prayer. *Stay out of my head,* she thought, knowing the futility of the command. Because he *was* there, swimming inside her, swirling around her thoughts and kicking at her heart; a ghostly presence that carried a worn suitcase bursting with a lifetime of memories, tied shut with that same dark string.

Then, without her consent, that black string gave a tug... and slid free.

THE KIDS WERE hidden from the larger world beneath a leaf-strewn canopy and the heavy shadow of surrounding trees. Storm clouds laid thick along the sky's underbelly like smoke from a house fire. In the distance, thunder rumbled.

"God wants in."

Carrie rolled her eyes at the joke for the hundredth time. Felt like the millionth.

"So let him in, dummy," she snapped, her bare feet folded beneath her knees in the matted tall grass. She picked at the rip in her dress, the fabric covering her bony knee having been rent by a splintered branch while she'd climbed a low-armed mulberry.

Eli lay supine, eyes studying the arching branches high above. He wore overalls and a white T-shirt stained with a young boy's persistence. His feet were bare like Carrie's, his heels blackened and rough. His light-colored hair was buzzed to stubble because of high heat and a recent bout with lice, his soft face reddened by a receding summer.

The makeshift creek whispered along beside them, a narrow ribbon brought to life by the wet season. The stream connected Jackson Pond to a state park miles away. When it rose high enough it carried trout. Eli's daddy had diverted the creek so it split the property between their two crops, running it through a dense thicket of basswoods, shrubby oaks and sugar maples. It also created a park for the children. A living playground of trees to climb, dirt to furrow for planting flower and corn seeds, a cold stream to mine for smooth rocks and minnows.

Rainfall pattered against the leaves that surrounded them, tapped against the covering above. Thunder rumbled a second time, rolling across the broiling gray sky from east to west. Carrie didn't hear the crack of distant lightning, so decided they'd stay a bit longer before heading home to schoolwork and chores. She slapped Eli's knee and he smiled at her.

"What?"

"Do something."

"Like what?"

She shrugged, scratched behind her ear, and looked around for inspiration. Her eyes fell upon the water, then twitched back to Eli, who watched her closely. She nodded toward the water and he gave a half-grin, then focused his eyes on the stream.

Carrie waited. After a few seconds, she felt a sharp gust of wind puff against her back, heard a whisper in the trees. A cool breeze tangled around her bare legs like serpents made of air, and she stared in fascination as the water of the creek began to bubble furiously, then rise in thin pillars from the surface, one-by-one, to form a line six-long and high as her hips. The pillars bent at their midsections in unison, forming a bow of water-stick soldiers awaiting her command. She giggled as more tufts of wind tossed her hair, struck her face in pockets like dissolving cotton.

Eli sat up and the water-stick soldiers collapsed into trickling chaos, the pillows of breeze vanished, and the air lost its magic. He smiled, pleased with himself. Pleased he made her happy. She started to speak, but he held up a hand, stalling her.

"Watch," he said, and began to lightly rub the pads of his thumb and pointing-finger together, his eyes intent on the motion. "Just watch," he repeated.

"I'm watching, geez," she said, but despite her tone was captivated. She'd hadn't seen this one.

A tendril of smoke rose from between his fingertips. In the next moment, there was a pop of spark and a soft snap of air, as if a million oxygen particles had simultaneously broken apart. A yellow sliver of fire rose from the motion of his fingers, then grew.

It reddened, fattened, and flickered. Slowly, as if releasing a butterfly without wanting to damage its wings, Eli spread his fingers apart so they splayed flat. He held his palm up to her; the lick of dancing flame lifting from his skin reflected in her wide brown eyes, her dark pupils quivering with an orange inner-light.

The storm outside their shelter grew. The wind beat more fiercely against the trees, battered and twisted the sheltering leaves above. Rain infiltrated their harbor. Fat cold drops dimpled the creek, tickled their faces, soaked into their hair.

"Eli…" she said.

He shook his head, eyes narrowed with concentration, then gently lowered his hand to the lip of the brook. He brought his face toward his palm – to within inches of the flame – and softly *blew*.

The fire, now deep red and yellow-hatted at its curling top, slid smoothly off his skin and onto the creek. It rested atop the surface, bobbing and jerking in place with the motion of the cuts and shimmers of the water. It bumped and swayed, but did not go out.

"How are you doing that?" she asked, a stunned whisper.

Eli studied the flame, eyes never leaving his new creation. "Air, mostly," he said.

Carrie got onto hands and knees, settled in beside the warmth of her friend. Together they watched the buoyed flame, now three inches in height and wide as a big toe. She rested her fingers lightly on the top of his wrist.

"Eli," she said. "Do it again."

TWENTY MINUTES LATER, they knew it was time to go. The storm had picked up and the wind and rain fell through the barrier of leaves with ease. Lightning had flickered in the distance, snapping the air like a whip, and was encroaching.

They stood shoulder-to-shoulder, not wanting to leave but knowing they could not stay. At their feet the stream continued mindlessly along its path, unaware of its riders.

Twenty flames flickered and danced atop the water. The children watched, transfixed. One in giddy awe, one in deep concentration. The light and heat of the flames were enough to warm their bare feet, illuminate his blue knees, her yellow dress. She imagined small fish rising to try and eat the fire, finding heat and pain instead. It was both cruel and beautiful.

"Okay?" he said, and she heard the strain in his voice. A tremor she hadn't noticed in her excitement. She looked at his face. What she thought to be rain was actually beads of sweat dotting his temple, forehead and cheeks. He looked pale in the gray-green light of their shadowed domain. She rested a hand on his back, as if her support would add to his strength.

"Okay, Eli," she said. "Let it go."

He exhaled, and she watched with wonder and sadness as the flames, as one, slipped down into the cold stream, and were smothered.

PARKER TOOK A long swig from the bottle and passed it back to his brother.

Too much, he thought absently, his reason a fluttering veil. He felt the whiskey go to his head and swore it off until the ceremony was over. The guys were getting shitty and that was fine with him. He'd be getting shitty, as well, if he could. But that would not go over well with Carrie, or her mother and nana, who, frankly, could both be pains in the ass.

"Guys, go easy," he said half-heartedly, wondering if Brock was going to do something stupid to ruin his wedding. Parker had already caught him taking a piss in one of Pastor Willard's potted floor plants, in whose office they'd been caged until the guests arrived. Parker thought maybe the plant was fake, and that the growing stain in the Berber carpet beneath the pot would be a tricky problem to explain. Brock was younger, but he was a big guy, a former all-state offensive guard who could lift a hay bale on each shoulder and carry them around easy-as-you-please. Parker had seen him do the same thing with giggling, kicking girls on a hundred youth-fueled nights under the lights, under the stars. To make things worse, Brock had a devil in his heart, a temper like no one Parker had ever known, and it was best not to chastise him when he'd been drinking. Henry and Tuck were easier, more manageable. They weren't smart or dumb, just bored and happy to go along with whatever made their little corner of flat-assed, cornfield-carpeted Iowa even a smidge more interesting on a day-to-day basis.

Brock tucked the fifth into the crook of his elbow and pressed it to his chest like a slippery baby. "Don't worry, Parker, we're not going to get drunk before your very first wedding."

Tuck snickered, and Henry went to the door for a peek at the church lobby. "Looks like folks are showing up, Park. Aren't you supposed to greet them, say hello?"

"No," Parker said, standing too quickly and fighting a wave of drunken dizziness before finding his feet. "That's you guys. You two are supposed to be ushers. Remember the rehearsal?"

Tuck pulled mints from the sport coat of his tuxedo. "Here," he said, taking two and passing the tin to Henry, who followed suit. "Don't worry, Parker," Tuck said, standing and dusting off his pants. "We got this."

"Thanks."

The mints got put away and the two groomsmen left the office. Tuck was about to close the door when he stuck his head back in, an eat-shit smile on his face. "Besides, smells like piss in here."

The door shut, and Parker sat back down, unsure why he'd stood in the first place. Brock sniffed loudly, then chuckled. "Shit, sure does. Sorry Park."

Parker waved dismissively. His stomach rumbled and acid coated his throat. The tuxedo was hot and the collar chafed his neck. The air-conditioned office *did* stink, and it was getting warmer by the second. Too many bodies.

"Crank the AC, huh?" he said. "And find me a glass of water, will you? I'm dying here."

Brock nodded, handed him the bottle, which was unpleasantly warm to the touch. He went to the straining window unit and turned the temperature knob all the way down. "I'll be right back. Drink that, relax."

Parker thought that if he drank the hot whiskey in his hands he's absolutely, one-hundred-percent, sure-as-shit be puking up his breakfast in the same planter Brock had recently whizzed in. Nonetheless, he nodded to his little brother, his best man.

Brock left, and finally – *thank God!* – Parker was alone. He set the bottle on the pastor's mahogany desk and lowered his face into his sweaty hands. He shook his head and moaned, felt revulsion slither through his guts, swimming through intestinal channels of black doubt.

"Parker, Parker... you dumb shit," he said, the words muffled, the stink and heat of his breath folding back into his face, stinging his nostrils. The stench was bad enough that he finished the thought internally:

Just what the hell *do you think you're doing?*

THE GUESTS BEGAN to arrive. Carrie heard a steady increase of voices from the front of the church, where the pastor and – if they hadn't run off to a bar – Parker's friends were greeting them. She hoped those assholes were behaving themselves and shuddered at the thought of being related to that mad gorilla Brock for the rest of her life. The halfwit's bulk was surpassed only by his idiocy and indecency. Twice he'd hit on Carrie... *after* she was engaged to his brother. When he drank he was a wrecking ball of violence, bad manners and worse decisions. It made her constantly worried for Parker and she could only hope that once they were married, and he was living with *her* instead of his idiot brother and their clueless parents, things would be better. He would be smarter. More responsible. It was possible, *wasn't it?*

"Carrie dear, how are you?"

She turned to her mother and smiled, her (recently whitened) teeth gleaming, brown eyes luxuriously darkened by mascara and eyeliner, lustrous brown hair pulled loosely back, awaiting the veil. "Fine, Mom. Just... you know, ready to get this over with."

"How romantic," cooed Trish, as she shoved what must have been her millionth lemon cookie between lipstick-smeared teeth. Carrie supposed she should be thankful to avoid the full eye-roll on top of the dripping sarcasm. "Stop it, you're giving me the jellies."

I think you have all the jellies you need, fatty, Carrie thought, then instantly regretted it. She was becoming a cranky bitch, and only in her twenties. It made her sick with fear how much worse of a person she might become as she grew older. She forced a smile at Trish.

"Poor choice of words," she said. "I'm just... you know... it's a lot of stress. But I'm happy. And excited." But Trish had moved on, already going back to Nana's cookie plate for crumbs.

Beth put a hand on Carrie's arm. "It's gonna be awesome, hon," she said. "I'm *so* excited for you two. Just focus on how amazing it will be to finally be *married!*" Beth's voice rose in pitch as she spoke, reaching a squealing crescendo at the M-word, and Carrie tried to feel some excitement, to unearth some sunken inner thrill to suit the supposed bliss of the occasion.

She had started to reply when Beth's buoyant face sank into a frown, her blue eyes narrowing and looking over Carrie's shoulder, out the window. A wrinkle crumpled her brow like she'd caught an invisible dagger between the eyes.

"Oh no…" she said quietly, as if remembering a childhood loss.

Carrie's smile faltered, and she turned.

Slipping through the sun-splashed corn was a lanky shape she would recognize anywhere, even in the darkest night. His blonde hair was combed – a first – and he wore a brown herringbone three-piece suit that looked short at the cuffs and ankles.

Likely the same suit he's had since high school… she thought.

And for the first time that day, Carrie's smile wasn't forced.

CARS LINED THE edges of cracked pavement that constituted the church's small parking lot. Relatives close and distant made their way from their vehicles toward the church entryway. A bitter fall wind had picked up and women held onto their hats as men shoved their hands deep into the pockets of Sunday suits. Children laughed and ran in their own moderate finery, enchanted with the idea of being at church when no sermon was imminent. Like attending a birthday party in a classroom.

As the guests filed into the foyer, Parker's friends were there to shake hands, a mixture of bourbon and mint on their breath. Henry and Tuck twisted wrists and smiled sheepishly at the older men and women, most of whom had scolded one or both of them at some time or another during the boys' childhood years.

Brock waved at a few familiar faces but made no attempt to engage. He stood like a immense bulwark near the door of the pastor's office, inside which his big brother brooded in solitude. Brock's dull eyes lit up only once as he watched the guests fill into the foyer, their happy chatter cluttering the space between heads and ceiling with inane remarks and forced reconciliations, overly-enthusiastic greetings for those they had lost contact with or secretly didn't care for in the first place.

When Eli entered, whispers intensified and eyeballs darted beneath floral hats and greased comb-overs. The boy was taller than most and his neat stack of blond hair was a furred golden bob resting atop a darker pallet of browns and blacks, a dark sea of heads. He smiled as he made his way through the throng, saying hello to those that held no animosity toward his peculiarities, his gossiped history as an oddity, as a close friend to the bride.

Brock's wide brown eyes became drunkenly alert and followed Eli as he made his way through the cluster. He scowled, jaw muscles bunched, teeth grinding behind meaty cheeks. He waited until Pastor Willard, with the help of those two toadstools Tuck and Henry, began ushering folks into the chapel for the ceremony, then pushed himself away from the wall, wobbling slightly. He belched acid and tapped the flask resting in his coat pocket for strength and reassurance. He was eager for another drink, but held off for the moment, savoring the sweet anticipation of feeding the dragon, the liquid lizard with whiskey-brown scales that lay coiled in his guts, one that whispered: *All will be well, Brock old boy. Just stick with me and we'll do great things.*

Great. Things.

Brock snorted and walked down the short hallway that led to the pastor's office. He opened the door without preamble.

He needed to have a chat with his big brother.

CARRIE OPENED THE door a crack, the width of an eye and a lightly-rouged cheek. She noted the faces of the guests, most of whom she knew immediately, a few she had never seen before. Her mother was hidden away along with her nana, the two of them holed-up in a cramped nursery waiting for the first chords of the opening music to signal it was time for them to be led down the aisle and seated. Carrie, Beth and Trish had wanted a few minutes alone (presumably to have some private girl talk) before meeting up with the older women via an antiquated bathroom the vestry shared with the nursery.

The real reason for their delay was to secure a moment for their own pre-ceremonial toast using the three airplane bottles of vodka Trish had tucked away in her purse.

"Are we gonna do this or what, sunshine?" Beth said to Carrie's back, holding her uncapped bottle aloft as if releasing a genie.

Easy, you lush, Carrie thought, and continued to scan the crowd, most of whom were now finding seats within the worn wooden pews – some for the bride, some for the groom. Frantically, she continued to search the chapel, knowing time was running out...

And then she saw him.

He entered, laughing and lightly touching the shoulder of Widow Brewer, the beatific old lady who had fed them slices of pie, cookies and great icy glasses of lemonade from her back porch on hot Saturday afternoons after they'd worked up a dirty sweat running through the fields, climbing trees, or playing in the creek.

Carrie watched as he helped the old woman sit down near the front on the bride's side. She studied his face, looked for signs of pain, of discomfort, of something dark hidden behind that cordial smile. In the end, it was the eyes that gave him away. They were constant whether he was laughing or studying the pews for an appropriate seat. She saw the sadness there, saw the void in those eyes she knew better than her own. *My blue eyes.*

Beth chirped from behind with increased urgency. "Carrie, we're running out of time."

Carrie dropped her eyes, let out a breath. She closed the door and turned, her smile strained. "Yes, of course. Here…"

She reached out as Trish handed her one of the small plastic bottles.

"To Carrie," Trish said grandly, "may she be happy forever." The three girls tapped the plastic necks together, and drank.

Carrie downed the liquor in three swallows and gasped happily, staring at the empty bottle as if it held magic. "Whoo-boy," she said, and they all laughed.

The alcohol burned her stomach pleasantly, lightened her head. A warm calm spread through her as she looked past her two friends and out the window that faced the fields. The September sky had turned a deep-sea-green and clouds were building like ink-stained cotton above the acres of stalks. The jostling crowd of plants waved gently, as if saying hello, or demanding her attention.

"Looks like rain," she said quietly, and the gentle push of alcohol released the tether tying her memories to the old wooden dock of her past. And, so released, the memories drifted through the seaway of time, into her present.

"LOOKS LIKE RAIN," she said.

He laughed. "You think?"

The rain fell in a deafening torrent all around them. A billion vertical broken lines of liquid Morse code repeating the same word into the earth: *LIFE... LIFE... LIFE...*

The repeated message was indefinable joy to their ears, the mad applause of every earthbound child. The riotous rushing sound of rainfall was disrupted only by the distant rumblings of an angry beast with a belly of white forked swords; a god who filled the sky, whose footprints were continents.

The gapped planks of the shed walls couldn't hold out the chilled October gusts, but the corrugated tin roof kept the rain off their heads. They'd made a dash for it from Wilson Road, along which they'd been trekking on a return trip from a matinee that she'd loved and he'd squirmed through. An epic love story. When the sky broke they detoured through a patch of ripe pumpkins at a dead run and into the beaten shed, the doors too rotted to hold a lock, the contents too sparse to warrant one.

The minutes stacked as they waited for an abatement in the downpour, but the storm appeared strong and long for this world. Flashbulb lightning split the window-shade of infinite blue-green above the horizon. Carrie rubbed goosebumps off her bare arms while Eli knelt by the shed's doorless entryway, stared at the growing puddles in the mud just outside their shelter.

"I suppose we should prepare some dinner," she said, hoping for a smile or another laugh. But Eli seemed to have wandered again, away from her and toward the elements of the earth, his playthings, his special bond. "Perhaps a hot bath? If we had a basin I'm sure you could manage something."

He stood smoothly, a long shadow tinted by the jade sky.

When did he get so goddam tall? she thought. They had both changed over the years, but even through life's alterations they stayed close throughout high school (the mid-summer graduation already becoming a distant memory). *Best friends forever*, she supposed, and fought to define the swell of emotion she felt at the thought.

Despite his size, she still saw him as the little boy whose flannel back she'd followed on a ragged sprint through cornstalk fields; the pale, skinny brother-she-never-had who always let her climb one branch higher simply for the enjoyment of hearing her gloat, who lay at her side beneath a midnight sky shattered by stars, clumsily holding her hand before she'd finally pull it away, turning his tension to gloom.

Now this boy, this *man*, stared toward the heavens.

Studying the clouds, she guessed. *Looking for his head, most likely.*

"Hey! Eli!" she snapped playfully, tapping his broad back. "These jokes don't write themselves, you know."

He spun with a jerk and stared down at her, as if surprised at her presence.

She gave him a sardonic *here I am* look, turned her palms up. She never once thought of her sleeveless cotton dress – daffodils on sky blue – and the way it clung to her wet skin, how it might have been giving him x-ray vision. This was *Eli*, after all, and she just couldn't relate to his perception of "them", despite her best estimations of his feelings. Carrie refused to apologize or acknowledge something so shallow, especially when they were part of something so much deeper. *And why doesn't he see that?*

"Funny as always," he said, but his eyes slid off her, focused on a dark corner of the shed. He scratched his scruff of blond hair. "Getting cold."

"Yeah, and I gotta get home. Promised Mom I'd help her decorate the house," she said, using her hands to express her Halloween vision. "I'm thinking paper skeletons, a laughing jack-o-lantern, some serious cobwebs. The kids will eat it up, don't you think?"

He nodded, his face a coal-black smudge against the backdrop of midday rain. "You figure it's what… half a mile to your place?"

"I guess." She shrugged. "I'm half frozen-to-death already, a little rain ain't gonna kill me. Seems we got no choice, unless you wanna sleep here."

He nodded again and turned toward the shed's wide opening. His arms hung at his sides, thumb-pads resting against the hips of his overalls, fingers splayed. After a moment of thought, perhaps the making of a decision, or the solving of a particularly hard math problem, he raised his hands to chest-height and began to rub them together, as if rolling a ball of dough. Carrie felt the air stiffen, heard the sound of rain grow muffled. She flexed open her jaw at the sudden pressure on her eardrums.

Eli turned his palms upward, as if carrying two trays made from air, and stepped to the mouth of the shed. "Stay close, Carrie," he said, and it sounded as if the words were spoken in a phone booth. Clear and intimate.

She pressed herself against him, pinched the back of his shirt. She clung to him lightly as they stepped onto the wet earth, and despite what she knew of his powers, she braced herself for the assault of ice-cold rain on her head and shoulders.

It never came.

He continued to walk, and after a few moments increased his pace. She clenched his shirt more tightly and stayed close as she could without tripping on his heels, as if he were holding an umbrella for them both.

After she fell into a rhythm with his steps, she let go of his shirt, slipped a hand onto his bare elbow to steady herself, then stared around her with amazement. She watched the spill of rain run off the surface of what she could only think of as a bubble; a protective shimmer of air he'd formed around them. Slowly she reached out, pushed her hand through the invisible liquid sheet of wind and rainwater. Rain splattered against her palm and she laughed with wonder. After a moment, she retracted her arm to the safety of the shelter, skipping to keep pace with his long strides over the soggy terrain.

They walked the half-mile wordlessly. She knew how much he needed to concentrate, having been privy to a thousand of his extraordinary enchantments over the years. When they finally reached her house, she stepped past him and onto the front step of the awning-covered porch. She danced up two more wooden steps and spun, wanting to embrace him and laugh at his miracle.

Her smile froze.

He was bent over at the bottom step, just under the lip of the porch roof. His breathing was hoarse and ragged, his face ghastly pale. He was shaking, as if burning with fever.

"Eli?"

He turned his face to her, and she stifled the scream that rose in her throat. His piercing blue eyes were gone, the sockets filled with muddy whites, as though he were a blind man. Dark blood ran from both nostrils, slid in dual lines down his face to embrace his upper lip.

"Jesus! Eli!" she yelled, and without thinking pulled his long body to hers, embraced his trembling form. "Let it go, sweetie," she sobbed into his chest, almost shouting in her fear. "Please let it go!"

Against her cheek, she felt his chest rise, then deflate. The thumping of his heart steadied and grew faint. A heavy breath slipped from him. The sheltering pocket of air surrounding them evaporated. The harsh sounds of the world poured in unfiltered. Wind rushed into her ears, the biting air snatched greedily at her arms and legs, a bitter chill smeared across the back of her neck as if traced by a ghostly hand.

His weight fell into her and she was barely able to lower him to the porch floorboards. She rested his head *his eyes, his ghastly white eyes* on the porch and rubbed his cheeks, pushed back his sweat-slicked hair. His eyes fluttered closed, and she rested a hand on his forehead. His skin was hot as fire. She pulled a blue handkerchief from his hip pocket – the one he always kept tucked there – and wiped the blood from his nose and lips. Without thinking, she kissed his temple, his cheeks. She sat back and waited.

"Eli?" she said.

After a few moments, his face softened, the strain left his forehead. Some of his color returned. He opened his eyes and she was sick with relief to see bright blue eyes staring back, a twinkle brewing deep within them. A smile curled his blood-smeared lips.

"Are you all right?" she asked, still worried but growing angry at the same time.

He nodded, then slipped his fingers behind her head and drew her gently to him.

They kissed, and she knew she would never love him.

Carrie pulled away, a hand on his chest. "You scared the shit out of me. What happened?'

He sat up and shrugged. "That was a long walk," he said, as if in explanation. She silently swore at herself for not paying him more mind along the way.

He sat up straighter, rested his back against the chipped white paint of a porch beam. For a while they sat together in silence, watching the rain, and that was enough.

"You should get going," she said finally, watching the gutters sluice water into flowerbeds. She held his hand and squeezed. "Eli, you shouldn't ever kiss me again. Not like that." She watched him closely, searching for a response. A stiffness; or anger, perhaps.

But it was like he'd simply disappeared, and in the place in which he sat rested a void.

He pulled his hand from hers and stood. He stepped into the downpour, was immediately drenched. He studied the horizon.

"You think I don't know how to love you," he said, his voice soft and broken amidst the harsh rhythm of the rain. She said nothing, unsure if she'd even heard him correctly. He twisted around and studied her, a quizzical look on his face, that crooked smile. "Or maybe love isn't what you're looking for." He turned his back on her once more. His face tilted to the sky and the spitting gray clouds, as if searching for something lost. "At least I kept you dry," he said. "I suppose there's that."

Without another word, or another look, he started home.

She watched him as he walked away. Watched until he was a rain-smeared blur of blue and blonde standing out against a distant copse of dark green firs, then vanish inside.

ELI FOUND A seat near the back of the church, a row empty but for a sour-looking pregnant woman he didn't recognize and a rough-looking man in a suit but no tie. He figured them for distant cousins dragged in from a cross-state farm, bitching their way to the church in a beaten-down truck and a morning fight unsettled.

Someone tapped him hard on the shoulder, and he twisted around to see Henry Munson, one of Parker's groomsmen (and all-around dickhead) staring down at him. Eli thought he looked a little drunk. His forehead was dotted with sweat, his toothy smile slippery.

"Hey man, what's up?" Henry said. His too-wide grin and sunken eyes gave him the look of a malnourished jackal.

Eli nodded and said nothing. Henry rested a hand on his shoulder, his eyes darting around the room before finally settling once more, albeit restlessly, on Eli. "Listen man, the bride and groom are doing some quick pre-ceremony photos while they can. Just, you know, with friends and such. They don't think they'll have time after because of, uh, other obligations and whatever."

Eli felt his pulse quicken but forced it to slow. He knew this day would be hard, but he was here for Carrie, whatever pain that may bring. "Sounds grand, have fun," he said, not wanting to hear the request. Not wanting, truth be told, to be here at all. He began to feel the heat of Henry's pressed palm making its way through the fabric of the thin suit, fought the urge to shrug it off.

"Yeah, well, Carrie wants *you* to come do a quick photo, dummy,"

Henry said, finally removing his hand and taking a step back, as if to lead Eli away. "So, let's go. They don't have much time."

Eli considered a moment, wanting to turn his back on Henry, to ignore the request and the slick weasel who'd brought it. He wanted to reject it, like he rejected the wedding. Like she'd rejected him. "I don't..." he started, then stopped.

He sighed, dropped his gaze to his lap, large hands resting on his knees. He turned them over to study deeply-lined palms, searching for answers. He noticed, with the sudden heat of shame, how the cuffs of his brown suit coat settled inches high from his wrists, how frayed thread spilled from the left cuff, a permanent ink-stain soiled the milk-white shirt beneath.

Who am I to demand anything? he thought. *And who am I really?*

He considered a moment more, then stood. He noticed the quick stagger of uncertainty in Henry's eyes as he rose almost a foot higher than the groomsman, whose smile had slid away to leave a twisted frown.

"When the hell'd you get so tall, man?" Henry said, then turned and walked quickly away, looking back only once to wave Eli after him.

Eli followed, wanting nothing more than to get all this over with; hoping that if he obliged he might find a moment alone with Carrie, offer reassurance of his support (despite it being feigned). He wanted her to be happy at any cost, even if he was part of the payment.

Henry led Eli through the foyer, then down a small hallway toward an office. Henry went through the door quickly, then let it swing back, nearly closing it behind him.

Eli heard laughter as he reached for the knob. Hesitated.

The door swung open and Parker's massive, hot-headed brother, Brock, filled the doorframe. His brown eyes blazed and his reddened face was scrunched into a tight-lipped smile of anticipation and hate. He clutched Eli by the knot of his tie and yanked him inside.

The door slammed shut behind him.

Eli's first thought was that he'd been pulled into a men's locker room. The small, stuffy office smelled of piss and sweat and liquor. He registered four bodies – all male, all in black tuxedos.

Shit, he thought.

Everything that came next happened very, very fast.

PART TWO
Red Night

WHEN ELI WAS three years old, he disappeared from his bed.

Upon making this discovery, his mother, Francis, ran screaming through the house, out into the yard. "Eli!" she called, the sound a tinny squeak swallowed amongst the billion acres of the earth, the great turning wheel of endless dimensions, the infinite reaches of space. "Oh, my dear God! Eli!"

She found Eli's father, John, working the crop, and frantically informed him of their son's disappearance.

Eli's parents spent the remainder of the morning searching their property but found no trace of their son. After a few hours, they called on neighbors to help them search. Soon thereafter, they called the police.

As afternoon turned into evening, John overhead some of the officers on a coffee break amidst the day-long search. They spoke in hushed tones about the blood moon of the night before, that rare blood-red tinting caused by a lunar eclipse. They shared the strange calls they'd received over the previous twenty-four hours: dogs going berserk and attacking their owners; livestock dropping dead so suddenly that farmers feared poisoning; a multiple homicide – the first one in more than twenty years in Gehenna County – that involved a mother drowning her three children, one-by-one, in the small pond behind their home.

John didn't want to hear such things, didn't take stock in some nonsense of a blood moon any more than he did vampires and werewolves. Despite his rejection of such ideas however, his pulse quickened and his skin grew cold as he left the officers to their coffee and bizarre conversation. Under a blackened sky, he shut out the voices and continued to search for his only son.

It was near midnight—more than twenty-four hours since the child was last seen—when one of the officers, while relieving himself along a nearby tree-line, heard what he swore were the dampened sobs of a child.

Led by Eli's parents, a corps of volunteers and six officers walked into the trees. Flashlights ignited the dark forest, sent ground critters scurrying for cover, erased shadows. They all heard it now – the unmistakable sound of a child – and John tried to keep Francis quiet as they walked deeper. Her wailing and constant beckoning bordered on a fractured mind, and it wasn't until the Sheriff himself took her by the shoulders and whispered frantically into her ear that she quieted to an oft-choked whimper.

They found Eli at the bottom of an old well, a forgotten, beaten-down shaft that had been covered with planks, now rotted through. The circle of stone marking its entrance was thick with Hosta leaves, ivy and wild ginger so dense they would have likely never seen it – never been aware of its existence – were it not for the child's complaining cries of hunger and cold.

They lowered John by rope (a span of nearly thirty feet) to fish out his boy.

Later, John would comment that when he looked up from the bottom of that well, clutching his cold, wailing child to his chest, he was struck at how the faraway moon seemed to look *back* from the well's opening, a bright white pupil centered within an ink-black eye, and how glad he was to see it pale milk instead of the fiery red from the previous night.

Although found (inexplicably) naked, and half-sunken into the soft muck at the base of the well's chute, Eli showed no signs of injury or long-term physical complaints.

His mother, however, never recovered.

Francis grew more anxious and fretful around her baby boy as the weeks passed. There were rumors she'd lost part of her mind, broken by the shock of the odd disappearance (and even odder reappearance) of the child. It was whispered she did not believe the child hers, that *her* boy had been taken away and replaced by another, the very one found in the bottom of the well that dreary night. John did his best to alleviate his wife's paranoid conclusions, but despite his tearful protestations he was unable to convince her otherwise.

Then, early one chilled morning, months after the incident, John woke to find both Francis and Eli gone. Panicked, he searched the home's immediate surroundings, and by the grace of God found them both.

She had taken him to the creek.

Her full weight was upon his back. His limbs thrashed in the ice-cold water's flow, his face completely submerged. John ran at her screaming a cry of horror and hate. He struck her head brutally with a clenched fist and pushed her off his child. He scooped the coughing and red-faced boy into his arms and ran for the house. Without hesitation, he called the police.

The Sheriff found Francis where John had left her, babbling and glassy-eyed with shock beside the creek, her eyes wide and distant with the loss of reason. A purple knob swelled at her brow where her husband had struck her.

Francis was hospitalized and heavily medicated, but did not survive the week. It was never discovered how she acquired the rusted razorblade she used to open her wrists and slice the carotid artery in her neck.

They found her lying in her bed, the thin mattress heavy with blood, the surrounding linoleum floor a red pool that stretched and channeled into thin, branching limbs, of which one had crept under the door leading to the hallway, where it was spotted by a nurse doing rounds.

Eli's father never discussed the incident of the well – or his wife's tragic suicide – with his son. He told him only that his mother had passed of a sudden illness and prayed their friends and neighbors would keep his family's dark history to themselves.

And so, as a child, Eli never knew different than a fictitious version of his past, and therefore never considered himself to be anything other than the son of a widowed farmer, growing up among crops in the heart of the Midwestern United States. He never considered himself unusual in any way. As anything other than human.

Not even when he performed miracles.

As ELI GREW older, his father often left him in the care of the neighboring Foster family, where he was watched over while becoming fast playmates with their youngest daughter, Carrie, who was of the same age.

Years later, when Carrie and Eli were in grade school, Mr. Foster suffered a savage heart attack that killed him faster than the swipe of a scythe, leaving both children now semi-orphaned and even more reliant on the other's friendship.

Gradually, for no reason either of them could put a clean finger on, Eli became more and more of an outcast. Despite his father's efforts of secrecy, rumors ran rampant about the strange disappearance on the night of the blood moon, and Eli's awkward demeanor and daydreaming manner left him open for attack from kids, gossip from adults. Some thought him a changeling, or a demon. Others suggested he was an alien from outer space.

Eli and Carrie would often laugh at the rumors, although Carrie knew, deep-down, that they deeply affected her best and closest friend.

"What would they call me if they knew the things I could do?" he said one day, and although he said it lightly, Carrie felt a rise of panic in her chest.

She clutched at him, stared deep into his eyes. "You musn't Eli," she said sternly. "You musn't ever. Not *ever*. That's between us, understand? Always."

He'd nodded and smiled in his melancholy way. His eyes left hers, found the horizon. "You don't think I'm any of those things, right?"

"What, like an alien?" she said, then kissed him quickly on the cheek, smoothed his thick wild hair. "Nah, if anything you're an angel, sent here to protect me."

"A guardian angel," he said, brightening. "I like that."

She took his hand and pulled him toward home, stepping through the field's high grass toward a dripping red sun. The sweet powdery smell of grain filled the air. She carefully pulled burdock burrs from her jeans as they went, brushed brown straw from his hair.

"That's right, blue eyes," she said, "and don't ever forget it."

PART THREE

Green Eye

A TERRIBLE SCREAM split the air.

Carrie was huddled in the nursery with Mother, Nana, and her two bridesmaids. A rectangular Plexiglas window – cut into the wall below a speaker used to relay the sermon for mothers soothing their bawling infants – allowed her to see into the chapel. Organ music had just begun to play, signaling the guests to their seats (and Carrie's entrance), when the horrible scream rang out.

Carrie leapt from her chair at the sound and flattened her face against the narrow strip of clear plastic, searching for the source. Through the scratched pane she noticed that a small contingent of guests had left the pews and gathered along the large windows just outside her field of vision. The scream had come from someone in that area – she couldn't tell who – but the faces appeared to be focused on something *outside*.

Frustrated, she turned around, as if to follow the gazes, but instead of windows she saw nothing but a scuffed white wall filled with pinned shapes of cardboard flowers, photographs of baby faces glued to their centers, the tiny bald heads sprouting cartoonish petals of gold, red and blue.

"What's happening?" her mother asked, already at the door leading to the foyer, where a tuxedoed usher would momentarily be waiting to escort her out.

"I don't know... I can't see," Carrie said, and spun to look once more into the chapel, craning her neck as if it might expose a wider view of the scene. More people were standing now, moving with purpose toward the east-facing windows. Carrie thought a few of them looked alarmed. Despite the commotion, she saw no sign of Parker or Brock at the front of the chapel. Just a bemused-looking Pastor Willard.

"They should be standing up there by now," she said quietly, and watched as the pastor – *why does he look so nervous?* she thought – eyeballed his watch, then left the altar to step down toward the pews, speaking hurriedly to the guests.

Carrie turned away from the window, confused and concerned, and saw all four women looking at her with expressions rooted in fear. "Something's wrong," she told them.

Her mother's crease-worried face suddenly smoothed as if frozen, a hardness that emptied the emotions from her features and made her appear as marble. Carrie noticed Trish take half a step away from her. *Beware a mother's love,* Carrie thought.

"Stay here," her mother said sternly. Carrie felt her protective force, her desire to be sure nothing ruined her daughter's special day, and was comforted at having such a stalwart ally. But Carrie also wondered what, exactly, was going on. What sort of incident was transpiring outside the church, and would the severity of her mother's ire be any sort of hindrance to its inevitable occurrence?

"Now you girls just relax, this is no time to be fussy," Nana said, sitting in a plastic blue chair that was designed for children rather than eighty-three-year-old women. She smoothed her cream dress over her thin knees and pursed her lips. "No reason for fussiness," she reiterated quietly, as if soothing her own nerves as well as those of the young bridal party.

Beth pulled Carrie's arm, offered her most disarming smile. "Whatever's going on, just know I love you, and that I'm really happy for you and Parker." Beth gave her a quick hug, then held her at arm's length, eyes beaming confidence. "Don't you worry. Everything is going to be fine."

Carrie smiled back, was about to say something in return, something equally assuring, a well-worn platitude... when the sound of an air siren rose in the distance.

The high-pitched whine carried across the fields and through the thin white walls of the church to caress the skin of those inside with icy fingers, to flood their hearts and minds with black fear.

"Oh no," Carrie said. She gave Beth's hand a squeeze, then a tug. "Come on!"

Carrie opened the door leading to the shared bathroom, pulling Beth behind her. They ran across the pale porcelain tiles and back into the vestry. They raced to the window, stared in awe at the scene forming outside.

Panting, Trish burst into the room just behind them. "What the hell is it?"

Carrie stared at the mountain of coal-black clouds suffocating the horizon. The entire sky had turned a spearmint green. Through a gaping hole along the roof of the angry cloud-cover, a bright aqua light shone through like a spotlight breaching the surface of the sea, the great eye of an alien god opening within the face of the storm.

As if coming awake.

As if coming alive.

ELI KNEW HE was in deep trouble. Even worse, he'd walked right into it. He'd been fooled by fools and he should have known better.

Parker had hated him for years, and had told him repeatedly, using different means of cruelty and violence, to keep away from Carrie. But now that the two of them were getting married, Eli had figured – with grave miscalculation – that Parker would move on from his childish paranoia, his obsession, with Eli and Carrie's friendship.

Because that's all it is, he thought, *whether I like it or not.*

Brock grabbed Eli's shoulders and shoved him into the seat facing the pastor's desk. Behind the desk, fingers folded as if preparing to lecture a naughty schoolboy, was a sly-looking, and somewhat intoxicated, Parker.

"Eliiii," he said dramatically, extending the name comically, almost amiably, as if they were old pals and Eli had just walked into the same bar Parker had designated as his evening's watering hole. "Eli Eli Eli..." he went on, slightly slurring the "L" sounds, and sounding – to Eli's ears – less amiable with each repetition of the name. "What... the *fuck*... are you doing here, boy?" Parker leaned forward, crossed his arms on the desktop, and grinned like a shark. "I mean... I know you and Carrie are friends from kindergarten and shit, but I thought... hell, man, I thought you and I had an understanding."

Without warning or provocation, Brock punched the back of Eli's head with a knotted fist. White light popped inside his skull, but he gripped the worn wooden arms of the old chair tightly and said nothing. One of the others laughed, and Eli had to fight against rolling his eyes at their sycophancy. Parker stood, strolled magnanimously around the desk.

"I mean, shit man… last time we had this chat it ended with you on the ground sucking piss-water in the alley behind Tom's bar, remember? God, that was just a few months ago, too. How could you forget that chat, Eli? I know you're dumb, boy…" Parker settled himself, ass pressed against the desk, his wrinkled black cummerbund not quite covering the beginnings of a beer paunch at his waist. He bent over and put a firm hand on Eli's shoulder. "But I didn't think you were stupid."

Surprising everyone, perhaps himself most of all, Eli sprang up, inadvertently connecting the crown of his head with Parker's nose. There was a loud *crack* as Parker's head snapped backward as if yanked from behind. Eli twisted and saw Brock coming at him, a mad bull in a very small china shop. In his peripheral vision, he saw the other two assholes squeeze their hands into tight fists but stand firm, at least for the moment. Behind him he could hear muffled cursing, as if Parker was screaming through clenched teeth and tight lips. Eli dared a split-second glance, saw with some satisfaction that the groom was stumbling backward, a hand pressed tightly to his face. Blood spilled down his wrist, soiled the cuff of his pressed, white dress shirt.

"Mothafutha!" he yelled through the slick palm of his hand, blood spraying between fingers, his watery eyes pinned onto Eli with deadly reprisal.

"Hot damn," Eli said under his breath, surprised at the potency of the unintended impact, and bolted for the door.

A boulder slammed into the side of his head and he flew into a wall hung with plaques and a framed visage of Jesus Christ. The impact caused the wall to shudder and Eli went down, the sharp, heavy corner of Jesus's image smacking into his forehead before flipping flat onto the carpet. Brock's foot stomped onto the glass, cracking Jesus in two, and grabbing Eli by the lapels of his cheap coat, pulled him skyward.

"Wait for it," Brock whispered, almost calmly, and then a second boulder pounded into Eli's guts. He folded over, breath stolen from his lungs. As he dipped, a black knee shot into the bridge of his nose, and a pistol shot popped in his brain. He collapsed to the floor in a limp heap, doing all he could to keep on hands and knees as he gasped. The room swayed, the frayed carpet blurred and shifting beneath him. He watched with a sort of wonder as a trail of blood dotted the coarse fabric beneath his face.

Reflexively – a pure survival instinct – Eli *shifted* the air around him.

Someone kicked him in the side but it hardly registered. One of the smaller ones must have done it. A coward's move.

"He's fucking hard as stone," a voice said.

Afraid to be hurt, but more afraid of arousing suspicion, Eli let go of the air, and immediately felt himself sag, as if his body had gained a hundred pounds of pain.

"You're just a pussy," a deeper voice said, and another kick came, this one heavy and pointed, dipped in the slick sheen of a tuxedo shoe.

This time the attack connected. Pain burst through Eli's side. He felt a rib crack as he crashed to the floor, sucking desperately for breath. He clutched his guts, his chest, and wanted to bellow for help before things got worse. Part of him knew he could end this now. Bring up fire and wind and drive them away, through walls if he must...

And reveal yourself? a voice asked, a voice that lived deep within the chambers of his heart, a voice that sounded suspiciously like a teenage Carrie Foster. *Attack my future husband? That would make my day memorable, wouldn't it? The groom, on fire, screaming bloody murder as groomsman were blown down the aisle, hmm? While the organ played Vicente Avella, perhaps?*

Eli rolled onto his back, terrified, slowly pulling thin ribbons of oxygen into his lungs. "Okay," he croaked, not knowing if his words were loud enough to hear, if they were being spoken at all. "Okay," he repeated, more clearly this time.

Four white faces appeared above him, all staring down at the shell of the man he'd become, the tattered remnants of his human spirit. Parker's chin was slathered in blood. His nose had swelled and was heading toward a dark shade of purple, but there was nothing Eli could do about that now.

"Okay *what*, asshole?" Parker growled, his eyes clear once more, his teeth clenched.

Eli raised a hand toward those faces, as if warding off evil spirits. "Okay, I'll leave," he said as loud as he could muster. Certainly audible. "I'll leave," he repeated, then added, "Forever, okay?" He fought back a sob, then said it again, as much as for himself as for them, knowing he meant it. "I'll leave forever."

Brock looked to Parker, who said nothing. Tuck pulled at Brock's arm.

"We need to go, man. The wedding is, like, *starting*."

But Brock only squeezed his meaty fingers into thick, hairy-knuckled fists, and Eli thought that maybe things like *reason* and *schedule* and *marriage vows* were no longer at the forefront of the brothers' minds.

Eli rose slowly to his knees, hands still raised in mock defense, in total surrender. "I'll go, man. Just… I mean, you're supposed to be getting married. What about Carrie? What about *her*? Don't you give a shit about her? This is supposed to be spec…"

Parker arched his back and shot his leg out like a piston, slamming the heel of his shoe into Eli's face. Eli felt his nose crack and twist, his jaw shift unnaturally, some string of key muscle and cartilage tearing free from the hinge. Two hard jagged teeth rolled loosely onto his tongue. White light fluttered in his mind like a strobe, and his eyes rolled back into his head.

Eli sank like dead weight, his body limp, his brain scrambling for consciousness. Blood ran freely from one nostril, his lip was badly split, and red saliva drooled from the corner of his mouth, down his cheek, and onto the urine-stained carpet. He gagged on the trickle of warm blood sliding down his throat, coughed once (spitting out at least one tooth in the process), then sickly swallowed. His face was numb, his nerves bullied into a state of shock. He knew he'd been badly, badly hurt.

Parker knelt in front of him, madness in his eyes, and Eli hated himself for the fear that leapt into his chest, the instinctive squeeze of his bladder whose release he fought against with every fiber of self-worth left in him. He lifted his hands, pleading.

"Please…" he said, more terrified than he'd ever been. Even more scared than the time they'd beaten him in the alley behind that bar, the same night Carrie had told him of her engagement. The night he knew his life with her was over. It was then that Parker had first warned him to stay clear of Carrie, of his best friend, of the very one he was supposed to protect. But he couldn't protect anyone. That had been made painfully clear, first that night in the alley, and now in this small, stinking office of the small church.

Eli had never felt more despair. Had never felt more hollow.

He dropped his hands and sighed, deciding it no longer mattered what they did to him. All the damage had been done, and he was broken inside. Shattered glass and shadows. He rolled over and hoped, for a moment, to rise, but instead let his face sink into the musty carpeting, too hurt to do anything more.

"Think he's had enough." Brock's voice. Eli could imagine him putting a hand on his brother's arm. "Let's get you cleaned up and get this shit over with."

Eli scoffed, kept his face to the carpet. A tear pooled in his eye and he didn't fight its departure.

"Not yet," Parker said.

And just as Eli was thinking what part of him they would attack next—was wondering, with a sense of inquisitive fascination, if Parker meant to actually *kill* him... he heard a loud scream from outside the door.

"What the hell was that?" One of the dickheads.

"I don't..." Brock started, then stopped. They *all* stopped.

Because that was when they heard the air siren, and the mounting screams that followed the first, hot on its wailing heels.

PASTOR WILLARD RAISED his arms and yelled over the heightening voices, the weeping children, the discordant shouts of panic, the distant warning cry of the siren. "Please! Please, be calm!" The interior of the chapel had taken on a green hue, reflecting the light coming in through windows, now filled with the most ominous sky he'd ever seen. *Where did this weather come from?* he thought, pushing the sudden burn of fear deep down while praying silently to his God.

Faces turned to him, pale and alarmed.

"We need to get out of here," one man said.

"Pastor, what should we do?" asked a pretty lady in a blue dress, her arm clamped onto the narrow bicep of an elderly man, who seemed confused as to what all the yelling was about.

Pastor Willard stepped forward, looked through the large windows at the building storm, the strange light that shone through the center of the sky's cloud-wrinkled face. "Let's just take our seats, please. Come on, this will be better if we remain calm." He smiled at them reassuringly. His sheep looking to him for guidance, for someone to lead. "Come on now, let's..."

His words were cut off as the roof of the church erupted in a hard clattering that echoed ominously throughout the open chapel, filling the room with a cacophonous, nerve-shattering racket. An image came to him of a thousand baby demons, born of the storm and formed by ice, banging their fists on the roof and walls of the Lord's house, commanding entry, demanding souls to take.

"What is it?" a child yelled, but the others said nothing, simply looked toward the ceiling as if waiting for it to cave inward, allow full access to the battering sky.

"It's hail," the pastor said quietly, then, clearing his throat and repeating the words with assertion, "it's just hail." He searched the group for faces he knew, for someone he could trust. He spotted the Marksons, who were smarter than most and had run a cattle farm in the county for decades. He decided to deputize them both. "Martha? Tom? Come on, you've both seen hail before. We all have."

Tom Markson nodded, as if trying to figure out why the pastor was addressing him specifically, then realization come upon him. He looked to his wife and nodded as she immediately started touching the shoulders of children, whispering reassuringly.

"That's right," Tom said, nodding ever more vigorously. "That's just hail, folks. I think we should all have a seat like the pastor said."

Pastor Willard smiled, feeling as if things were coming to hand, when he happened to glance over the heads of the group and out the large windows toward the beating heart of the storm. Lightning flashed, illuminating the sunken dark shadows of the tumultuous clouds. Revealed what lay hidden there.

A massive, twisting funnel extended down from the ceiling of boiling sky, pushed its way earthward. The tip of it curled like a witch's finger, digging a hard gray fingernail across the earth. The pastor could see, through a swirl of dirt at the twister's base, black specks rising from the ground to feed it, pulled upward like confetti falling in reverse.

Those are corn stalks, he thought.

But deep down, sulking within his hidden subconscious – where nightmares fester and all of our greatest fears are harbored – was the truth. *Cars!* His subconscious shrieked, piercing his brain like an ice pick. *Houses! Livestock!*

And then: *People!*

"Oh no." The words fell from his mouth like a dead prayer, and all heads followed his wide-eyed gaze out the windows...

... and inside the small church, hell broke loose.

CARRIE SAW THE funnel and clutched Beth's hand in a fierce grip.

Behind them, through the door that led to the chapel, came raised voices. Alarm. Pastor Willard was speaking loudly, urging for calm...

"We have to get out of here," she said, surprised at how level, how *reasonable*, her voice sounded, when inside panic whipped through her chest and stomach faster and more urgently than the thrashing storm outside. "We need to get to the cars and get the hell away," she said more insistently, as if giving instructions to hardened soldiers instead of scared bridesmaids wearing dresses of cauliflower blue.

Beth and Trish nodded. Fear held fast in their eyes, but their mouths were set with determination and forced calm. Trish grabbed her clutch and tucked it beneath a bared arm. Carrie had a beat to think how beautiful she looked in that moment.

"I don't have anyone here, I'll take your mom and nana with me..." Trish said, then hesitated. "Where do we go? We should meet..."

Carrie thought for a moment. "City Hall," she said, remembering what she'd been taught as a child, if ever caught in a storm near town... "There's a shelter at City Hall."

"Why don't you come with us?" Trish asked, already moving for the door.

"I have to find Parker, I'll leave with him," she said, the words coming automatically. She tasted the lie on her tongue as she spoke it and was surprised at what her true thoughts were, the face her mind conjured the second she realized the peril was real. That their lives were in danger.

I have to find Eli.

She pulled Beth's arm and went quickly through the door, Trish already ahead of them and calling for the older women to get in motion.

Carrie entered the nursery to loud voices. Trish was gently lifting a complaining Nana from a chair in the corner, and her mother was at the door, yelling at both of them, tears in her eyes. "I don't understand... Carrie, what's happening?"

"A tornado, mom. Just east. A big one."

"Oh my God…" her mother said, then held a breath, sniffed, and straightened. "Okay, let's all go, come on."

"I'll meet you," Carrie said, and went to her mother and hugged her fiercely. "I'll go with Parker. I'll be fine. Now come on."

Carrie yanked open the door that led to the foyer. She had one last moment to think, despite her fear and the impending danger, that her wedding day was over. Vanquished in an instant. There were no ushers to take her elbow and lead her to the aisle. No turned, expectant faces watching her step gracefully through the small chapel, toward the handsome groom, the smiling pastor. There would be no veil covering her face, no ring on her finger, no vows spoken.

They stepped out of the nursery. Directly across the foyer, at the end of a short hallway, another door swung open, breaking Carrie's momentary reverie. A man walked out.

Parker.

He stopped short, met her eyes, then looked down and away, as if ashamed. She noticed his face was smeared with… *is that blood?*

Behind him came Brock. He saw Carrie and froze, mouth agape, as if already searching for an excuse to whatever new mess they'd gotten into.

She took a small step to the side, just slightly, in order to make out what lay on the floor through the open door behind them. A shock of blond hair. A face, bloodied and beaten, resting against the carpet, one blue eye wide, and then wider.

"Oh God, no…"

She took a step forward, her face already burning with the heat of fury, her heart pumping hard beneath the white fabric of her tight dress. Parker was already raising a hand toward her, as if to say: *now just wait a second, it's not what you think, baby…*

Carrie had just started across the foyer, fingers squeezed into tight fists, when Pastor Willard strode between them, a large group of wedding guests on his heels, quickly filling the space between bride and groom. Tears spilled down Carrie's cheeks as she tried to cross the space, push through them, toward Parker, toward the bloodied Eli that lay hurting on the office floor. The pastor had been heading for the exit but stopped when he saw Carrie fighting her way toward him. His alarmed face went slack with worry.

"Carrie, darling, it's okay. Look, I know this all seems horrible right now, but it's going to be all right. Please don't cry," he said, and gripped her by the arms, held her fast.

She looked at him in amazement. "It's not that..."

But he only nodded, squeezed her arms so tight she felt the pain of his hard thumbs digging into her biceps. "I know you're scared, honey. But there's nothing to worry about. We just need to get to shelter, underground..."

Outside the wind grew with such force that the building shook and rattled. The warning siren still wailed but it was muffled now by the battering hail and the whipping howl of the wind. The front doors of the church began to clatter, as if poltergeists were on the other side, slapping their ghostly hands against the sun-bleached wood from their mad purgatory, desperate to reach the living.

"Damn," Pastor Willard whispered, and released his hold on Carrie. He raised his arms up high, addressed his gathered flock. "All right folks! Let's do this orderly now, we got time. Let's get to the cars safely and get to the shelter in town, that's the safest place..."

"I got a storm cellar a half mile from here!" yelled Mr. Daniels, who owned a modern ranch up Route 33, settled nicely within three-hundred acres and a hundred head of milking cows. "I can fit at least twenty of us."

Pastor Willard nodded, as if placating a child who was showing off his newest finger-painting. "That's fine, Bob, just fine. Now, let's move orderly, okay?"

The church doors battered their frames, harder by the second, the wind screeching outside the thin walls like a swarm of banshees. Pastor Willard nodded to his flock one last time, turned, and stepped briskly to the entrance. He pushed the arm-bar that unlatched the door.

There was a sharp *BANG* that made Carrie jump despite the other commotion. The door had whipped open, torn from the pastor's hands and slung hard against the outside wall by a violent slap of wind.

"Oh!" he cried, and reached for it, as if to pull it closed again. People began to surge, to shove at him from behind. "Just wait a damn second!" he roared, trying to be heard over the tumult. The wind pushed his silver hair away from his head, flowers blew off a nearby table, and Mrs. Hallemann's wide-brimmed hat flipped and soared like a wobbling flying saucer back toward the chapel. Hail spattered the floor of the entryway, sprinkling across the blue-gray carpet of the foyer like beads spilled from a pearl necklace.

Something outside cracked louder than thunder. A hand grabbed Carrie's arm and tugged her backward. She had time to see the pastor struggling with a man in a dark blue suit. A woman was fighting to get past them both, pulling a little blonde-haired boy with her, the terrified child screaming at the top of his lungs.

The roof above Carrie's head exploded. The wall above the doors burst inward with a plume of drywall dust and splinters, blasting a cloud of debris into the foyer.

The mighty oak had been ripped free of its poisoned roots and now finished its fall, the enormous trunk crashing against the aged doors with the bulk and velocity of a school bus dropped from the sky. Pastor Willard, the man in the blue suit, and the woman holding the hand of her tow-headed child evaporated in a floor-shaking crunch. A dousing spray of red mist decorated the people surging forward in crimson, coating their faces, their fine dresses and suits.

Carrie fell hard to the ground, pulling Beth down with her, and noticed her dress had gone from white to pink, the blood that burst from the crushed bodies of the pastor and the others, like juice from a fat grape, had coated her from toe-to-chest. She opened her mouth to speak but was surprised – *and a touch concerned* – when nothing came out but an incoherent wheeze.

The reasonable part of her brain, the logical override that had been flipped to extinguish the unbelieving sensory organs, stared blankly at the exit, now blackened by the bark of an oak tree high as a man, littered with pieces of church. *And churchgoers!* part of her mind insisted. But she shoved that thought away, let logic take the controls once more.

As you can see, dear, Logic said, its inner voice steady, almost relaxed in its precision, *the exit, quite obviously, is now blocked. And time, I fear, is of the essence.*

"There's a door in the back!" someone yelled, but now things seemed lost. Carrie realized, quite lucidly, that things had suddenly spiraled completely out of control.

The panicked mob surged back toward the chapel, colliding with those who had either waited patiently or were trying to push their way into the foyer to see what the hell had happened. The two forces collided and there were more screams—men yelling, children crying, women clawing to get through, to get back, to get OUT.

Carrie felt arms reach around her waist from behind and try to lift her to her feet. But she couldn't move, couldn't think of what to do with her legs, with the muscles of her body. *How do I stand?* she thought, and looked at her blood-smeared hands in a daze, as if the answers were written upon dripping palms. She watched, emotionless, as a little girl in a pink dress and white leggings fell – no, was *pushed* – into the edge of a pew, her head smacking the dense wood hard enough that Carrie heard the thud of impact amidst the chaos. The girl fell to the ground and was stomped upon like a rag doll, her mother *Mrs. Baker, I think, yes, Mrs. Baker my senior high school teacher I loved her she always brought in cookies on Fridays* was trying to yank the girl to her feet, screeching and baring her teeth at the others crowding past her in a frenzy for escape.

More hands grabbed Carrie and this time she was able to find her feet, allow herself to be lifted from the floor. Her mother stared at her, shook her, pleading. "We've got to go, honey! We've got to get out of here!"

Carrie nodded and started to let herself be pressed toward the chapel, where the crowd heading toward the back had soundly defeated those who had been heading toward the front. She spun her head back toward the hallway, toward the office where she had seen Eli lying on the floor. But she could not move, could not free herself as she was shoved mercilessly forward, into the chapel where people were filling the aisle, tearing to shreds the white paper runner that had been laid for her walk to the altar. Others were climbing over the backs of pews, rushing toward a distant door...

The tall arched windows that lined the east side of the church burst inward as one. Shards of glass flew like a hail of bullets toward those trapped inside. More screams rang out and a few people collapsed, grabbing at their heads, at legs, at necks. One woman had both hands over her face, an inhuman howl coming from within, blood spurting between her knuckles.

"Oh no!" her mother screamed from beside her. "Oh God, no!"

Carrie turned toward the windows. The view of sky and cornfields had been obliterated by a funnel wider than a football field. It filled the world. She watched in stunned amazement at its sheer *power*, at the fibrous musculature of the churning air, blackened and pulsing, and hungry – God help them, it was *hungry*.

The building shook, and Carrie saw pieces of the church vanish, sucked away, pulled toward this embodiment of earth's vengeance, this smoky, churning fist of a deadly god. She raised her eyes to the ceiling as part of the chapel's roof blew apart and vanished. Those nearest the gaping hole were pulled into the air, as if lifted by invisible rope.

There was another surge of bodies and Carrie was shoved to the floor between two pews. Beth and her mother fell with her. They clutched at each other, as if one of them had the power to save the other.

Then the east wall of the church disappeared, replaced by a broad veil of indescribable force, the thick foul funnel having finally arrived, late to the ceremony.

THE SIREN WAILED as if from a distant harbor, the office windows rattled ceaselessly with the force of hurricane-force gusts, and the sounds of panic from the foyer made evident what was happening to the wedding guests. Parker and his mates had heard it as well, and their interest in Eli waned with each passing second of the growing tumult, both outside *and* inside the small church.

"What the hell's going on out there?" Brock asked, his foot resting with almost nonchalance on the back of Eli's suit coat, pushing his belly into the ground.

"Storm," Tuck said.

Parker looked down at Eli, then at his brother. "You think it's bad?"

Brock shrugged and turned his bulbous head toward the screams coming from the foyer, just outside the pastor's door. "Shit," he said.

Parker nodded, stepped over Eli and opened the door to the office. Brock removed his heel from Eli's back and followed.

There! Eli thought, the very sight of her a jolt of hot current to his brain. *Carrie...*

From his vantage point on the floor, his head swimming, his jaw throbbing painfully, he saw past the legs of the brothers and into the lobby. He saw Carrie standing white as an angel, more radiant and beautiful than he'd ever thought possible. He would have smiled if the muscles of his jaw had deigned to respond to his brain's commands.

He watched the pastor take her by the arms, then a swarm of people surged into his line-of-sight, and she was pulled away. The roof above was being beaten by hail, and the winds, already at a seemingly impossible pitch, were picking up speed. Eli forced himself to his elbows, then his hands and knees. Tuck ran out the door, following the brothers who had disappeared into the thicket of guests crowding toward the exit like a dressed-up murder of hungry crows fighting for a spill of fresh guts.

Eli heard more yelling, then the loud *crack* of a slamming door. He put a hand to the desk to steady himself, stood shakily. He heard a whimper and looked down to see Henry huddled on the floor in the corner of the room, hands between his knees. *My God... he's praying.*

As if realizing he was not alone, Henry looked up at Eli, his eyes white eggs of fear. "I always hated storms," he said, his hands visibly trembling. "Even as a child, I had a recurring nightmare – night terrors, really – of a storm blowing me away. A tornado eating me up. I can't..."

But an enormous crash from the foyer drowned out his words and shook the building. Henry screamed, then moaned loudly. Eli was sure the kid had wet himself but couldn't find the time to care because through the open door he watched the entire front of the building crash inward, saw the gnarled limb of a giant tree stick its length into the church foyer as if reaching for a life to take. Blood was everywhere. People were screaming full-throated and pushing away from the doors, back into the church.

"Carrie!" he yelled. He had just taken his first step toward the chapel, toward the destruction, when a hand clutched his leg. He looked down to see Henry holding him back, still crying, yelling something about being alone, about being taken away. Heat built in Eli's chest and with wide red-rimmed eyes he bound ropes of air tightly around Henry's body that raised him from the floor, his arms and legs locked, his eyes slipping from fear to shock to horror.

"Eli!" he shrieked, eyes wide with shock.

Eli's lip dipped into a snarl and with a singular thought he *pushed.*

Henry's body flew backward hard enough that his palms met his shoe-tips. He crashed through the window like a foul ball and was swallowed by the raging storm.

More shouts rang out, mingled with the sounds of the building being ripped apart. The jet-engine whine of the great whirlwind had fully manifested, devouring and destroying all in its path.

Without a second thought, Eli ran toward it.

IT WAS THE loudest thing she had ever heard, could imagine ever hearing. It was as if the entire world were being torn to atoms, ground to dust. The wind roared, and although she knew she was screaming—screaming so loud she could feel the pain in her throat and the burn in her lungs—she could not hear herself, could not hear the cries of the others, could hear nothing at all save the wind, so deafening as to make her vision shake with the force of it.

Still flattened against the floor, Carrie turned onto her side. Beth's face stared back at her. She was yelling something, eyes wild with fear. Carrie looked away from her, from those terror-filled eyes, and toward the aisle. She saw the approaching wall of the cyclone and knew she would soon be dead.

People had stopped running and were now holding on to anything they could lay hands on – the ends of the pews, the altar, each other. There was the sense of an unveiling and Carrie looked up to see the roof of the church peel away like the lid of a soup can.

The sky above was demonic, the ceiling of hell itself. Black pulsing clouds shoved and jostled against each other, filled the dark green heavens. Hail and rain fell in a deluge through the open ceiling, soaking those inside within seconds. Carrie sat up, then tried to stand. She had to run, to escape. A hand gripped hers and tried to pull her back. She turned and saw her mother hiding under a pew, reaching for her, beckoning her to lie with her, to be with her at the end of everything.

The air inside the church – or what was left of it – was circulating like a blender at high speed. Pieces of wood and glass filled the air. As Carrie watched in a sort of senseless shock – distantly aware of the mosquito-bite pain of debris cutting her arms, legs and face – a red pickup truck crashed through the rear wall as if thrown like a child's toy, decimating the twelve-foot cross that hung there and crunching grille-first into the large altar. The small cluster of people that had been clutching at the slab were crushed or thrown. A small old lady, stripped to her underwear, flew toward the missing east wall and never found the ground; she simply traveled higher and higher, spinning, white limbs flapping, through the air and into the sky until she vanished within the immense funnel, as if sucked into it through a giant straw.

More of the wedding guests were being lifted away, and Carrie could feel her dress – her long, beautiful bridal dress – being pulled toward the vortex. She hurriedly studied what was left of the church interior, hoping to see Eli one last time before it was over, to say she was sorry, perhaps to say she'd been wrong.

Instead she saw the man she was to marry, and with emotionless cool she watched as Parker and Brock threw people aside as they pushed their way toward the front of the sanctuary. Before they made it halfway, there was a blur of brown, and a honed splinter of wood the size of a baseball bat slammed into Brock's chest, opening him like a red mouth, rib bones for teeth. Parker groped for him as he fell, then looked around in a panic, as if someone could help. As if anyone could be helped, or spared.

For a moment they made eye contact, but Carrie saw nothing in his eyes but fear. He thrust his arms up over his head, warding off the singeing splinters of wood and glass. She watched, with that same sensation of numbness, as her own nana grabbed him around the waist. To his credit, he embraced her as a flailing limb of the storm swept across the pews, snatched them from the earth and tore them away.

No longer able to watch, Carrie spun and dropped to her knees, wanting to hold her mother once more before it was too late.

She looked at the floor where Beth and her mother had been only moments ago, but the space underneath the pew was empty. They were gone. *But how?* she thought, and an icy cold shook her. She slumped and let go of her feelings, of her life. Felt it drain out of her like sand. Deep down, she hoped maybe they'd escaped. Found a way out. A miracle.

The cyclonic mass was here now, and it was time. The beast roared in triumph, bellowed with enough violent force that Carrie's hearing became buried beneath a high-pitched whistle as the great god of destruction bore down on its final sacrifice. She felt herself sliding toward it. Her mind, her thoughts, her fears, were consumed completely by the mad howl of the monster. She put her hands over her eyes, closed them tight. She did not want to see the end of her life.

And then… from one heartbeat to the next… *silence.*

"Carrie."

Hands landed lightly on her waist, just above her hips and bent knees. The thunderous roar of the storm had stopped. No… not stopped… *muted.* The ringing in her ears remained, but the pull of the wind had vanished. The sounds of death, of nature's fury, were nothing but dim white noise.

"Carrie, look at me. Please."

Is this God? she thought. *Is this what happens when you die?*

Gentle hands moved from her waist to her wrists, pulled her hands from her face.

"Open your eyes."

Carrie did, and joy swelled in her heart.

Eli sat before her, his face bloody and already bruising, his beautiful smile slanted to one side and gapped by two missing teeth. She smiled back at him, briefly in relief and with a mad surge of love, wanting to hug him, to touch him… but she saw something else in his face beside the pain, that crooked smile.

He was shaking. And his hands, though gentle, were tight on her wrists with tension. Despite her shock – and her happiness at seeing him, at holding him – she could not resist turning to look behind her, madly hoping the storm was impossibly gone, hoping she would see only blue sky and a green harvest splitting the horizon.

But it *was* there, filling every inch of her vision. The great writhing face of the twister, ready to feed.

"Don't look at it, Carrie. Look at me," he said quietly, his voice soft and clear, as if they were lying side-by-side on a cool autumnal night, watching the stars. "Keep your eyes on me."

She did, and looked upon him with wonder.

The cyclone that had consumed the church now completely surrounded them. They knelt, each facing the other, holding on almost peacefully before the approach of the swirling colossus. Carrie could not feel it, could not hear its frustrated wailing as they passed – somehow – *into* the funnel. The world went black as they slipped inside the great heart of the beast, and she was spared by deep shadow the sight of meat and metal flying furiously around them, bouncing off the surface of the protective bubble, vanishing into the folds of wind. An insane fury encapsulated them, and if she had looked up (*she dared not!*), Carrie would have seen a great green eye staring down at her from the heavens, glowing bright with cosmic hate, with its frustrated desire to consume.

"Close your eyes," he said, his voice muffled, his breathing heavy. "And know that I love you."

She obeyed, relishing the peace of her own darkness, the silence of his protection. He held her slim wrists tightly and they waited together, not speaking, as death passed them by. After a hundred rapid beats of her heart, after minutes that seemed without end, the world finally lightened from complete black to a shadowy gray. The edge of the tornado licked at their protective shield with its last deadly whips before moving past, off to find other victims, other worlds to rent and tear.

Carrie could stand it no longer. She wanted to grab Eli fiercely, pull him to her despite her fear of distracting his focus. She needed him to know what she felt for him. What part of her had *always* felt for him.

And so, she opened her eyes, and screamed.

Carrie screamed in fright, in horror, in absolute despair. Her body and soul emptied itself with her cries, gutting her. A sorrow she had never known, a maddening pain, tore at her heart.

Eli knelt before her still, but his pale skin sagged on his bones, as if the fat and muscle inside him had melted away. His eyes were gone, replaced by blue water, twinkling in his sockets like the surface of a creek. It poured down his cheeks in an impossible, constant flow.

"Eli, let go!" she yelled, and could already feel the pocket of air around them dissipating, the noise of the departing twister growing steadily louder.

He shook his head and she thought maybe he might have smiled one last time. He opened his mouth as if to say goodbye, but only dark sand poured from between his lips. The skin covering his hands grew hot, and she tenderly pulled her wrists free with a wince, saw the red bands around her arms, the charred lace of her dress where he'd held her. Parts of his flesh sparkled with yellow flame, and where it met water, steam rose in silky tethers.

"Eli, let go, let go! Please let go!" she screamed, for the world had returned and she could feel the rain once more, the playful push of now-harmless gusts of wind in her hair; heard the rumbling of the dying storm. "I love you, Eli! My blue eyes, oh no please no..."

She wept and pressed what remained of him to her chest, felt the heat of the flames eating his skin, smelled his flesh in the smoke. The water that poured from his eyes ran cool over her neck. His suit sagged in her arms, then collapsed in the growing pile of warm mud that had once been her only true friend.

She lifted her eyes from him only once, to watch the monster moving away, off into the distance, a black mountain of corn stalks rising through the air to feed it, to serve.

Carrie looked down through a distorted lens of tears at what remained, pushed her hands into the charred wet fabric of the suit. Sobbing, she laid her body flat to rest with him. She kissed the mud, let it stick to her face and hands, mingle with her blood and tears. She smelled the deep minerals of his lost body, the enchanted elements of earth mixed with his sacrifice, with the magic of first love, with love forever lost.

THE WHEEL

1

It takes three men and a furious fate to destroy Mary's life.

There she is. In a bra. Buttoning new jeans. Twisting to the mirror to inspect her ass. Strawberry hair spilling over freckles, spread out and faint as faraway stars in milky space, a universe exposed in negative.

The soft bump and flex of a shoulder bone.

Everything looks how she wants it. The clock says ten minutes until Rob arrives. The window is glazed with custard sunshine, soon to be caramel dusk. She must hurry.

It's a casual date. But still a date. No T-shirts. A blouse then. Red. Yes, red and fiery. And the leather jacket. It'll be cold at the pier. It's September now, it'll be cold. The ocean will be nipping at the beach, frigid. Cooling the air.

Heels or sneakers? Shit. No time for this. Sneakers. Fine.

There she goes to check her hair, make-up, practice a smile that will light up her royal blue sparklers. Love, youth, vitality. So excited for the night she feels ready to burst. Tonight with Rob. A palpable excitement, a buzzing electric wire tapped into a hot-light Saturday night. Quickly, what to bring. Clutch will do. Essentials only.

Wait, do you hear?

And now she's flying to the stairs because there's a knock at the door that means Rob has arrived.

Time to go because time is short.

OUTSIDE THE FOUR-UNIT building just off Lincoln Boulevard, that messy urban strip that runs parallel to the coastline but bears none of its fruit, Rob waits.

His hand touches the pocket of his jeans. Fingertips find the secret. A silver ring, encrusted with diamonds, crowned by the largest, the one he'd saved for. Tonight is the night. It was all planned, etched in his popping mind, neuro-scraps scribbled upon over the last several months while driving, at work, half-asleep before rising.

They will have dinner, drinks. A stop at the arcade. Then, when the silent dark blue dusk settles completely and night falls, stars winking, they'll ride the Ferris Wheel. Dashing strips of neon tubes, an eternally shooting star at its hub; red, blue and yellow lights pulsing outward from the wheel's core, to its ends, to the floating cars, hinged and rocking. When they arrive at the top – the very highest point – the whole of the city will be spread out to the east, the dark blanket of the Pacific to the west, the coast snaking blisters of runway lights terminated by the distant smokestacks of Long Beach to the south, the bent elbows of the Santa Monica mountains – that stagnant herd of hunchbacked Mastodons, wooly with forest green – to the north.

But not yet. Later. Footsteps. He takes a deep breath, lets it out. Smiles in readiness.

The door flies open. She dovetails into him and they kiss.

"You look beautiful."

Neither know anything of the man sleeping in the small plane a few miles away, snoring in drunken slumber, as if in wait to be summoned like a Kraken, destroyer of worlds and true love.

FRANK IS KNEES-TO-CHIN in the Cessna's seatless rear cabin. The wind-tossed tarp lies across the windshield like a dead acrobat, letting the late-afternoon sun drink the interior shadows like a golden cat laps cream.

The snores stutter and Frank wakes, slow and dumb. One lid lifts half-open, the other remains sealed. There's a crust at the corners of his eyes and lips. His mouth is an ashtray dipped in sap and left in the hot sun for an afternoon. His brain is pudding with a heavy skin. He manages to rub the sealed eye open. A watch ticks on his wrist. Later than he thought. Much later.

"You're kidding me," he says, voice slurred and ragged, breath foul. Then remembers.

The Typhoon Restaurant, just off the tarmac. Pilots and "in-the-know" tourists. Leslie working the bar, passing him freebies because they hadn't slept together yet. Votes of confidence. Frank a regular, and regularly alone. The Cessna 172 had been a gift to himself after the divorce. The property in Brentwood a gift to his wife, now ex'd forever. Which left him with the bungalow in Venice they'd been renting to a couple LMU grad students, and if he'd felt bad about terminating their month-to-month, he didn't notice.

Now it was nights out at clubs, bars, hip-lobbied hotels. Spending more than he should, a fifty-year-old man trying for thirty all over again; but youth is slippery and does not play well with the older you wanting it back. It shucks and jives, laughs as you leap and cross your arms, hug empty air. All the dancing for coins made Frank a bitter, tired old bear. Desperate. The loneliness, after the divorce, at first nothing but a distant point in space, now a meteor bearing down, hellfire from the sky, big as a moon, plant-wilting heat, soul-wilting doom. No big red panic button in sight except for the shot glass, Leslie filling it up so he could hit it again, destroy the destroyer.

Last night he'd hit the big red button until it broke, split down the middle. His black-out started shortly after midnight, lifted momentarily at closing. The manager played orderly, ushered him out by the armpits. A cab was called, but fuck that. He'd *fly* home. And so, evading the night guard, he'd snuck through the dark, under the bulging white corpse-eye of the waxing gibbous moon, to the Cessna.

And, oh, what fortunes awaited him! A gift, a forgotten gift. A full bottle of the good stuff. The old stuff. Hunched in the rear, sucking on the glass tit. Brown sustenance. The great curing poison, swallowed, swallowed down.

Now, awake, blood still thick with the devil's elixir, he knows his task. *That bitch*, he thinks. And then, the next shoe drops.

Catalina Island.

Of course! That's where she is all right, walking through herds of buffalo with Jim What's-his-fuck. The new guy. Yeah, sure.

Frank knows what to do. A quick sweep of the tarp, a topping of the 172's tank, and off, off he'll go, high into the sky, due west for the island. If he leaves now, he'll land at Island in the Sky airfield well before nightfall, twenty short minutes. Then he'd rearrange things a bit. Get some shit *organized* with the ex and old Jim What's-his-fuck.

Frank belches, then cracks the door and pukes onto the tarmac. Wipes his mouth. Better. Much better. Stepping over the slop, proving himself worthy. Note the dexterity! He smiles as he pulls loose the knots of the splayed tarp.

Time to fly.

2

Santa Monica. Strips of commerce surrounded by stucco clusters of apartment housing, swaths of Zen architecture interiors, bamboo-fenced bungalows, minimal, traditional pastels with postage-stamp lawns and overpriced brushed-chrome wine coolers, grandfathered craftsmen filled with orange shag and elderly surfers. Parks and strollers. Pot bellies and tans. Money.

The beach city hugs the coast like a desperate lover. Traffic backs up from the east on concrete arteries, fresh unwanted blood from inland districts stream in like a temporary flu, filling the beaches, the boardwalk, the boutique studios, the overpriced restaurants (newly opened and already in the red). Food trucks serve gourmet burgers, lobster on a stick.

The Inlanders, tourists and locals all agree on one destination, a plank-board middle finger pointing west from the mighty knuckles of the coast, the massive digit held aloft upon shoulders of sand-sunk pillars, bases slick with algae.

The Pier.

A paved two-lane road pushes into the beach, extends beneath the great neon sign: *Santa Monica Yacht Harbor: Sport Fishing. Boating. Cafes.* Sidewalks lining the entry are packed with people filing onto the pier, hitting that first massive wood plank like a piano key, water shushing far below, over the ocean now and still walking. A wonderland. Vendors huddle along the right. Drawing caricatures. Your name written in dolphins shaped like letters. Seashell jewelry and hash pipes. T-shirts. On the left, more shops. Fast food. Hot dogs and soda. Cotton candy. Past that, the housed carousel, where Horace McCoy thought they shot the horses. Now the arcade. Filled with beeping boxes of light that used to cost a quarter, now a dollar. Maybe two. Sixty seconds of confused adrenaline. Skee-Ball, lined up mini-bowling lanes ending in raised bulls-eyes, delicate thunder of the rolls humming beneath the electricity. And look up! The rollercoaster! Twisted steel swooping and dipping like pulled taffy. No screaming yet. Rides open at dusk. Not quite time. The sky is still mandarin, the orange sun still sinking. Buddha-belly in a shimmering bath, surrounded by rose-colored walls. Pink clouds so bright it's fantasy. All of it unreal.

Here's Rob and Mary, hand-in-hand, continuing their stroll toward the end of the pier. Smiling. Heading toward the sunset, wanting front-row seats. Rob looks to his left, past the roller coaster, up higher, higher.

The great wheel.

Already blushing neon-red in the husky haze of sundown, the wheel stands like a sentinel god, benevolent. But demanding sacrifice. The priest at its feet fills flesh into its rotating row of iron mouths, sending them up and around; stomachs sink as they go up and up and up. This high the people are ants on the boardwalk. Toy cars filing into rows back toward land. Distant seagulls are black drifting flakes of ash over the water...

But not yet. Not yet...

Rob and Mary walk past the great wheel. Butterflies flutter in his guts. It's on the wheel he'll show her the ring. It's at the top he'll ask for her hand. *She'll say yes, and we'll kiss in our private cabin, high above the world.*

THE PRIEST OF the great wheel arrives unshaven, a former carnie wearing a ball cap and dark blue T-shirt. Black jeans and high-tops. He readies the ride as the sun sinks, distant and bored, tired of this day. It slashes its own belly, bleeds fire into the cold sea. Seppuku sunset.

51

THE FUMES FROM the fuel truck are withering. A wall of stench deadly in more ways than one. Frank waits, head down, tries not to bring up more of last-night's drink.

"I'll be back."

The mechanic waves, not caring, and continues to fill the plane, fuel truck rumbling behind him like a beast. The gray tarmac turns charcoal in the encroaching dark. Frank shuffles across the cooling asphalt to the administration building, strides briskly through the empty lobby, past double-doors and into the parking lot where his BMW sits hunched and impatient, black skin reflecting the lot's phosphorous lights. Frank walks by the car without a glance, heads for Centinela Avenue. He reaches the sidewalk, cars zip by both ways. His head is fuzzy, his stomach gurgles. He punches the button to cross, punches it again. Watches the orange hand showing *Halt*. Works his feet, chews his cheeks.

"Come on."

Beyond the busy street and up a block to the next corner lies a small strip of commerce. A watch repair and sales shop. A tailor. A tanning spa called Golden Buns, can you believe it, and a store with posters of bottles hanging in the window, neon signs of beer names with logos. The stretch above the door lit up. LIQUOR. The R sorta flutters, as if a bulb has gone funny.

The orange hand becomes a white pedestrian, frozen in mid-stride. Frank hustles across the street to pick up a bottle of Jim Beam and, god willing, some Twinkies.

Whiskey and processed sponge cake. A sad man's last meal.

Ten minutes later he's paying the old guy behind the counter, sticks the bulging paper bag under an arm. Hot-foots it back to the plane. Frank wants to get to Catalina before dark, but realizes now, tilting his head to the sky, that it's not going to happen. The gold-hued horizon is already bleeding out, red swelling into purple shadow. The clouds above the bruised miasma ruffle toward heaven like the bottom of a wave you'd dive beneath to avoid the water-palm slap, holding your breath. Clouds the color of cotton soaked in fluorescent tie-dye, rippling and vast.

"Ain't never been lucky," he mumbles, feeling childish and petulant. His head throbs as he crosses Centinela again, and he debates going back for a pouch of aspirin. A car blares its horn. White walker has become orange hand. Cars wait as he debates.

Has he stopped? Yeah. He has. Flicks his eyes toward a red Honda, a fat face rages behind glass. Mouthed profanities, muted.

He mutters curses at himself, at his ex, at the asshole in the Honda, then scurries up the curb, eager to be into the bottle.

THEY STAND AT the wooden railing, look over the wide sea. The sky is a light show, the water a glassy blue canvas upon which the sun paints its dying colors. Rob grasps Mary's hand. Her fingers squeeze his greedily, but their eyes never leave the glowing horizon. He asks if she's hungry. She shakes her head. Behind them, the pier swarms, rides arch into the sky, laughter and noise blink and sizzle in the air like popping stars. Before them only the brilliant flat Pacific, the black triangle silhouette of a faraway sailboat. The muffled racket of sea birds, piercing and hungry. It's hypnotic.

A rough tugging at Rob's sleeve. Reverie broken, he looks to Mary, who still gazes outward. He smells sour and ashes. Piss and body odor.

"Hey man, give me a buck."

Rob grimaces, sensing the intruder's degraded state before actually seeing him. He turns, sees an old man buried in a heavy brown sport coat, corduroy and patches. His skin is brown as mud, wrinkled as the ocean surface, eyes ice blue and bloodshot. His knit hat too large on his narrow head, tasseled like a child's toque; dirty cartoon eyes, woven into the brim, spring out above his temples. Rob sees bugs crawling within its weaves.

"I don't..."

The man opens his mouth into a snarl, exposing two rows of solid yellow teeth, two wooden fences you'd climb over as a child. A shortcut to the park. To a blackened tongue. He pulls hard at Rob's arm, as if expecting coins to fall from the boy's palm. "Gimme something!" he says, harsh and guttural.

Mary turns from the ocean, from the sunset. Her blazing blue eyes still reflect the dying light. She sees a wrinkled black thing pulling at Rob's arm. Glazed and dripping, vacuous eyes, sharp yellow teeth springing from a small mouth, punching through lip and cheek. Black saliva spits from the hole, a tiny geyser, puckered. Rob's arm is covered in the spray.

"Easy!" Rob yells. Heads turn. Families. Teenagers with bad skin and sodas.

He pushes at the man and the man swipes at him. Sharp nails tear into his skin. A cat's hiss comes from the foul mouth.

"Hey!"

Without another word the man turns, walks briskly away, cursing into the air.

Rob raises his arm, examines the scratches. He wants to go after the old fucker. *Let it go,* he thinks. *Don't ruin the night. Not now.*

Remember that weird bum in the cartoon hat? they'd say, years later.

"Rob," Mary says, reaches for his gashed arm.

He smiles at her, pulls away. "It's nothing. Just a scratch." He looks at it slyly, then smiles at her again. He had rolled up his sleeves because of the warm day, and he quickly unrolls them, covers the damage.

Mary sees the mix of blood and black saliva seep through the fabric. She looks for the thing that had attacked him, but it's gone.

"Hey, forget that guy," he says, clutching her hands, forcing her attention back to him, away from the escaping attacker. "Let's eat."

JEREMIAH PETERS IS no priest. Yes, he feeds the great wheel. Fresh flesh, round and round. But he holds no belief in a greater power. Be it God or Devil. Eastern gods, Western gods. None of it matters a shit to him. Jeremiah worships Man. Or, more precisely: Woman. He's done a little prison time, yeah, sure. Been in some nasty scrapes over the years. When he was a traveling carnie, he'd been fired twice for inappropriate behavior toward some of the clientele. Bounced around every state there was with whatever outfit would take him on.

See, here's the thing: everyone needs a good machinist. Jeremiah can fix the gearbox of a Tilt-O-Whirl or refashion a snapped metal clasp on a chair swing, replace the wheel of a bumper car easy as spit on it. Even repair the motor of a Merry-Go-Round. If you can do all these things, then the *other* things about you (things that are not so helpful) get overlooked. Bad behavior is more easily forgiven.

To a point.

For example, when working a carnival, Jeremiah had the nasty habit of sneaking into haunted houses. He'd slip in through an employee maintenance entrance, wait for a couple women to come by in the dark – clutching at each other with overstated fear – then step in behind and grope one of 'em like a monkey in heat. In the dark, they never saw him coming. Some of them took a while to react, unsure. Maybe part of the experience? Not fully understanding... and some of them would just stand there and let him do what he wanted, hell, for a minute. Sometimes more. He'd shock them, see. *Surprise* them into acquiescence. Of course, there were always the strong ones, the ones who would turn and attack with spitting fury from the get-go. Jeremiah just gave those women a hard shove before slipping away – disappearing via a secret door, or through a hidden opening behind one of the displays. By the time they made their way out of the house, hissing and screaming, he'd be long gone, yessir. *Long* gone. Having a smoke with a fellow carnie behind the hot dog stand, innocent as you please.

Not a bad system. Not, that is, until the bitch with the six-gun-quick smartphone. Flash in the dark. Profile shot. Busted. Police, charges, the whole bit. Fired. Jail time. When he got out, it just meant a different state, different carnival.

He could fix anything, after all.

More importantly, he could run a wheel. A much-desired skill. Much in demand. Most folks don't realize how complicated it is to operate a Ferris Wheel, that it's easily the most complex of all the rides at a carnival, despite their evolution.

The newer ones are automated, full hydraulics, but you still need to balance the tubs just right. Can't have them tipping. More importantly, you have to keep the wheel itself balanced just *so*. Modern wheels are nothing like the ones from the old days. The universally-used clutch-and-brake systems created by the Big Eli Bridge Company were death traps. The cable drive systems total nightmares. An operator would need to time the brake *just* right so the rotating tubs would stop dead on the platform. Quick math and a certain touch, that's what it was about. Older models relied almost purely on *feel*. No easy task on a long, hot day. No sir.

But now? Now the controls are just buttons and a brake override. Jeremiah would never admit to it, but any dummy could likely run the newer models. But folks still wanted someone with experience. *Just in case.*

And Jeremiah has decades of that. He can run a Big Eli or an Aristocrat with his eyes closed, get those tubs to rest exactly where he wants them on the downturn. Knows just how much pressure to give the clutch, get everyone spinning, all the weight distro'd correctly. When you're a wheel operator, you learn quick to shake hands with gravity and make nice, because you're running things together. You're partners.

Jeremiah hardly worries about such intricacies these days. Now that he runs the big white beauty at the Santa Monica Pier. This baby's even solar powered. Only one in the world. Jeremiah was proud to operate such a fine beast. Yeah, he was living the dream. Hugging the ocean. Running the Ferris Wheel. He's learned his lesson. Couple of times. He's better now. Keeps to himself. Internet provides all sorts of freakish pleasures for him, he doesn't need any more trouble, thanks very much.

Of course, sometimes... well, he just can't help himself.

He looks at the sky, at his watch. Little on the early side, but he's already checked in, so what the hell. He unlocks the cable securing the power switch, pushes the paint-chipped heavy metal lever up, flips the lights.

The Wheel comes to life.

Beyond the platform, a long chain holds the gathering crowd at a distance. Folks give a cheer. Jeremiah smiles, nods to a few of the little ones who look up at the massive wheel, the lights reflecting off shiny faces. It's kinda sweet. He looks at their mothers, as well. Thinks them even sweeter.

He makes a few inspections, walks underneath the wheel, across the metal platform, to the operating panel and clutch system. He'll send her around a few dozen times, like he always does, make sure everything is running smooth. Check each tub, confirm they close and latch proper. Then check them all again. No doubt tonight would be the night the insurance inspector would make an appearance. They like to come when it's good and busy, when you least expect them. Jeremiah would be damned if the City of Santa Monica gets flagged on his watch. He isn't planning on moving again. No, this is the last stop. He likes it here. Likes the ocean. The big wheel. He and the wheel have an understanding. She'll keep on spinning, and he'll keep feeding her fresh meat.

Apparently, Jeremiah believes in gods after all.

He just doesn't know it.

3

FRANK SITS IN the Cessna, stares at the controls with blurry eyes. He has the plane powered on but the engines are silent. Airport chatter of other pilots and the controllers fill the cabin. White noise.

"Okay, here we go," he says, and dons his headset, turns off the chatter, prepares to run the checklist. He does so mechanically, aviator-training kicking in despite his inebriation. He double-checks the mixture, switches, breakers. Gauges all acceptable levels.

"Clear prop!" he yells, then realizes the windows are closed. He opens the vent windows on both sides of the cabin. "Clear prop!" he yells again, starts the engine. The propeller roars to life, a monstrous mosquito. "SMO tower, this is Cessna 172 Tango Charlie," he pauses, belches wetly. Continues. "Requesting taxi to runway two."

Static. Prays he sounds sober. He waits, continues the after-start checklist.

"Cessna 172 Tango Charlie... are your lights on? We're not seeing you."

"Fuck," he mumbles, and reaches under the control wheel to flip the white switches, turning on navigation, beacon, strobe and taxi lights. "Fuck fuck." If they gave him shit he'd have to feign sickness. "Uh, roger that. Lights on. Sorry, tower, distracted by a passenger having seatbelt issues. Checks are all clear. Request taxi to runway two."

For a few seconds, the only reply is hissing static. The propeller roars in front of him, eager to chew air. "Okay, Cessna 172 Tango Charlie... we see you now. Proceed to runway two. Slight delay there, so standby for takeoff. Busy night tonight. We'll give you clearance momentarily."

"Copy that tower."

Frank releases the brake and throttles gently. The plane rolls forward.

ROB AND MARY at Buddy Tub's. Splitting the breaded shrimp and a basket of fries. Sipping Corona. Grease stains on the paper lining of the fried shrimp basket. Mary thinks Rob is acting strange. Distant. He isn't talking much, eyes everywhere. She's worried, then afraid. Is it *her?* Is something wrong?

They've been together three years. Oddly, although they'd both gone to the same college, it wasn't until after graduation that they started dating. Throughout their tenure at Cal State they'd been merely acquaintances. He a friend of a friend. Occasional parties. A few words in passing once. A baseball game when the Titans were in the playoffs. A few months after graduation, she'd been invited to a dinner party. Her old roommate's new apartment. A housewarming. Rob was there and when they saw each other that night it was like they *knew*. They'd had their flings, their experiences. And now. Now was the time for that next level. The real relationship. A night out minus the handle of cheap vodka, the drugs she was always too nervous to try. Sure, she'd pop the occasional tab of ecstasy, maybe a small line of coke. But she wasn't into it like the others. She supposed she was boring for a college girl. Only two boyfriends. Very little experimenting, sexual or otherwise. At the party, they talked about their mutual college experience, and she could tell he'd led a similar path. Over the course of that evening, they'd separate, as if not stuck to the other, but she'd find herself searching the room while everyone mingled, music played too loudly. A wistful homage to dorm life. With increasing tension, she'd try to find him. At one point, she'd thought he'd left, was caught off guard by how hurt she'd been. Panicked in search for a trace of him. She found him on the small balcony, chatting with another girl she didn't know. Relief mingled with new hurt.

Then his eyes found her. He smiled, and she knew it was private. For her. The hurt went away, and she relaxed, knowing – at that *moment* – things would be fine.

They shyly exchanged numbers. Words bumped awkwardly in the air between them. He called her later that night, and she floated. Adrenaline capsized rationale. Her words forgotten the second they left her lips.

They dated voraciously, fed off each other like starved cannibals. It was obvious from the first date it was going to be forever. The realization was a shock, both frightening and luxurious. Together.

Three years later. She wondered if he knew it was the anniversary of their first date. A bad horror movie and drinks at a tucked-away speakeasy in Culver City, where the bartenders wore suspenders, grew beards and waxed their hair. She'd been snapped at by the bartender for stirring her newly-prepared drink too vigorously, and she and Rob had rolled their eyes, laughed, enjoyed the pride of the mixologist. It was strange to think it was only three years in the past. It seemed to her a lifetime with him had already been lived.

ROB ACHES. THE fried food sits in his belly like lead. His nerves are rattled. He's anxious for the moment to arrive. He glances out a window, sees people beginning to climb aboard the Ferris Wheel, feels a new surge of delicious panic. He's decided they'd skip the arcade, go straight to the wheel. He wants to get through it, then they'd have all night to revel, to celebrate. He looks at Mary, tries to smile, but she looks wary. She knows something's up. He was always been terrible at secrets. He nearly laughs out loud at his own tension. It's time to go.

"You done?" he blurts. Mary nibbles a lone French fry survivor.

She pops the fry into her mouth, sips her Corona, eyes darting up and left as she does so. She's annoyed. He knows. That's her tell. If she had locked eyes with him while drinking, they were good. If she looked down, or absently away, no problem. Up and to the left? Danger Will Robinson. He almost laughs again at his nerves, relishing the fact she's pissed at him. He imagines her relief, her joy, when she discovers the reason he's acting like a distracted, pushy idiot.

"Sure," she says, curt. "Didn't know you were in a hurry."

"I'm not," he lies. "Just done eating."

She softens, worry filtering her features like a black-and-white movie star. "Are you okay?"

He smiles and can tell it relaxes her. She'd know if the smile was a lie. "Totally. Just a little antsy tonight. Sorry."

She shrugs. Apology accepted, but he knows she's waiting for him to mention the anniversary. Maybe he'll mention it after. Part of him enjoys playing the lout. Like the friend forced to lie to pull off a surprise party. It only feels gross until the shouting starts.

He drops a twenty on the table. "Let's go."

"Like... go home?" Brow furrowed.

He wants to hug her, kiss away the pain in her eyes. "No. Hell no. I want to ride the Ferris Wheel."

She laughs, relieved, confused. "Really?"

"I've never done it." He stands, put out his hand. She takes it. "Come on, let's go see what's at the top."

4

JEREMIAH ISN'T FEELING so good. His heat is up. The women… my *god*, the *women* tonight.

It isn't even high summer. Not yet. Early June. Traces of spring still in the air before the heat of August and September. In Los Angeles, there are no winter months. There are hot months, warm months, cool months, and some weeks when it rains. The warm months are March through June. Heat kicks in at the end of July. Really gets cooking, then. Stays that way through November, typically. If residents are lucky, it'll cool down for December and January, but no promises. If they are incredibly lucky, it'll rain a few weeks around that same time. Off and on, if you please. Just enough to avoid the perennial drought, to keep the reservoirs and basins full, to keep the hills green. To wash away the pollution, the smog, the filth on the streets. Push it all back into the massive sea, the all-consuming sea. The great devourer.

No, June isn't too hot. But it's a warm night. Jeremiah wipes sweat from his brow, despite the encroaching night. Normally, he can contain the urges – the *intensity* – of his desires. But the way they dress! In all the nights Jeremiah has worked the pier, he has never seen a parade such as this. Beautiful young women, lined up in butt-clinging, thigh-grabbing shorts. Sheer tops, for the love of Christ. *So much flesh, so much flesh!* he thinks. *In you go, dear, in you go, watch your head, my god your thigh right there* and he restrains his own hand from reaching out, from touching a barely-covered breast, an ass. Rub his fingers along a long bare leg. Torture.

Jeremiah keeps loading them in, loading them in. His heart beats fast, his brow leaks tendrils of salty sweat from under his ballcap. His neck wet, his crotch swampy and hot. "Okay, miss, in you go." He's trying not to do anything stupid. That last one's boyfriend, the tough guy with the tattoos and permanent scowl? He saw Jeremiah's lust. The men often do. Hard to hide lust from another man, especially when it's directed toward a girl that man is with. Sixth sense. Primitive radar. But Jeremiah only nods and smiles, latches them in. Up they go, up and away until the next girl comes up, and he fights the battle all over again.

And now this one. Oh *sweet lord!* Look at this one. So pious, so innocent. Sweet tangerine. Twenty-two, twenty-three? An angel.

"You two are next. Uh, tickets please."

The young man with her, a bit of a model type himself. Fit and athletic, but not dumb, no, not stupid. But innocent like her. Naïve like she most assuredly is. Jeremiah takes the tickets from the young man, studies the girl more closely.

No. Wait a second, now... maybe not so innocent. But for him, yes, for him she would be. He tries to rein in the rabid stallions of his desire. *Sure*, he thinks, leering at the young couple, *I'll tame that gorgeous thing.*

"How long is the ride?" Mary asks the sweaty guy running the wheel, who she is already thinking of as "the old pervert who works at the pier." I mean, look at him. Gross. She clutches Rob's hand, steps closer to him.

"Oh, ah, usually around five minutes. I like to give everyone a few times around."

Rob barely hears Mary and the worker guy. His heart thumps in his ears. The ring in his pocket burns against his leg. It's so damn hot. A lot of people. Too close. Crowding him. He takes a deep breath. Feels Mary's hand clutch his.

For the millionth time that night, he jams his free hand into his pocket. He's been so paranoid about losing the ring. That morning he'd turned the jeans inside-out, studied the pocket lining to be sure there was no hole, no loose thread that could *become* a hole. But now he feels the prick of the small rock at the bottom. There. It's there, waiting. *Chill, dude,* he thinks. Tries to relax. The gondolas or whatever they're called are spinning around, around. He and Mary will be put on next. Red, green, yellow, blue. Each bears a faded number. Roofs like umbrellas. Open-air. A waist-high tub keeping the riders safely inside. The lights are frying his eyes. The music too loud. The crowd...

"Okay!" the man says, and Rob snaps his attention back. Sees the rotation of the massive wheel has slowed to a crawl. "When this group gets out of, let's see, number nine, you two hop in."

Nine? Is that a good number? A lucky number? Rob doesn't know. He's panicked. Okay, ride stopped. Four girls jump out, giggling. A waft of marijuana slams into his face. They were smoking up there. They're laughing and the old guy is smiling at them and Mary is pulling his hand, leading him forward, forward. The old guy opens the door, turns to help Mary in...

Mary steps in, then stops. What's happened? She spins, red fury. She slaps the old guy – *hard* – across the face. *What the fuck is going on?*

JEREMIAH CAN'T HELP himself. He opens the door, turns. The girl, holding her boyfriend's hand. It's safe, dear, of course it's safe. He lightly places a hand on her elbow, guides her inside. He's breathing heavy. My god, the smell of her. His dick so hard. Fucking hell. He slips a hand to her hip, as if to steady her. The other hand quickly to her other hip, slightly lower. *Just a little boost.* His hands are shaking. She puts a foot into the tub and, without his brain's consent, without his even fucking *thinking* about it, both hands slide *up*, over her breasts, lightning-quick, then away! A slip of the hand! An accident! She won't say anything, she'll be too confused... but she's turning. *Shit shit shit.* He smiles, starts to put his hands up, as if saying, *an accident, miss, an accident!*

No go. She smacks him a good one.

Damn.

"WHAT THE FUCK!" Mary screams, her eyes furious. She looks from the old man to Rob, who looks more confused than upset.

"I'm so sorry," Jeremiah says. "I didn't mean to... I'm so sorry young lady."

Rob now. Up close. Between them. Crowd in line paying attention. A couple cell phones out, aimed at the trio. At the drama. Someone yells down from one of the gondolas, angry at being stopped for so long. Rob turns to Mary.

"What happened?"

Mary looks into Rob's eyes. Sees the concern there, the fear, the potential madness that comes with loving someone. She looks over his shoulder at the old pervert, hands still up, shaking his gray head. Her eyes narrow. Back to Rob, who's put a hand on her shoulder, asking what's wrong. She wants to push his hand off. She wants to tell him what the fucker did.

No.

There it comes. Unbidden. Something... something deep inside her. A whisper. A warning.

No.

She doesn't want to listen. She wants to tell Rob that the creep copped a feel. Wants to have Rob kick his old tired ass up and down the pier. And he would, she knows he would. He'd beat the guy senseless.

Then what? Police. A scene. Their date night spent in a squad car, giving a statement. A complaint. Future trial, maybe. The night ruined. An ugly blemish on their lives. Something they'll remember forever. That night at the pier, when the old man grabbed you. The fight. The police. How it dragged on.

Yes, they'll think how horrible it was. How horrible the man was. How stained. And that stain would rub off. Just a little bit, onto them. It would become *part* of them. Part of who they were. Their lives. He'd be a piece of their puzzle. Somewhere down in a shadowy corner, a small piece tying their young lives together, a part of the tapestry that would be *them*.

No.

She drops her eyes, puts her hands on Rob's chest.

"Can we go?"

To her surprise, Rob does not acquiesce. Does not immediately take her hand, lead her away. Does not soothe her, kiss her, protect her. He only looks at her stupidly, mouth hanging open. His eyes wide, scared. No, not scared. Panicked.

"Go?" he says.

"Rob, I want to get out of here."

"Why? What's wrong? Mary, what happened?"

Mary says nothing. More people shouting from the ride now, from above. Squawking birds. It's been a couple minutes but it feels like an eternity. The people in line restless. All eyes on her. She looks quickly toward the man, who is now showing more impatience than apology. Eager to get this over with, one way or another, she guesses. Rob grabs both her hands.

"I want to go on the ride," Rob says, and now it's Mary's jaw that drops. "Seriously. I don't know what's wrong, but we can talk about it later. Please, Mary. For me. Let's just go on the ride."

Mary is flabbergasted. Unsure of herself, of him.

Hypnotically, without emotion, she finds herself nodding, then turning toward the open door. Toward the beet-red tub, rocking loosely on the hinge that connects it to the massive wheel. She feels hands on her again and wants to fucking slap them away but she knows it's just Rob, and that's okay. He's helping her up, and they're inside.

The seat next to her is sticky with spilled soda. She slides to the far side. Rob is opposite her, smiling uncomfortably. *How did this all get so twisted?* she thinks, then sees the smiling asshole operator stepping quickly to the door.

"No hard feelings, huh?" he says, and slams the door hard, almost clipping Rob's knee which lingered too close to the opening. She hears the latch snap firmly into place. She looks away, toward the hard white strut of the wheel, and beyond that the ocean, the coastline. People. Careless people and a distant moon. The sky otherwise full dark.

Mary feels a sickening jolt and they're moving. She can't look at Rob. She feels sick. Weak. Stupid. She feels taken advantage of. She's disgusted with herself. Why didn't she say something?

Because Rob. She studies him. Tries to understand why he's acting so strangely. Is he...*nervous?* Yes. Very nervous. Why hadn't she noticed it? Why hadn't she immediately understood? He wasn't acting aloof, or angry. He's scared shitless. Mary's rage subsides, buffered with the question of *why?*

What could Rob possibly be scared of?

The wheel stops. Below and behind them, more people get off, more climb on. Laughter. They are a little higher now. Away from the pier, the people, the creep. The breeze is light, cool.

ROB WATCHES MARY. He wants to ask her what happened, but he doesn't have to. Not really. It's obvious. The guy did something. Grabbed her weird. Touched her inappropriately. Something. But Rob doesn't want to ask. Doesn't want to know. *Not now, please, not now. Don't let it spoil things*... please, Lord.

Don't let anything spoil his plan.

5

FRANK IS IN the air.

The propeller drones. He studies the controls, but his mind is wet, slippery. The console of switches a blur. The black eyes of gauges wink at him. Taunting.

He finds himself losing altitude and jerks up. At one point he nods off, just as the plane crosses the line of cooling beach, the rustle of white-capped waves.

He comes to, but it's as if all the booze has kicked in at once. Panic gives his body the shakes. His eyeballs are vibrating, his hands full of tremors. A stabbing thought drills white-hot through his sluggish brain.

Just how drunk am I?

With a burst of clarity, Frank realizes that flying an aircraft is not a good idea. In fact, it's a horrible, terrible, idea. He's over the water now. Black, icy Pacific. He tries to focus on the meters, but they're fuzzy. *Shit shit shit! Come on!* he thinks, raging at his mind to SNAP OUT OF IT!

Frank vents the window, gulps in cool air. He clicks on the radio.

"Uh, SMO tower... uh, god, this is Cessna 172 Tango Charlie...I got a little problem here..." he begins, but doesn't know how to finish. *Help me? I'm drunker than I thought and I can't fly?*

"Go ahead Cessna 172 Tango Charlie..." comes the crackled reply.

Frank shuts off the radio. The coast is disappearing behind him. He's afraid. Catalina is twenty minutes if he flies straight... but what's straight? It's pitch dark, he needs to rely on the plane's compass, the controls... but *he can't fucking see them!*

He begins to hyperventilate. This is bad. Oh, so bad. How had he been so stupid?

"Okay, okay… think, dammit."

And he does think. Right before fear comes raging at him like a pissed-off jackhammer rattling itself into his brain and he knows right then – *at that moment* – that he will never make it.

If he tries to fly, he'll die. One hundred percent. He'll go down into the black ocean; the frigid water will fill the cabin in a heartbeat and he'll sink like a stone. Food for fishes.

"Fuck that," he mumbles.

He wipes a shaky hand across his sweating forehead, turns the control wheel. His altimeter flashes briefly – he's flying too low – and he pitches back, gains altitude. *Christ*, he thinks. He starts to straighten out, but he can see nothing but a curtain of black. He fights the plane like a drowning man fighting a lifeguard. Blind fear. Sheer panic.

I can't see! He pulls back too hard, the plane whines and bumps against pockets of air. He's under five hundred feet. Too low! His gyroscope is slipping around, he has to keep it level.

There! Lights! He focuses on the lights. Needs to center himself, devise a plan. If he can get back to the coast, find the airport… if he can only clear his goddamned head!

His stomach twists into a hard knot. He drools and moans, his eyes glassy. Without warning, vomit gushes through his throat, burns him inside, splashes the console, the control wheel, parts of the windshield. It runs over his chin and soaks his chest through his shirt. His arms are rubber. His jaw hangs like a wet hook.

He is close to blacking out. If that happens, it's all over.

He curses his body, his mind, for the betrayal. He sobs like a child stuck in a bad dream. He recalls his own childhood nightmare. Hidden in the closet. The boogeyman's shadow filling the light wedged beneath the door. The handle turning. How he would wake, screaming.

He wants to wake now. In bed. Hungover, but on the ground. Alive. This whole thing a nightmare he'd laugh about. He'd go directly to a meeting, get his shit straight again. Forget about revenge. The past. If only he could wake up…

His eyelids flutter like mosquito wings. His eyeballs roll white.

The cockpit is a blur. Gauges spin madly. The plane lurches through the wind-blown dark, toward the lights, the pilot careless anymore to stop the inevitable, knowing with a broken heart that it's too late, too late.

SILENCE.

Rob and Mary are almost at the top. They haven't said a word since being locked in. Rob is tense. Nerves frying like oil on a hot pan. Mary is a two-faced doll. One minute fuming, eyes fire. The next docile, smiling warmly at him.

There's no such thing as a perfect moment.

That's what Rob's father had said to him. Rob confessed the plan. The ring. Mom on the line crying. Both parents talking over each other in excitement. Rob not sure when, how. His father, wisdom embodied from Chicago: *There's no such thing as a perfect moment. The perfect moments will come after.*

After.

Rob hopes it's true. The night could not have gone worse. The homeless man. The tense dinner. The creepy Ferris Wheel operator. Is this the night he wants them to remember forever? Or does the night not matter? Does the *moment* not matter? Is it truly all about what comes after?

He feels the lump of the ring through denim.

The ride stops and starts. Stops and starts. Each gondola emptying, filling with new riders. They are at the top now. The highest point of the wheel.

It's so beautiful up high. The lights dazzling. The ocean terrifyingly vast. Rob can hardly tell where the night sky stops and the great sea begins. It's all a giant, earth-consuming abyss. Eternity dressed in funeral black. Part of him wishes he could take Mary's hand, fly from the metal box they're confined in, soar into the moonlit eye of that great void. Fly forever through the cold dark. Past stars, past galaxies. To a forever land. He'd like to take her there. To forever. To whatever it held in its cupped palms, filled with mystery and starlight. Locked in the ever-present, past and future blown apart, forgotten.

"It's pretty."

Rob turns away from the night. To Mary. Her smile more genuine. Relaxed now. It's okay up here. Up here, above the noise, the crowd, it's okay.

"I'm sorry," he says, and the remaining words stay unspoken. That's okay, too.

She shakes her head. Reaches out a hand, takes his. Leans forward. They kiss. Nothing magic. Just comfort. Trust. More unspoken words. "Let's forget it," she whispers into his cheek, and he nods.

They sit back, study each other. Rob swallows. He reaches into his pocket. Tips of padded fingers find silver. Cool against his warm flesh.

"Mary…"

The ride jerks into motion.

Rob is thwarted. Flustered. *Is that it?* he thinks. There's not enough time. They're moving too much. It's herky-jerky. Rushed.

This isn't working, he thinks, fighting tears. He knows he won't be able to go through with it. Not tonight. He'll need a new plan. They'll be off the ride soon, there's no time. It's all wrong.

They begin to descend, the wind picking them up as gravity takes over. The great wheel spins.

As they near the bottom, Mary looks toward the operator. Her eyes meet his, shadowed under his cap. His eyes narrow and his lip turns, a scowl. He looks away, and then they're gliding through, past the platform, past the upturned faces, a Doppler effect of crowded voices and tinny music. The voices mute as they fly up and away and into the night.

JEREMIAH LOOKS UP at tub number nine as it comes down. Catches *her* stare.

He's loaded all new riders, he'll spin them around a few times, then stick number nine up there like a head on a post. Give him some time to think. To figure out his next move. His mind is racing. He doesn't want to be here when she gets out. What if they've spoken? What if the boyfriend is up there, right now, working himself into a lather? Or maybe they're on their phones. Calling police. Friends in high places.

He pulls off his ballcap. Wipes sweat from his brow with a sleeve. His long gray hair hangs down his back in a ponytail. He wishes he was back traveling with the carnival. Running the Merry-Go-Round. Those were sweet days. The girls would get off and they'd take his hand and they'd dance with him. Dance to the hick band the carnival hired local, each city different. How he loved to hold those girls. How he loved to dance.

Jeremiah smiles. His gold tooth glimmers fiery red in the neon light.

Number nine passes again. She's looking away this time. Smiling. Good, good. There they go. The slut and the idiot. One more time around and then he's gonna let them sit up there a while. Cool down a bit.

He watches, waits... timing has to be just right...

He pushes his foot to the brake. Harder than he should, and there are some happy yelps of surprise from the riders as the wheel slows, almost jarringly so.

Number nine is at the top. All right, all right. He'll leave the lovebirds up there a bit while he figures out what to do.

In the meantime, fuck 'em.

THEY ARE HELD at the top. The ride settles. Their tub rocks and groans. The world is all around them. Waves crash on a distant planet. Music comes from a satellite. They are in a spaceship floating along an orbital path. Forgotten by mankind.

A minute passes.

Rob hears a distant plane whining through the night sky, like the far-off cranking of an old air-raid siren.

Another minute.

Mary thinks: *How long is this ride?*

Rob's mouth is desert dry. His neck bathed in sweat. He knows, it's now or never. Mary is distracted, looking toward the coastline.

Now...

There will never be a more perfect moment in this imperfect night. The music of the ride dampens, the crowd buzz washed away by a Pacific breeze, the ocean's impatient exhale. Rob reaches into his pocket, pulls out the ring, palms it.

"Mary?"

She turns. A smile, just for him. The one he'll hold onto the rest of their lives. The welcome of her.

He takes her hand. She's startled at his urgency, but her face is alive. She smirks at the seriousness on his normally carefree face. "Mary," he says. "I love you. I love you so much."

Her smile widens. "I love you, too."

Then she sees something in him. His eyes, wide and eager. His hand trembling.

Her stomach turns. Her nerves go ice cold, the back of her neck prickles. *My god... no, it's impossible... my god oh my god please... is he? Is he?*

Rob tries to look relaxed, happy, but fails. He settles for the adrenaline of excitement. The thrill of the biggest step of his entire life. Of their lives. He kneels and her free hand shoots to her mouth, her eyes show whites. She screams something into her palm. A tear falls from her eye, drifts over her cheek, her knuckles.

Rob lifts the ring. The diamond glints kaleidoscopic colors of the night.

"Mary, will you do me the honor of being my wife?"

She can't help it. She laughs. A jailbreak of tears. Now he's crying, and she cries all the harder while nodding, nodding frantically. Yes. Yes. Yes! Rob starts to put the ring on her finger, hesitates. She extends the correct one. He smiles shyly, appreciatively.

The fit is perfect.

The tub rocks on its hinges when they kiss.

6

JEREMIAH HEARS THE crowd's growing voice surrounding him. Number nine is rocking at the top of the wheel. He pretends to study the gearbox, as if there's something wrong with it. *How could he have been so fucking stupid?*

He takes a deep breath. Rubs his eyes. A verse from the Bible, one he has written in his AA book, comes to him.

"I know the plans I have for you," declares the Lord, *"plans to prosper you and not to harm you, plans to give you hope and a future."*

"Shit," he says, ready to take his chances. He can't leave them up there any longer. It's already been more than three minutes, and the assholes stuck in the tubs are beginning to act stupid. Throwing shit down at the laughing crowd. *Maybe I deserve whatever I get,* he thinks. He moves to release the brake. Stops.

Someone is screaming.

Jeremiah spins, scans the crowd. The folks waiting to get onto the ride. To feed the great wheel. Some of them are still chatting. A few of them look outright horrified. Two of them are pushing away, through the tight group. A woman is knocked down.

There's a... *whining* noise.

A few of the kids in line are holding cell phones to the sky. He's not sure if it's an offering or a prayer.

He turns as something drops in front of him. The platform shakes. A white-faced teenager. He jumped from one of the lower-hung tubs. Number thirteen. *What the hell?*

"Hey!" Jeremiah yells, but the kid is running. "Hey!" he yells again.

Now the crowd is backing away. The screams are becoming more prevalent. The whining sound growing louder. Jeremiah looks wildly at the sky, tries to see what they're all on about. Toward the ocean. Toward the moon. But the wheel is between him and *IT*. Whatever *IT* is.

He ducks under the rim of the wheel, steps onto the opposite side of the platform. Twelve feet of dimpled metal flooring followed by a giant gearbox the size of a compact car, then a fire lane that runs the length of the pier. Beyond that, there's nothing but a wooden handrail and the great sea facing due south. Jeremiah searches the sky. It doesn't take long. He sees it now. Sees what many of them have already seen. Knows why the kid jumped from number thirteen.

Holy hell, he thinks. *It's a goddamn airplane.*

MARY CAN HARDLY breathe. She's never been so happy. Rob is sitting beside her now and they're clutching at each other's hands, almost desperately. His fingers still shake. Hers now, as well. They're so young. Children deciding to become adults. Partners. He kisses her again.

"So it's a yes?" he says, swiping at his wet cheeks with the palm of a hand.

"Yes," she replies, and laughs.

"I..."

Rob starts to speak. Stops. His eyes flicker off hers, focus over her shoulder.

"Rob?" She hears it now. From behind. A noise so loud… she can't believe she hadn't heard it until this very moment. "Rob?" she says again, not daring to turn.

His eyes are wide. He looks to her, then over her shoulder once more. The screams from below more evident. Mary's terrified stare won't leave his face. She's petrified.

"Oh, shit," Rob mumbles, dreamlike. Then, "Mary?" The inflection of a question. As if she's just arrived here. He grabs her hands tightly. His face twisted, grotesque. A snarl. His eyes pure terror, brown irises being devoured by white. "Mary!" he shouts, and she is so startled and flushed with fear that she can physically feel the blood draining from her face. "Oh no, Mary!" he sobs.

The noise fills the air. The roaring of an engine so loud she can barely hear him scream her name. She can't take it. She turns.

A plane.

Coming right at them.

Fifty yards out she'd guess. A private plane. The ones that are always running into phone lines and crash-landing on golf courses. It's dipping and swaying, as if being throttled by a hurricane.

She stands, bangs her head against the metal top of the gondola, yells out in pain. Sits back down. He clutches at her, drowning. "Mary!" he screams, as loud as he can, because now the world is nothing but that *sound*. That engine, so loud her teeth chatter.

IN THE CESSNA, the cabin rattles. Wind whips through the open vent window. Frank makes one last effort to steer the plane. His only thought: *Toward the lights*. His soused mind tells him the lights are the runway. The lights are safety.

His mind flickers, goes out. Passes out. A mercy. He lurches forward. His body – never buckled – gives up, slumps forward. His chest flops into the controlling wheel, slams it down.

He dreams of the life he'd hoped to have as a child. Those hazy thoughts of a bright future while playing baseball with friends. Girls strolling through the outfield. A summer day. Nothing but hope in the grass beneath his worn sneakers.

In Frank's dream, the sun explodes like a nuclear bomb. His teeth fall out, then his eyes. He grabs at his face, catches bits of himself like falling debris. He has no time for fear. A flash of light wipes him from the fantasy like a bug from a windshield.

MARY SCREAMS. SCREAMS until her throat goes raw. The plane consumes the sky, only seconds from smashing into the giant wheel. As she claws at her cheeks, she sees other riders climbing from the gondolas in front and below them. One guy jumps toward the ocean from thirty feet up. She has time to watch him fall short. Crash into the pier. His body seems to snap in half. He flops into an 'L' shape upon the planks, unmoving. A woman in a yellow dress dangles from one of the lower ones, half-in, half-out, crying. She drops with a shriek.

Rob grabs Mary, pulls her away. He's yelling at her: "Get down! Get down!" She's thick-headed. Confused. Rob's on the floor of the gondola. Weeping. Pulling at her. She understands but casts one more look toward the plane. She stares, transfixed. The plane whines ever louder, screeching like a banshee falling on its prey. Mary waits to die.

Suddenly, the propeller of the plane dives downward, as if slapped away by God. No longer coming right at them, it's shooting down like an arrow toward the pier.

It's going to miss us.

She grabs Rob, yanks at his arm. "It's turning!" she screams at him. His wide eyes flicker, register her words. He shoots to his feet, eyes searching. He sees it cutting down and away. A boulder dropped from the sky.

He looks down. The plane so close as it cuts away they can feel the heat from the engine wash over them. The smell of oil. They watch as the plane crashes into the back of the restaurant next to the Ferris Wheel. Flames erupt from the point of impact. They hold on as the whole wheel shakes. Shrieks of horror and pain and death fill the night.

Mary has a split-second to think how lucky they are. They had just been in that restaurant eating fried shrimp, not an hour ago. Now the building is decimated. Caved-in. Burning.

The second and third explosions steal her relief. Twists it into fresh terror.

THE CESSNA SLAMS into the rear of Buddy Tub's. The fuel of the plane does not immediately erupt upon impact. The kitchen crew and approximately a dozen patrons are killed instantly. As the plane spins and rips apart, one wing swings like a massive machete, tearing through the midsections of two line cooks and the steel of an industrial stove. Gas hisses into the air from a cut line, catching a spark from the engine and blowing the cockpit. A ball of fire disintegrates the plane interior – including Frank – before blowing out the glass of the surrounding windows.

Located within a mesh cage at the rear of Buddy Tub's are two industrial 420-pound propane tanks which feed into the main gas line of the restaurant. Each tank is a couple feet shorter but just as wide as those blue porta-potties you often see at construction sites. The plane's propeller, spinning free after the cabin's explosion in a blur of sparks and chipped metal, slices through the head of one of these tanks – essentially decapitating it – before planting itself into the second, bending it inward at the waist. This creates enough pressure for the gas to punch outward, where it meets the gushing flames of the Cessna's burning engine. Tank number one erupts with a violence that immediately triggers a second explosion to tank number two, blasting the entire structure which once accommodated Buddy Tub's shrimp house, along with the near-capacity 136 souls inside, into nothing but a mushroom cloud of spattered metal, wood, bones and meat. The fuel tank of the plane absorbs the heat of the fire, catches, and blows the Cessna apart. The plane's bellyful of gasoline detonates eastward, spraying liquid fire toward the main body of the pier, engulfing the base of the Ferris Wheel, the adjacent roller coaster, and the crowds that had yet to flee.

Within ten seconds of the plane's impact, nearly five-hundred square feet of the Santa Monica pier has been obliterated, transformed into dust and fire flying high into the air like a massive geyser of death before raining down to earth, littering the surrounding ocean and beaches for hundreds of feet in every direction. Nearly a third of the remaining pier is engulfed in hungry flames that devour the dry wooden planks like kindling. Fuel and oil spill into the water, still aflame, coating the surrounding sea in a blanket of fire.

Jeremiah, who had remained stuck to the ground in shock as the plane exploded (along with over three hundred other equally stupefied locals, tourists and employees), was incinerated by the secondary blast. His ponytail and flesh turned instantly to ash, his eyeballs and brain liquefied inside his skull, his corpse blown free of his shoes to land, ungracefully, near a vendor selling mugs, T-shirts, and other assorted such shit.

As the survivors scream and run for the mainland, or leap over the edge of the pier into the waves or onto the forgiving sand of the beach below by the dozens, the riders of the Ferris Wheel (other than those nearest the bottom, who were instantly broiled within their metal confines by the intense heat of surrounding flames), can only cry for help and pray as they watch the crowd stampede toward safety.

Thick smoke fogs their surrounding view, the mural of horror clouded by black billows. The heat from below grows in intensity as the great wheel itself catches fire and begins to burn.

7

ROB'S HEAD IS propped through the opening of the gondola. He pulls himself back in, shifts to the other side, repeats the action.

"I can't see shit," he says, voice shaking.

Ash-filled smoke billows thick all around them, the heat from below palpable. The whole world is screaming. The whole world is on fire.

"We can jump!" Mary says, her leather jacket tossed to the ground. Red sleeve covering her face like a bloody bandage, a worthless attempt to keep from inhaling the smoke.

Rob shakes his head. "No way. We're like fifty feet in the air."

"No, the ocean. We can jump for the water."

Rob shakes his head again. Stands on his toes, looks desperately toward the water. The smoke, a misty gray veil, clears on and off enough for him to see the lights of the coast, pieces of beach, a patch of black ocean. Below them, there's nothing but flames and death. "It's too far, Mary. We won't make it. You know that. We've seen people trying... I don't want to die like that."

Mary thinks about the first guy who jumped. How he'd landed on the deck, crushed like a stepped-on beer can. More people had jumped. Rob was right, they'd both seen them. They had watched two, then three people leap from the gondolas. Into the floor of hellish fire. Or jump toward the water, fall short. Scream as they burned. It reminds her horribly of 9/11, and the poor souls of the Twin Towers, who chose to leap rather than burn alive. Now it's happening to them. Irrational is it is, she wants to try. The whole fucking wheel is beginning to burn. She feels like a marshmallow rammed through with a stick, heating over a campfire. Getting too hot. They'll soon be dead either way.

There is a loud *CRACK*. And a *SNAP* that vibrates the gondola.

The wheel shudders. And begins to *lean*.

Rob and Mary look at each other, stunned.

We're going to die.

"I think…" Rob swallows, coughs. "I think we're going to fall."

He grabs her then, and she can't stand the heat of him. The hot flesh that will soon be nothing but ash. She pushes him away, but he is so crazed, so deeply in shock, he only looks at her wild-eyed. "I love you!"

She nods, too afraid to speak. The smoke chokes them both. Every breath is hot air that burns her mouth, her throat. Flames lick the air next to their gondola. The rubber mat of the floor is melting. Sticking to their skin and clothes like hot paste. They are being cooked.

CRACK!

The gondola lurches, drops, then steadies. Rob and Mary scream, thinking death has come. Rob pushes Mary roughly to the side, then kicks the gondola door open. The latch snaps and the door splays outward. Mary puts a hand out to steady herself, but the metal is too hot. She pulls it back, cries out more from desperation than pain. She slumps onto the bench, skin hot, hair matted with sweat, dazed.

On hands and knees, Rob looks down through the opening where the door had been. Mary looks at his body, hands splayed on the sticky, liquefying floor. His black sneakers, his blue jeans that hug him perfectly. The nice blue dress shirt he'd worn just for her.

My God, she thinks suddenly, the thought rushing into her like cool water. *That's my fiancée. I'm fucking engaged.*

Mary can't help it. She smiles. The saddest smile she will ever wear. Tears stream from her red-rimmed eyes, evaporate in the heat. That is her future husband, staring into hell itself. Searching for a way out, a way to save them. She reaches out, touches the back of his leg. She's filled with so much love at that moment, an internal surge of core heat. Somehow hotter than the flames which surround them. Hotter than the sun. "Rob?" She wants to kiss him one last time.

He springs from his knees. His face is streaks of gray, bright reds. Soot and heat. He clutches her shoulders.

"Mary!" he says. "You're not going to die! I won't let you die!"

She nods at the lie. Sweat and dried tears cover their faces. He puts his hands to her cheeks, looks into her eyes. *So much love.*

He helps her to her feet. Mary looks around, sees more flames licking upward. The people in the gondola adjacent to theirs are looking back at her, hopeless. She ignores them. Below, people are screaming as flames coat their shelter, frying them. Something dark falls through the smoke like a fleeting shadow. *Another body,* she thinks, and wonders if they'll jump next.

Mary looks down, past the open door, into the flames.

She sees them down there.

Black writhing figures, like the one who had attacked Rob. Untouched by the flames.

All the devils have come to feast on the dead, she thinks, watching the clawed black demons tear at charred flesh, climb the wheel itself, scale burning beams toward them. *We're still too high for you.* Her mind is jarringly dislodged from sanity by her terror. *Too high for you,* she sings to herself, wanting to laugh. *Too high for you-hoo!*

Mary smiles, her eyes flutter, and she tries to step through the open door, drop herself into the flames. Rob catches her, wraps his arms around her tightly. Screams something. She stares at him, numb. He is yelling, crying her name, touching her face. But she feels nothing. Is not able to feel any further. She wants to burn. To have it over with. To feed those demons with her flesh.

"Mary!" he screams. "Please hold on!"

There is another loud SNAP, loud as a boulder splitting, and the great wheel lurches and groans. Even in her shocked state, Mary realizes something very important is happening. Something very *vital.*

"Oh god," Rob murmurs.

Suddenly the air is clear. The smoke blown away by a surge of ocean breeze. Mary sees clearly through the open door of the gondola. Sees the blanket of fire below, on the pier, in the ocean beyond. She tilts her head skyward. The stars in the night sky are still there. Still watching. The lazy moon sits above the horizon, glib.

Are you enjoying the show? she thinks, not knowing to whom she is addressing the question, nor why it has come to her.

At the shore, where the pier meets land, Mary can see what looks like a thousand flashing lights. Fire trucks, police cars. Lined up for miles. Announcements through bullhorns, or speakers, carry through the air. She can't make out the words. So many people. Running. Running. No one can get *in*, because all the people are trying so very hard to get *out*.

The wheel staggers. A snapped cable sings past, whips against the side of their metal *coffin it's a goddamn coffin* gondola with a sharp *smack*.

Rob has torn the shirt off his body, is wrapping it around a hand. His feet are on the lip of the open door, his half-naked body leaning back, into the open air, one shirt-wrapped fist clutching the vertical metal rod that connects the bottom and top of the gondola.

The sight breaks Mary from her shock.

"Rob!" she screams, and reaches for him.

He shoves her away. "Stay back, Mary!"

She sees the ocean behind him. The floor is tilting downward. Following his example, she snatches up her own jacket, lassoes it around a post on the opposite side – the *pier* side – of the gondola, and holds on.

8

FAR BELOW WHERE Rob and Mary are perched, awaiting sure death, the pier has burned through the base of the ride. The giant metal triangles supporting the wheel's core crunch through the burning wood of the pier. The platform slants, sinks slowly through charred timbers toward eager water.

The great wheel is defeated.

Half-burned, free of its moorings, it begins, ever so slowly, to lean.

Then, when it can hold itself upright no longer, and with the dying groan of a great god, it falls.

9

MARY STARES IN horror as Rob's feet leave the metal lip, float outward into the air, as if he's entered zero-gravity. She clasps her jacket tight. Looped around the opposite side of the tub, she holds it like a lifeline. The pads of her sneakers are melting into the rubber-matted floor, the heat unbearable. *Like standing on a frying pan.* She stares at her fiancée, wide-eyed. She watches in rapt fascination as the landscape behind him changes, like a vertically sliding backdrop, from the night sky, to the ocean, to a sea of flames.

We're falling, she thinks, and knows it to be true as her bottom rises, slides toward the open door. Toward Rob. Toward the flames.

"Rob!" she screams, not sure what scares her more: him leaving, or him coming back. She wants so badly for him to comfort her, to hold her in these last moments.

"It's gotta fall toward the water!" he yells, red-faced, and she can see now what he's doing. He's *pulling* the great wheel. Using his meager weight to throw the balance in the sea's favor. Helping it to fall toward the water versus the flaming pier. She knows it's meaningless. Knows his scant one-hundred-eighty pounds won't have sway over which way the massive, burning wheel tumbles. *But my god, look at him,* she thinks. She was never more proud. Never more in love.

She feels something – something final – give, far below. Her body lifts away from the floor. The jacket she holds no longer a reassuring support, but a rope to dangle from.

They're tipping.

"Mary!" Rob screams, now fully horizontal, his feet hanging away from the gondola, toward the flames and raging water below. "Mary! It's going to fall! Be ready to jump!"

Mary nods, but doesn't move. This is no movie. The physicality of the metal, the heat, the flames. All too real. The force being consumed will take her down, her life nothing but an afterthought to the great devouring.

"Mary!" he says, his face full shadow. "I love you, Mary."

And then, before she can think or hear any more, they are tilting over… they are *falling*.

She watches in frozen horror as the world rushes upward.

There's a flurry of sparks, and only Rob's hand remains, clutching the post. Their descent picks up speed, the world splinters.

Rob disappears. Sucked away into the night sky.

Her body lifts higher, toes tapping the roof of the doorway, but her eyes never leave the onrushing landscape. She dangles, legs kicking, from a great height. Though she is stationary, the world accelerates toward her.

A world made of flames. The speed of her descent spreads to her cheeks, her fluttering eyes. Wet hair is blown away from her face. The raging fire rushes at her, eager, and then falls away frustrated and hungry as she pushes outward past it. Now only the dark water fills her vision. Coming to kiss her. Flames and pieces of flesh or wood she doesn't know fall all around her – down, down into the sea.

She does not let go, but hangs on tight, sticks a heel against the metal wall, rides the gondola down. Her stomach lifts into her throat, gravity pulling her apart. She does not yell out as she slams into the frigid waves, an avalanche of water crashing upward. Swallowing her. She wants to scream at the shock of it, but it's too late.

The weight of the burning wheel lands on top of her, overwhelming.

It pushes her down, down into the cold black sea, which devours her with an insatiable, giddy greed.

THOUSANDS OF ONLOOKERS, from the beaches to the streets, watch in horror and fascination as the pier burns, and as the great wheel finally succumbs to the flames, belches a death rattle groan and crashes, lifeless, into the sea.

They know that nothing on it could have survived.

THE SOUNDS OF death fall silent.

Mary sinks. Pushed down into the water, the weight of the massive steel gondola presses at her back, the wheel itself – what remains unburned – sinks quickly, hundreds of thousands of pounds of dead weight plummet toward the bottom of the ocean. Taking Mary with it.

It is shallow near the end of the pier. Only about thirty feet until you reach the settled muck at the ocean's shoreline floor. A buried world of seaweed and mud, crabs and other creatures that live and feed in the kelp forest below.

Mary lets go of the jacket she'd been clinging to, holds her breath as she sees the black seafloor come up at her, illuminated from above by the oily flames now settling on the roiling surface. She can't move, can't swim. Can't escape. The weight is forcing her deeper, deeper. Writhing kelp arms slip through the open door of the gondola, reach for her. She kicks out. A silver fish swims past her field of vision.

Then the tub slams into the sea bottom, the floor coughs a cloud of mud.

And still the weight of the wheel presses downward, burying the gondola and Mary into the soft floor of the sea. Dark sand billows into the water, blinding her. Mary feels her feet, then shins, knees, *sinking* into the cold sand. Past the weeds, into the soft sea bottom as the colossal weight presses impossibly hard upon her back, driving her into the mud, folding her over. Terror overrides her mind and reflexively she wants to scream. Eyes widen as she fights the impulse, manages to keep her breath. She twists her body, convulsively, desperate for escape. One arm pushes up, expects to meet metal, but finds open water. She spins, blind, chest burning, the great weight pushing her down... but realizes there is still time.

Seconds.

The opening between the base of the gondola and the roof. She can squeeze through. She grips the metal lip with both hands, forces her body rigid, lifts her head through the descending opening.

Seaweed entangles her legs. Mud sucks at her feet.

She shakes her head violently, needing so badly to cry out one last primal scream of survival. She keeps her lips sealed tight and grips the edge of the metal and pulls herself – using all of her strength – through the space and into open water. Her legs slide free and, as the gondola sinks into the mud, she rises through, into the dark, gloomy sea.

Alive. Still alive.

She spares a glance down, watches the gondola sink deeper into a haze of disrupted muck, knowing she was nearly buried forever beneath it, then kicks upward, tries to center herself. The entire ocean seems to be illuminated by flame. She looks up. The surface impossibly far. A bed of fire rests upon it, a flickering orange canopy spread out as far as she can see.

A blackened beam sinks past, smoldering, trailing liquid smoke as it drifts downward.

Running out of breath, she allows herself one last look around, then down, where the wheel is settling into a gray cloud, its white limbs like fossils. Mary takes a second to study the surreal entirety of the drowned Ferris Wheel. Flickering orange, green and blue in the flashing depths. It's bigger than she would have imagined. Like an alien spacecraft, crashed and sunken.

Arms and legs of trapped riders dangle from the gondola openings, waving at her like the seaweed, beckoning, blackened by death.

She does not see Rob.

She searches the foggy black water once more for a glimpse of him — the illumination from the fire lighting great patches of dark blue — but there is no sign, and there is no more time.

Desperate to surface, Mary sees no opening in the sheet of flames, doesn't know which way to swim. Toward the beach, or into deeper water?

She makes her decision and begins to swim toward the beach, and in doing so floats higher, near the surface. Too near. She feels the heat of fire above her. Despite the burning in her lungs, she forces herself deeper. The wheel passes beneath her as she glides over it, praying she can hold her breath a few moments more.

Motionless bodies drift up toward her. Released from the clutches of the wheel, corpses in tennis shoes and T-shirts and fifty-dollar haircuts rise toward the surface, where they will burn. Mary tries to not panic, to stay level-headed, to keep swimming. She pushes through the water, over the wheel, away from the flames, toward safety. The world beneath is akin to being trapped inside a globe, the topography of hell its surface, the sunken wheel its broken core. Mary floats beneath a continent of fire. She's running out of oxygen, her eyes search frantically… there! Open water! An amoeba-shaped clearing amidst the flames. No more than ten yards away. She pumps her arms through the water. Faster. Kicks harder. She can make it.

A heavy, rising weight bumps into her midsection, knocks her off stride. She lets out a mouthful of air at the impact, spins.

A young man. A teenager. Sixteen perhaps. His skin melted into doughy red splotches. Scalp red and flaky, the hair burned away. He floats into her. She starts to push him away.

His sealed eyes open.

Mary does scream now, and the last of her breath flees her lungs, dissolves in the water. The teenager's lips twist in what Mary thinks of as a smile. His charred hands seize fistfuls of her red blouse. He yanks her down.

Mary kicks, chest burning, panic in full force. Her air is gone. She beats at the corpse but feels herself sinking back toward the wheel, toward the ocean bottom. The water grows more frigid. She twists one last time – hard – feels her blouse tear away.

Free!

She continues to swim, head jerking side-to-side. *Where is the open water?* There's nothing but burning sea above her. She's lost her sense of direction, cannot tell which way is the beach, which way the pier. She looks down, sees more corpses floating up, eyes open, staring at her. Swimming for her. Her long, floating hair tangles with a red-hot ember, begins to smolder and burn.

Coarse hands of peeling skin grab her heels, her arms, her hair, her flesh. She writhes and struggles, kicks and beats them with her fists.

Slowly, she weakens. Her vision tunnels. The oxygen to her brain gone for too long. It's shutting her down. One limp hand floats upward as the wheel's minions pull her deeper.

The diamond of her new ring dazzles bright orange. A star in the black sea.

A beacon.

A warm hand wraps around her fingers, another grips her forearm. With the last of her will, her strength, she looks up. Sees the dark shadow of a man floating above her, the flaming canopy of the ocean a dramatic backdrop to his figure. He tugs at her hand, his feet kicking, pulling her skyward. The hands of the dead reluctantly release her, unable to hold on. She is propelled through the water, feels it surging past her. Up, up, away, away.

She is limp. Helpless. Can do nothing but let herself be saved.

No more air, no more energy.

She feels icy water surge down her throat, fill her lungs. Her world begins to fade.

The surface is broken. Cool air kisses her face.

She is surprised to not feel the heat of surrounding flames.

Her body rejects the invading fluid. She vomits out a lungful of saltwater, coughs and hacks, releases everything inside her. Sucks the air in deeply. Greedily. The oxygen restores her body, clears her mind. She knuckles at her eyes, wipes drool from her lips, and looks around feverishly…

… and sees nothing but sea.

She turns, looks another way. Then another. There is nothing but vast, flat black water in every direction. No land. No pier. No people. Mary is confused by the sudden, vacuous quiet. There are no sounds on the air – no riotous flames, no screams. Nothing but the soft lapping of the endless black sea.

Her rescuer floats a few feet away, motionless, his face turned away from her, as if studying the vacant horizon. She stares at the back of his head. Hair matted to a skull. Bare shoulders licked by the water's gently rippled surface.

"Rob?" she says, surprised at how flat her voice sounds. How dead.

She looks skyward, expecting to see the familiar heavy blanket of night. Distant stars. A hazy moon.

But Mary sees only a flat pale sky, white as bone. Below that, an infinite horizon.

She starts to speak again, when her savior turns to face her.

SODA JERK

ELLIE LOOKED DOWN from her bedroom window and watched the yellow moving van pull out of their new driveway, into the street, and disappear behind a large shaggy tree that craned upward from their front yard toward blue so bright and clear that the clouds were nothing more than bursts from far-off cannons, small puffs of smoke crawling along the surface. The sky was so perfect it seemed creation itself was smiling down on her – her new home, her new life. She looked into that vast blue and wanted to smile back, feel the joy it offered, but found she could not. Perhaps it was too blue, she thought. Too expansive, too true. The sky was a lie, after all, a shiny trapdoor that hid the whole universe behind its fragile, curved shell. She drew a humped line on the thin glass of the window to match the shape of her frown, brushed her fingers along the lace curtains hung prior to her arrival, and turned away.

She sat down heavily on the bare mattress of her bed and stared at the neat stacks of boxes that held all her worldly goods. She eyeballed the furniture placed haphazardly around the room, moved them piece-by-piece in her mind to different parts of the space. Nothing seemed to fit just right, and a knot of frustration tightened inside her. She smoothed her cotton dress over her knees, calming herself. She studied the tips of her white sneakers while fighting back a swell of tears. *A sixteen-year-old girl should not have to start over*, she thought.

She'd spent the last ten years building her *life*. Now that life might as well be a million miles away, on a distant planet for all the good it did her. She had loved Chicago, her school, her girlfriends, her old room...

All gone. Swept away like dust.

"Ellie Miles, you are the unluckiest girl in the whole, wide world," she said, the words drifting to the floor like dead autumn leaves.

Downstairs, someone knocked at the front door.

Momentarily distracted from her self-pity, she ran back to the window and looked down, expecting to see a wide-assed neighbor holding a Bundt cake, or the local pastor, bible tucked under one elbow, ready to welcome new sheep to his venerated flock. She put her palms to the frame, lifted her heels to stand on tiptoes, strained to see who would visit them on the very day, near the very *hour*, of their arrival.

A sun-kissed, shimmering cherry-red Chrysler ragtop sat in the driveway, but the jutted roof blocked her view of both the porch and the stranger standing upon it. With a low growl of frustration, she ran to the bedroom door and pushed her ear against it, listening as her mother crossed the floor below to answer, her clipped, subterranean steps echoing off the walls of the starkly-furnished home.

The front door opened and she heard excited voices. A young man's voice by the sound, and her mother's high-pitched fake laugh, the one she used at cocktail parties and while on the phone with old friends. Ellie slipped out of the bedroom and moved deftly to the top of the stairs, looking down at slanted squares of bare white walls and polished wood floors. She leaned over the railing, saw the back of her mother's calves and a pair of black sneakers pointed forward, then moving.

The door closed and Ellie pulled away from the railing, out of sight, inexplicably held her breath.

"Ellie!" her mother called, her voice bouncing off the bare floors and walls.

"Yes?" she replied flatly, her porcelain-skinned hands resting on the bannister, her chin lifted regally in anticipation of being introduced.

"Can you come down please?"

As no faces appeared beneath her to look up and notice her perfect positioning, Ellie blew out a breath and walked down the stairs, stopping just short of the bottom to maintain superiority of height.

She saw the lithe frame of her mother, dolled up in a white dress with light pink polka-dots, her blond hair pulled back from porcelain features. Beside her stood a tall, skinny boy. He smiled down at her mother with stunning white teeth; his high, tanned cheek-bones shone like polished brass. He had a bold pompadour of slicked black hair, glistening like a black ocean wave atop a broad forehead.

Ellie coughed lightly, announcing herself. She felt color rise to her cheeks when the boy's eyes met hers. They were of the brightest blue, piercingly so, like the sky above her new town. Blue eyes were her favorite.

"How do you do?" she asked politely, staying on the stairs for now.

"Honey..." her mother started, as if to reprimand, then brightened. "Ellie, this is James. James... what was your last name, dear?"

"Honeycutt."

"Of course," she said, giggling as if he'd goosed her behind. "Honeycutt. James Honeycutt. James has come to welcome us to the neighborhood. Come here and say hello. He won't bite, will you James?"

"No mam," he said, those white teeth shining.

Ellie went to them slowly, lifted a hand and allowed James to shake it.

"James goes to your new high school. He's the class president, isn't that something?" her mother said, all but scribbling out wedding announcements in her head while she did so.

"That's true," James said humbly, "and as such it's my job to come meet any new students, show them around, make them feel welcome."

Ellie nodded. Even she was taken off-guard by the boy's sincerity and obvious kindness. And he was such a strong, handsome, obviously popular boy; traits she rarely found in combination with generosity of spirit, at least with the boys back home.

"I see," was all she said in response.

"I gather you have a lot of unpacking to do, but perhaps, when you're settled, you'd allow me to escort you around our fine town, show you some highlights, introduce you to some of the locals."

"Oh, well, there is a lot yet to do..."

"That is the most wonderful thing I've ever heard of!" her mother interjected, giving Ellie a cunning look. "You two should do exactly that.

James, dear, what are your plans today?"

"As it happens," James said, "I'm quite free. I was going to offer to take Ellie this afternoon, but then I saw how much work there is to be done here... hey, I'd be glad to stay and help move some things around."

"Nonsense!" her mother said, so loudly Ellie jumped in her skin. "Harry, that's my husband, will be home from his new job in just a few hours and he and I will get everything in its place. You two kids should go and have fun, really. Ellie, you should take a sweater in case the night gets chilly."

Night? she thought, hesitating.

"Go on, dear," her mother said, in a polite yet firm tone that was not to be denied. "Go get your blue sweater. I hung it in your closet with a few dresses so you'd have something to wear until we got settled. Go on, hurry up, James doesn't have all day."

"Oh, no hurry at all, it would be my pleasure," James said silkily, and smiled at her, those blue eyes twinkling like melting ice on a sunny day. "I have a few things I think you'll be real interested to see."

"So," SHE SAID, warm under the glass of the wide windshield, but not wanting to put her window down for fear of mussing her hair, "how long have you lived in Sabbath?"

"All my life, of course," he said, steering the massive red car out of the suburban street and onto Lakeview Drive, the town's one main road that circumnavigated the lake it surrounded. She felt the power of the car beneath her as he sped up, the purr of the engine belying its unleashed force.

"Why 'of course'," she said, trying to subtly catch her face in the side mirror to check her lips.

"Oh, I guess I just mean, you know, why live anywhere else? As far as I'm concerned, Sabbath is the most wonderful place on God's green earth."

Ellie laughed, not able to help herself. "And how would you know that, James Honeycutt? Have you been everywhere else on earth?"

He turned and smiled at her, as if playing along, but his blue eyes weren't twinkling like they had been. They looked hard and flat, like dead sky. She made a point to not break eye-contact with him, despite his steely gaze, and she wondered if this boy, no more than a year or two her senior, perhaps *had* been all over the world. There was knowledge in those eyes.

"Jimmy," he said, his gaze softening.

"Sorry?"

He looked toward the road once more. "Call me Jimmy. All my pals do."

Pals, eh? That'd be a first for me, she thought. *The boys back home certainly never wanted to be "pals."*

"Thanks," she said shortly, making sure not to sound impressed. "So, Jimmy, where are we headed on our whirlwind tour of the wondrous, God-given, eighth wonder of the world that is the town of Sabbath?" She laughed a little so he wouldn't think her bitchy, and he smiled along this time.

"First stop is the lake. It's the heart and soul of our little town, so it makes sense we introduce you first thing."

"Well, I'll be sure to be on my best behavior," she said, pleased to have a new boy to flirt with.

"That'd be wise," he responded tonelessly, and her smile vanished.

THE LAKE WAS larger than she'd expected, larger than it looked in the pictures her father had shown when he was selling her on the move. Staring at it through the sun-glazed windshield made it seem somehow unreal, a projection from a different world made entirely of contrasting blues, a canvas of sea and sky.

Jimmy had pulled the car off the paved road a half-mile back, cut onto a broad dirt road leading into a dense cluster of trees. Ellie was on the cusp of being nervous – being trapped with a strange boy in the ever-darkening woods and all – when the dark green canopy abruptly vanished and the tall tunnel of trees gave way to expansive yawn of open air. The dirt road terminated into a gravel-covered parking lot at the edge of the calm surface of Sabbath Lake, after which the surrounding town was named. Jimmy pulled straight to the edge of the gravel so they could stare at the water from the car, the warm apple-skin red leather sticking lightly to the backs of her bare legs.

"You want to get out? Walk around?" he said, fingers dancing on the steering wheel.

"Sure," she said, opening the door to a light breeze, the air warm but not as dense as it had been in the car.

They walked down a slight grass slope to a skinny stretch of coarse beach. She saw a few folks seated along the edge of the lake, small dots of dark color smudged against the rough sand.

It came then what had been nagging at her since their arrival. It was the *calm* of the place. There were no boats on the water, despite the docks dotted every few hundred yards. There were no swimmers in the shallows, no laughing kids on the beach. No sunbathers. The people here just seemed to be... watching.

"So, where is everyone?"

Jimmy strolled along the lake's edge, inches from where the still water lay dormant. She followed, hurried to his side as they walked. "What do you mean?" he said.

"It's Saturday afternoon. It must be eighty degrees. A perfect day for a swim, don't you think?"

"Sure," he agreed, watching his feet.

"So... why isn't anyone swimming?"

He stopped, his head tilted, as if thinking, then those blue eyes fell on hers. A small smile played on his lips, but he seemed to fight it off. It was a look you had when trying not to laugh at someone. To spare their feelings, perhaps. "Ah," was all he said, then turned to face the lake.

"Are there no fishermen in Sabbath?" she teased.

When he didn't answer, she turned to the lake as well. Across the water she saw miniature houses with toy cars in their driveways; tiny people watering lawns or seated on back porches. The lake itself, she noticed, was free of waves, almost solid-looking. As if frozen. The water, although blue, looked black as sodden soot toward the middle, gradually darkening as the bottom fell away beneath.

"It's not the biggest lake in the world," he said. "But I'll tell you what. It's deep."

He put a hand on her elbow, and she nearly flinched at his touch. His fingers, long and firm, pressed into her skin; not painfully, but forcefully, as if he were about to guide her to the water's edge and shove her down into the shallows. She wondered, almost hysterically, if she should pull away, rebuke him. In the end, surprise and logic eclipsed anger and fear, and she stayed perfectly still, almost curious to see what would happen next.

"Anyway," he said, dropping his hand, his voice cheerful once more, "you'll find out all about the lake once you live here for a while. You'll come to love it, just like we all do." He turned and walked abruptly away, up the weathered grass and toward the parking lot. "Come on, Ellie," he said loudly, not turning back, "afternoon's a wastin'!"

She nodded, but found herself transfixed by the water. Yes, she could sense it now. How very deep it was.

As she stared, a moving cloud must have sprung free and drifted across the sky to blot the sun, for an enormous shadow passed along the water's surface. She looked up but saw nothing that might have created such an effect. When she dropped her gaze once more to the lake, the shadow was gone.

She turned to go and noticed a small cluster of people seated a few hundred yards away at the top edge of the beach. She could have sworn they were all staring straight at her, their faces placid as the water, pale as foam.

Gooseflesh broke out on her arms and legs. She put her head down and walked quickly after Jimmy, doing her best not to run.

THE AFTERNOON SUN was waning, there were hints of red at the horizon, and Ellie was getting hungry. She'd never admit this, of course, not unless she wanted Jimmy to think her a cow.

The Chrysler cruised smoothly along the lakefront. Ellie caught blinks of blue where the trees thinned, then vanished altogether, the lake flashing into full view, exposing its naked splendor to all comers. She turned away, saw the road to downtown slip by on their left, but Jimmy never lifted his foot.

"Where now?" she said, trying to sound nonchalant but growing tired and irritated, which was unlike her. Something about the way the people at the lake had looked at her, something about the stillness of that massive body of water...

She sighed heavily, then caught herself, embarrassed for her own rudeness, even if it was only in her head.

But Jimmy just turned and smiled at her with those brilliant teeth and sparkling eyes. "We're heading out of town a ways, then we'll come back, hit main street and grab a bite to eat. Sound good?"

"Sure," she said, watching the white dashes of the road slip beneath them like Morse code, snatched up by the powerful engine. $S - O - S$, she thought, for no good reason at all.

SHE SAW IT from the distance. Drab heaps of metal columned against the horizon, an expanse as disproportionate to her reality as the lake was. A large, surprisingly clean metal sign was strung up by heavy chain between two wooden posts the size of telephone poles. Jimmy slowed the car and turned to go beneath, stopped in the shadow of the creaking sign overhead.

"Riley's?" she said, looking up to read the name printed in large yellow letters against a rust-red metal backdrop.

"Yup, this is one of our star attractions here at Sabbath," Jimmy said, humor in his voice. "Folks come from miles around to visit old man Riley's, check out the soaring vistas, explore the rugged terrain, search for buried treasures."

She looked at him, gawping. His face stayed rigid for a moment, then he burst out laughing, and she with him. Ellie fought to compose herself, but Jimmy was busting more than one gut at her reaction.

"But it's a junkyard!" she said, too loudly, her laughter spilling out among the words.

"Yeah, sure it is. But *what* a junkyard."

She opened the door of the car and stepped out, looked at the seemingly endless acres of piled cars, ambiguous metal scraps, toilet seats and bicycles; at things so rusted up and run together it was nearly indistinguishable where one thing ended and another began. *Good Lord*, she thought, *how does a small town accumulate so much garbage?*

The flattened cars were stacked forty, fifty-feet high, the mountainous heaps of debris at least half that and twice as wide. A narrow dirt road twisted through the massive piles, like a path leading to a mystical land where everything was broken and rusted; an extinct civilization where only jagged ruins remained, massive paperweight reminders of a dead race.

"I've never seen so much crap in all my life," she said, amused at her own vulgarity. "My god Jimmy, look how high it goes. I wouldn't be surprised if there was a whole city underneath all that stuff, hidden from human eyes. I bet the dumps in Chicago aren't nearly as big."

He laughed, and she could feel him watching her. But she kept her eyes on the towers. *A wonderland of shit*, she thought, keeping *that* vulgarity to herself.

"You know, there's a story..." he started, then stopped. "Well, it's gonna sound crazy."

"Tell me," she said, not knowing – not *really* – whether she wanted to hear the story or not.

"It's kind of an urban legend," he said, "that there's a car down there, way deep in the yard, sitting all by itself. An old Ford or something. It's rusted right through, big holes in the roof, in the hood. It's got wheels but no tires, and it's missing a door, and all the glass is broken out. But what's really weird is the car's color – as it first was, I mean. They say it's painted a bottomless, empty black. Dark as outer space." He paused, as if reflecting. "The kids like to say the car was built in Hell. Crazy, right?"

"Geez," she said, scanning the piles of cars.

"What's really scary about this car," he continued, "even though it's junked and old and useless... well, it's said that anyone who dares sit inside of it..."

She looked at him, eyes wide. "What?"

His soft smile was amused, but his eyes had that hard look again. The look of ice so frozen it could never be thawed. He stepped behind her, lay his long fingers over her shoulders.

"They never come out," he whispered into her ear as she looked on at the broken towers of metal, the vast field of a used past. "A few kids *have* disappeared over the years," he said. "More than a few, actually. And lots of us hear rumors about dares and stupid stuff like that, stories about how kids like to go into Riley's to hunt for that car, dare each other to sit inside and see, see if anything happens. And *something* must have happened, right? Something pretty terrible. Because those kids, the ones that went looking for that old rusty Ford, the ones who found it, who sat inside... they never came back. Not ever."

Ellie noticed the reddening sun peek at her through the columns of junked autos and suddenly wanted to cry. An ache had settled into her guts

93

like a cancer. She didn't know why, maybe it was the thought of those kids who had disappeared. Or maybe it was just hitting her, full-force, that this was her *home* now, and these were the highlights. The day was almost gone, and what had they made of it? A creepy lake and a haunted junkyard. She wondered if she'd ever be happy again.

"Say, I have an idea," he said, breaking her train of dark thoughts.

"Jimmy…"

"Let's give it a try."

She spun to look at him, saw his wide grin, his flickering eyes, his sculpted hair coming loose. A greasy strand hung over his face like a scythe.

"Try what?"

"To find it!" he said, grabbing one of her hands so tightly she winced. "We can try and find the car together. See, I think it's a portal, you know?" he said excitedly, his words pouring out of him in a rush. "Like a doorway, between this world and another. Only, you can only go one-way, or maybe not, but maybe when you come back... when you come back it's another time. The future, maybe… or the past! We'd leave and maybe never come back. Not ever. Can you imagine, Ellie?"

Ellie could imagine, and more than ever she wanted this day to end. She pulled her hand away, not as forcefully as she might have, but enough to wipe the smile from his face. "Jimmy, you're scaring me."

She turned away from him, looked down at her shoes. *What a mess*, she thought.

"Come on, Ellie, I was just joking," he said to her bowed head, and she thought he sounded sincere enough. She felt hands rest lightly on her hips and pushed down the rising thrill of his familiarity. He turned her to face him. "It's just a dumb story, okay? I was only fooling around."

She nodded, but said nothing, couldn't meet his eyes.

"Tell you what?" he said brightly, "Let's get out of here. We'll head back to town, get some food, then I'll take you home so you can get your room set up before bedtime, okay?"

She *was* hungry now, and getting very tired. "I guess," she said.

"Good," he said, sounding relieved. "Then come on, there's one more thing I want to show you."

She followed, somewhat petulantly, but was glad to go. She twisted her head for one last look at the junkyard, squinted at a dark shape hunched atop a stack of faraway cars. She imagined wings wider than the car it rested upon unfurl from its core and spread against the backdrop of hazy red sun before the dense shadow dropped away, disappeared into the eroded world beyond.

How strange are the shadows here, she thought, then settled into the warm seats of the convertible, reminded of the fabled old Ford that made children vanish, a doorway to other worlds.

THEY PARKED AT the corner of Aylesbury Avenue and Dean Street in the heart of downtown Sabbath. The Chrysler trembled, then went still.

The streetlights popped on as they got out of the car, the glow of the bulbs rising from brown to beige to white as they walked along the broad sidewalk. She had her sweater on now; the sun was gone and the evening had grown cold and surprisingly damp. The streets were quiet, nearly empty. In the distance she thought she heard the lapping of waves from the lake, and wondered if the stillness of the watery expanse had finally been curdled by the wind, re-animated by nature.

Dean Street was wide and glistening, the lamps fully amped against the misty evening encroaching upon them, the small stores that lined each side of the street well-lit, although most were closed. A flower shop, a bakery, a clothing store, a bank. The young couple passed beneath the shadow of a theater marquee and she eyeballed the darkened poster stretched behind glass on the side of the lobby entrance, but didn't recognize the image, or the title. The words seemed like gibberish. *Perhaps a foreign film,* she thought, but couldn't fathom it in such a small town. The poster was blotted with vague, intense imagery, as if it might be a horror film, or a monster movie.

They passed by and she didn't look back.

They approached the stark white window of a small drugstore. Bright white letters that hung against the brown brick façade read DOOGAN'S, the name bordered by a thin double-band of red-striped neon.

"How about a burger and a malted, on me?" Jimmy said, and Ellie just nodded, too exhausted now to argue or discuss. She was growing more and more depressed. She missed home. Not the house waiting for her a few short blocks away – the bedroom of blank walls and boxes, with curtains framing vistas of a world she did not recognize – but *home*. Chicago. Her friends, the house she grew up in, the neighbors whose names she knew like the back of her hand. Safety.

"Here we are," he said cheerfully, and opened the door for her.

She stepped inside, blinded by fluorescent light. There was a row of small booths set into a clean white wall to her left, and a long counter to her right, lined along its length by red-backed swivel chairs. It reminded her, in a way, of Chicago, of the fountain shop she and her friends gathered at when they were younger, although it was much busier than this one.

This one was nearly empty.

One of the booths to her left harbored a morose-looking younger couple, and there were only two people sitting at the counter. She saw the Pharmacy sign hung against a sleek wood-paneled wall in the back, the word CLOSED hung on a rope triangle above a boarded-up window. Behind the counter stood a very tall man, his face white as egg yolk beneath a paper hat. He had a tiny bowtie at his neck and an apron around his bony hips. He held what looked like an ice cream scooper in one hand while the other rested on the counter in front of a teenage boy with ginger hair and freckles.

Both turned to look when Jimmy and Ellie entered, the bells strung to the heavy glass door stung the air, ringing their arrival.

"Here, sit down, Ellie," Jimmy said, and she did, right next to the teenage boy with freckles. "This here's Fred," he said, indicating the man behind the counter, "and Fred will get you whatever you want, won't you, Fred?"

"Sure I will," Fred said, nodding to Ellie and smiling through his putty face. "Always happy to welcome a new family to the neighborhood. How are you enjoying Sabbath so far, young lady?"

"It's fine," she said, trying to smile but feeling weak and out of sorts. "Just fine."

Fred smacked his hand lightly on the counter. "You look a little pale. Has Jimmy not been feeding you?"

She gave a wan smile. "He's been showing me the sites." She shifted her eyes to the right, saw the boy with freckles staring at her intently, and looked back to Fred. "I admit, I'm a little undernourished," she said, trying to sound light about it so as not to hurt Jimmy's feelings.

"I have just the thing," Fred said. "House special, and it's on me."

Someone clicked on a jukebox she must have missed when they entered and a crooning voice floated through the room. Fred turned away, grabbed a large metal cup, and began to pump white syrup into it from a steel sprocket.

She swiveled her seat to look behind her. The couple in the booth were watching her, and she noticed they were drinking what appeared to be vanilla milkshakes.

Feeling queasy, she turned back to watch Fred do his work.

He dolloped in a scoop of ice cream from a freezer before moving the metal cup beneath the spout of a massive keg which sprang directly from the wall. She watched as he turned the nozzle and carbonated water flooded in. He turned off the water and jammed the cup under a mixer, let it roar for a minute, then poured the thick wet shake into a tall ridged glass.

"Jimmy..." she said.

Fred dropped a long spoon into the glass then put the drink on the counter in front of her; a square red napkin nestled beneath, catching the perspiration.

Ellie looked down into the white, frothy shake. Bubbles rose and popped along its surface, and when the smell of it hit her she thought – she *knew* – it smelled like the lake. She thought the bubbles looked like eyes.

"What kind is it?" she asked, trying to keep her voice steady.

Fred, both hands on the counter, smiled as best he could, a crooked thing that cut into his face, making his eyes shift unnaturally. "That's a hometown special, young lady. Cream and syrup that's made right here in town, and water straight from Sabbath Lake itself. Carbonated, of course." He gave her a grotesque wink. "That's what makes it tickle."

She looked around for... she didn't know what. For help? For guidance? All eyes were on her, and the jukebox had switched songs and was playing "Rag Mop". She tilted her head to Jimmy, spoke quietly to avoid a scene.

"Jimmy," she said under her breath, her eyes no higher than his strong chin. "I just want to go home."

"We will, angel," he said, "but first have something for the road. I'm telling you, Fred here is the best soda jerk in the county."

She looked back at Fred, his smile now gone.

"That's a hometown special," he repeated, as if surprised she didn't understand. "Once you drink that, you'll want nothing else. That there's a big cold glass of coming home."

She looked down at the shake, saw something the width of a spaghetti noodle slither along the surface then dip down into the rich contents of the glass and disappear. She put a hand to her mouth, turned and cried out despite herself, "I'd like to go home now!"

Jimmy put a hand on her shoulder, squeezed it lightly. "Yeah, sure, Ellie, no problem," he said flatly. "You must not be feeling well."

"No, I guess I'm not," she said. Relief flooded through her and she started to rise.

Jimmy slid his hand from her shoulder to her neck at the same instant Fred pulled her drink back toward his side of the counter. Jimmy's hand reached into her blond bob of hair and gripped it with a fierce tightness. She started to scream when he jumped to his feet, still clutching the back of her head, and slammed her face onto the hard countertop.

Ellie felt her nose crunch. White light exploded in her head.

Jimmy tugged her head back, then rammed it down onto the rock-solid countertop once more, harder this time than the last. Her mouth and chin took the brunt of it and her thoughts became blurred steam, drifting away from her like dead memories.

He pulled her head off the counter, cursing. Her eyes rolled wildly and her nose was bent. Blood covered her mouth and her chin and the countertop where her trembling hands spasmed. Jimmy wrenched her hair back with a hard twist so that she found herself looking at the ceiling. A slow-turning fan faced her, the blades spinning rhythmically to the song from the jukebox. She groaned and was surprised to find herself gagging on a dislodged tooth.

"Give it here," she heard Jimmy say, and she wondered why no one was helping her. Wondered why they were all just sitting there, watching. As the shock abated, the realization of her great danger flooded into her and she began to squirm, to wrestle from his grasp.

Strong hands grabbed her wrists, held them tight. *The freckled boy,* she thought.

Her hair was yanked back even harder. She winced and cried out. A calloused hand gripped her jaw and squeezed painfully until she opened wide.

She felt the cold, frothy shake being poured into her mouth, coating her tongue, pushing against the back of her throat. Reflexively, she gagged, hacked it out, then, almost convulsively, began to swallow. The taste was chalky and sweet and mixed with the tang of her own blood. The flavors exploded in her mouth, numbed her senses, and swam down into her.

The hand on her head released her hair and she was allowed a breath. The fingers on her jaw lightened. She stared up at the fan – dared not look away – as she felt the rush of the drink settle inside her stomach, begin to spread through her.

A tickle at the back of her brain almost made her smile.

"More," she said, and Jimmy, holding her head gently now, supportively, emptied the rest of the shake into her mouth.

She gulped it down.

Doorways in her mind burst open and her consciousness folded outward like the petals of a black flower as big and ethereal as the universe itself, as a thousand universes. In her mind's eye she soared among ancient ruins buried beneath a façade of rusted metal, inhabited by winged guardians and sleeping gods. She flew past and dove deep, deep into the lake, past the white god that slept there, slid along the edge of the great bubble, then passed beyond.

I am the gateway.

The words echoed in her mind as she blasted past galaxies and hit light speed, spinning into an endless abyss of stardust flesh, a million worlds at her fingertips.

Then, with a blinding flash of light and a thunderous *CRACK*, she slammed abruptly back into her flesh. Her body convulsed and fell from the swivel chair, landed hard on the clean linoleum floor, writhing. Blood and white cream sprayed from her mouth and nose as the kids watched in silence. After a minute, the convulsions stopped, her body went limp.

Jimmy knelt down, put a towel to her chin, wiped a tear from her broken face.

"How do you feel?" he asked.

She smiled back, her mouth smeared in blood, a new root already climbing from the gum where a tooth had been knocked free. She felt the bones of her nose shift and click into place, and her eyes, she knew, were bright as his own. "Fine," she whispered, and he helped her to her feet. People on the sidewalk stood watching through the window. She looked at all the faces and knew them. She turned to Jimmy, her mind a buzzing hive of voices, and slipped a hand into his.

He squeezed it reassuringly. "What now?"

"Now?" she said, as if waking from a sweet dream. "Now..."

She wiped blood from her chin, hungrily licked the last of the white froth from her lips. She smiled like a serpent, like Eve.

"Now it's time to go home."

SYMPHONY

FATHER DOESN'T KNOW about this journal and if he ever found out he'd kill me.

ESTHER HEARD THE music again.

It played over this scene: she with her mother, running through fields of impossible green. The birds-eye view of an omniscient observer would have noticed specks of bright blue, budding wildflowers among the tall grass. There were also flecks of white, beads of yellow. The meadow lay the width and breadth of heaven, and no matter how fast or far she ran, holding her mother's cool, soft hand, she never tired, never felt her chest grow heavy or her brow grow hot. Mother wore a white linen dress, Esther crimson silk that flowed and trailed behind her, riding the tips of the grass, giving her blood-red wings.

It came from above. Always from above.

Horns, gentle and rising in a chorus. Strings plucked and run across with a taut bow, interrupted by bright bursts of staccato wind chords, as if through flutes or sagging bagpipes. Simultaneously cacophonous and melodic. A mathematical movement stuck with barbs, an orchestra created by a genius and performed by a thousand madmen. It came from a distant point and Esther looked past her mother's face to the sky, seeking the source.

The hovering clouds were white cotton stretched thin, with puffs of gray near the horizon. A mounting storm. From there the sounds emanated, and it was toward that gray swirling cluster that the women ran, headlong, faces stretched into smiles.

The clouds climbed higher, spreading like smoke from a house fire, reaching over the expanse. Esther started to slow, to cry out for her mother to stop, to turn back. She pulled at her mother's hand, but it was no longer soft, no longer cool. The fingers were thick, hard, long. The fingers entrapped her own and pulled her along at the same breakneck speed. She tried to get her mother's attention but could only see the back of her head, blonde hair flowing, the thin white dress a writhing sack of pumping arms and legs.

"Mom!"

The head turned slightly, and Esther saw a chin, a nose in profile. The skin appeared strained, wrinkled, scabbed.

The music amplified—*and, oh, it was beautiful*—filling the sky end-to-end like swelling twines of muscle, straining against the atmosphere, the vibrations of chords strong enough to shake the earth. The gray clouds were above them now, and still they raced on. Rain fell in sweeping sheets, the hands of Neptune slapping across the plains, dousing them both. The linen dress clung to her mother like translucent skin, revealed her body's slight, elfish frame. Her hair, like Esther's, no longer flowed, but spilled over their heads like jars of paint. Mother's pale yellow, Esther's inky black. Esther no longer tried to scream, the raging harmony was too loud. Her vision juggled, eardrums tickled, teeth chattered from the physical strength of the music, so big it filled the world, split the sky like broken plaster. The shattered pieces fell as hail.

And still the music grew, a heaven's worth of angels shouting down Jericho's walls.

Above them, charcoal clouds circled in masses large as cities. A spiral funnel formed, a finger of God that pushed slowly through the fabric of the world, thrust itself down, down toward the firmament, toward Esther.

Her mother stumbled, collapsed face-down and motionless into the grass. Esther fell with her, her crimson dress running off her like warm blood. She clutched her mother's prone head, lifted it from the ground to face her.

Mother's eyes were hollow, her skin stretched, flaking and calloused, her teeth crooked shards. "Stay away, Esther!" the hag that was her mother screamed. "Stay away from him!"

Esther screamed but could not hear her own voice. The song crescendoed. Thunder rumbled alongside pounding drums. Great horns wailed, cymbals crashed. Lightning rode the rain down and spit fire into the earth. Dirt flew and Esther felt the heat from the electricity.

The rushing wind tugged at her with invisible fingers, lifted her small body from the earth, gently as a soul rising from the grave toward heaven. She spun her arms, reached for her mother but she was there no more; only a charred black chasm remained, into which her body had fallen. Esther could see downward into the great fires of Hell.

And still she rose.

She began to cycle with the twister, the world spun while falling away. Higher and higher she flew, into the gaping maw of the storm. Her body flipped to face the sky. She saw slits of golden eyes above an expanding, swirling mouth. Sonorous laughter came from the great aperture, and lightning crackled at the edges of the portal like fire-born teeth. She was pulled inside, swallowed. It was darker than she'd imagined, the earth seen only in dancing slivers. A spark bit her dress and it caught with flame. Her skin burned, the meaty smoke filled her nose and her mind screamed at the hungry storm which had engulfed her to *let her go or let her die.*

But the music did not stop.

Even when she woke from the dream, surrounded by the banality of her shadowed bedroom, it lingered.

Rain spattered the windowpane, opaque against the night. She sat up, her shirt and pajama bottoms soaked through with sweat, strands of hair sticking to her cheeks and neck. She slowed her breathing, her rapid heart. Listened. The melody remained, as it often did. Persistent. As if to say, *this time, child? This time will you heed the call?*

She squinted at the window, eyes adjusting to the gray-toned sketches of the landscape: the flat shadow of large meadow, the thin smoke-trail of road that led to a larger world snaking away from its edge. It was the middle of the night, and the moon shone strong despite the rain. Esther nodded to the dark in acquiescence, pushed down the covers and swung her legs out of bed. Her toes dangled inches from the floor as she faced the window and studied her spectral reflection.

This time, she would heed the call.

THE RAIN WAS different than in the dream world. The haunting music was still distinct, but faint, as if pressed against a massive membrane that separated this world from that of dreams. The sound of the drops hitting earth and flora was like the arguments of fairies, soothing with an underlying hostility. She felt observed by the rain, but did not mind.

Her clothes absorbed the cool water, turned heavy and chilled against her skin. Esther turned back once to view the pale house, misty and beaten by shadows; its half-open window a sleepy eye in the western wall of the one-story ranch home. The milk-toned walls wore sepia shingles like a sharp-angled hat. Father's room was on the opposite side, and she did not fear his seeing her, nor did she fear his coming to her room late this night. She had learned his patterns, sly though they might be.

The sky danced with flashes, popping bulbs of lightning. The music above her swelled. Horns fattened and swayed, a melancholy dirge. She turned and ran across the knee-high grass toward the trail head. The trees that surrounded the meadow and enclosed their home were old and dense, protruding fingers of oaks, maples, birch and cedars. Beyond the woods, up and over a ridge, was the trail, an old Chippewa path kept alive by the occasional Sunday hiker and the environmental leanings of the local council. The trail was hardly ever used this close to Paw Creek, where her and Father lived, but would take you six miles north if you let it, winding along the big lake to Little Bluff, a quaint tourist town that thrived in the summer and hibernated, like they all did, in the cold months. Esther had never walked the entire way, but she and Mother had often explored the trail, marveled at the long tunnel of trees it afforded those who passed through. Just ahead was the flute where the trees opened, a dividing not unlike the Red Sea, a clear path of thin grass, rock and dirt piercing the old woods like an arrow shaft.

As she strode into the forest's moon-dipped fissure, she closed her eyes. As rain pattered her head and cheeks and shoulders, she debated whether she truly wanted to continue. She took a breath, smelled the life in the rain.

Took another.

A whip-crack of thunder, and her eyes sprang open. A chorus, sweet as a swarm of locusts, sang in her ears. The orchestra bellowed, not from the sky, but from the trees. A swelling coda of dancing keys infiltrated the surrounding wood, and as the rain slapped against earth and leaves it stopped being random white noise and instead took on a melody, a rhythmic beat, a fantastic pulse of notes flowing through her like waves of energy, a complex and torrid symphony as haunting as it was blissful. The wind gusted at her back, pushed her forward despite her uncertainty. The trees were bent unnaturally, the hardwood creaking as the tips arched into deep courtship bows, branches reaching into pointed bark-coated fingers.

This way, they said.

She ran, let the wind lift her off the ground every few steps, gently place her back in stride, heel-to-toe on the wet earth. She entered the trees, felt them watching her askance as they bowed deeper, uniformly directing her steps.

Esther saw the tunnel take a turn just ahead, darker here than at the entrance, the moonlight not breaking through. The crook in the trail was called the Devil's Elbow, and her mother had said it came from an ancient Indian name, translated roughly to "where the spirits live." Esther didn't believe it of course, knew her mother was teasing, trying to frighten her. But now, alone in the dark, Esther thought it an appropriate name. She felt energy here, a tingling that carried from the bottom of her spine up through her neck and along the back of her skull.

There was a sharp break in the song, a stuttering record skip, and the trees groaned and lifted themselves straight as soldiers. She slowed, then stopped. Waited. She was confused, lost without the music. When it started again it was soft. A sonata. The trees cracked and leaves murmured. She watched in wonder as they swayed, gravitating to a synched point, the ones to the left of the path bent nearly horizontal in their reach, the ones to the right dipped so sharply as to be upside-down U's. She stepped forward to where their leaning tips directed, a sole spot in the earth along the shoulder of the trail. She looked up, spun around, saw the tops of the trees looking back at her with stern, leaf-skinned faces.

The music rushed back like a sharp wind, frenetic and hurried. Gasping, she dropped to her knees and ripped at the soft earth with her fingers, yanked at the top layer of grass, then into the pale brown mud, pulling away rocks and small roots, tossing it behind her as she dug.

She was elbow-deep, fingers bleeding, nails chipped and split, when she finally felt something cold, unnaturally smooth. She wiped and scraped away the remainder of the mud to uncover an object shining and black. Six inches in height and intricately shaped. She pried her fingers beneath it, pried it up.

A ray of moonlight broke through the canopy and she lifted the onyx carving into its shine. The head was a unicorn, the twisting horn protruding from the raised forehead as long as her pinky, the tip sharp as a needlepoint. The body, however, was that of a large man. Brutish, hairy, and hunkered into a sitting position. Unnaturally long fingers sagged over his knees, his chest a mighty barrel, his stomach a protruding gumball. Legs, bent and knobby, ended in hooves.

Esther stood, swayed, felt sleepy. The moonlight was fading, her adrenaline waned. She was cold, wet. Clutching the object to her chest, she sighed and headed for home.

Minutes later she crawled through her window. The carpet squelched wetly beneath her dirty bare toes, the half-open window having allowed in the rain. She set the statuette on her nightstand, then went to the bathroom to dry herself, wash the dirt from her hands and feet.

She found clean sweats, a long-sleeve thermal, and dry fluffy pink socks. Warming slowly, she climbed into bed, scribbled blindly in her journal, then fell into a deep sleep, where no dreams could catch her.

Too tired to write much tonight. Sorry.
  Another nightmare and some found treasure.
  New friend, perhaps.

"Eat your eggs."

Esther looked down at her plate, the pile of moist yellow scrambled eggs on one half, greasy fat-tipped bacon on the other. Her stomach clenched at the thought of putting any of it into her mouth, so she nibbled at the edge of an unbuttered piece of toast and studied the meal, wondering what she could do to get out of eating her father's failed attempt at a healthy breakfast.

She kept her eyes lowered as he pulled out a chair from across the table, sat down heavily, picked up the morning paper and slurped his coffee.

Saturdays were Esther's least favorite day of the week. Monday through Friday she spent at school, and often tried to extend the time away from home by asking for playdates with her friends, or volunteering to help with after-school projects. Anything to keep her from returning home to her secluded prison with Father, who still had no job, paying their bills with the insurance checks that came every month since her mother died.

She poked the eggs with her fork, head bowed, then subtly lifted her eyes to examine the man across the table. Hair graying, thin, and much too long. He looked pale and gaunt, but she knew how strong he was. He had looked different when Mother was alive. Or, perhaps, he had only *appeared* different to her. Rose-colored glasses of a young girl in love with a daddy who adored her, smothered her with love, *protected* her.

Now he was the boogeyman. A stalker of the night.

When he drank, as he did most nights, he got depressed, then, especially of late, hostile. It started with visits shortly after Mom's death. He'd sit on Esther's bed and cry; she'd hug him and *she'd* cry. Then he would stay in her bed, hold her, sleep with her until morning. At first, she loved it. But as the months went by, the visits became too ritualistic, too invasive. Esther was getting older and realized how very *odd* it was. She'd tried to play it off at first, made a joke of it. "Daddy, go sleep in your own bed!" she'd say and throw a pillow at him, or a stuffed bear. Often he'd laugh, take the hint, leave.

But the more he drank, the less of a game it became. The less in control he was. The warmth became a chill that never left her body, the games a sullen acquiescence. When he first started groping her, she'd squirm and jump out of bed and yell at him to *stop!* And he would. For a while. Until he came home drunk again.

He started tying her down. Used pieces of her own clothing. Sweats or leggings, whatever was around. He'd tie her to the bed and put his hands on her. Angrily so. Sometimes, as if sickened with himself, or with her, he'd push her into the closet and jam a chair beneath the doorknob. Leave her there for the night, often well into morning, until he woke up and summoned the courage to face her.

After a while, she stopped lashing out. Stopped fighting. He never went too far, kept the damage mainly psychological, which she supposed was a blessing. But it was also, she knew, temporary. She was getting older, her body maturing, and he had noticed. It shamed her. All of it shamed her. She would look in the mirror at her own body and break down in tears, hating her own womanhood. Hating the female of her. Hating that she drew him to her in that way. Hating him, but herself more.

During those first months, when he'd become more abusive, the nightmares began. Dreams of storms and music, of being with *and losing always losing* her mother. Again and again and again.

He looked up at her, caught her eye and held it.

"Eat your eggs."

She stuck a fork into the bright yellow mush, lifted a small bite to her mouth. They were cool and wet and she wanted to spew them out, but she managed to swallow. Maybe she should start handling the cooking duties. At least then she wouldn't be eating shit every meal.

She recalled the statuette sitting on her nightstand and smiled to herself. A secret was always a good thing to ward off feelings of worthlessness, of abjection. Secrets *empowered*.

Then she realized a sad truth: Secrets did empower, but in their case they empowered *him*. Because his secret, in this particular scenario, was her.

HOLY SHIT.

Okay, how can I put this into words? How do I describe last night?

I was laying here, falling asleep and staring at the unicorn. Thinking about the music I'd hear in my dreams and the night I dug it out of the dirt, near the trees.

I heard a loud… I don't know… scratching sound, and the room got very, very dark. Like I was underwater, like my whole room was sinking in a submarine, diving into some dark abyss. My ears plugged up and the air got hot… and then, a minute later, my ears popped and I could sort of see again. Everything was fine. Normal. Except when I looked around my room, I saw him.

I turned on the lamp by my bed, ready to scream.

He stood by the window, and he was big. Massive. He was, I don't know, seven feet tall or something. Hairy and wearing weird clothes, sort of like a robe but it only covered his middle, not his arms or head or feet. But they weren't feet. They were hooves, like on a horse, or a goat… but way bigger. Hard and nasty-looking.

This giant man with horse feet… was just standing there, staring at me like a big creepy shadow. But here's the thing—he wasn't *creepy, or scary, not at all.*

He was nice.

I liked him right away, even though I was obviously startled at first.

At least it wasn't Father.

So he stood there, watching me, and I didn't move because I was too freaked out, and then he smiled, and he had big white teeth, and he said…

"HELLO, PRINCESS."

She didn't respond, didn't know *what* to say. The beast of a man had just appeared out of the shadows, standing between her bed and the window. In her fright and surprise, Esther looked first to the bedroom door, as if expecting to see it open, Father standing there, arms folded, watching and smiling.

But the door was closed. The house quiet.

"Hi…" she managed.

The man laughed. A big, deep, wide-open laugh that she was sure Father would hear.

"Ssshhh!" she said, sitting up urgently, stealing another look to the door.

The man covered his mouth, dark eyes wide, as if sorry. Or amused. He took the hand away, crouched so he could be more level with Esther.

"Pardons, my dearest. Don't want to wake your dad, do we? No, not that."

Esther shook her head, and the man pounded one hoof against the floor reflexively. He stepped closer to her bed, out from the shadows.

He had long, bushy black hair. His face was stretched and narrow, but strong-boned. His mouth protruded, the giant teeth pushing against fat lips. His eyes were smooth black stone that glinted like diamond when they caught a stray sliver of light. His hooves were tapered black pots, scarred by use. His draped woolen robe couldn't conceal the geometric shapes of his protruding, spherical belly, his massive square chest. His naked arms were thick as trees and roped with taut muscle. His hands were twice the length of a normal man's, and they curled in on themselves like eagle talons, the dark nails of each finger honed to a point. She knew they weren't hands but claws, each one big enough to wrap easily around her head, powerful enough to squeeze until the skull snapped.

She could feel the heat of him. Wispy black smoke drifted off his skin.

And yet, she *liked* him. Liked him immediately, and was not afraid. She studied him, overtly sly. A look she had perfected with her mother, one that always got a laugh.

"What's your name?"

"Whatever you wish it to be," he said, his voice rumbling, head dipped in a bow. "I have many, but care for none of them."

He said this in such a manner as to make Esther giggle and smack her palm to her forehead in the slapstick fashion of television sitcoms. "Oh gosh. You are frustrating!"

He bowed more deeply, and she laughed again. "A name, if you please. For I will soon vanish without one."

She thought about it, searched her mind for things that made her laugh, or smile, that made her think of the way things used to be. "Hobbes!" she commanded, pointing a finger at his black eyes for emphasis.

He nodded, as if not unexpected, and took a small step back into shadow. "May I stay, princess? I'll sit on the floor over here, like a good dog, and you and I can speak to one another, speak of things that we could not say to anyone else in the world. Would you like that?"

She nodded, smiling.

"Wonderful," he said, eyes sparkling, chunky white teeth a slice in the dark. "Where shall we begin?"

She shrugged, said nothing. He pretended to ponder the issue, then gasped and lifted one long, needle-tipped finger, his face brightening as if struck with a most brilliant thought.

"Tell me, princess," he said, and she heard the murmuring intrada of violins whisper from beneath her bed. "What does thee know of Hell?"

THEY WERE IN the kitchen, argument full steam.

He arrived home late and drunk and there was no food in the house. While he was away, she'd made herself a dinner of shredded wheat without milk, tried to lose herself in whatever was on television so she wouldn't have to think about how sad she'd become. There was a great, constant weight on her shoulders, a tiredness she was not mature enough to identify as the early stages of deep, clinical depression. It wrapped around her, a cursed hauberk that sucked the joy from her, bogged down her spirit.

When he finally came through the door, Esther was seated at the kitchen table, finishing a family mural assignment that was to be a combination of pictures, drawings and text on a sheet of yellow poster board given to the students by Mrs. Holmes, her sixth-grade teacher. She'd been gluing a picture of her and her mother taken one day in their backyard, Esther sitting in a small red wagon, arms around her kneeling mother's neck, both smiling. Beneath the photo she'd written a paragraph about how much she missed her mother, and what her favorite things about her were. *The funny voices she used when telling me a story at bedtime. How she would comb my hair with her favorite brush, made from silver. When we went shopping on my birthday and I could try on whatever I wanted. Her smile.*

"I will call the police, you fucker!" she screamed, pushing his thin-fingered hands away from her. "Don't touch me!" She swung her fist at him, hit him wildly in the hip. Her father jumped back, his face shocked and slackened by alcohol. She could smell the whisky on his skin.

"How dare you cuss at me!" he roared, then tripped over his own feet and almost fell, grasping the edge of the kitchen counter. He started to cry. "I just wanted to hold you, princess. I love you."

"If you come near me I'll kill you!" she screamed.

She fled to her bedroom, slammed the door. Her heart hammered. She was gasping, could feel the sobs in her throat, but refused to cry.

"Push that dresser in front so he can't get in."

Esther spun and saw Hobbes laying on her bed, hooves crossed, long fingers interlaced behind his shaggy head. His black eyes were wide and filled with stars. There was a quarter-sized hole in the center of his forehead she had not previously noticed.

"Jeez, thanks," she said, and tried to push the heavy dresser across the carpeting.

"Stand back," he said, and he whistled, or made a face as if to whistle, but a swinging lick of horn came out instead, like a jazz trumpeter tuning up for a midnight performance.

Lithe figures made of smoke slipped from the hole in his forehead, danced across the floor to the dresser. She smelled the sour of sulfur and the dresser jerked free from her fingers and slammed against the door with such force that small chips of wood flew into the air, the peach-colored wall which spread outward from the doorframe dented where the edge had struck. "There," he said, and the devils slipped back into his head, as if inhaled.

There was an immediate pounding at the door. Her father in the hallway screaming now, screaming that he was going to punish her, punish her for what she said. For disrespecting him. The screams were muffled, as if his face was pressed flat against the other side. The handle rattled, fists slammed into the wood.

"I'm coming in there," he said, and it did not sound like her father, but like someone else. Like a stranger in their home. "I'm going to come in there and take care of some business. You hear me! I'm gonna take care of business tonight!"

Esther ran across the room to the window, meaning to escape into the dark. She pulled up on the handle, but the window would not budge.

"Help me!" she screamed, crying now, releasing her fear and misery. Hobbes sat up slowly, razor-tipped fingers punching effortlessly through her blankets, into the mattress. The hole on his forehead cycled open wider, the size of a silver dollar.

"You don't want my help, princess. If I helped you, it would be to take you away from here. From all this. Into Hell."

She ran to him, threw her arms around his massive frame, her small hands only making it as far as his biceps. The heat of his skin so hot, almost burning, the smoke coming off him covering her like oil. He did not move.

"He's going to come in here, and he's going to get me." She stared into his deep black eyes, wide and round as a mad stallion. "You don't understand what he'll do to me."

Hobbes looked at her, nodded. When he closed his eyes, a tear, black as ink, slid down his roughened cheek. "Listen to the music, princess."

HELL.

He took me there. I don't know how, but he did. Shit... it's hard to describe.

First off, it was way worse than you'd imagine. Very dark and cold and Hobbes wasn't even Hobbes when we got there. He didn't look much like a human anymore. His head was that of a huge black horse, or a unicorn, but it was NASTY. The horn was long as I am, it stuck out forever! And it was drippy and twisted, moving up and down like it was covered in little skinny snakes. He'd pretty much doubled in size, and even though he still had his normal body, it was bigger. WAY bigger. All covered in thick hair and he had a tail and when he walked everything shook, like tiny earthquakes.

And—yes, I know how this sounds—that's when Satan arrived. But he wasn't like I'd been taught. He was beautiful and radiant. And sweet. All smiles and power. He glowed like a giant angel. He must have been ten feet tall, because he was even bigger than Hobbes.

This is when it got crazy. Satan (or Lucifer, he said, call him Lucifer), wanted me to stay. He didn't want me to come back. Which, frankly, I wasn't all that upset about. Come back to what? Father? A shitty house in the woods with no friends and no relatives and nothing but a horrible man who couldn't keep his hands to himself? Who is supposed to LOVE ME GOD DAMN IT.

Then Hobbes got mad, and they argued. Lucifer said he would let me return if Hobbes performed for him.

And he did. It was unreal.

The most incredible thing I'd ever heard. He unleashed a thousand creatures inside a deep, massive bowl in the ice, and I sat with Lucifer and they performed this insane symphony. It was like what I hear in my dreams, but a million times louder, a million times better. It was beautiful, and scary. Melodic, but violent with bursts of sound and wide swinging melodies. Sometimes I cried, and a few times I laughed, but I loved every second.

Lucifer told me that the world I was from was being destroyed by the music. He said giant waves were destroying cities, hurricanes were flattening towns, and millions of people were dying. I nodded. I didn't care. Not really. I hoped my house was flattened by a giant tree, or hit by lightning, or blown apart in a tornado, like the one in my dream, and that Father was cut to ribbons and destroyed.

I think Lucifer knew I was thinking this because he laughed, but I didn't mind, because Hobbes was beautiful, and brilliant, and all those creatures—

they looked like humans, and animals, and other things I'd never seen (some were horrible and ugly, and some were so gorgeous you couldn't even look at them)—were playing for HIM, and I could hardly breathe until it was finished.

At the end Lucifer stood, an audience of one, and clapped. Hobbes bowed his great unicorn head, and then everything was gone, and it was only me and Hobbes left. A lake of fire burned in the distance, but I stood on black ice and shivered.

"WHEN ARE WE going back?"

"I'm not, princess. Just you."

He kneeled. His giant head and spiraling horn towered above her. He looked down, white teeth reaching, thick gray tongue bobbing inside his mouth as he spoke. "Listen to me. I will tell you something not everyone knows. It is very hard to kill a unicorn. Almost impossible. Do you understand?"

Esther nodded, not understanding but desperately wanting to. She waited, eyes on his, attentive.

"Only a virgin can kill a unicorn," he said, licking at his teeth and huffing out a great warm breath. He shook his mane and continued. "And when all the virgins become whores, nothing remains which can destroy the beast. Do you see?"

Esther knew she was still a virgin, despite her father's nighttime visits. And she swore, right there, to remain that way forever.

And then she cried. Sobbed at her despair, her loss. All her mournful life crashed in on her, suffocated her in what could have been. Her feet were numb from standing on the black ice of Hell, and the massive unicorn looked down at her sadly, the flames from the lake of eternal damnation dancing in his mournful eyes, reflective as windows at midnight.

A WEEK PASSED. She did not see Hobbes, and her father made no late-night visits. She went through the motions of school, of being a normal girl. She cleaned the house on the weekend, and her father spent the day working on a nearby farm, making extra cash and, shockingly, staying out of bars. They didn't say much to each other, but it wasn't as strained as it was pregnant with possibilities. Potential future dangers.

Esther remained guarded. She was sad her new friend had disappeared. All that remained of him was the six-inch statuette hunkered on her nightstand, long spiraled horn puncturing the air, thrusting skyward.

The dreams also had ceased. She almost never heard the music anymore. She wondered if her visit to Hell had stolen that right away from her, if the symphony played for Lucifer had burned out the lingering tendrils of the song in her mind, left her devoid of beauty—be it raging or melancholic—and filled her instead with the tuneless every day, with the repetitive, identical note-plucks of normality.

The devil would have told her, had she asked, that only suffering is eternal, and bliss is almost always short-lived.

FATHER'S DRUNK AGAIN. He's in the kitchen hollering for me, but there's no WAY I'm going out there. I've got the dresser in front of the door and if I have to I'll go out the window. I checked to make sure it wasn't stuck like last time and left it open a couple inches just to be sure.

And what else? Hobbes came back! He's laying at the foot of my bed as I write this. I can't tell if he's really asleep or just faking, but he's all curled up in a big hairy ball. I have to keep my knees tucked up just to fit on my own bed because he's huge. I hadn't seen him for a week, but when I heard Father's car pull up and him get out cussing, I knew he was drunk and ran for my room, and there was Hobbes, snoring and curled up like a pet dog instead of a demon bigger than two men.

Oh shit. Father. He's at the door. Banging again. Damn it...

I kick Hobbes but he's not waking up. Father's yelling some crazy... he sounds out of control! DAMN IT! I hate this.

I'm scared.

Hobbes better wake up. The dresser's not holding this time. I'm going out the window. I've got to run for it.

THE DOOR BURST open another foot, the dresser pushed against the resisting carpet as her father shouldered his weight into it again. She tucked her notebook back under her pillow and stared, petrified, at his pale, sweaty face, his arm reaching through, slapping the dresser.

"You think you can hide from me?" he said. "You're my daughter, Esther, and you will do what I say or I will punish you!" His voice rose into a slurred squeal. "You hear me, princess? I'm coming in there and you and I... well, we're going to have a little talk."

He shouldered into the door, began to squeeze through the opening. Esther cried out, shook the giant sleeping at the foot of her bed.

"Hobbes!" she screamed. "Hobbes, wake up!"

Eyelids popped open, onyx shining. "I'm awake, princess."

"Then *do* something!" she yelled.

Her father was almost through, his belt seemingly caught on the metal door handle. She leapt for the window, turned back as Hobbes stood, rolled off the bed, his hooves clumping to the floor, and stretched. His fingertips scraped the ceiling. He looked down at Esther, gave a toothy smile. "Not much I can do, princess. My boss won't let you leave a second time, and I can't hurt him without hurting you." He shrugged, his face cragged, muscles writhing. "Such is my power."

"Please!" she screamed, backing for the window.

Her father pushed through the half-open door and into her room. He circled around the bed toward her. "Beg all you want, but I'm done playing games with you," he said, his mouth a twisted snarl. "Shit, I don't even think you're my daughter. Your mom used to cheat, did you know that? She had lovers, who knows how many! And when she died, I was *glad*."

Esther shook her head, weeping, hands up in a useless warding gesture. "Please stop."

"I was hap-hap-happy!" her father said, then giggled like a madman. "And you? You're probably one of 'their' babies, someone else's little girl that I gotta take care of, gotta feed and all that shit."

"Daddy..."

He paused a moment, face softening. His blurry eyes roamed the room, as if confused as to how he arrived there. Then he smiled, and straightened.

"I'm done chasing you. Get over here."

He pointed to the ground. Esther turned, sprang for the window. She grabbed the bottom of the window frame, tugged it upward. Before she could lift a leg he was there, arms wrapped around her waist, pulling her back, howling. She screamed out and he twisted and threw her across the room. She crashed hard against the side of her bed, the back of her head cracked into the nightstand, rocking it. The statuette wobbled, then steadied. She looked up in time to see him coming at her.

Her eyes found Hobbes standing silent in the corner. He studied her for a moment, sighed, then said, "Remember what I told you." His voice sounded as if he were in her head and not across the room.

In the next heartbeat, Hobbes roared and sprang his full girth at her father. She felt a surge of exultation, of hope, as the giant demon crashed into him, slamming them both into the far wall. The room shook, the window rattled in its frame.

Esther stood, ready to run for the door, waiting to see if Father was conscious after such a blow, waiting to see what Hobbes would do next.

"No..." she said.

Hobbes' body began to push itself *into* her father, the two of them morphing like liquid, becoming one. Her father's eyes were open wide, staring at the ceiling. His mouth was a long, perfect 'O' of shock as Hobbes somehow, someway, forced every inch of himself into Father's flesh, one long black fingernail slipping in last, disappearing in a wrinkle of the dingy white T-shirt her father wore above his jeans.

Hobbes was gone.

She waited, unsure of herself. Father was hardly moving. His head swayed side-to-side, eyes wide and unfocused; a string of drool dangled from the corner of his mouth. She took a step toward him.

"Dad?"

His mouth snapped shut. His chin dropped, and his eyes expanded to twice their size. Silky ink flooded from the distorted pupils like black blood, covering the whites and irises. He stood as if pulled up by a string. He was taller, broader. Esther took a step backward, not understanding. She studied his face as he dropped his new eyes to stare down at her. A black spiral opened in his forehead and widened, two inches across and funneling deep into his head. She saw the stars in his eyes, and the funnel howled like a killing wind.

"Hobbes?" she said weakly.

Her father shook his head, smiling. Teeth oversized and thick. "Afraid not," he said.

He lunged for her and she screamed, dashed for the door. But he was too fast, too strong. Fingers closed around her arm and she looked down, saw fingernails like chips of black coal, sharpened to pinpoint tips.

From the ceiling, she heard the plucking of strings. A wild rumpus of a thousand violins being sprung, broken, tugged and pecked. A mad, broken pizzicato.

Then she was flying.

She slammed into the wall with a great crash of cymbals, dropped face-down on her bed. Her arm hurt bad and she wondered if it was broken. He came for her again.

Panicked, she leapt from the bed, grabbed the statuette, began to spin toward him, hoping to defend herself, when something impossibly hard slammed into the side of her head. She dropped, senseless and limp, to the floor. She moaned. The room swung out of focus, sideways.

Her ears rang, and all else was muted. She stared dumbly across the great expanse of her carpeted world. She recalled a pink doll house that used to stand in the far corner, where she would play for hours and hours. She thought of her mother telling her stories; remembered a small easel her father had given her on her 6th birthday. She'd painted watercolor flowers on sheets of thick, rough paper from the art store. The day her mother died she'd burned all the flower paintings. Made a bonfire in the backyard and turned them into sheets of ash. Later, she exiled the easel and dollhouse to the dark of the closet.

She had only a few moments left in her life to wonder why she'd let her childhood go without more of a fight. Why had she let it go so easily if this was growing up?

Her father's feet filled her vision. His brown work boots had split apart and she saw rough hooves behind torn leather, pushing through the stretched, shredded fabric of wool socks. One foot kicked her over, and she could only stare, arms sprawled to the sides, at the towering beast. He offered a grotesque smile, raised his arms like a bird taking flight and lifted a giant hoof high off the ground. With a grunt, he stomped onto the middle of her chest, like a mule kicking a rusted bucket. She felt something snap inside her and she spasmed, then spilled tears and groaned, her body sliding into shock.

He bent over her, long fingers coiled around her neck. She heard knuckles clicking as fingers twined around her throat like snakes, the point of each fingernail digging into flesh. She was lifted off the ground like a doll. Despite her body's shock, her fingers tightened their grip on the cool statuette and held on as her feet hung limp in the air. She found herself looking directly into her father's deranged, alien face. His liquid black eyes stared back at her coldly. The hole in his forehead swirled and gaped like the mouth of a hooked fish, pulsing with excitement and pleasure.

"Almost done here," he said, his voice deep and ancient.

A million miles away, she heard rumbling thunder. The strumming of cello strings that pranced through the room had been joined by bursts of a baritone horn, a thumping, bumping orchestra that might accompany a jaunty dance, a Strauss waltz.

She swung the statuette at her father's head. The long spiral horn went in through his left temple, sunk three inches deep, smoothly, as it might slide through butter. She gritted her teeth and pulled it free, blood spitting from the wound, then rammed it in again, this time just above the ear. She felt a *snap* as the horn broke free from the rest of the figurine, and when she dropped her arm there was only a nub on the unicorn's head where the long spiraling horn had once protruded.

Her father blinked, but no sound came from his clenched throat. His fingers opened and she fell to the ground, cried out in pain, felt a dagger punch into her chest. He stumbled backward clumsily, a horrid dance that fell sickly in time to the waning melody, then dropped against the far wall, head lolled to one side.

Esther waited, panting, fisted hands clutched to her pained chest.

Her father's head elongated, skin breaking with black bristles, teeth reaching, eyes bulging. A stunted shard extended from the hole in the black forehead – the broken base of a unicorn's horn.

She crawled to him, cradled the enormous, sagging head in her arms. "I'm sorry, I'm sorry," she said, over and over. She wept as she held him— wept for her mother, herself, her father. For Hobbes. For all that had been lost.

A sound came from the dying creature. She resisted her cries and leaned close to its mouth. "One more thing," it said, its voice a scratched whisper, brittle as a winter leaf.

She listened, and nodded. When he stopped breathing, she laid him down gently on the patch of floor that once housed her childhood, in the room that once cradled her innocence. She stood slowly and staggered to the window, still open wide, and pushed herself into the night.

She didn't look back.

Outside she could smell a brewing storm. The sky was the color of plum, the wind calm but charged. The jagged music played on behind her, but drifts also now came from the air, from the earth. The wild bleat of a horn, the rumble of a bass drum. But not symphonic, not whole.

She saw a flash of lightning in the distance but heard no thunder, felt no rain. She ran awkwardly for the trees, her chest broken, stabbing her with every step. The remains of the figurine still clutched tight in one small hand.

The tunnel of trees swayed, arms lifted. Melodic voices came from behind their trunks, a sad chorus paving her way deeper, deeper into the wood, toward the Devil's Elbow.

She went on as best she could, breath hitching, head pounding. Finally she reached the hole where she had found the statuette, and returned the thing to it. She coughed, a flood of bile and blood pushed into the back of her throat. She gagged, then coughed again. Even in the dark she could see the splash of liquid splatter against the moon-tinged glimmer of the object.

She looked around, desperate. A few feet away she saw the protuberance of a smooth stone. She crawled to it and began to dig, relieved there was more of it hidden beneath the earth. It would serve.

Free of the dirt, the rock was the size of an oblong baseball, and she gripped it easily in her hand as she crawled back to the hole where the statuette lay. She saw it there, at the bottom, already broken but still alive, still throbbing with power. She sensed the rustle of the trees around her. The chorus grew, rose like a high tide, warning her. The beating of bass drums came from the heavens, and the soft mumbling of horns, carried by a soft breeze, drifted through her, slid into her ears, nuzzled against her slowing mind like a ghostly feline.

She gritted her teeth and brought the rock down on the statuette, felt the satisfying crack as something inside it separated. She raised the rock again, slammed it down again. The chorus was rhythmic, a rising tremolo. Jagged horns surged, beating against her like shadowy fists. Jolting percussion vibrated her bones. The mad swipe of a thunderbolt bow against sky-wide strings, angry and frightened, pitched through the trees, filled the breadth of the tunnel with thick, crackling air.

Esther shrieked, the last of her strength pouring from her, and brought the rock down again, and again, and again.

Spent, she released the stone, stared down at the splintered fragments; the once beautiful figurine now a jumble of dead shards. She felt weak. A surge of fresh blood shot up from deep within her, spilled into her mouth, coated her tongue and teeth. She gagged and spat, and when the dark blood splattered onto the smashed idol, the music stopped. The strings, the drums, the horns... all of it... stopped.

There was silence.

She swayed on her hands and knees, but could still push the earth she had dug free back into the hole, filling it. When finished, she fell to her side, stared upward. The trees looked down at her, impassive as the moon and stars and gods beyond.

A sharp, splintering sound, like a massive sheet of ice slowly cracking into fragments. She turned her head, which felt heavy, so heavy, and saw the trees twisting and bending unnaturally, as if they had joints being broken by an invisible force. They splintered in snapping blasts of bark. The leaves upon their branches browned as one, dried up, and crinkled into small flutes that fell around her softly, a rain of feathery death. Slowly, each tree tipped, and fell. There was a splashing crash that she felt as much as heard. All around her they pulled free of the earth, disjointed and misshapen, and tumbled, collapsed to the ground, lifeless.

She rolled her heavy head the other way, far as she was able. Her breath came slowly, each intake hurting worse, each gasp shorter, her lungs slowly shrinking, filling with blood where rib had punctured lung.

All the trees had fallen, blackened as if by fire, and she could now see the entire ceiling of night sky, unbroken by their withered trunks. A meteor shot across the firmament of her wide, staring eye, captured a final frozen image of the stars and planets shimmering like fireflies on bruised parchment, the moon a quiet mother.

Esther lay in the open field, surrounded by a woven circle of deadwood that enclosed her like a witch's funeral wreath. She had time only for a prayer: *No more dreams.* Her eyelids closed like curtains on a play, and darkness flooded her.

LIGHT.

Bright enough to turn the skin of her closed eyelids to pink. She flickered them open, stared at a clear blue sky. A nimble, warm wind swept the earth, fingered her hair, tickled her skin. She sat up, the pain in her chest gone.

She looked about, confused and sleepy. The day seemed to sing a sweet silent coda to her of its perfection, its absolute beauty.

She stood on wobbly legs, but felt good, felt strong. She took a few deep breaths, let the analeptic oxygen clear her head, feed her heart.

"Esther!"

The voice came from beyond the line of trees stretching before her, a line that would become a tunnel leading home.

"Esther!"

She knew that voice, and with a gasp, she *ran.*

She cut through brush to the path, hopped over a fallen trunk, landed on her heels and pumped her legs around the bend. The tunnel appeared before her, and in the distance, the familiar meadow, and her house. She could see her bedroom window, closed now. At the front of the house she saw a woman looking toward the trees, hand shielding her eyes, blonde hair whispering out from the sides of her neck. A man came and stood next to the woman. He wrapped an arm lovingly around her shoulders.

He waved at her, and Esther, smiling and sprinting, waved wildly back. She ran across the vast plane of meadow, thrown wide in all dimensions, covered in brilliant green and dotted with flowers, the colors of which she'd never seen.

Bells chimed where her feet crushed grass, and the trees lining either side of her bent, creaking, as she ran past; long trunks curving to point her way home. The wind pushed at her back, lifting her.

Earth and sky melted away as she leapt through electric silence.

ATEUCHUS

"I am a worm and not a man..."
Psalm 22:6 (attributed to Jesus)

1

ALFIE DROVE THE Jeep hard over the rough, rock-strewn road that led to the find. He was up high now, altitude of at least 10,000 feet, the wind brittle cold. He kept the windows down, relishing the clean air, even if it turned his knuckles to blue bolts as they held the steering wheel.

The Jeep lifted high on the passenger side, came down with a thud, then dipped left into a gulley, rocking Alfie so hard his feet momentarily left the pedals. He jerked back into the seat, laughed, and gave it more gas.

James had said "not of this earth," and James – an Oxford man through and through – wasn't one for hyperbole or metaphor. Quite literal, his geologist friend. He'd also said the sample showed dramatic aging that held no relation to its geological position or depth. Put the two together and you had a nice fat meteorite, a juicy bit of space right here on planet Utah, only a few hours' drive for Alfie from his home-based lab near the university. He praised the heavens that the thing wasn't found a bit further north, across the border, or James might have been calling Jim Robinson at Wyoming instead. Even so, Alfie figured the find was technically on federal land, part of Ashley National Park, but he wasn't about to bring that up with James. Hell no, this space rock was his and by God he meant to have it.

The Jeep bounced over a ridge and Alfie saw the tents in the distance, navy green pimples dotted along a butte a half-mile ahead, the thin dirt road twisting like a brown snake right for it.

"ABOUT FIVE-THOUSAND YEARS, I'd say. More or less. Just a baby, really."

Alfie nodded, stared at the blackened chunk of rock lying in the middle of the miniature crater the geologists had dug around it. Its surface was jagged, almost crystallized, and gave off a black, chalky residue when touched. It looked, to Alfie anyway, rather unstable. More like shale than stone. James' crew, all students, stood absently around the dig, some of them likely hoping to be included in whatever this discovery ended up being, the rest simply cold and homesick. Alfie smirked, remembering his own years as a student, having to take whatever shit the professor or project head doled out.

Hate to break it to you fellas, but your claim on this meteorite went out the window when your boss brought my sorry ass up this mountain, he thought, itching to be gone but not wanting to seem overly anxious, lest James rethink the importance of the discovery.

"Pre-Egyptian," Alfie mused, as if bored, each word punctuated by clouds of breath in the frigid air. "Any similarities?"

James jammed his thin white hands into the front pockets of his vest to warm them, stuck out his lower lip. A posture he took often, and one that Alfie always thought would go well with a pipe and a stuffed hawk in the background, decorating the mahogany of whatever Oxford study room the professor most often postured within.

"Nothing on record, not anything like this, at least. She's a rare bird. The composition is strange for a meteorite. As you can see it's flaking, oxidization must have been slowly cooking this thing for the last few millennia, killing it from the inside out. But like I said, the material is completely alien. I may not know much about this little guy, but I know it wasn't born on planet earth. I've already taken my samples, pictures, measured, weighed, catalogued. It's not a chrondite, I can tell you... some rare achondrite I've never come across, and since you're the only meteoritic within a thousand miles, I figured I'd hand you the baton. I have my hands full with the shit I actually came out here to do."

Alfie nodded, only half-listening, not entirely caring about James's considerations on the matter, since the man knew as much about meteorology as Alfie knew, or cared, about the archeologic bone-digging mission the Brits were on about. Besides, he was entranced by the object before him; it consumed every ounce of his attention. "Iron prominent, I assume?" he asked, knowing the answer but wanting to build some goodwill by asking the idiot his opinion.

James looked at him strangely, his voice lowering, as if nervous of being overheard. "That's the thing, Alfie. You'd think it'd be packed with ferrous, yeah? But it's not. So far, our tests have shown no iron at all."

Alfie gave him a hard look. "You've got to be mistaken."

James scoffed, pulled the front of his khaki archeologist vest down neatly. "I don't think so. If there's one thing I know, it's how to test the chemical makeup of rock. Or, in this case, meteorite. Ergo, I'm curious what the university will come up with."

Alfie nodded. "Well, I better load up and get it over there. People are waiting to see this baby," he said, knowing damn well he had no plans to take the find anywhere but his own home lab. He didn't want – or need – the university's premature meddling in a case like this one. If he was ever going to raise his personal profile within the scientific community, he knew it had to be outside the purview of his employer. He stepped down into the belly of the crater the team had dug out, his eyes dancing over the rock in anticipation.

You ready to go home? he thought, kneeling down beside the meteorite, noting it was about the size and shape of two bowling balls side-by-side, joined at the corpulent hip. He rubbed the surface with his fingertips, gave a little yelp and flinched, jerked his hand away. He could have sworn he felt a *pulse*, as if he had touched an electrical wire thrumming with current – not enough to shock, but enough to make him want his fingers back, thanks very much.

He stared at the black smudges on his fingertips, rubbed them together, the dust staining his skin. His hands were trembling.

"Don't tell me it shocked you, mate. I'll have to call the Star," James said without humor.

"No, it's fine," Alfie said, the strangeness of the meteorite only building his excitement to study it more closely. "You're the composition expert, so tell me. What's it made of James?"

"Beats me," James said irritably, beckoning for two nearby assistants to come over and help with load-in. "What the hell you think I called you for?"

2

ALFIE DOLLIED THE large, latched titanium case through the front double-doors of his slate-gray home, the 201 freeway roaring above and behind him as he weaved the hand truck through the entry and into the carpeted living room, rumbled over the linoleum kitchen floor and slowly lowered the hand truck's wheels down the basement stairs to his lab, step-by-step, careful not to jostle the docile contents, despite knowing the case's interior padding held the meteorite firmly in place.

He set the case in the middle of the lab floor, turned on all the lights and ran back up the stairs, nearly bursting with anticipation. He was sure *this* would be the Big One that finally raised his profile to national, if not global, heights. He imagined the grants pouring in, the book offers and, inevitably, the substantial raise in salary from the university. That's if they could even keep him, of course! He had, after all, always enjoyed the idea of an ivy league professorship, and there was always MIT. Why *not* dream big?

Outside, Alfie locked up the Jeep then ran back inside, where he hurriedly closed and bolted the front door. As he flipped the deadbolt he gave a last look through the door's small window. His front yard, a large half-acre weed-riddled thing surrounded by a low metal fence, and the giant, adjacent vacant dirt lot that served as his only neighbor, were both as empty and quiet as ever. Chastising himself for his paranoia, he turned and strode deliberately for the underground lab.

Midway to the basement stairs, he changed his mind and went through the living room to the glass double-doors leading to the rear of the property. He checked the backyard, found it clear, then locked the sliding doors and pulled the brown woolen curtains closed, robbing the room of light, leaving him in musty darkness.

He went through the rest of the house, pulled every curtain, closed every blind. On his way to the basement, he activated the door alarm, the one he usually only set when traveling.

Just in case.

ALFIE HAD CONVERTED the basement a few years back, having realized he could get more work done — without prying eyes constantly peering greedily over his shoulder — in the privacy of his own home. He'd installed a reinforced metal door with a load bar lock, put up fluorescent lights throughout, drywalled over the exposed beams and painted it all a stark, clinical white. He'd built in an industrial washing station at one end of the open room, an end-to-end stainless steel countertop along the adjacent wall, mounted cabinetry, and purchased two mortician tables that he'd wheeled together to form a workstation in the center.

It was upon the mortician tables (thoroughly steel-brushed and sanitized once purchased) that he placed the meteorite for inspection.

Alfie checked the two digital cameras mounted inside the lab — one above the counter, one on the opposite wall — and made sure they were recording to a two-terabyte cloud drive the university provided. Satisfied everything was in order, he donned goggles and surgical gloves and approached the foreign object. He shifted the rock — just a bit — so it rested easily on the table, without any wobble, and prepared for testing.

Using his lightest hammer, he chipped a fragment off the side of the dusty black rock, then another, and another. Enough to get started. He put the respective samples in their own enclosed petri dishes, labeled them One, Two and Three. He walked them to the counter where his equipment was set up, including a microscope (on loan from the university), a series of acids and solvents, brushes and fine tools and other refined equipment, some of which was his, most of which he had borrowed and not yet returned.

"One more, I think," he said, wanting to test a particular oxygen generator mixture on a clean sample. He turned, hammer in hand, back toward the meteorite. And froze.

A thick, wriggling, maggot-like creature, white as a sunken corpse, slick with moisture and peppered with dusty black residue, protruded from a crack in the rock. From the exact spot where he had chipped away.

At first, he assumed the thing must have been somehow attached to the *exterior* of the rock, something he had missed while packing and pulling it from the crate. *Something James missed while taking his measurements and weights and pictures?* he thought. *Fat chance.*

He stepped closer to the meteorite and spun the table slightly on its smooth wheels, wanting a better view of the rock's surface without having to touch it. He fully expected to see the worm sticking to the side of the strange object.

But it wasn't.

It was obviously – quite unbelievably – pushing its way outward from *inside* the vessel.

"Impossible," Alfie said aloud, his mind already racing for explanations, scientific rationale of how the worm might have been trapped inside the meteorite... possibly trapped under years of sedimentation, perhaps as other materials had slowly built themselves up around the surface, somehow trapping... *alive*... this creature? Or did its initial heat melt surrounding matter to its core... or maybe something burrowed itself *into* the rock... laid eggs...

Alfie knew how ridiculous it all was even as he thought it.

Not, however, as ridiculous as the alternative. That the worm had been living inside the rock for, what, five-thousand years? That it had been inside while the thing hurled through space for who knew how long? Impossible! Ludicrous! Nothing could survive, especially something that appeared to be in its larva state... just recently hatched...

Unless.

Unless there were dormant eggs inside the meteorite. Somehow... suspended. And then, perhaps... just perhaps... when supplied with a certain life-giving element... namely oxygen... a *trigger.*

Alfie bent over, his face less than a foot from where the larva slowly, persistently, pushed itself through a small, almost invisible, crack in the shell. A clear, syrupy residue leaked down the black surface of the rock as the larva continued to thrust its way into the world. *Into our world,* Alfie thought... and the ramifications of his discovery suddenly exploded in his mind.

His back straightened. Behind the goggles, his eyes went wide. His body had gone a tingly sort of numb all over. He realized, with stunned wonderment, what may have just happened inside the basement of his home.

His home. In *his* laboratory.

Alien life, he thought dumbly, drunkenly. He smiled, almost laughing at the sheer ridiculousness of the potential reality.

"I've discovered alien life," he said out loud, testing the words, the idea. *Maybe I have*... He looked at the worm once more. Nothing else made sense. He knew it in his heart, in his scientific mind... there was no other possibility.

Like a stretched piece of elastic, his thoughts snapped into place, his body rediscovered its nerve endings, and the whole world glowed with brilliant possibilities. "HOLY SHIT!" he screamed, and spun in a circle, dropped the hammer to the floor, ripped off his goggles and howled at the ceiling, "WOO-HOO!! Alien life, baby!"

He laughed loudly, hysterically, then caught himself, realized he was drooling, breathing heavy, his heart pounding. He wiped his mouth, stared at the worm still extracting itself, his face hurting from idiot grinning. He rubbed his stubbly cheeks.

"Get a grip, Alfie," he said, realizing there was a mile of testing and analysis before even considering such a wild claim. He would have to be sure. Unequivocally, undeniably, *positively* sure. If he revealed his finding and was wrong he would be the laughing stock of the scientific community. He would be done, finished. So yes, he must be *absolutely* sure...

Oh, yeah... he thought, *but what IF!*

"I'll be famous," he said, addressing the visitor, who didn't seem to care or notice Alfie's state of pure exaltation. "I'd be the most famous person in the world," he said, slowly and surely, tasting each syllable as it rolled off his tongue.

"Okay, okay," he said, trying to calm himself, to slow the rush of blood to his head, the adrenaline-fueled pumping of his heart, and focus as best he could. "First things first," he said, and took a deep breath. "My little friend, I'm gonna need you to put on your game face."

Alfie ran a hand through his hair, cleared his throat, and stepped up to one of the mounted cameras. Assured by the red light, he looked directly into the lens and began to speak.

"My name is Alfred James Monroe. It is August 21st, 2016. I have recently returned from a sample-gathering trip near Athena National Forest, just *outside* the federal perimeter, where I discovered what I immediately deduced to be a meteorite. Subsequently, I brought the meteorite back to my lab for further study and, in order to analyze the rock, I proceeded to chip off a sample of the exterior shell. Having done this, in no great extreme, I produced what appeared to be a small fissure leading to a hollow in the interior of the meteorite. Stunning, I realize." He paused for effect. "Even more stunning, and still hard to believe, is what's inside."

He turned slowly, hand laid out like a game show model revealing the Grand Prize, letting the tension build for future generations, and pointed at the white, fat larva. As the camera recorded the moment for posterity, the larva finished its expulsive journey through the rock's shell and fell with an inglorious *plop* to the lab table's surface, a trail of clear goo thin as a spider web stretched between it and the hole it had burrowed through.

"Shit!" Alfie yelled, immediately forgetting the camera and lunging for one of the petri dishes and a glass stirring rod on the counter behind him. Grabbing the items, he spun back to the steel table on which the meteorite sat and gently – *oh so gently* – rolled the larva into the petri dish where it lay, relatively docile, slowly squirming and bending this way and that.

"Hello," Alfie said, mesmerized, holding the clear dish and its lone occupant so close to his face he could almost smell its dank alien excretion. "My name's Alfie, what's yours?" he said, and laughed at his own stupidity. "I'm sorry? What was that?" he said, putting the thing in the dish close to his ear, "it's hard to hear you because you're so very small. Wait, let me guess," he said, setting the dish down on the work table, anxious to get a closer look, "take me to your leader, am I right?"

The larva squirmed like a living slick white thumb as Alfie put it under the microscope, beyond curious to know the detailed makeup of the bug-like creature. He would need to extract tissue, study its composition. He'd have to send it off for analysis, but how to do it without letting the proverbial cat out of the bag? He shook his head. *A problem for another time,* he thought, and stuck his eye to the microscope's eyepiece, his hand absently reaching for a notepad and pencil.

"Rub-a-dub-dub, there's a grub in my tub…" he mumbled, and began making notes.

He was so immersed in studying the alien that Alfie did not see the emergence of a second larva head, protruding from the same slick crack of the meteorite, push its way stubbornly, and with great purpose, toward a new world.

3

IN THE DAYS that followed, Alfie was forced to leave the house twice for supplies and equipment. Otherwise, he did not sleep, or shower, and hardly ate. He had called his supervising professor at the university and given a cock-and-bull story about his mother (long deceased) being gravely ill, saying that he'd be leaving town a few days, maybe a week, maybe longer. The professor had given his regards and assured Alfie to take all the time necessary. Which was just peachy for Alfie, because since that first larva had poked its head out from the meteorite, he had forgotten about anything other than studying the strange creatures, going through the identification process, and seeking madly to positively identify them as truly, undeniably, extraterrestrial in origin.

Now, as he stood and stretched after a short nap on the cold steel mortician's table adjacent to the one that held the meteorite, Alfie thought the lab looked more and more like an incubation chamber. There were now six rectangular aquariums lined along the full-length of the counter, each holding about a dozen of the alien larvae. He had filled each aquarium halfway with thick, dense black soil, roots and other vegetation, hoping the creatures would be able to feed off the earthen offerings.

After those first two larvae had wriggled free of the meteorite, many more followed, and followed, and followed. Alfie decided to cut to the chase and, as delicately as he could, split the rock with a hammer and chisel. Inside he had found two nests, each containing a giant's fist of squiggling, slimy larvae, feeding themselves on the carcasses of who Alfie assumed had been their parents, for lack of a better label. Once he had moved each of the larvae to the incubation aquariums, he was able to better study the remaining husks of the host creatures.

His initial thought, followed quickly by a stomach-dipping surge of disappointment, was that they weren't alien creatures at all.

They were beetles.

Large beetles to be sure, and most closely resembling the *scarabaeidae* or, more commonly known, Scarab beetle. The carapaces were a foot in length, wide as a hand, and heavy as brick. Alfie was no entomologist, but he knew enough about the science of insects to know the hosts had likely given birth only very recently, possibly upon the discovery by James and his team just a week or so prior. *Something triggered the birthing process,* he thought again, knowing it impossible but too intrigued to let it go. *Like they were waiting, dormant, in some sort of hibernation...*

Alfie allowed the scenario to work its way around his head as he studied the creatures, whose biology was so similar, but also so very different – very *alien* – from earth's own insects.

They were much denser, for one. The gravity on the world they came from must be vastly different from Earth's, and when he looked at the meteorite he began to think of it less as a rock and more of a spaceship of sorts, despite it being composed of mineral versus machine. Primitive, and yet, somehow superior to mankind's technology. It had landed five thousand years ago, struck the earth hard enough to be deeply buried, hidden, all that time. What remained of it, anyway; what hadn't burnt to ash upon entry through earth's atmosphere. And there the inhabitants had lain, for thousands of years, awaiting discovery...

Awaiting release.

He knew it was true. There are no coincidences in science. The beings had lain stagnant, been unearthed, and when something released inside the chambers... a ticking clock had begun. The four creatures, two of separate sex in each chamber, had procreated, laid eggs... given birth to the masses of larvae, then been slowly consumed by them, nourishing the offspring with their own flesh until the time for release came.

A release Alfie had single-handedly manufactured.

By studying the remains of the host creatures, Alfie figured the larvae could have likely sustained themselves another six months, perhaps as long as a year. Keeping one of the hosts for his own research, he dissected the other three, dropped them into each of the aquariums, unsure of whether the nutrients were essential to the successful growth of the larvae, in addition to the decomposing vegetation and soil he himself had provided. They were so similar to grubs, down to the shining extended buckeye head and protracted limbs, that he assumed they could consume similar nutrients. And so far his theory proved correct. The grubs seemed to be thriving – not one had died – and the pieces of the adult hosts were being devoured as greedily as the roots and vegetation he'd provided. He knew it would be months before any of them developed into pupa, and possibly years before they reached the full imago stage. But he would be patient. He would make sure his research was thorough and held to the highest scientific standard, so when he revealed his findings to the world he would already be the leading (if not *exclusive*) expert for the first alien species ever discovered. Books, guest appearances on every major talk show and news program, speaking engagements... he'd have to hire a publicist, a manager, an agent. Perhaps even a movie deal... Why not? His story would be one told throughout the ages. His name would be in every textbook, on the lips of every scientist throughout what remained of the history of mankind.

Sitting on a hard stool at the long counter, Alfie scratched at his unruly beard, watched the aliens thriving in the aquariums, and thought hazily of all the possibilities the future held. All he ever wanted was to be remembered.

To be immortal.

ALFIE WORKED THROUGH the day and into the next. Not eating, not sleeping, driven by thoughts of fame, by the excitement of discovering new life from another world. Finally, his body yielded to its limitations, his vision grew fuzzy and his hands shook when he tried to write. Eventually he collapsed across the work table, midway through writing a note on the alien's feeding habits.

He slept, but not deeply. There were whispers in his mind, whispers that crawled through his subconscious like a million microscopic lice. They were words... but not any that he could understand. The words were constant, consistent in tone, a steady flow of instruction, of knowledge, being delivered to him in a rhythmic fashion, driven directly into his brain. Whispers, so many whispers... too many... thousands of voices, all speaking at once, all telling him something new.

Images pulsed through his mind as well: sunbaked vistas, hazy pyramids in the distance; an expanse of outer space, colorful galaxies flowing like cotton candy in black ether; a broken army of strange, stalk-like savages, swarming to escape a ravaging enemy attacking from above and beneath; bizarre cities razed to the ground, planets reshaped, civilizations destroyed by an army with countless numbers…

The whispers and images quickened, faster and faster, driving into his head, erupting like a supernova in his mind's eye.

The frantic, overwhelming invading thoughts were *hurting*. His sleeping body began to shake, blood spat from his nose as he groaned and coughed. In the half dream-state (if it was a dream at all), his head felt like it was *swelling*, his brain bursting apart, bubbling with the acid of alien thoughts, visions of unknown worlds no human mind could comprehend. He winced and barked broken denials, as if in a nightmare… fighting the whispers, the *voices*, now wanting them out of his head… *Stop!* he screamed in his mind. *Please*, he begged, afraid, *please get out… it hurts… you're hurting me… you're HURTING ME! GOD DAMN YOU I SAID STOP!*

With a jerk he woke, raised his head from the cold surface of the laboratory counter on which he'd been dozing with a gasp. His temples pounded viciously, a migraine behind his eyes so sharp and painful that the room wouldn't come into focus. His stomach flipped and gurgled as if filled with acid, its meager contents wanting, quite badly, to rush up and out. He lurched drunkenly off the stool. His legs immediately buckled and he fell hard, cracking his forehead on the concrete. A stack of notebooks and papers filled with notes, sketches and data collapsed on top of him, scattered across the floor. He moaned, rubbed the butt of one hand into an eye that felt like it might very well explode.

I need a drink, he thought, and then, more rationally, *and some fucking food*.

Alfie wasn't sure the last time he'd eaten anything of real substance… didn't think he'd eaten anything at all for days, other than the dregs of a giant bag of greasy chips, whatever beer had remained in his fridge and a couple granola bars he'd dug out of a dusty backpack he'd found tossed into a corner, remains of a former expedition.

He slowly, carefully, got to his feet, one hand resting on the lip of the counter, and let the room sway a moment, then, after a few deep breaths, steady. He wiped a line of drool dangling from his lip, scratched at the week's growth of beard growing like unruly moss just below. *Jesus*, he thought, *I'm a mess. I've got to...*

Then he heard it.

He froze, listening, holding his breath. He didn't move, didn't make a sound, heard only the beating of his heart throbbing in his ears, the sealed room devoid of all other noise... except for... and there it was...

Scratching.

He looked at the aquariums, eyes wild.

While he'd slept most of the larvae had transformed, entered the pupa stage. He was shocked. What should have taken weeks, or months even, had happened in mere *days*.

But even so... regardless with the speed with which they were developing, they certainly shouldn't be *moving*, and they most certainly shouldn't be *digging!*

Alfie moved closer to one of the aquariums, saw that the pupae had, miraculously, burrowed deep into the six or so inches of earth, and a few of them were now pushed against the glass, as if trying to continue their path, to go deeper, as was their nature in the adult stage (or at least the nature of their earth sister, the beetle), in order to build a wider, broader nest.

And now pupae were trying to dig through the damned glass. Their undeveloped legs protruded like jagged broken matchsticks from their thick, jelly-like bodies, claws tenaciously flicking blindly against the aquarium sides. To Alfie's relief, the glass was holding.

For now.

The pupae themselves were unlike any he'd ever seen or studied. Each was easily the size of a baby's fist, and had a deep, golden hue pulsing beneath their slick mucilaginous surface. Other than the size, however, they didn't seem to be all that irregular from the earth pupa of a beetle. What *was* strange was the strength and vitality of the aliens. A normal beetle – an Earthen beetle – in the pupa stage would be completely stagnant, essentially developing within a chrysalis, awaiting their transformation to full imago before shedding the pupa layer and emerging. But these were active workers. Diggers. The pupae appeared as nothing more than a fat lump of worm with a shining bronze head, complete with new antennae; while the tarsus and claws were emerged, working frantically, the femurs were still hidden beneath the wet golden shell.

As he looked more closely at the undercarriage of one particularly tenacious creature, Alfie could actually see thin scratched lines in the glass where the pupa's claws had grooved the interior surface, as if their claws were made from rock, or diamonds.

The sound of the hard, scratching limbs on glass filled the lab. Combined with his headache, and the nasty dream he'd had, Alfie was suddenly overwhelmed. His heart raced, his breath came in gulps, black spots crowded the corners of his vision. He felt suddenly panicked, perhaps even a little *frightened*. He staggered for the stairs, wanting suddenly free of the lab, of the strange creatures growing there, of that incessant sound.

Once upstairs he went to the kitchen, all but lunged for the refrigerator. He was out of beer but there was a half-filled bottle of orange juice, a somewhat pruned apple, and an unopened packet of cheese slices. He ripped the top off the orange juice and gulped it down, nearly vanquishing the remains in one breath. It wasn't until he lowered it and breathed in deeply that the sharp tang of spoil hit his taste buds. His stomach lurched and gurgled loudly enough to reverberate in the small kitchen. He picked up the apple, prepared to eat it, but thought he may need it for the bugs, so he stuffed it into his pocket and instead unwrapped three or four slices of American cheese and stuffed them into his mouth, the processed dairy turning to mush as he chomped and swallowed it in a dry lump; it sank into his stomach like a ball of grease, slowly digesting in the rancid juice and percolating stomach acid.

He dropped the plastic juice jug to the linoleum, where it clanked, fell over and sloshed out part of its remains onto the floor. He lurched to the bathroom, hoping he wouldn't have to throw it all up, but needing to pee and brush his teeth. His mouth was dry, pasty and sour.

He used the toilet and turned on the faucet to scrub his hands. When he looked into the medicine cabinet's mirror and saw himself, he nearly gasped in shock; there was a brief moment where he, quite literally, did not recognize his own face. His hair was mussed and plastered oddly in places, clumped wildly in others. Facial hair covered his mouth and cheeks and chin in a hazardous tangle; patches of crust and particles of meals long-past clung to the beard like the last survivors of a sinking ship. His eyes were bloodshot, and worse. One eyeball had ruptured a vessel, flooding the sclera with red, giving the right side of his face a monstrous look.

"Damn it," he said, and splashed water over his face, his eyes, his beard and hair, sloppily grooming himself to a relatively respectable level. "Gotta get it together, man," he told the dripping reflection, and vowed to have a shower and a proper meal before the day was through.

And what day was it, anyway? he thought, then shuddered. He'd lost track of time so completely he had no idea. He hadn't followed up with the professor; had left his cell phone, the battery certainly dead, somewhere in the lab. He wondered if his associates, his friends, had grown suspicious of his extended absence without communication. Surely, by now, curiosity would have grown to concern, fictitious dying mother or no. *Have they come to my door? Have they tried? Have they called the police?* He doubted the last. He only had a few friends, and most of them traveled on their own projects, had their own busy schedules.

Just how long had I been down there?

The thought of not knowing panicked him slightly, as did his grizzly, wild appearance. "Screw it," he said, and decided a break was in order. A shower, a shave, and a trip out of the house to get himself a solid, cooked meal.

The bugs will be here when I get back, he thought, and smiled weakly at his reflection, feeling good – feeling confident – about taking control once more.

He was just about to take off his stinking, sweat-soaked t-shirt, eager to get into the hot spray of a shower, when he heard the muffled sounds of breaking glass.

It came from the lab.

ALFIE TORE DOWN the stairs and pushed through the reinforced door into the lab space beyond. He slammed it behind him, eyes scanning the aquariums, the tables, the floor. He saw that two of the aquariums had shattered. The other four seemed to be holding, but he could still hear that constant, determined *scratching*. He ran to the aquariums that had broken, saw that heaps of dirt and most of the pupae had spilled out over the table and onto the floor. At first, he went to pick them up, thinking to put the spilled ones into the other aquariums, but as he looked more closely, he noticed that the pupae seemed quite alive and, almost disturbingly so, active. The dozen or so that had dropped to the floor were writhing on the concrete, but not without purpose.

They were still *digging*.

And, by the looks of it, making progress.

Alfie stared as the frenzied pupae tore at the concrete floor, deep scratches already evident where two or more seemed to be working – somewhat impossibly, Alfie thought – in unison.

Mesmerized, and more than a little curious, Alfie stepped over to the other aquariums, careful not to accidentally step on the pupae, although a part of him wondered if it was to keep from smashing them or from hurting himself. *Those claws must be razor sharp.*

He picked up the first aquarium, the glass sides vibrating with the efforts of the aliens within scratching for freedom. He tilted it over, let the contents pour down onto the floor. Dirt, roots, and golden, wriggling blobs of the pupae all fell into a giant pile, joining the rest. They too, without hesitation, started attacking the floor with their claws, the tibia on each creature a blur of frenetic motion.

Alfie turned over the remaining aquariums, one-by-one, creating a great pile of dirt and alien bugs on the lab floor. He pushed the mortician tables to the side of the room, clearing as much space as he could for the bugs to work, and for his own observation.

He stacked the empty aquariums against a wall, then backed to the doorway, shower and food forgotten, and slid to the floor, his back against the door, amazed by the power and tenacity of these creatures that had not even yet reached the imago stage of their lives.

He pulled the shriveled apple from his pocket, thought about taking a bite, then tossed it overhand into the pile of dirt.

It was immediately devoured.

4

THE FIRST ADULT spawned three days later.

The Meketaten, as Alfie had come to refer to the scarab-like creatures, for reasons he didn't wholly understand, had burrowed through the basement

138

floor, the foundation, and into the earth below the house. Alfie hadn't gone down into the tunneled earth to thoroughly investigate, primarily because he feared the tenacity of the workers (he didn't want his limbs perceived as an obstruction, to be sawed through the way they had torn through concrete, rock and earth). But he had crawled to the edge of the massive crater in his floor, easily big enough to drive a car through, and flashed an industrial flashlight down into the depths the Meketaten had created.

At first, there didn't seem to be a bottom, but then he noticed the deep tunnel that they'd dug curved northward, so that he saw only the tunnel's bend and, not having a powerful enough light to illuminate it, assumed it a bottomless void.

They had gone on to dig multiple tunnels extending outward from Alfie's property – each wide enough for a human being to walk through, if slightly hunched over – to unknowable lengths. He assumed, based on his early study of insect life, that they had built a nest somewhere down there, deep in the belly of the Earth. As if to prove this theory, it was from one of these tunnels he saw the first adult emerge.

It was the most beautiful thing he'd ever seen.

The large creature caught the beam of his light as it climbed up and out into the main sunken area just below the home's foundation. Alfie had been shining the flashlight downward, trying to count the number of tunnels the Meketaten had created, when the alien scrambled into view. It was a massive thing, long as a small dog, perhaps, and wide as a baby sea tortoise. Its antennae were long and black, tensing and twitching in the depths. The shell was a solid bright gold, shiny and clean as chrome, with three bright green luminescent dots set neatly across, about midway down its shell. The creature had looked up at Alfie, as if sensing him, and immediately skittered up the sloping dirt path, as if anxious to say hello to a new friend.

Alfie panicked, suddenly very afraid of what the fully-adult creature might do to a human, given the strength and cutting ability of the pupa spawn.

He wanted to stand, to run, to regroup. He tried to get his legs under him, but the room swooned and he fell back on his ass with a grunt. *Too weak,* he thought in a panic. His head was pounding to raise the dead, his eye throbbed like it would burst from its socket. He groaned, nearly sobbed at the thought that he'd let himself get this bad, ignore his own needs, the needs of his body. He turned his head, looked back toward the hole.

He watched with wide bloodshot eyes, in fascination and horror, as the creature emerged, first the long antennae, then the jet-black head, its mouth wet and dripping, eyes shining like burning black suns. It had slick jaws and a monstrous beak. The beak was shaped like jagged teeth.

Alfie let out a terrified squawk and shuffled on has ass back and away from the hole, kicking wildly as he pushed himself to the far wall, his eyes never leaving the emerging creature.

The adult heaved itself easily, nimbly, onto the concrete floor and skittered straight toward Alfie, its sharp legs clicking like tiny pistol shots as it crossed the floor. Terrified, knowing the thing wanted nothing but his insides for a meal, he looked around desperately. The handle of the rock hammer jutted from over the edge of the mortician table he had pushed aside, the one still bearing the vessel these beings had inhabited on their trip through space. Adrenaline and fear fueled his movements and he reached up and snatched the hammer, fingertips brushing the black leather of the handle just as the creature scrambled onto his foot. With a pathetic cry he swung the sharp edge of the hammer down at the alien, putting all his remaining strength and terror behind the blow, hoping to spear it and keep himself alive a little longer.

The hammer hit the golden shell and clanged off without even scratching the surface. The creature didn't, in fact, seem to notice Alfie's effort.

The hammer clanked to the ground as the alien climbed higher, its front legs already gripping one knee like a steel clamp. Alfie tried to kick at it, in vain, he supposed, but the monster – the *Meketaten* – only clambered faster, its hard sharp claws poking into Alfie's thighs and hips like spears. In trying to pull away from the thing Alfie only managed to slide his body off the wall, his torso flopping to the ground as the creature moved higher, undaunted, before settling heavily on his stomach and heaving chest. Its onyx eyes stared emptily at Alfie's own, its antennae stroking his face with soft, wiping slashes. Alfie couldn't believe the *weight* of it. Despite being no bigger than a shoebox, the creature felt like a cinderblock weighing down on him.

Alfie was about to do something – to scream, to fight – when the creature *spoke* to him, its audible voice an inhuman series of squeaks and clicks.

You are dying, it said.

140

Alfie couldn't believe it. The thing was communicating with him... speaking in indecipherable sounds... but Alfie could understand it. *Alien insect speaks English*, he thought, almost laughing aloud at the idea.

Not English, Khepri, it said, reading his thoughts, its jaws working as it hissed and clicked, tendrils of warm liquids sliding from its mouth, wetting Alfie's shirt. *But you CAN understand, because we will it so. You are dying, Khepri. You must not die. It is almost time now.*

The creature stared at Alfie another moment, its glassy black eyes studying him, then turned nimbly and scrambled away, off his body, across the floor, disappearing over the edge of the hole, down into the tunnels, back toward the nest.

Alfie watched it go, his body going limp with relief as it vanished from sight... at which time he promptly, and most thoroughly, passed out.

WHEN HE FINALLY came to, groggy and drained, Alfie wasn't sure how much time had passed. He laid face-down on the cool surface of the basement floor, too weak to stand, too tired to do anything but watch the coming-and-going of the now very large quantity of adult Meketaten that clambered in and out of the hole in his basement floor. Unlike the first adult, who had made a point to visit him straightaway, the rest of the scrambling creatures seemed to be completely ignoring Alfie's presence. So he just laid there and gawked at the amazing alien beings and their hectic building pace.

The lab itself was unrecognizable.

They had layered the walls and counters with dirt and dung, smashed through the reinforced door and created the head of an earthen tunnel leading upwards toward his home. The fluorescent lights still shone, and some counter-edges still protruded through the packed earth, but Alfie felt as if he'd been taken from his home and dropped into a faraway cave on a planet not his own.

As the Meketaten worked, Alfie passed in and out of unconsciousness, wondered absently if his wasted body would be used for food.

During a particularly cognizant moment, he noticed a massive adult emerge from the hole, twice the size of his previous visitor – *my god they're getting bigger*, he thought – and walk toward him. It was long and wide as a wheelbarrow, and Alfie didn't want to even think how heavy it must be. He prayed this one didn't clamber onto his chest, confident it would crush his ribs like toothpicks.

As it got closer, Alfie noticed the giant creature held a large membrane, sagging from its jaws like a veined water balloon, a rubbery-looking sack that wiggled and writhed. A womb with a hundred feisty babies eager to get out.

Alfie's eyes fell closed once more, his exhaustion complete. He watched through a blurred haze as the sack hit the floor, saw the bundle of fresh larvae spill out. The giant creature angled its face down to look directly into Alfie's own, its mouth hissing and clicking, its breath surprising clean and earthy, like the inside of a cave, or the bottom of a new grave.

There is good news, Alfie heard, his mind somehow translating the language. *We have begun mating, Khepri,* it said, all squeals and wet clicks. *The time is near, and you must eat.*

Alfie tried to respond, to question... but could only moan and drool into the dirt-smattered concrete beneath his head. His eyes rolled up into his head, something deep in his brain *popped,* and Alfie's dimming consciousness was only slightly awake to the sensation of a strong, stick-like object entering his mouth and pulling his jaw open. His tongue lolled, rubbed against the coarse hairs of the creature's limb.

Something moist and wiggling was shoved into his mouth. The taste was bitter and the mushy, twisting body pressed against his cheeks. Warm juice ran down his throat. He tried to gag, to spit it out, but instead his mouth was gently – but firmly – closed, and it took hardly any effort at all to compliantly swallow the thing down.

A hard claw opened his mouth once more and another larva was pushed inside. This time Alfie swallowed greedily, then, like a blind baby bird, opened his mouth for more.

With the patience of a mother caring for her young, the creature continued the feeding.

5

ALFIE SLEPT, AND dreamed of great things. A boundless golden army that could attack by air, by ground, from *beneath* the ground. Millions strong.

A raging storm cloud of creatures, nearly indestructible. Flying sun-fueled warriors the size of tanks – swarms of them.

He was shown visions of destroyed cities, of nations, of every people. The extinction of entire civilizations.

In a state of semi-consciousness that lasted an indefinable period of time, Alfie felt the bustling legs of the creatures – so many creatures – upon him, ripping and stripping away his clothing, tugging at his hair, his face, feeding him, whispering to him, *teaching* him. Their voices filled his mind, spilled their history, and the history of mankind, into his own memories, and he took it all in... he listened.

As his mind continued to be bombarded with images, it was as if he were reliving his own memories. Alfie could see vast sand-filled plains, vistas of wild green forest, vegetative planets with flora beyond his ability to fathom, burning landscapes where creatures of fire were laid waste, mountainous horizons, cities of blue metal populated by giant men.

There are others, they said.

In his own world, thousands of years ago, a leader was chosen by Earth's Meketatent, the army of Aten, the Sun God. That leader united civilization, demanded their worship, their compliance. It was a new world order. One of peace, of intelligence. One God for all humankind. An end to wars, to tyranny, to terror. He saw a species of giant Meketaten working side-by-side with Earthmen, building impossible structures, beacons to their brethren's own home planet, billions of light years away, where the true Aten resided, the creator of suns, the creator of life. The One God.

These Meketaten, these travelers, had built civilizations before, but man and Earth had failed. And now the time had come to try again, begin the rebirth, start the world over, hope mankind could survive and build, carry the light of the supreme being that humans called Aten, Itzamna, Yahweh, Amun, Shiva, Nugua... too many to count, too many to name.

As the thoughts persisted, some distant part of Alfie could feel the larvae bursting apart inside him, the fluids and alien bacteria from the creatures rushing into his bloodstream, expanding his heart, reshaping his delicate, intricate brain.

His body was lifted, placed by sharp legs onto the back of a giant creature. He could sense more than see being carried down, down into the depths, toward the nest. His world lifted up and away as he went lower and lower, his fingers dragging in soft dirt as darkness encompassed him completely.

He was set down inside a chamber as vast as Solomon's palace, an entryway to the massive honeycomb of caverns and tunnels already reaching beyond the city, spiraling downward and outward; new catacombs being even now created and traveled, reaching even further. His eyes prickled, sharp needling pains shooting through them. He opened them, blinking, and was surprised he could now see clearly within the depths – a duotone yellow showed every crevice of the cavernous fulcrum.

The vast walls crawled with countless golden shells.

He was no longer fed. He was so full now, and he could digest no more. He defecated, his body emptying itself, and the creatures methodically combined it with their own waste, spread out in great piles throughout the cavern. The Meketaten covered Alfie with the waste, then rolled his bloated body – his stomach a giant flexed womb of nutrients pumping through his system – into a great pile of dung. They continued to roll him into a massive ball of dirt and shit, inside which he laid, dormant, at the center of a chrysalis, awaiting transformation.

In the quiet, warm dark, Alfie curled into himself like an unborn child; could hear his heart beat faster, faster. Visions and information translated into his mind like a hurricane, expanded his brain, physically reshaping his human skull into an oblong cranium, the parietal plate breaking and pushed backward, stretching new skin. His mind reformed into an antenna which could communicate with the One God as well as the other Meketaten; to receive and provide information, relay the will of the great one.

Lead them.

As the transformation slowly continued, he felt – numbly, with awareness but no pain – his limbs crack, reshape, lengthen, then quickly heal. Stronger than before. Stronger than bone, than steel.

A thick secretion spilled from his pores, hardened around him, over him. His back broadened, shoulders separated and extended, muscle ripped apart and regrew, sinew sprouting like weeds inside as his skin became shell.

His new mind started to finalize its ultimate form, and the part of him still human wondered if he would fly, if he would swarm with his brothers, his children, and watch the destruction of what mankind had built from high above, caressed by the cool mist of clouds, the warmth of the One God spread across his impenetrable carapace like a guiding hand, the hand of a father.

They will call him Ateuchus, and when he emerged the new world would begin. His creatures, having created this new man, will scream like locusts, "*See him! See the great one, uniting the earth!*"

And he will rise, burning like the golden sun.

ID

1

WE MET IN a mental hospital.

Wow. What an opening line, right? Doomed from the get-go. Why go on?

It's okay, it's okay. It all ends up just fine.

Trust me.

SO YEAH, I was suffering from a spike in my lifelong battle with chronic depression, one that led to a sad attempt to kill myself by popping twenty-plus Ativan while blasting Foghat and drinking a bottle of cheap California Merlot before settling myself into a hot bath in a lightless bathroom save for a flickering scented candle (that was supposed to smell like vanilla but came off more like perfumed cake batter) while waiting to pass out and drown. I woke up at 3 a.m. freezing my ass off and jittery as a blue bottle fly high on cocaine. I took a walk around the block, lugged a brick through an ex-girlfriend's window then drove myself to the ER where they promptly admitted me for an abnormally high heartrate and a nasty hard-on for classic rock suicide.

When I say admitted me I don't mean for general health care. I mean they admitted me for psychological evaluation. Which I passed with flying colors, ha-ha.

THE MENTAL WARD was part of the main hospital. To get into the mental ward, however, you needed to run a gauntlet of locked, oversized metal doors that separated the sane and stable from the confused and emotionally-challenged. Upon entry, security would beep you through the first door, which literally said MENTAL WARD on it, plus there was a big red lightbulb that popped on when the door buzzed open for access, and a security camera so the guard inside could see you clearly. Once through, you entered a stunted hallway, not unlike the cleansing chambers you sometimes see in movies when the guys in white hazmat suits get sprayed down before going back into society so as not to carry any rogue bacteria that might be clinging to them.

Once you're in the decontamination chamber, you must sign in with the glass-shielded guard before being escorted through one of two internal doors.

The first door had a green stripe across it and the tightly stenciled words: Green Ward. The words hovered carelessly above a small, likely bullet-proof, window, that revealed only a maddening tease of what lay beyond. This was the door for depressives, the socially anxious, mildly disturbed, paranoid, moderately delusional, fringe psychotic, et cetera, et cetera. This was the path for the soft ones. The passives, you might say. My diagnosis was clinical depression, anxiety and mild schizophrenia. In other words, *soft*.

The other door went to the Blue Ward. This area housed the folks you see in horror movies. Guys bumping their heads against concrete walls, patients in white gowns shouting curses, dudes in straightjackets... you get it. These were the psychotic and borderline dangerous, the patients who would not only hurt themselves, but potentially others. Not murderers or anything, but the ones who lived nowhere but in their own heads. The ones who could hurt you and not even know they were doing it.

If they steered you toward the Blue Ward, you were nine kinds of fucked, to put it mildly. If they steered you toward the Green Ward, you most likely had bandaged wrists or a sullen disposition, potentially comatose.

Maybe you heard a voice or two, but nothing, you know, *too* crazy.

By the way this isn't foreshadowing. You'll never see the Blue Ward. Not in this story. Trust me, I'm doing you a favor.

My first night in the Green Ward my roommate was a guy named Milo, a pretty laid-back fella, especially since he was strapped to his bed at his wrists and ankles and force-fed meals. We didn't talk much.

I remember that first night vividly because Milo woke up screaming. A few nurses came in and gave Milo a needle to shut him up. I was so absorbed by my own depression and altered circumstances I barely registered the experience before falling back into an anxious sleep.

The next morning Milo was gone. I never did get another roommate.

Which brings us to Crystal. The moment you've been waiting for, right? Yeah, well, it wasn't that glamorous, believe me. Don't bother cueing the slo-mo.

My third morning in the bin I was ditching the group session (again) and sitting in the hallway sort of rocking and moaning (again), my brain anesthetized by hospital-grade tranquilizers and mood suppressants. I was just debating going back to my Milo-less room to groan in private when I heard the already too-familiar buzzing of the entry door.

Then I heard loud, urgent voices. Then screaming.

A nurse ran toward the inner door that stood between the decontamination area and the ward to assist in whatever the hell was going on at the entry.

Let's take a moment here to note two things for imaginative purposes. First, the nurses. These are not skinny ladies in hip-tight starched white dresses with napkin-fold hats and a bobbed-head of hair full of pins, their tugged follicles stretching the skin so tight as to force a permanently scowled appearance. Don't picture Nurse Ratched from *One Flew Over the Cuckoo's Nest*. No, in reality, the nurses are primarily dudes in pale blue scrubs with hairy arms and bored eyes.

The other thing was the ward itself. It wasn't that bad, honestly. Imagine a cross between a Motel 6 and a community college commissary and you're close. The floors were carpeted. There was a large recreation room with plush chairs and couches, but no television (not allowed). There was a pool table, but it was missing one of the balls. The red 3 I think. The cue sticks themselves were warped and cracked and no one ever played. It was still sort of comforting to have it nearby, though. Just the idea of being able to play a game of pool made you feel a *little* bit normal.

The ward had a small tangerine-colored cafeteria where a lot of patients hung out, opting for the sanitary round tables and plastic chairs over the soft pleather furniture of the rec room. And it *was* more comfortable in there for some reason. Couldn't tell you why. It's also where we ate, of course. Personally, I spent most of my time there building puzzles. Building them as fast as I could, all my senses totally focused on putting the pieces in the right places, creating a picture that offered a sense of cohesion. I burned through all the puzzles they had in just a few days, and then they brought in more just for me. Nice, right? I guess it must have been helping. Cathartic, perhaps. Or maybe it just kept me from groaning in the hallways.

There were no computers or cell phones, and the only way to reach the outside world was via this one sort of beat up, solitary payphone. And the only way you could use *that* is if you asked a visitor to bring you a calling card, or by calling collect. The second day I was there a woman I hadn't seen before, wearing the standard newcomer uniform of blue gown and bandaged wrists, stood dopily in front of the payphone, staring at it with lost eyes. Without a word between us I took a calling card out of my pocket – one that I had found on Milo's nightstand after he was taken away – and placed it beneath the phone, just inside the faux wood cabinet that housed it. She looked at me and smiled, then called someone. I wasn't even sure it would work, I hadn't had time to try it. She didn't offer it back and I didn't ask. I never saw her again after that, which is saying something because there weren't many of us in the Green Ward. Not as many as you'd think. Twenty tops. The regulars, folks who stayed more than a day or two, counted to no more than eight or nine. In a strange way, they became my friends, despite my not really knowing them at all.

But I digress. Someone was screaming, right?

Okay, so the door banged open and here came two nurses carrying this girl along between them. Peroxide blonde, thin and pliant as a tent pole. She wore a loose V-neck T-shirt that had the word PEACH written across the front in glitter and skin-tight blue leggings. I couldn't see her face very well, but noticed her mouth was sort of hanging open and her eyes were heavy-lidded. They'd obviously stuck her with something to calm her down, because a thin line of drool leaked from her mouth, strung like a glistening spiderweb from the corner of one dark-red lip down to the hint of a left breast lumping her shirt just above the CH.

I watched sullenly as they walked her past me and then, just as quickly, forgot about her before she'd even turned the corner and disappeared from view. Just another nutjob in a room full of them, I thought. And I was right.

IT WASN'T UNTIL dinner that evening, when we all gathered in the linoleum-floored cafeteria with the steel-countered kitchen and the pale orange walls, that I saw Crystal again. This was only my third night at the ward, but I'd already found a clique of friends who I sat with at meals. Even in the loony bin you form tribal connections. Although, studying each of the faces at my table, I couldn't tell you what our common denominator might possibly have been.

There was Charlie; a pimply, overweight teenager with long black hair and thick-framed glasses who liked to smile but rarely talked. He wanted to write children's books, a fact he confided to me one day during breakfast. But Charlie also suffered from seizures and bouts of screaming at voices, so they ended up treating him with electroshock therapy. Yes, they still do that, believe it or not. For twenty-four hours or so after one of those sessions, Charlie's brain was "reset," and he'd sort of slump over, expressionless, unable to remember my name much less any of his fanciful story ideas. He still sat with us though. I suppose habits die last.

Then there was Sarah, a housewife with three kids and an investment banker husband. They lived in Bel Air and were disgustingly wealthy. She'd tried to hang herself using a towel hook and the belt of her bathrobe but was discovered unconscious, and very much alive, by her oldest daughter. "Just choked myself out, I guess," she said one night, unperturbed. That very same night she checked herself into the psych ward. She said she was "taking a break while I figure some things out." Weren't we all.

Lastly, there was Stan, who I think of as a close friend even though I never spoke with him once since I left the hospital. Stan was a homeless guy who, before his admission, had been spending nights in a prostitute's motel room, paying his rent with dope and babysitting her little girl while she, you know, worked. Stan would put the kid in a grocery cart, cover her in a blue tarp and wheel her around Hollywood while he gathered recyclables and did small menial tasks. Or begged. Once he squirreled away enough money, he'd buy a little dope, go back to the hooker's motel and they'd shoot up.

He had a dog as well, at some point. It was hit by a bus.

Or maybe it was the little girl who was killed by the bus.

Maybe there was no dog.

These things get jumbled up in my head, to be honest.

The other thing about Stan was that he volunteered for an experiment being done at the hospital. It was all very Kubrickian. They'd give him drugs, strap his arms and ankles to a chair and make him watch movies and old news footage, just like in *A Clockwork Orange*. It's true! They'd gauge his responses to see how the different drugs (or placebos on some days) affected him. According to Stan, they were paying him for this guinea pig service, and all-in-all he said it wasn't so bad. I visited his room once and he showed me the chair with the straps, and the television, and talked about how it all worked. It was the only time I ever went into Stan's room. I never wanted to see that chair again.

But none of these folks are important to this story. Sorry, they're just more drab window dressing. B-characters whose roles – whose lives as seen through your eyes – ended the second I left the hospital. Like them, we are narrow. Snuff out one perspective, and you likely snuff out the whole lot. We are shadow's opposites; our stories need the light to survive. I adjust the beam, and you follow.

Besides, this story is about Crystal, right? Okay, so let's cut to the part where she entered the cafeteria that evening for dinner, just a few hours after she'd been dragged into Green Ward, screaming and drugged and drooling. She entered the room and it seemed that everyone looked up at her, like she was the guest of honor, or a celebrity. She, in turn, smiled at us. A big, silly smile that radiated... not warmth, but a sort of manic glee. You couldn't help but smile back, despite whatever psychological impairment you were fighting off at the time. She came straight to my group's table and sat down, folded her hands in front of her and looked at each of us in turn.

Her hands, I noticed, were bone-white. Her fingers narrow and twiggy.

Her exposed wrists and forearms were... rubbery. Freckled. Sickly. She was still wearing the PEACH shirt, and I could see the gray patch above the CH where the drool had stained an amoeba-shaped spot. She sat ramrod straight and her moderate but pointed breasts were pushed out against the tight white fabric. You could tell she was used to thrusting them forward like that, as if she were bellied up to a bar and trying to get the attention of a busy bartender, or a nearby male patron in the hopes of a being offered a free cocktail. My study of her continued to the neck, a goosey stem that was slim and deathly-white as her forearms. Her flesh was... not wrinkled, but sallow. Dry. Like an old person. Or a corpse.

But it was her face that *really* threw me off.

She'd obviously had some time to apply whatever makeup she'd carried in with her, because her lips were thick and deep-red, her cheeks blushed with some rosy powder, her eyes darkened, her lashes long and stringy as black weeds, her eyebrows drawn-on and arched like highway tunnels. Her hair, that peroxide blonde I mentioned, was dry as a stretched tumbleweed. Frazzled. Also, when you studied the way her face was all... inter-connected, I guess, you could tell she'd had plastic surgery. Lots of it. Her nose was pinched and looked disproportionately small between her cheek bones. Her lips were too full. Her forehead and temples were so tight it reminded me of the woman from the movie *Brazil*, creating an almost dystopian sense of beauty that was hard to look at for more than a few moments before it became unsettling, like a bout of vertigo.

But it was her eyes – her wide, large, deep brown eyes – that stayed with you, that erased the strangeness of the rest of her. That took you in and held you. They were beautiful and, if we're being honest, completely mad.

She introduced herself to the group but she and I both knew she was really introducing herself to me, and I, in turn, to her. She was vivacious, energized and hyperactive. I assumed she was bipolar because you can assume things like that when you meet a person in a mental hospital. She was loud and brash and had a wonderfully unhinged laugh that made us the envy of the cafeteria, more than one patient sulking in their suicidal tendencies and wondering how it would feel to experience joy. To laugh, if even for a moment.

Crystal spent a total of three days in the Green Ward, and she and I spent a significant chunk of that time together. At first we'd chat idly over meals, then face each other, cross-legged on the floor, in the rec room. By her second day our shoulders were mashed together on the couch, staring at a black wall where a television would normally sit, making up movies in our heads we couldn't watch, whispering about our respective suicide attempts and how much we hated the world.

On the day she left she wrote her cell phone number on my hand in red Sharpie, and I promised to call her once released.

And I did.

Dumb, right?

2

WHEN YOU'RE LONELY and socially inept, you don't choose your friends, you simply glide through life and keep your exterior sticky, hope to hell someone grabs onto you and holds on long enough to eventually discover the *real* you, the buried you that isn't so bad, or scary, or insane. Folks like me daydream about this. That someday, just maybe, somebody might really care about you. And wouldn't that be something?

So while you're shaking your head and thinking what a terrible idea it was for me to befriend Crystal, my ward-mate, my equal in sickness, my friend in mental disorder, realize that loneliness breeds desperation. Even the deranged need contact with another human or else the illness stays internalized; the delirious voices, the wicked thoughts, the confusion of self, the self-flagellation. It eats you alive.

When I first called her she literally *squealed* with excitement, which to a guy like me is the most powerful elixir in the world – to know that someone out there is actually *excited* to hear from you. It's like no other feeling in the world. The anxiety is blown apart, the social awkwardness releases like a snake uncoiling in your chest and slips away, biding its return. You feel welcomed. Wanted. Maybe not loved... but *liked*. God damn, it's beautiful.

We got together that very night and literally did the one thing we were both legally mandated *not* to do within sixty days of our release from the hospital.

We went out drinking.

As a patient of the Green Ward I was regularly taken to a conference room full of doctors, who questioned me. During one of these sessions I completely lost my cool and I screamed at them and slammed my hands into the smooth reflective surface of the brown table again and again and again.

SLAM!

SLAM!

SLAM!

SLAM!

I would be sobbing during all of this which they noted.

I PICKED HER up at her house and she bounced out like a kid on their way to Disneyland. She jumped into the car, banged the door shut and gave another little squeal before pulling me toward her into a tight hug. When she pushed back I could see her face — her real face, her true mask — for the first time since the hospital.

The first thing I noticed was that the makeup job she'd done in the Green Ward was nothing but a whisper of the whole works that screamed across her skull that night. Her ghostly pale skin was blotted with blood lips and blackened eyes. Her lashes so long and thick I immediately thought of Venus Flytraps every time she batted them open and closed. Her hair had been sorta puffed-out, blow-dried to enhance the body of the bleach-white cornucopia that lifted up from her forehead and bowed away and down the back of her neck. She wore jeans that glittered and looked sprayed-on to her stick-thin legs and an equally tight black T-shirt. I checked her feet and saw bright red heels, three inches high at a minimum. I almost felt underdressed, even if we were just going to a sports bar near her house to watch the Kings game (she was a rabid hockey fan, if that helps complete the picture here), but she assured me I looked "darling."

I smiled sickly and tried not to recoil when I noticed that, astonishingly, she'd had another surgery done in the couple weeks since I'd last seen her. Her big brown eyes were still as glorious as ever and glowing with that bright inner-light, but now one seemed, uh, *lower* than the other. I stared at her flesh, tried to understand what had been done and why. It was not unlike attempting to solve an unfinished puzzle, not unlike the ones I did in the cafeteria of Green Ward to pass the time, to ease my anxiety.

She kissed my cheek and the spell was broken. While I drove us to the bar she put a cold hand over mine, and a shudder went through me at the skeletal feel of her clutching fingers, the chilled pad of her palm. But amidst all that revulsion huddled a satisfied pleasure. An elation. Despite it all — and as insane and poorly constructed as this idea was and as mildly deranged and physically unsettling as Crystal appeared to be — I was happy.

I'd made a friend.

3

I DON'T KNOW how or why the sleepovers started.

The first one occurred a couple weeks into our new friendship. We'd been hanging out a few nights a week, neither of us having jobs and both of us in need of companionship. One of those nights, after a movie I think, she asked me in for a drink. I accepted, and we hung out in her living room watching television and splitting a pitcher of margaritas she'd...

No. Wait.

That was the night I met her mother.

It was her *mother* who made the margaritas. The mother is important, so keep her in mind as we go. If it helps, I'll tell you that there was nothing extraordinary about her. She was smallish and drab. Wispy. Borderline translucent. I'd wager you could spend hours in the same room with her and never even know she was there. Mrs. Cellophane, you know? Her wardrobe consisted of gray knit sweaters, generic black slacks, tired sneakers. She wore little or no makeup and was always *extremely* happy to see me. You'd think, knowing full well where her daughter and I had met, that she might be cautious. Wary. But she embraced me that first night, insisted I take off my shoes and get comfortable. She suggested we take the couch, Crystal and I, and then offered to make the margaritas.

While Crystal and I shoulder-snuggled on the puffy leather couch, a position I was quite familiar with from our mental hospital days, her mother made the drinks. She brought out glasses, crackers and bland cheese. A perspiring pitcher. She handed Crystal the remote control and said, "I'll be in my room. You two have fun." Adding: "I won't be able to hear anything."

Crystal had giggled and dug her shoulder playfully into mine, like a hairless cat burrowing in for a comfortable spot on a quilt. I found the whole thing a little strange, and having the pale-skinned, misshapen girl rubbing against me did nothing to assuage the feeling of discomfort. If anything, the creepiness of the situation enhanced. I felt as if the older woman not only expected us to fool around while watching the late-night talk shows, but was endorsing the idea.

But since I had nothing else to do, nowhere else to go (the idea of drowning in the dark thoughts waiting at my apartment was terrifying), and no one else to hang out with, I convinced myself that this was all very *nice*, and that her mother was very *nice*, and that Crystal herself was extremely *nice*. Nothing to see here, folks. We're all good.

Or so I thought. Or so I hoped.

Like I said, when you're a depressive you'll close your eyes to almost anything if it means a little bit of comfort. A touch of human warmth. A shred of joy. So, I stayed over that night. We slept together on the wide, soft couch. No, not sex, although I think she wanted to do… something. But the idea of touching her in that way was too much. The thought of being fully exposed, flesh on flesh. Repulsive. Instead, we cuddled fully-dressed and let ourselves sink into sleep and the psychotic's dark realm of troubled dreams, our heads thick with anti-depressants and tequila, with only a late-night comedian's monologue to escort us.

FROM THERE IT became a sort of ritual.

Every time we went out, or nearly so, we'd end up on the couch watching television, drinking ourselves into submission, an unspoken agreement between us that I would inevitably stay.

But, man, if the evenings were odd, the mornings were downright bizarre.

I'd wake, open my eyes, and see her brown eyes staring back at me. Focused. As if willing me to wake up, to sense her heightened awareness of me and miraculously become alert to the strength of her desire.

I'm not going to lie, it wasn't the most pleasant experience. Usually her hair would be matted, the straw-like fiber knotted or smooshed against her head by whatever product she'd pumped it full of the night before. Her face was puffy in the mornings, pale and lined, facial powder crusted in the creases. Her lashes, more often than not, were clumped and gluey. One morning I couldn't help but stare into an eye that was half shut, the right-side of the eye's lashes clinging to each other in desperation, a mock bridge keeping the thin flesh of the lid sealed in a sloppy, perpetual wink.

When Stan watched television during the experiments, they'd strap a device around his bicep that monitored his heart pressure. Some of the stuff on the television was silent, some of it turned up very loud. Gangster movies. Old news footage. Cartoons.

Stan once confided to me that he thought every day was a "placebo day" because he never felt a goddamn thing.

After shock therapy, Charlie drooled in a wheelchair during meals and never ate.

Sarah tried to kill herself again. She snapped a pool stick over her knee and ripped the flesh of her wrists with the splintered tip. Wrists to elbows.

INEVITABLY, HER MOTHER would make us coffee and toast, or bagels, and we'd all sit at a small table in the kitchen, foreign early morning light slanting into us as we nibbled and sipped. The older woman would constantly study me with laughing eyes over her cup, all but bumping me with an elbow in a glee usually reserved for those cultures that displayed bloody sheets to an entire village, the marriage consummated.

"I'm so glad Crystal has you," she said one morning while Crystal excused herself to go brush her teeth, put her clumped hair in a ponytail and unglue her sticky lashes. "You like being here, I can tell," she went on, while my eyes darted toward the hallway where my friend had vanished, hoping she'd bounce back any moment to disrupt the moment.

"She's very nice," I'd say awkwardly, then lamely add something along the lines of: "Thank you for breakfast."

Upon my release, I'd stumble out the door into dewy morning light, a strange platonic version of the walk of shame, and drive myself home. I wondered nearly every time why the hell I ever stayed over there in the first place.

Why didn't I just go home?

OCCASIONALLY, I WOULD ask about her father, who apparently lived with them and was wildly adored by both mother and daughter. They spared no praise when speaking of his generous nature and supermodel looks, but despite my numerous visits and extended overnight stays, I never once saw him. Further, there were no portraits of the family anywhere in the house, and the one time I asked whether she had any siblings she laughed so loudly it made me want to scream.

Once, she mumbled something about having a brother, but did not elaborate. My curiosity, however, had been peaked.

During a pre-sleepover evening her mother had stayed to sit with us, all of us drinking from what she described as a "very nice bottle of red." I repeated my inquiries – both about the absent husband / father and the mysterious sibling.

Her mother smiled at me, her teeth stained like shiny rose petals. "Crystal's father is a wonderful provider. He pays for all of her, you know, *work*. My god, I've lost count of how many nips and tucks our little girl has had."

"Twenty-three," Crystal announced proudly, her eyes not leaving the television screen. "And I'm getting my boobs done next month. Daddy said so."

I opened my mouth to ask about the brother, but before I could get out a word she turned on me, eyes wide with excitement, lips stretched in a wicked smile, teeth bared. "Oh shit!" she screamed, then clutched my shirt in one bony fist and put her other hand over my mouth, as if to keep me from also screaming. "I fucking forgot to tell you! I'm getting new tits!"

Her hand was firm on my mouth and nose, and I shook my head in annoyance. She removed her hands from my shirt and face and placed them on her breasts, gave them a little jostle. "I mean, look at these things. Worthless."

I turned my head slightly to look askance at her mother, concerned at the reaction she might be having to the bizarre turn in conversation, fearful she'd be shocked at her daughter's behavior in front of a young man. A guest. But she only nodded and smiled, sipped at her wine, seemingly as comfortable and anticipative of this twenty-fourth surgery as Crystal herself.

As for me, I could do nothing but nod along, dazedly giving my own approval for the latest wave of Crystal's surgical sea change. "Well, if you want to. I don't think you need it, personally, but..."

"Bullshit!" she screamed, and slapped me hard across the face.

Her mother immediately started to laugh, cackling so hard it sounded like she was choking on her wine. Crystal also started laughing wildly, eyes too wide, looking from me to her mother and back again. She jabbed a finger into my chest. "You know you love a woman with big honkers!"

I was too stunned to speak. My cheek stung and I guess I was in shock, my brain jammed into neutral, a fit of paralysis that immobilized my ability to process, to react. I stared absently at the television and pretended nothing had happened while my face reddened.

Sensing my disinterest, Crystal shrugged and slumped back into the couch, docile once more. "Whatever, sometimes people are just friends, right?"

I caught a flash of disappointment flicker across the face of her mother, but did not pursue it. Suddenly, despite the medication and the therapy and the booze currently dulling my brain, a very alive part of me was beginning to realize that this situation – this relationship – had become increasingly, maybe dangerously, out of control.

4

LET ME TELL you about the Blue Ward.

Oh, right.

I did say that, didn't I? About not going back to the Blue Ward in this story. That you'd never see it again.

Sorry. I lied.

Do you still trust me?

The Blue Ward's accommodations were straight from a Penny Dreadful. A hellish theater. Unlike the hunting lodge comforts of the Green Ward, the Blue Ward was more akin to what you'd expect when you hear the words *insane asylum*. The floors were smooth concrete. The walls, inexplicably, were constructed of cinderblocks, their rough surfaces glazed over with thick coats of dark gray paint. The lighting was industrial – not the soft whites and bedside lampshade browns of Green Ward, but harsh fluorescents housed in cages strung high overhead. The Blue Ward version of the "rec room" was essentially a cement box lit in dim deep-sea blue, so that all the patients wore a translucent, navy-tinted duotone. An almost ghoulish quality. When they moved, it was like the walls themselves were moving, the floor writhing with their flesh and shadow. It created a sensation not unlike being submerged among slow-waving creatures of the deep. Just as a coral reef is a biological structure, so the patients inside these walls are the room itself – its very existence reliant on the bodies and souls of those trapped inside.

Whenever it was time for the Green Ward to have "outdoor activity," the patients were led, under guard and single-file, like a line of scuba divers, through the Blue Ward rec room and out onto a sunlit industrial patio where we could wander around in circles, smoke cigarettes, talk amongst ourselves or stare in solitary silence at the traffic jostling along the freeway horizon of the 405...

Or... wait...

The puzzles I put together in the cafeteria were not complex. I mainly competed against an internal clock, trying to create the picture as fast as I could with doped, trembling fingers. Five hundred pieces tops.

The final image was often something I recognized. A place I'd been on a long-ago childhood vacation. Or one of the rooms in the hospital.

Familiar scenes.

5

GIVEN THE INCREASING strangeness of our relationship (and by "our" I mean the one between Crystal, myself and her mother), I should not have been surprised by what happened on the last night I saw either of them, despite her subsequent pleas via messages and ALL CAPS texts, the ones with lots and lots of !!!!!!!!!!!!!'s and xoxoxoxoxoxoxoxoxoxoxo's.

I had been at the gym, taking my doctor's advice to exercise more as a way to clear my head, increase endorphins and thereby, theoretically, reduce the severity of the depression. It never worked, but it did make me feel better to know I was at least trying. So, I guess it did work, just not in the way it had been presented. Regardless, for the first time in a long time, I looked forward to getting home, having a beer and a microwave pizza, watching a movie. The idea of relaxing, so foreign to someone suffering from the anxiety I suffer from, was now so tangent as to be *alluring*. I had, if nothing else, exercised enough to tire myself out; tire out the black hamsters spinning the wheels in my head, the ones that propelled dark thoughts, created the depressive fog that condensed behind my eyes, poisoned everything and anything that was good.

I hadn't even made it to the car when my cell phone rang, the screen flashing CRYSTAL at me like an insult. I honestly debated. For the first time in the few months we'd been friends, I considered whether I wanted to answer her call.

Yeah, of course I did.

"Hey."

She was crying. "Can you please come over? Please?"

I told her I was sweaty, stinking. I needed to change. It was late. I was tired.

"Please? Oh my god, please." More sobbing. More hysterics.

In the weeks that passed since my stay at the hospital, I had begun to feel more clear-headed, more normal. More like an... "everyday" kind of guy. Therapy and medication and the occasional visit to the gym all combined to grind down the jagged edges of my dark thoughts, smooth them to wrinkles; hiccups versus disease, speedbumps versus walls.

And with a stronger, healthier mind came realization. Clarity.

I began to see Crystal for what she truly was. Not a fun, hot girl with an overly constructed face and a passion for makeup, but a truly disturbed individual. I finally accepted that it wasn't normal for a girl her age to do to her face, her body, what she had done. The obviously neurotic need for more and more surgeries, fixing and tweaking and moving her features like puzzle pieces. Her mother, too, I now understood, was disturbed in her own right. The way she acted with Crystal. With me. Her strange way of pushing us into each other.

All these thoughts were tinkling like wind chimes on a breezy porch when I saw her name appear on my phone. It was like a door of sanity inside my head shot open and all those coherent pontifications poured into me, a waterfall of understanding that stopped me in my tracks and halted my thumb's progress over the word ANSWER, the pad hovering above it like a man about to press the big red button that sent nukes trailing sky-wide cottontails to start the end of everything.

But I did answer. And then the sobbing, like I said. The hysterics.

"I'll come over," I said. "I'll be there soon."

I knew before I got into the car I'd made a mistake. I also knew I didn't want to keep doing this. Seeing her. I needed to move on, get things back to normal. Get normal friends and find a job. My savings account was running thin and I felt more emotionally and psychologically stable than I had in years.

Resolute in my thinking, I started the car, let out a kept breath, and drove to Crystal, knowing in my heart I would be seeing her for the last time.

6

THIS IS A great time to tell you about the one and only group session I ever participated in, and I'd only done it because Crystal had insisted. "It'll be hilarious," she'd said.

In group, everyone talks about how depressed / upset / scared / fucked up they are. About their horrible lives and their chemically-imbalanced brains. About their suicide attempts or the fight they had with their girlfriend / boyfriend / parent / kid / husband / wife that finally pushed them, arms flailing, over the edge and down.

It was during this singular group session that I learned, for the first time, about Bobby.

Bobby was Crystal's ex-boyfriend. It was his dumping of her that sent her into the final, deathly spiral, her own futile run for death's door and ensuing psychotic break. Apparently, she'd been caught outside his house a few hours after he'd delivered the bad news of their relationship's demise (the deed apparently done in a red corner booth at the neighborhood Denny's). After said pronouncement, he quickly left, dropping enough cash to cover the bill and a generous tip before high-tailing it out of there, riding bent-for-hell on his Kawasaki before she could come to her senses and chase him down. Later that same night, the police, who'd been called by a neighbor, spotted her hiding in a cluster of bushes beneath his living room window. She tried to run but they chased her down easily as she struggled to locate where she'd parked her Honda, her clothes muddy and ripped.

It's a testament to her slight frame and nightclub appearance that they didn't use the cuffs until they spotted the kitchen knife she clutched in one tight fist.

She spent a night in jail despite Bobby's refusal to press charges (later she revealed that a restraining order had been put into motion), and after a psych eval had ended up assigned to the Green Ward until such time as the supervising psychiatrist deemed her stable enough to release.

At the time, I'd thought the story pretty funny. Like an episode of some cable comedy. But as I spent more time with Crystal, I became more attuned to her "off" moments – like the slap – or the time she pretended to run me over with her car and then almost inadvertently did just that. Or the way she acted around her mother at times, sulky and absent both, as if she'd gotten lost in a memory that was too sad for her mind to properly process.

I think those lost moments was her thinking of Bobby.

7

I ARRIVED AT Crystal's house twenty minutes after we spoke on the phone, simultaneously worried and sickened the entire drive there. Worried about her, about what might be wrong, hoping it wasn't a serious relapse. Sickened that I had to go there again, not able to shake the feeling I was somehow being trapped, ensnared in this strange web she had spun, a surreal funhouse friendship that clung in tatters to parts of my mind like elements of a bizarre and troubling dream; nightmares of the distorted physicality of her reengineered visage, the ghost-like way her mother plied us with alcohol at every given turn then slipped away like a wraith, face split with the not-so-sly smile that intimated the blessing for a conjoining that would never occur.

Almost as haunting were the absences in her life. The holes between the taut webbing. The father always spoken of but never seen. The mysterious, nameless brother mentioned only as if by accident, and always dropped abruptly, as if it had fallen into the conversation like a spilled drink that's quickly sponged away before it can do any real damage.

And the ex-boyfriend. Bobby. What had ever become of her obsession with him? Was her love cured so quickly? A raging, burning flame extinguished with nothing more than the passing of a few weeks and a slight alteration in medication? Was it possible? But if not, then why the silence? Why wasn't she still mooning over him, or insulting his name, or insisting on some form of revenge?

Unless *I* was the revenge. Ah, yes. Of course. But I was being an uncooperative weapon. A dulled knife. An empty-chambered pistol. I mean, what was the point of finding a new lover, someone who allowed you to throw the heat of newfound burning lust into the face of the one who had hurt you… if only to be spurned? Rejected once more. And worse, denied the satisfaction that comes with one-upmanship. With dominance.

I was as futile to her as I was to myself.

And yet I had a role to play. The platonic friend who came running when she called. The balm to soothe her ragged, frayed feelings, erase the despair of loneliness, to be steadfast in the face of the rising storm of anxiety that I was also so very familiar with.

When she answered the door, I had physically braced myself for the impact of her pushing herself into my arms, her waxen face smeared with tears, her body hot with the feverish exertions from sobbing her heart out.

Instead the door was thrown open to reveal a smiling, almost giddy, Crystal. Her hair was yanked into a tight ponytail, pulling her eyes – wide and glassy as a stuffed deer – even further apart than normal. She had a drink in her hand (gin and tonic by the looks and smell of it) and wore a tight black tank top above what I was *fairly* sure were black panties, and nothing else. She grabbed me roughly by the scruff of the shirt and yanked me inside.

"Oh my god what took you so long!" she yelled dramatically before releasing me, stumbling under my own forward propulsion toward the living room. "God damn I need another drink." She tilted the remaining contents of the glass into her mouth, belched, then bellowed, "Mom!"

I heard glasses clinking in the kitchen. Ahead of me the television was on and turned up loud. A police drama by the sound of it. Sirens and screaming. Beyond the living room was the hallway that led to the back bedrooms. One of the doors in the hallway opened and Crystal's mother stepped out.

It was as if *she* had been the one crying. I looked at her and saw what I had expected from Crystal: red-rimmed eyes, a slack, puffy face, clotted hair, blank expression. She wore a ratty bathrobe and appeared to have, possibly, just woken up, despite it being nine o'clock at night. Her feet were bare and her hands were clutching repeatedly at the fold of her pinkish robe, as if fighting to keep it tightly secured. She was mumbling to herself like a madwoman.

Then she saw me and the caul of madness and despair slithered off her face. She lit up, smiled wide, her eyes scrunched in a sort of delirious joy. "You're here," she said, then did something she'd never done before. She walked up to me, slipped her arms around my waist, lay her head on my chest, and squeezed me tightly.

"Jeez you guys, get a room."

I turned my head, not wanting to move any other part of my body while being embraced by the small, frail woman, and saw Crystal approaching, a wicked smile on her face. She thrust a drink toward me. Her own, I noticed, had been adequately topped off.

Her mother let me go and I accepted the drink, my eyes not leaving Crystal's as I looked for signs of her distress.

"Are you okay?"

She slurped from her glass loudly, studying me. She finally lowered the drink but said nothing. Her mother had moved. Circled around to now stand behind Crystal. She whispered something in Crystal's ear that I didn't catch. Crystal, her eyes never wavering, nodded, as if in agreement, then leaned into me and gave a couple loud *sniffs*.

"Mom's right," she said. "You really do stink."

She looked me up and down, as if just noticing my sweat-stained gym clothes.

"Do you have anything else to wear?" she said, as if condemning me for showing up to a formal event underdressed.

"No..." I said, dumbfounded by the attitude of both women, overrun suddenly by that confused, confined feeling once more. "I came straight from the gym. You called..."

"Oh, *that*," she said with a wave of her hand and another gallant pull from her drink. "I'm over that."

I stood there, stupidly, not knowing what to do next. The television blared at my back. Guns were firing. The drink was cold in my fingers, the perspiration giving it the same texture as a slowly melting, fist-sized ice cube. I wanted to set the drink down. I wanted to get the hell out of there. I wanted to go home, shower, and crawl into bed with a book. But instead I just stood there, waiting to be told what to do next. *Confined*, I thought, wondering at the context of the word.

"Okay, well, first you need to drink *that*, because you look like you just ate something gross, or you're tense, or something." She eyed me suspiciously, and I had to look away. I was afraid she could see my thoughts, my desire to flee, my sense of being *done* with her. "Something's wrong. I don't know... you're acting weird. He's acting weird, isn't he Mom?"

I looked up, saw the older woman nodding over Crystal's shoulder.

The Blue Ward was filled with damp abyssal creatures.
The Green Ward had carpet and no visitors were allowed.

A pool table.

"So," SHE SAID carefully, as if talking to a child holding a loaded gun, one frightened fingertip on the trigger, frozen with the fear of what they might do next, whether purposeful or by accident. "Here's what's going to happen. You're going to have a big sip of that drink, then you're going to turn around and go into that bathroom. You're going to take off your disgusting gym clothes and take a hot shower. We," she motioned to her mother with an extended thumb, "are going to wash your clothes and bring you some clean stuff to wear in the meantime. Then," she continued boldly, not giving me an opening to counter her plan, "we are going to lay down on that couch, watch a bad movie, and I'm going to rub your back and shoulders until... you... *relax*."

If this were a horror movie, this is the part where the audience would be shaking their head in disbelief, am I right? Of *course* you don't go into the shower. You put the drink down, politely excuse yourself, and walk without hesitation to your car, where you get in, lock the doors, and drive your ass as far away from those women and that house as you can, never to return. But the thing is, at the time you just aren't putting it all together. You're too... *involved*. You have no perspective. When you're watching characters on a screen, it's easy to shout "Get out of there!" at them, because it seems so damned obvious. But when you are *in* it, when it's real life, the idea of running seems, well, stupid. Over-the-top. Excessive. Outrageous.

Crazy.

So, I did what I think a lot of men would have done in my situation. I mean, a relatively hot girl in her underwear is handing me a drink, telling me to take a shower so she can give me a back and shoulder massage? There's a lot there to be argued for. Yeah, of course, it was weird that her mother was sort of lurking around the whole scene. And yes, Crystal was attractive, but sadly not to me, due to her amphibian white skin and nip-and-tucked features, but nevertheless I turned on my heels and allowed Crystal's cold hands, now pressed firmly into the middle of my back, to push me gently through the open door of the bathroom.

I even took a sip of my drink. Just like she asked me to.

"Get those clothes off so we can wash them," she yelled through the door. I looked at myself in the wall-length mirror, saw my matted hair, my baggy sweatshirt and knee-length athletic shorts. I set the drink down on the counter, sat on the toilet, and began peeling off my socks and shoes, shaking my head the whole time at what a complete and total idiot I was being.

I put my clothes in a small pile next to the sink, turned on the water, waited a few moments while it heated up, then stepped into the tub, pulling the two sections of the blue plastic shower curtain closed around me.

The water was hot, and I'd be lying if I said it didn't feel good.

"I'm coming in, hide your penis!"

The door opened and I froze. *What the fuck?*

The room was immediately invaded by the not-so-distant blare of the television. I heard her rustling around just a few inches away from me in the narrow bathroom. *She's getting my clothes, that's all. Just getting my dirty clothes.* I knew I was being stupid. Of course I needed clean clothes. They had said that.

I waited for the sound of her exit. For the door to close behind her.

There was nothing.

I continued to wait, not moving, breathing shallow, as if not wanting her to hear me. To know where I was hiding. The sound of the water hitting the tub seemed explosive, like thunder. I closed my eyes tight. Why wouldn't she leave?

"Peek-a-boo."

I turned so fast my heels almost slid out from beneath me. I steadied myself, put a hand on the while tile wall.

Her face hovered there, stuck into the cut of blue plastic, the two sides tucked tightly beneath her chin, as if she were sneaking a peek at the audience from behind the heavy red curtain of a stage. She appeared as the visage of a playful god slipping its broad head through the fabric of space, or a creature rising, pale and bloated, from some dark body of water, surfacing with wide alien eyes, a sharp mouth jammed with ragged teeth.

"Christ!" I yelled, startled and embarrassed.

Her eyes moved up and down my body. Her smile distant now. Not faltering, not exactly... but absent. A melting mask dissolving due to the carelessness of its wearer.

"Crystal, what the hell?" I said, not knowing how to begin to cover myself, only able to turn away to give her a view of more ass than anything else.

"I just wanted to tell you," she said slowly, "that I brought you clean clothes. They're by the sink."

"Okay, fine…" I said, and then, because the thought struck me so suddenly: "Whose clothes are they? Not yours I hope."

She didn't laugh like I'd expected her to. Her face just sort of… went blank. Her mouth hung slack. Her eyes continued looking at my body, as if confused. Confused or, possibly, thoughtful. The way you'd look at the photograph of someone, or something, you missed very much.

"No," she said, finally. "Bobby's."

Before I could respond her face disappeared.

More shuffling outside the curtain.

I heard her mother come into the bathroom. They were whispering. I heard the word *Bobby* more than once. Her mother laughed and I thought if that wrinkled sad face poked itself between the shower curtain and whispered "peek-a-boo" ala her daughter that I would scream and possibly punch that crazy bitch square in her fucking red-toothed mouth.

I turned away from the curtain and looked at the white tiles lining the wall, breathing heavily. Anxiety and panic tightened my chest. I stared hard at the tiles, tried to focus, prayed they'd just *leave*.

Then something emerged from between those slick white pieces. Where there had previously only been clean, white grout, there was now a seeping blackness. Like spilled ink being absorbed through white fabric.

I lifted a hand, ignoring the women's scratchy murmurs, and touched the bleeding black with puckered fingertips. When I rubbed my fingers along the edge of one tile, it loosened, as if stuck to nothing but air; as if it were a child's tooth, dangling by a single thin fiber, ready to leap from the gums with just the slightest *tug*.

I did so, and watched in amazement as it fell away. Then the black began to spread more quickly, seeping through the grout between a second row of tiles, and then sinking to cover a swatch of ten, now twelve, forming a bizarre mosaic – an image of a white checkerboard. I pulled each one away from the wall, tearing the puzzle apart, carelessly flicking each smooth ceramic piece backward into the tub, where the cooling water still sprayed. The inky dark leaked down the wall in runlets, splattered into the churning water at my feet, blackened it.

When the opening was big enough, like that of a window, I stared through to what lay beyond. I recognized it right away.

The Blue Ward.

It was the rec room, the one lit in dull blue, with the concrete floor and cinderblock walls. I stared at the patients who laid on the floor or were sunk into corners; at the ones who stood facing a wall, hands roaming the porous surface, speaking as if in prayers.

I thought of stepping through, but I was already there.

I stood not too far away, wearing the same smock and pants of the ward's other inhabitants. That version of me studied the back of his hands, which moved rapidly over open air, as if putting together an exceptionally large puzzle. I was talking out loud, yet calmly, to no one. I strained to listen to what this "other-me" had to say. Once I tried, the words he spoke became so clear I didn't need to focus at all.

"Put it together, put it together, put it together…" the other-me said, over and over and over again. A mantra.

The door to the bathroom slammed shut and I jerked my head away from the vision. I turned off the water.

"Crystal?" I said, not too loudly, but loud enough so she would hear me if still inside the bathroom.

There was no response. I clenched the split in the blue curtain with wet hands, paused to take a breath and steady my nerves, then jerked it open.

The bathroom was empty.

A fluffy green towel sat on the counter. Next to it, folded neatly, was a T-shirt and what looked like track pants. A pair of athletic socks lay balled-up next to the clothes.

I grabbed the towel, began urgently wiping myself down. When I was relatively dry, I stepped from the tub and went to the closed door. Quietly as I could, I pushed the button in on the knob, locking it.

After I finished drying off, I picked up the T-shirt, put it on. I glanced into the mirror. I could still see the Blue Ward rec room hovering behind me, past the curtain, past the fallen tiles.

There was a heavy knock at the bathroom door.

"Hold on!" I yelled, trying to sound stable. Unshaken. Sane.

I put on the pants, then sat on the toilet and pulled on the clean, warm socks.

The banging on the door came again. Louder, more insistent. Violent.

The clothes, I noticed, were a perfect fit.

I stood up and studied the mirror. I stared at myself. I leaned in slowly over the countertop, watched in amazement as my two sets of eyes drew closer, closer together. Soon, our faces were only inches apart. My breath fogged the reflection.

The doorknob twisted, rattled, but held. There was giggling from beyond the door. The shuffling of feet. Another hard series of banging fists, a pounding so forceful that the door shook in its frame.

I ignored the pounding, ignored the voices. I stared hard into my own eyes, forced myself to focus. Pieces floated and fell like rain drops through my mind. I thought, *put it together, put it together, put it together.*

Over the reflection of my shoulder I could see the wall of white tiles was back where it had always been. I closed my eyes and let out a choked sob, rested my forehead against the cool glass. A hot tear ran down my cheek. I opened my eyes. The face in the mirror smiled.

You know who I am, right?

Come close and I'll tell you...

The door burst open with a crash.

I'm me.

FRAGILE DREAMS

1

WHAT'S IMPORTANT RIGHT now, he thought, straining to study himself in the warped bronze plating of the elevator walls, *is that you remember to breathe.*

He pinched the knot of his grandfather's favorite tie, tugged down his newly-dry-cleaned dark blue suit coat, tightened his grip on the handle of his attaché, and lifted a hand to smooth his gel-slicked hair.

He thought again of losing the handkerchief in his suit pocket. He touched the top of the square fold Diane had worked so hard on. "It's sexy," she said, but he thought it might be too much. He leaned closer to the wall, looked at each of his bright blue eyes closely. He didn't see circles, at least not obvious ones. He hadn't been sleeping well. Money was becoming an issue, Diane restless, the school loans a burden with no foreseeable relief. Without a job...

He stopped the train of negative thoughts before it could build steam. He stepped back to the middle of the elevator, turned away from his reflection to face the doors.

"Fuck it," he said out loud, and allowed himself to smile. A warming lump of confidence expanded outward from his belly. He exhaled, there was a distant *ding*, and the polished metal doors slid open with the soft sound of a broom swept over a clean floor.

The firm's address was listed as a Suite, but despite the line of doors to his left indicating other businesses — accountants and other legal offices primarily — *Baskin and Associates* took up a majority of the entire fourth, and top, floor of the downtown Burbank building. As he exited the elevator, his polished black Oxfords sunk into a rich green carpet, soft music was heard from invisible speakers, and a gold-and-glass reception desk the size of his Prius loomed from his right, pulling at him like a magnet. He stepped up to the desk and the slim brunette sitting behind it, her expensively-framed eyeglasses tilting up to him, her wide dark eyes sending a quiver though his spine.

They must use a modeling agency, he thought to himself, and almost smiled again, then thought better of it. He rested the tips of his fingers on the spotless glass ridge of the crescent-shaped desk, lightly cleared his throat.

"Matthew Calvert. I'm here for an interview," he managed, then did smile, albeit apologetically. "With Mr. Baskin," he added, leaving her eyes to scan the surface contents of her desk, as if an appointment ledger or sign-in book awaited his mark.

The receptionist had sucked-in bronze cheeks bookending glossy lips that made Matthew think, rather oddly, of two fat babies lying back-to-back, covered in blood. She tapped something into her keyboard, her languid eyes searching a hidden screen. When she flicked her head back to Matthew, he flushed, realizing too late he'd been caught staring. She smiled, though, and he relaxed, as if he'd passed some mysterious test.

"You're early," she said, and Matthew wondered if there was a degree of flirt in those pretty hazel eyes.

"Yes, well, traffic wasn't too bad," he said, trying to sound casual and failing and *knowing* he was failing. "The 101 was wide open for some reason, so..."

She held his eyes another beat, as if considering, then swapped one smile with another. This one more officious. "It'll be a few minutes. Would you like water or coffee while you wait?"

Matthew was about to reply that a bottled water would be lovely when he felt a vibration thrum through the plush green carpeting, a vibration strong enough to tickle the pads of his feet through the thick soles of the shoes. The receptionist's smile didn't falter, nor did her eyes leave his own. He looked at the floor, then back at her — as a fellow human this time.

"Did you..."

His thought was truncated by a loud, bottomless rumbling, as if God were clearing his mighty hallowed throat. This time the floor beneath Matthew *shifted*, and he was forced to take an unsteady step.

The receptionist felt this one, springing up from her desk and stepping backward, her tight skirt and high heels making it an inelegant movement. She eyed her desk in horror, as if the glass monstrosity had bared crystallized gold teeth and snapped at her.

She glared at Matthew, almost accusatory. Things grew quiet. Matthew spotted other movement around the office, saw heads bobbing behind eye-level office windows set within clean white walls. A young lawyer emerged, minus his suit coat, from a nearby copy room, looking up and down a distant hallway, seeking assurance, desperate to share his fear. Somewhere deep within *Baskin and Associates,* something heavy fell with a thump. From another unseen area, a husky-voiced woman yelled an obscenity, as if she'd been badly hurt.

Matthew and the receptionist faced each other, the desk between them an abandoned lifeboat, the ink-green carpet beneath their feet a calming sea after an eruption of storm. Matthew smiled at her reassuringly, almost amused by the affect the earthquake had on his anxiety. *Perspective,* he thought impulsively.

"That was a big one," he said calmly, his nerves iron now, testosterone and the realities of the world's true dangers steadying him.

The receptionist was not smiling, and still looked off-balance. Her pinned hair had come disheveled; one sweeping dark arc lay forlornly along the side of her face. She opened her mouth to speak – Matthew had just enough time to notice how very *white* her teeth were – when the building was slapped hard enough to knock people to the ground. The world beneath him began shaking with a mad, volcanic violence, as if they were stuck inside a snow globe being throttled by a malicious child.

Matthew stumbled, dropping his attaché and holding his arms out for balance. He looked to the walls surrounding him and watched in disbelief as jagged, lightning-shaped cracks coursed through them, spreading rapidly in webs of thick black veins. He jerked his head back in time to see the monitor on the glass desk topple and spark, the receptionist fall to the carpet, drowning in her fear. He wanted to run to her, help her, but the shaking was so violent, and the noise so ear-shattering, he could barely keep his own feet. He took a step toward her, saw her frantic eyes, her wide-open mouth an O of shock. Was she screaming? Calling for him? If she was, he could not hear her, not over the otherworldly noise of the building being ripped apart, the terrible growl of the rioting earth.

He watched helplessly as the ceiling burst open and a long rectangular tube of metal venting crashed on top of her, a plume of bright pink insulation dangling like a monstrous tongue from the shattered mouth of the broken panels. A cloud of drywall dust hovered low over the scene like a fallen cloud. He couldn't see clearly, couldn't hear anything over the tumult. Massive, desk-sized pieces of ceiling were smashing down everywhere, filling the air with more dust and debris. His eyes darted around the office space. People were under their desks, lying on the ground, running, falling. They were all screaming now.

Beyond the reception desk Matthew noticed a conference room, a long, polished wood table surrounded by empty swivel chairs, all of it behind a floor-to-ceiling glass wall. The outer wall of the room was also made of glass, large blue-tinted panes made to shield conference room attendees from L.A.'s hot summer days. As Matthew watched, the blue-tinted panes split, then shattered, then fell away. Sunlight invaded the office interior like a spotlight exposing a rat's den.

The receptionist had found her feet. She climbed over the fallen vent awkwardly and stumbled toward Matthew. She steadied herself momentarily against the edge of her familiar desk. Matthew was able to get a good look at her. The side of her face had been torn open, gashed from ear to chin, and blood was slithering down her neck in pulsing ropes of red. Her terrified eyes, smaller without her glasses, locked on Matthew, yearning for assurance, naked and desperate. He started to say something, and then, to his disbelief, parts of *Baskin and Associates* began to simply... *disappear*. He caught her eye and frantically motioned for her to look behind her. She turned.

They watched in a frozen daze as the conference table dropped away from view, as if the floor, and the construct of the floor beneath it, had been erased from existence.

Next to the conference room, a well-dressed Asian man in a dark suit was gripping a large copier, hanging on as the floor tilted toward the crumbling exterior of the building. The man leapt atop the copier, as if the elevation of a few feet would save him. The machine slid, bumped and almost tipped, before spinning out into the expanse. Matthew had caught the man's expression as he prepared to die, and would have sworn he had been smiling like a demon. Matthew thought of the moment in *Dr. Strangelove* when Slim Pickens had *Yahooed* while riding the bomb as it fell to the earth, flung like an insect to his own death, to the death of millions of other insects.

The remaining walls lining the far side of the office bent away, folding in half before flying into the open air, the people behind them long since gone.

Matthew backed toward the elevator, caught in a nightmare that did not have a panic button to jar him awake. There was a jolt and the building seemed to buckle and snap. His view outside the building *tilted* and he fell hard to the ground, his hand sinking into the sea-green carpet, so soft and solid. He looked up from his sitting position and heard the receptionist shriek, loudly enough that it pierced the rising, rumbling sounds of destruction. It was the kind of scream created from way deep down, leaping up from the abyss of absolute terror that came with knowing your life is about to end. There was a *rising* beneath Matthew as the building itself, or what remained of it, was lifted from the ground, as if it were *elevating*. A split-second later it crashed down so hard Matthew bit off the end of his tongue. He felt blood rush into his mouth and his eyes leak tears at the stab of sharp pain. A blast of stinging white dust filled the air, clogged his eyes, nose and mouth. He had no time to think of anything other than *GOD HELP ME* before the carpet beneath him disappeared—pulled away as if by a magician—and he dropped into empty space.

The building gave in to the earth's desires, and it too fell. Graceless as a dying giant it collapsed in an implosion of glass and concrete and iron, heaping itself atop the bodies within, burying everything inside of it in a tangled black mass of clumsy, angry death.

2

DIANE KISSED HIS ear, but Matthew continued to feign sleep. He could feel her smile hovering inches from his neck. He waited, wanting her to kiss him again.

She did. Longer this time. Her soft lips were warm on his ear, then his temple, and then, as she gently rolled him, on his forehead. He kept his eyes closed, but his mouth betrayed him with a smile of his own.

She was face-to-face with him, so close he could feel the warmth of her breath on his cheek. When she spoke, he caught the sweet minty smell of whatever toothpaste she had found in his shared bathroom. She whispered.

"Matthew..."

He groaned, not wanting to wake. He wanted to stay in this *in-between time*, when the sensations of his body were peaked by his half-dream state. It was a bit like being on ecstasy, walking that padded corridor of consciousness that separated sleep and waking.

Dream, and reality.

He opened one eye, saw the soft curve of her cheek. *You are so beautiful*, he thought. Her black hair was mussed, her green eyes darted playfully from one side of his face to the other, as if she were memorizing him, a rushed portrait painted in her mind. The sunlight coming through the far window gave her a soft halo, her skin luminous.

"Morning," he said, his throat dry, his mouth pasty. She slid a hand over his forehead, smoothed it over his clumpy hair in a way that made him want to close his eyes again and just *feel* a few moments more...

"You have class in twenty minutes, tiger," she whispered.

The dream state evaporated, and Matthew woke fully with a rush of unwelcome thoughts about school, grades, career, money. He groaned again, meaning it this time.

"Right," he said, twisting over in his tiny bed to gaze blurrily at the digital clock, the green illuminated digits mocking him with their vibrancy. "Right," he repeated, and fell back to look at her again.

She was still naked and tangled in the sheets he'd brought with him from home, the same ones he'd slept in as a teenager. *And how awesome was that?* he thought happily. The same material that had covered his sexually frustrated fifteen-year-old body was now tangled sweetly between the thighs of a gorgeous coed who he'd spent the entire night having insanely great sex with. Fifteen-year-old Matthew would be proud.

"What?" she purred, sensing his amusement.

"Nothing. You're just hot is all," he said, kissing her. She responded, her hand running across his chest, then down it. He felt his body calling him to action, like a general screaming to rally the troops before battle... but then he remembered his Ethics class, and the thought of Professor Bruker's monotone lecture voice was like a pail of ice water dumped pitilessly on his young lust. He clutched her hand in his, set it down on the bed.

"Don't start," he said. "I have Ethics. Like, literally."

She laughed at his mock seriousness and, in that moment, he loved how they were doing that *thing* couples did. Like in the movies, or on TV, the hot actors saying their lines while lolling around, naked and perfect, the morning sun rich and hazy through their bedroom window.

The realization that he loved her came quietly, fitting into him like a puzzle piece.

"I have to go," he said insistently. He sat up, kissed her mouth, and rolled off the mattress, planting his feet down onto the scratchy, thin brown carpet of his dorm room floor.

"If you must..." she teased, lounging gracefully in his narrow bed, letting the sheets fall to her waist as she extended a perfectly-posed nonchalant arm. "I'll just be here, waiting for someone to have sex with."

"Well," he said, "Kelly will be back any minute, so I'm sure all your wishes will be fulfilled."

Kelly, Matthew's roommate and best friend, was a dashing, handsome guy who (besides being tall, intelligent and athletic) had known since middle school that he was, as he had put it to Matthew one day when they were kids, "without-a-doubt" gay. Kelly carried the confidence and inner peace that came with vast quantities of self-assurance and the unflagging love and support of family and friends. Matthew always envied him for having parents that were there for him, who cared and nurtured him. Something Matthew never had. Quite the opposite.

"Hmm," Diane murmured thoughtfully, "that may be an uphill climb."

"Don't know until you try," he tossed back at her as he disappeared into the small manila-lit bathroom he and Kelly shared with their dorm-neighbors, and closed the door.

WHEN MATTHEW CAME back into the bedroom – clean, naked and towel-wrapped – he found Kelly at his desk and Diane gone.

"What'd you do, scare off my girl?"

"She made a pass at me," Kelly replied, not bothering to turn around from whatever heavy textbook he was busting though.

"Right," Matthew said, and dug through a laundry basket at the foot of his bed for a t-shirt and jeans. "Fuck I'm late," he murmured.

"Better you than her…" Kelly said, tick-tocking a finger over his shoulder, his eyes never leaving the textbook.

Matthew continued dressing, saying nothing, letting his non-reply dangle. When he glanced Kelly's way again, his friend was turned around, giving Matthew his full attention, his dark eyes staring punctuated expletives.

"I was kidding, of course. Jesus, don't tell me…"

Matthew laughed and shook his head. "Nah," he said, then gave an embarrassed smile. "But I honestly wouldn't mind… I mean, obvious practicalities aside."

Kelly frowned and turned back around. "There's plenty of time, Matthew."

"I know," he said. Then… oddly… forgot what he was doing. *Going to class,* he thought, but his blood ran cold. "I…" he started, staring around the dorm room, confusion coursing through his brain like black smoke. "Kelly…"

"There's plenty of time, Matthew," his friend said again, although this time his voice was muffled and slurred, as if speaking with a numbed tongue.

Matthew started to ask why he was repeating himself when Kelly turned around. But it wasn't Kelly. Or, it was, but this Kelly had no face. It was just… blood. A face of blood. The large naked teeth were slicked with it, the bulging eyes piercingly white and roving.

"Kelly," Matthew said, eerily calm. "Your face."

"Yeah, I know," Kelly replied, the words gurgling. He wiped at it lazily, smearing blood on his hands, then his pants as he rubbed his sticky hands against them. "You too," he said calmly.

Matthew raised fingertips to his own face, felt spongy wet tissue and tight, pulsing threads of muscle, the hard round edges of bone. Moaning, he ran into the bathroom and looked in the mirror, stared in shock at his face which was no longer a face—the flesh torn away, the pulped tissue seeping droplets into the yellow-stained porcelain of the sink.

"Kelly!" he screamed, terrified, his pulse racing. He looked back toward their room, could Kelly through the open bathroom door, watched as his friend crawled awkwardly across the shit-brown carpet, one of his legs bent unnaturally so his toes pointed upward, his knee loose, calf and foot dragged behind like dead weight. His collarbone was caved in on one side, his tilting head a gruesome pile of blood and eyes and bone.

"I know, I know..." he said, a guttural laugh coming from somewhere within the gore of his mouth. He sounded exasperated, as if losing his face was the most frustrating part of his morning. "I'm sorry, boy-o," he said, then collapsed, his jaw working into the carpet. "We're dead dead dead, man..."

Matthew started for him when the door slammed shut, smacking like a fist into the exposed tissue of his cheek. Matthew felt one of the bones in his face crack and pain surge to his brain. All his senses were screaming that he was *damaged*, his brain tapping his consciousness, repeating in a steady mantra that something was very wrong... wrong... wrong!

He spun and fell hard to the gray linoleum. He moaned, rolled over, the stained bathroom floor pressing into what remained of his broken face.

Something incredibly heavy landed on top of him, collapsing his lungs, bearing down on his lower spine and the back of his legs. He heard a creaking and raised his eyes toward the door, which had opened a few inches. Matthew prayed it was someone coming to help him *help me up please* and could only watch in horror as a torn, flayed hand slipped through the narrow opening, stamping smears of red on the wall as it groped for the wall switch.

He started to scream just before the fingers found their target. There was a *click*...

...and the lights went out.

3

MATTHEW OPENED HIS eyes but could not see. It was black. A thick, rich black pressing against his shock-wide-open eyes, slathering his skin, dampening his hair.

It took him a few moments to place himself, to understand... everything was so fuzzy, his thoughts slow, as if drugged. He was lying on his stomach, his face pressed downward, his cheek mashed against rough concrete. He tried to lift his head, found he could not, so left it where it lay. It felt so damned *heavy*.

A minute passed. Another. Matthew didn't move, lying deathly still, trying to piece together what, *exactly*, had happened to him. He had to think...

He focused his breathing, blinked rapidly, attempted to formulate a clear, sensible idea of where he was.

Then he remembered.

The memories came in a mad rush to the forefront of his mind, freefalling through his rousing consciousness in hot, darting flashes, a lapping wall of flame eating its way to the surface. The horror of it flooded him. The unbelievable, unfathomable realization that he must be lying *deep within* the collapsed building. The terrible knowledge that above him—on *top* of him—rested a mountainous heap of bone-crushing weight.

The thought kickstarted a surging panic. A heavy blanket of claustrophobia smothered his brain, his flickering awareness, a defense mechanism built by blind terror. The panic beat against it with tireless, angry fists; a diseased, irate moth with a broken wing, bouncing and bashing against the inside of his skull. Without caution, he tried violently to twist his body free, but realized – in a blinding assault of horror approaching madness – that he was *stuck*. An object, unimaginably immense, had pinned him down. A fresh wave of terror ignited his nerves aflame and he wanted to scream until his lungs were emptied, lash out at something, anything. But his prone body refused, the synapses in his brain not firing the necessary instructions to his muscles, as if he had been cut off from himself. A dead, crispy butterfly pinned neatly within a boy's insect collection. He imagined himself inside a frame, hung on a wall like so many other captured insects, awaiting the boy-god's pleasure.

He gulped in deep breaths and the hysteria began to ebb, the moment of contested interaction between mind and body depleting his strength, allowing Matthew to take a moment to refocus, to calm himself. *Stupid!* he thought. *Do I want to bring the whole building down on my head?* He knew he must use greater caution, at least until he had a better handle on his situation.

Fine, fine... I'll get my shit together. In the meantime, just how bad are we?

He waited for the surge of panic to subside fully. He closely monitored his breathing and kept his body very still, no longer daring to move. As his muscles relaxed and his mind quieted, he recalled a memory from when he was a child. His grandfather, when putting him to bed at night, would shut off the lights, stand by the open door and instruct him softly, his comforting voice so soothing in the dark. "Relax yourself slowly, Matthew. One body part at a time. Start with your toes," he'd say. "Tell them, very nicely, to go to sleep."

Matthew, just a small boy, would close his eyes, focus on his toes.

Then he'd think: *Go to sleep, toes.*

"Good," his grandfather would say, watching him. "Now, tell your legs. Then your fingers, then your arms, then, finally, your head. Got it?"

Matthew would nod to the shadow by the open door, then, closing his eyes once more, follow the instructions exactly. *Goodnight legs*, whispering the instructions in his mind. *Goodnight fingers... goodnight arms...*

He rarely made it to his head.

Matthew decided to use the same technique now in assessing his injuries. Slowly, calmly, he did his best to let the suffocating fear slip away. Then, one-by-one, he began exploring individual areas of his body.

He started with his mouth. He closed his eyes and felt around with his tongue. He winced and inhaled sharply as he slid his gashed tongue slowly up and down, then side to side. The inside was sloshy. But what he thought was saliva, he realized with revulsion, was his own blood. He tried to spit but pain shot through his face, so he simply tilted his head, barely able to tuck his chin to chest, and let it spill out. The blood waterfalled over his lips and down his chin, soaked into the rough carpet of rubble.

Matthew let his jaw to hang open a moment, panting like a dying dog, breathing in the stale, dusty air. When he finally closed it to swallow, he was sickened by the slick of blood and bits of flesh that slid down his throat. Worse yet, with his mouth closed, he discovered he could not breathe through his nose. With effort, he let that thought alone for the moment, still trying to take inventory as slowly, as stolidly, as he possibly could. He wouldn't panic, not yet. Panic wasn't an option. He tried to relax, to take *hold* of the situation. In the meantime, he would just have to breathe through his mouth, although the taste of the air sickened him.

His face, he knew, was badly damaged. He tried to breathe through his nose again and failed. It felt... wrong. He could sense that the bridge wasn't where it was supposed to be.

Let's move on, he thought, and reached out with his senses to feel his arms, his hands. His right arm was immobilized, but he thought it was all right. It didn't seem broken, and he felt no sharp pain, and he could wiggle his fingers all right. But whatever was pressing down on top of him *the building the whole fucking building* was also pressing down on his shoulder, keeping it immobile. But he could move his hand without pain. He tilted his wrist up and down, twisted it left... then right. All good there. *Not so bad, considering*, he thought. *It's okay everybody, we're just a little stuck at the moment.*

He tried his left arm next, almost weeping with relief when it moved freely and with ease. He slowly bent his elbow, brought his fingers toward his face. Again, he felt no pain, and he thought it a very good sign, overall, that his arms seemed to be undamaged. The right one, for now, trapped. The other, for now, completely operational.

Feeling more confident, he went back to his face. He gingerly pressed fingers to his nose. He sucked in sharply at the pinch of pain even the gentlest touch caused him. Lightening his touch, he very carefully moved the pad of one finger along the bridge, trying not to panic when he felt the break just below his eye-line. He could feel the swollen knob of gristle, the sharp edge of the broken bone where it shifted at a decided angle. More probing revealed a wide, deep gash running from the break in his nose to just below his left eye. It was sticky to the touch. When he pinched and wiggled the askew tip of his now rather loose nose, it gave sickeningly, moving too easily under his fingers. An internal grating sound of shifting gristle filled his ears when the dislodged pieces rubbed together.

With a deep sigh, he left it alone once more, moved on to his eyes and forehead, pawing at himself like a blind man seeking recognition of a stranger's face. He found no cuts, no painful spots or anything else terribly out of sorts. He thought it possible that one cheekbone might be broken, but it was too tender and swollen to tell. The skin felt slack under his right eye where it should have felt like a facial bone, and despite the swelling he knew something had been dented permanently. He didn't want to dwell on it, the thought of his face disfigured not helping his spirits, so he quickly moved probing fingers to his lips.

Praying silently for good news, he pushed two fingers into his mouth.

He immediately felt the jagged, tender edges of two broken teeth along the top left. He felt around some more, touching the tip of each tooth, and was pleased that everything else seemed in its proper place. He next tapped the pad of his swollen tongue and, with some astonishment, realized he'd bitten the end of it completely off. There was a raw stump where the tip had been. He could only assume the missing bit had been swallowed, or spit out, with the rest of the blood that had settled in his mouth while unconscious.

He fought off a bolt of nausea while reliving the meaty stew he had swallowed upon waking. *Moving on,* he thought, and pulled his fingers from his mouth. He patted the top of his head, then around to the back, and then felt his ears.

Grateful for the knowledge that at least his skull was still in one piece, he allowed his mind to feel out the remaining parts of his body. It was as if he were opening a sealed door in his consciousness, one that had been closed off to protect him from the knowledge of what lay beyond.

He could neither roll his body nor raise his torso in any way, his lower back pressed down by the great weight from above. Beneath him, something bulky and sharp-edged jammed hard into his pelvis and guts. Luckily it had not broken the skin, or any bones that he could tell. The weight on his spine was not severely painful, but it was immense, as if the slightest increase in pressure would snap his body in half, like shears pressing through the middle of a thick twig, leaving it in two.

He shifted his attention from his back and let his mind float down his legs. They were, he thought with a degree of confusion, *exposed*. He could *feel* the space around them, and when he gently tapped the toe of one foot *where were his shoes he was missing his shoes* against something hard he let out a held breath of relief at the welcome surge of feeling that ran through his foot and up his right leg. He tried to do the same with the left, but that leg was bent awkwardly, the ankle wedged into something heavy and twisted, like metal ribbing or, possibly, a piece of the building's iron framework. But he could *feel* that trapped foot, which meant, he was pretty sure, that his back was not broken. At least, he thought less optimistically, not severely so.

Okay then, where does that leave me? Broken nose, certainly. Maybe broken cheekbone. Trapped arm, trapped leg. Back hurt, but likely not broken, because I can feel my fucking feet. My insides, though, this pressure in my stomach.

He broke off his thought, let his mind go blank, tried to be positive. He knew he was lucky to be alive.

His assessment complete for now, he tried to think back, to remember the moments prior to the building's collapse.

An earthquake, he thought, straining to piece the jostled memories, filled with panic and terror, together. He recalled how the office disappeared in large chunks, slipped away before his eyes as the earth shook. *The receptionist*, he thought, *she was injured, her face...*

Matthew didn't want to think of her, or the fate of the other fifty or so people in that office. Dead, of course. They're all dead. The whole firm wiped out with a snap of God's fingers, a swipe of his mighty hand.

Unbidden, the thought sprang to him – with a twinge of instant shame – that he would not be getting the job.

He laughed, shook his head and let a few tears spill from his eyes as he did so, chuckling between gasps while lying down, down, in the deep dark. The laughter turned to coughing, then hacking. Blood spurted up his throat, sour on his tongue.

Is that internal bleeding? he wondered. *No, dummy, you just swallowed half your tongue, remember? That's your goddamn brunch today, boy-o.*

What about Mr. Baskin? he wondered. What had happened to the elderly lawyer he was supposed to interview with? He'd never even met the man. Matthew wondered what the old coot had been doing when his world literally collapsed and he was dropped forty feet down, crushed amongst the bodies of his subordinates? Had he been chatting with his wife, the lovely Mrs. Baskin? Making dinner plans, maybe? Or had he been reviewing Matthew's CV, boning up for the interview? Preparing the hard questions, wondering if this young man would be the right fit for his prestigious firm. A protégé, perhaps? A future partner in the making?

Doesn't matter now, Matthew knew. Baskin's firm was done. Literally wiped from the face of the earth. *Force Majeure*, Matthew thought involuntarily. The big Delete button. He couldn't help himself thinking about all the life insurance policies that would not be paid out, the property damage that would not be reimbursed. Although, if Baskin was half as good a lawyer as Matthew had heard, the old man's assets were likely fine. An old eagle like Baskin would cover all his bases, allowing for such things as lightning strikes, tsunamis and, yes, earthquakes.

For his part, Matthew had no life insurance. No savings, either, for that matter. What Matthew would be leaving to Diane and their child was debt. Shitloads and shitloads of debt. Student loans upward of a hundred thousand dollars. For what? A law degree he might never be able to use.

"If it please the court," he mumbled, choking out the words, "this really fucking sucks."

He wanted to laugh again. To find levity... but could not. He rested his head down lightly, forehead pressed against something cool and hard, a pillow that stank of concrete and dirt. He closed his eyes and waited for someone, anyone, to rescue him.

"NOT ADOPTED. DUMPED," he told her, she with her Pinot and he with his lager.

Their second date. Time for storytelling. Time for *This Is Your Life*. If you think there's a chance, if you think she's the one. Then you give it up. You let if fly.

"My grandfather raised me from infancy. I never even met them. They left the country, never came back."

She spun her glass, treading carefully. "You never tried to find them?"

Matthew shook his head. The din of the restaurant disrupted his thoughts, irritated him. "By the time I was old enough to give a shit, to fully understand, they were dead. Well, at least that's what I was told. I got a letter once..." he trailed off, not ready to let her into the place that talking about the letter would take him. The painful doors it would open, showing her the twisting insides. He swallowed some beer, waved his hand dismissively over the spattered remains of their shared plate of grilled Brussel sprouts and mini Ahi tacos. "Plane crash somewhere in Spain. I was sixteen when my grandfather told me. He woke me up one Saturday morning, sat on my bed, and said 'Your parents were killed yesterday. I'll be gone a week or so. Get up, there's things you need to do.' And that was it. He left. A week later he came back, and we returned to our lives."

"Jesus, a real sweetheart," she said, appearing to instantly regret the words. The reaction of a college girl who knew nothing of the world. "I'm sorry, I mean…"

"No, it's okay." Matthew tried to smile, sensing her self-admonishment, hating the idea of her feeling uncomfortable. "He wasn't a real emotional guy." Matthew hoped his words, his smile, would relieve her apprehension. *Because she could be the one, couldn't she?* "He's a good man, a fair man. I love him." He shrugged. "Besides, he's all I have."

Diane slowly spun the spine of her glass. "He's alive, then?"

Matthew nodded. "I talk to him every day. Well, almost. He still works the farm, although it's smaller now. No animals, just the fields. He's a good man," Matthew repeated lamely.

She reached out a hand and he took it.

I'll take care of you forever, Matthew thought. *And we'll have children and I will love the shit out of them.*

He pulled his hand away, laughed self-consciously as he swiped a stray tear from his eye. She smiled and handed him a clean napkin. He laughed again, falling, wondering if she was falling as well.

4

MATTHEW JERKED HIS head from a half-sleep, a sharp pain immediately stabbing his neck. He became abruptly alert as the earth beneath him, and the rubble of the building surrounding him, began to violently shake.

Oh fuck oh no no no no… he thought as the world trembled.

The slab of heavy concrete wedged against his back vibrated like a mountainous chainsaw, sending tremors up his spine, turning his legs cold. It pressed into him *harder*, as if he were not yet bearing the full weight of the thing. As it slowly shivered loose from its anchored position, he realized with horror it was sinking – *inch by inch* – into his lower spine; deliberately settling itself into his lower back, crushing him with agonizing slothfulness. He gritted his teeth and screamed, out of pain or fear or both he didn't know.

As the earth continued to shake, small chunks of debris fell on and around him, choking the air with concrete dust. As he was pressed downward, downward, the hard object beneath him pushing into his pelvis shifted, but *thank you God* it miraculously shifted away from him, creating open space in that small area below his stomach and hips. As the great weight continued to sink, he felt his spine curve, his feet raising higher as his midsection bowed. He flayed his one free arm outward, waiting for that moment when his spine would snap, his stomach burst and his insides rip through his skin and spit themselves over the dark ruins.

He screamed again, louder, praying his lungs would allow the air back in once he'd expelled it, that his compressed body would not reject his next breath.

When the shaking stopped.

He could barely breathe, the pain unbearable. He groaned, gritted his teeth. There was the sound of a deep rupture – a land mass being snapped in two – loud but muffled, down in the belly of the ruins beneath him. A monster's belch.

There were a few more splintering snaps, as if two-by-fours were breaking in half – *SNAP – SNAP – CRACK-SNAP* – and then everything beneath him sagged a few inches, and Matthew's body sank along with the debris. Mercifully, the slab ramming itself into his spine did not lower, and the pressure released itself from his back, guts and groin as his body leveled out. Breath leapt into his lungs.

"Thank you, thank you, thank you," he whispered in a hushed, torn voice, breathing in more easily now as the incredible pressure, threatening to break him, ebbed. He could feel the blood in his body racing to his legs and chest, free once more to flow without obstruction.

After a few moments of nervous gratitude – waiting for another aftershock, praying his body was not too badly damaged – Matthew took a deep breath and made an attempt to once again assess his position. He was still unable to turn or twist his body, the weight of the slab still resting on top of him heavily, if not with the deadly force of a few moments prior. He imagined the Thing, that rock monstrosity from the *Fantastic Four* comics and movies, was resting his bony ass on Matthew's spine, waiting for backup to arrive, and Matthew could do nothing but squirm and try to keep breathing beneath Thing's bulk – a trapped, feeble villain.

For the moment, at least, the ground had ceased its final vibrations, and Matthew was still alive. But with the release of that sharp fear came cold despair, an icy blanket that wrapped around him, filled him, and he abruptly began to sob like a child. Tears ran down his face and into the broken concrete. He realized, with no small sense of shame, he had pissed himself, whether from terror or the immense pressure on his bladder he did not know, but he could feel the urine cooling along his hip and thighs. He wiped his face with one dirty hand, then cried some more. The sobs became louder, more ragged, soon pitched into the air as panicked screams. It was the weeping and cries of hysteria – of terror – of a person slowly, and quite painfully, dying.

Am I going to die? he wondered. He desperately wished he could see what was around him. *I'm so goddamn sick of the dark!* he thought, straining to make out anything, any shapes that made sense, that brought an element of reality to his slowly unraveling mind. He wondered how deeply he was buried, how precariously. Was he ten feet above-ground, or twenty-feet below? If above, would he collapse downward with the next aftershock? Sliding down and down into the bowels of the earth? And if below, what if the rescue teams *because surely there were rescuers they always showed them on TV always always always* brought in heavy machinery and accidentally drove over the rubble sitting on top of him, squashing him beneath like a bug?

He felt panic rise again and wanted so desperately for the ability to just *turn over* and look above him. Would he see light? A pinprick, perhaps? The proverbial ray of hope?

Or would there be nothing but more darkness? The total inky black submersion that did not let you see the hand in front of your face. The kind that muffled the sounds you made as if your body was trapped in warm outer space, wedged between dimensions like a dead rat between the walls of a rickety old house.

Matthew started to hyperventilate. He had to get out. He had to get out. He *had* to get OUT. With a fresh surge of mindless panic, he began to push and twist, crying out in pain as the edge of slab on top of him dug deeper into his flesh. He felt skin tear and a warm gush of blood spill down his side, seep into the waistband of his boxers.

He stopped, exhausted, knowing he was making things worse. "Damn it!" he screamed, feeling more helpless and alone by the moment. He tried desperately to get a grip, to slow his breathing, to calm himself. The beat of his strained heart began to slow... his breathing steady...

He was just regaining some of his composure, when something – something behind him in the dark – *pulled* at his foot.

His head snapped up, eyes wide with surprise.

He had time to think: *Wait... did something...* when he felt another quick, sharp *tug*. Not his foot. His *toe*. Or, more accurately, the sock of his toe. It felt as if two tiny fingers were pulling at the very tip of his sock, teasingly trying to pull... it... off.

Matthew had just started to wonder how he had possibly lost his shoes when that unseeable *Something* pulled at the tip of his sock once more. He almost laughed through his misery, the sheer madness of someone pulling at his foot...

His smile died. It died quickly, between one heartbeat and the next.

The next tug was more insistent. More frantic. More *needful*. He felt a sharp prick, as if a pin had poked the bottom of his big toe.

"Ow!" he snapped, then held his breath, focused all of his attention on the sound reaching him from around his feet. He closed his eyes, listened closely to the dark.

He heard his own heartbeat, the pulse of his life thumping steadily in his head. And then, so faintly he would have never heard it were he not focusing every fiber of his body to receiving the sounds made in the space around him, he heard a *scuffling* around his legs.

He let out his breath. *No.*

This time the tug of his sock was more certain. This time he felt the undeniable pinch of *teeth* sink into his toe. And then the thing... and then the thing was *chewing*.

Despite himself, despite knowing he was defenseless, that his body was likely on the precipice of life and death, that the slightest jostling of his position could bring the bloody black-robed rider crashing laughing down upon him, he screamed! He kicked! He thrashed his one free hand around, swiping madly, invisibly, at the blackness!

"Get away!" he shrieked in a strained, broken cry. "GET AWAY!"

He kicked his foot toward the scuffling sound and heard a satisfying, tiny *squeak* of pain. *Or frustration,* he thought. His breath became quick and ragged as he thrashed defensively. He knew his toe was bleeding, probably quite badly. He prayed the smell of blood would not bring more of them.

How many would it take to eat all of him?

"Stay away from me!" he cried, his strained voice sounding alien and weak in the darkness, any reverberation muffled, as if he were screaming curses from the inside of a padded cell.

He stopped, waited, heard nothing. He slowed his breathing once more, willed the panic to subside. He waited for the scuffling sound to come again, the scurrying of the tiny rat feet...

"Hello?" came a voice.

Matthew held his breath, cocked his head. *A woman's voice*, he thought wildly. *From where, from where...*

"Hello? Can you..." she said, the voice thin and wavering. The woman was somewhere... she sounded just beside him. No more than a few feet away. Was it possible someone had been down here this whole time, and he hadn't heard her? Didn't sense her presence?

Yes, he thought, *yes, of course it was possible. She was injured, unconscious, but alive, alive!*

Hope coursed through him and he forgot about the weight on his back, forgot about the foot, long-since fallen asleep and grown numb, intertwined within coarse hard metal. Forgot about his trapped shoulder, about the rodent feasting on his toe... *Alive!* he thought once more, the word a blaring trumpet in his brain.

"I hear you," he said urgently, loudly as he could. But his voice was so feeble it surprised him. It was as if something inside him had gone wrong. As he strained to look through the dark, toward the voice, he was suddenly light-headed, dizzy. What was left of his tongue was slimy with blood, and when he tried to spit he only managed to drool more slick fluid over his chin. He shook his head, tried to clear his thoughts.

"Are you there?" *Or am I going crazy?* he thought.

"I'm here," her voice replied, from so close he felt as if...

He reached his free hand toward the origin point of the woman's voice. His fingertips found dusty chunks of rubble, something coarse and metal, but nothing more. Just a shattered wall between him and whoever was speaking. He started feeling out the chunks of debris blocking him from the woman, straining his shoulder socket to its maximum flexibility to try and find a piece to remove. If he could dig through...

"What are you doing?" she said, sounding panicked. Scared.

"I'm sorry," he said. "I'm trying, well, this is stupid, but I'm trying to dig to you."

"Please don't," she replied. "I'm afraid. I don't want anything else to fall on me."

Matthew paused, let his fingertips rest on the rough, dusty barrier. They were such small pieces of rubble. He could feel around their edges, could imagine their shapes. Much of it was loose, not like the thing pressing him down, crushing him to death.

"Please," he said, almost a whisper. "I'm so scared."

There was no reply, and Matthew wondered, again, if he'd imagined it all.

"Hello?" he said, praying. "Lady?"

After a moment – a long moment – she spoke.

"I'm here."

Matthew felt sweat running into his eyes and tried to wipe it away, lick the blood and dust from his lips. "Are you... are you all right?" He could almost sense her taking stock of herself as he waited.

"I don't really know," she said finally, and he could have sworn he heard her lightly chuckle. "I think my arm is broken. And my legs. Something is wrong with my legs. I can't feel them."

Matthew felt an icy cold wash through him, but stayed silent.

"My head hurts terribly," she said weakly, absently, as if she were trying to understand how she had become so badly injured.

There was a long pause. Matthew didn't know what else to say. He began to search for anything to tell her, just to keep communicating.

"I think a rat was eating my foot," he said finally, feeling idiotic but also needing to share the terror engulfing his heart.

For a long time, the woman did not reply. *Great, she probably thinks your nuts, boy-o*, he thought. *She probably thinks she's stuck down here, in the bowels of a destroyed building, with a raving lunatic. Some comfort you are.*

"I kicked it away," he added, hoping the rational response would allay any fears of his insanity.

"What's your name?" she said, so softly and sweetly Matthew wanted to hold her and cry.

"Matthew."

"Matthew," she said, as if tasting it. Her voice rose a bit, more reassuring now. "Matthew, I'm Dee."

Now Matthew did cry, the tears running hot down his face. He smiled, unconsciously covering his eyes with his free hand. "Hello, Dee."

"I think it's safe to say," she said, her voice much stronger now, "that I wish we had met under better circumstances."

Matthew started to laugh, but a bubble of blood erupted from his throat, and he gagged on it. Something in his stomach was *burning*, burning so badly and he prayed the works in there weren't fouled up, prayed his liver hadn't been crushed, that the contents of a torn intestine weren't dumping out into the clean rivers of his bloodstream. He tried to respond, but could only cough.

"You sound hurt, Matthew," Dee said quietly. When he said nothing, could say nothing, she said: "You should rest now."

And when Matthew heard those words, he thought there was no better idea in the world. He lowered his forehead to his concrete pillow, and immediately fell asleep.

5

"Is it serious?"

"What's the phrase?" Kelly said into his ear, the connection beginning to crackle and fade as Diane drove them deeper into the mountains. "As a heart attack?"

"Yeah, that does sound serious. Plus, you know, at his age, not the worst metaphor."

"Oh ha ha," Kelly replied. "Let's get it all out of your system now before we meet up. C'mon, here we go, please, cut loose," he urged.

"Well..." Matthew said, sparing a look at Diane's focused expression as she wound the old Ford up the narrow tree-lined road into the frozen heart of Big Sur. She saw him watching and gave a half-smile, then put a hand on his knee while expertly steering with the other. "I did have a whole folder of daddy-issue puns I was planning on using this weekend."

"Uh-huh," Kelly said drily, distracted now. "Whatever, Matthew. Tell Diane to keep you under control, please."

"Kelly wants you to make sure I behave in front of Stanley," Matthew said to Diane.

"Don't worry, Kelly," she said loudly. "He's on a short leash."

"Great," Kelly said in Matthew's ear. There was a pause.

Being best friends with someone since childhood gives one certain superpowers when it comes to said best friend. Such things as the strength to raise them up when they've been knocked down. Conjuring up the right joke to make them laugh, even when you know it's the last thing they feel like doing. X-ray vision that tells you their heart is broken. Another helpful best friend superpower is the ability to read their minds, a sixth sense that tells you when something isn't "all-the-way right," as his grandfather would say. And best friends want each other "all-the-way right." Every day. Every goddamn minute.

"What?" Matthew said, probing. Diane's smile flickered, her brown eyes darted to him, then back to the road.

"It's nothing," Kelly sighed, morose now.

"Oh, okay, great," Matthew replied, sarcastically chipper. "Guess I'll see you tomorrow. Bye!" Kelly said nothing for a moment. Matthew knew the fact he was not scolding him was a bad sign.

So he waited.

"Listen, let's talk when I'm there, okay?" he said finally, quietly. Too quiet for Kelly.

"Dude," Matthew said, a little alarmed now. "What's up? You're freaking me out."

"You freak out far too easily, Matthew," Kelly replied, but Matthew noticed his heart wasn't in it. "Look, so you won't make Diane crazy, it's just... god, I really like Stan. Like, not the usual Kelly crushes I used to have in college, the ones that end in ambivalence and heartbreak for the poor sod I fell out of crush with, or whatever, but like a real deep thing." He paused again. "God, I sound stupid."

"No," Matthew said quickly. "No, man, you don't. I get you. It's good, Kelly. You should think of it as a positive. I mean, shit dude, real feelings? That's pretty sweet, right?" He looked to Diane, smiled. "Our little boy is growing up. Puttin' on big boy pants."

Matthew could feel Kelly smiling on the other end of the line, and knew he had him right where he wanted him. "I'm proud of you, brother. Whether this works out or not, it must feel good to know you've got it in you to really care about someone. How cool is that?"

"Very cool," Kelly said quietly.

"Okay then."

"Yeah, okay," he said. "Thanks."

"It's the sole reason of my existence, to be there for you. You know that."

"Good lord," Kelly said, sniffing now, and Matthew could see him wiping his face in that weird way he had, with just the pads of his hands. "You're really going for it."

Matthew laughed, missing him so much right then his heart hurt. "Listen, we're getting up there in them thar hills, and Diane's driving like a bat out of hell. Likely gonna lose you. You good?"

"Yes, god, I'm fine." Kelly sniffed loudly one final time, and when his voice returned, it was stronger. "So, do we need to bring anything or what? I don't want to sit around all weekend drinking your cheap... if that's..."

"Kelly?" Matthew said, unreasonably alarmed. Hearing the struggle to keep reception, Diane slowed the car a bit. "Kelly?" he repeated, straining to hear. "I'm losing you."

"Yeah, whatever, we'll bring booze!" Kelly yelled loudly, as if that would help the connection. "Kiss Diane for me, and I'll see you tomorrow. Excited to... big... ay..."

"Can't hear you dude. I'll see you tomorrow."

"Good... Matthew, I..."

There was a crackle, and the connection cut out.

They arrived at the cabin a few hours later. Snow covered the ground all around it, and the tall crimson planks of its exterior were a broad red stain against the stark white in which it hunkered. Hollow black windows watched them approach, the worn second-story deck, facing West for best views of the sea and sunsets, jutted toward them like a defiant chin.

Once inside, Matthew built a large fire and the young couple relished a night of sitting near the warm blaze. Outside, the clouds dumped a couple more feet of snow, enclosing them in nature's dark wet bosom, where they twined and used each other for warmth, sheltered and safe.

She'd made him dance. He remembered that so vividly. They had spun in front of the fire, a Benny Goodman swing record spinning on his grandfather's RCA Victor, the frayed cabinet speakers laying out the bouncing, whipping horns and rumbling drums while they did their best not to stomp each other in their semi-drunken attempt at never-before-used dance moves.

Later that night Diane conceived. In the thousand days since, they'd gone over it time and time again, but the math worked out the same each time. Matthew wished it were not the case, and tried to see grace in the timing, but all he could feel was guilt, as if this new life was a betrayal, one that would haunt him forever.

MATTHEW WOKE TO the metallic shrilling of the cabin's analog phone. He hadn't heard an honest-to-god phone ringing in so long that at first he thought it was a fire alarm. He sat up quickly, looked around, took a beat to remember where he was. He looked down at Diane, who looked around sleepily, also caught in that daze of being somewhere unfamiliar when woken suddenly.

He got out of bed, wincing at the frigid air attacking his naked body. The floors were bare wood but for a few large Southwestern-style rugs. He looked for something to cover himself with, then, knowing time was an issue, shook his head and walked briskly to the dining room, his flesh covered in goosebumps, his arms crisscrossed around his thin torso, his teeth literally chattering. He smelled the old smoke from last night's fire, and decided they'd use the central heating today and keep the fire for romance purposes, because there was cold and then there was fucking *cold*.

He made it to the phone on the third ring, instinctively reached for it, then stopped. He was sideswiped with a realization that sickened him to his absolute core. His hand actually paused above the green rotary phone, hovering, trembling inches from the receiver as the bell inside the antiquated contraption pealed like devil's wings.

Only one other person had this number. His grandfather. This was his place, and the phone was kept alive because there was no cell reception.

Matthew had time to think, *why the hell is my grandfather calling me...* he looked at the digital clock over the stove... *at 6:45 in the morning?*

Out of time, he picked up, said "Hello," and listened to his grandfather's calm voice explain to him the manner in which his best friend had been killed.

In slow, gentle terms, he told Matthew how it had been the other guy's fault, a truck driver cutting a turn on a particularly nasty switchback. Kelly's car had driven straight into the rear wheels, which had drifted far into the oncoming lane, at forty miles an hour. He and his "friend" – as my grandfather put it – were both killed instantly. *Coming around the turn like that,* he had said, *they probably never had time to register what was happening. Then it was over.*

Matthew didn't remember the next few hours of his life, and it never came back. Those few hours, the ones where he had screamed, and cried, and slumped down to the floor, hugging himself. Diane had held him while she also cried and soothed him in that frozen cabin, where they thought with such cleverness they had hidden from the horror of the world, and been proved wrong.

A month or so later, Diane found out she was pregnant, and it helped him think forward instead of back. Slowly, he crawled out from under his depression. He started looking for work, started thinking about the big picture of their lives. They decided to name the baby Kelly, regardless of gender.

They were married on Catalina island. Matthew's grandfather was his only family and only guest, but Diane's large clan made up for it, bringing an air of vibrancy and joy to the event, filling the seats on both sides of the aisle.

The ceremony took place on a pale stretch of beach behind a seafood restaurant on a breezy, but warm, spring day. Diane's older sister stood beside her as the maid of honor. The space beside Matthew, while he held her hand and said his vows, was empty.

6

WAS IT DAY? Or was it night?

Matthew opened his eyes, and saw nothing.

Maybe I'm blind, he thought without emotion. *Maybe... maybe there's light all around me, but I was hurt, and now, without even realizing it, I'm totally blind.*

He lifted his one free hand as close to his eyes as possible without touching his face, wiggled his fingers.

Nothing.

He put his palm over his eyes, then removed it. On. Off. On. Off. No difference.

He tried not to think about it. He had felt his head and there were no severe cuts, no tender bruising.

It's just dark, he thought, chiding himself for panicking over nothing. *It's just really, really, REALLY fucking dark.*

"Dee?" he called out, tenuously. "You there?" he said again, a little louder.

No reply.

He closed his eyes in exhaustion. He didn't know how long he'd been asleep. Didn't know what time it was, or how long he'd been stuck amidst the rubble. He tried to think. Anything to take his mind off the weight crushing his back, his trapped, possibly broken, limbs. *Okay, think dummy, let's figure out what time it is. Let's keep it under control.*

His mouth felt like sawdust, his hobbled tongue fattened with swelling, an engorged leach stuffed between his cheeks. His broken nose was throbbing and clogged. *C'mon, Matthew,* he thought. *Focus.*

He took a deep breath, let it out, and tried to think.

The interview was Monday at 10 A.M. He figured he'd been stuck in the rubble for at least twelve hours. Not knowing how long he'd been asleep, it might have been longer. His watch was on the arm which was jammed and trapped, and he wouldn't be able to see it anyway, not in the dark. His phone had been in his attaché, and for all he knew it was sitting right next to him, but he didn't think so. He thought it was buried elsewhere, his phone likely vibrating stupidly underneath a hundred pounds of rock and steel, the "smart" technology inside too stupid to know how useless it was.

So let's assume it's midnight. That felt right to him. He was tired, and it was cold. He realized, with some surprise, that he wasn't hungry. *Likely because my stomach is being squeezed to the size of a grape,* he thought, praying again that his organs weren't permanently squished to jelly.

"Dee?" he croaked, the word coming out as if he had a lisp, more like "Thee" due to his swollen tongue and dry throat. He wondered why rescue crews hadn't come yet. He strained to listen, but heard... nothing. No alarmed voices. No sirens. No vehicles or bullhorns. No help.

Nothing at all. It was as if he was deaf as well as blind. Complete and total sensory deprivation. Except for the pain, of course. There was that. The cramping of muscles stuck in the wrong configuration for too long, the spasms shooting up his spine, his broken mouth and bent nose, all reminders that he was alive, that he was a physical being.

And don't forget about the rats, Matthew, a small, high-pitched voice said inside his head. *The rats are REAL, oh yes, boy-o, they're very real, and very, very hungry.*

Matthew shook his head, clearing the voice away. He began to whimper, fear and panic surging into his body once more. He tried to tamp it down, to think of something else, anything else.

Kelly, another voice said from deep inside his head, a different voice this time. A kind voice. *Think about Kelly and Diane. They're home, they're worried about you. They're coming for you.*

"Yes, of course," he croaked. "They're coming."

He thought about little Kelly. It wasn't that long ago he first learned to smile, then to laugh. His sweet baby's laugh that sounded like heaven, that gave you chills and let you believe the world was good, that life was good.

Life is good, he heard the other Kelly's voice *the dead Kelly* saying in his ear. *Don't forget that you're a very lucky guy. Now why don't you stop bitching and try to help yourself out of here, eh boy-o?*

Matthew nodded to the voice, took two deep breaths, steeling himself. His confidence growing and, knowing he would be losing more and more strength as his body tired, felt a renewed determination to do something, anything, to better his situation. To fight against this twist of fate he'd been so savagely dropped into.

He decided to free his arm.

He held his breath, allowed his mind to feel its way down the length of his trapped limb. He began the process by wiggling his fingers, just to see how much room there was. Only his pointing finger could move at all. He let out the breath he'd been holding, nodded to himself.

"All right, all right," he said, and started to rotate his shoulder. First to the left, then to the right. *If only I could see,* he thought angrily, but kept at it. Left, then right. Left, then right. The pieces of the demolished building moved like dry gristle, and he blew away the puffs of dust and grit that fell onto his face, into his eyes and panting mouth.

After working his shoulder around a few minutes, he couldn't tell if the arm was any looser or not. *Damn.*

Time to try pulling.

So he pulled, and twisted, and wiggled his finger. Sweat broke out on his forehead, and he began to breath more heavily. He smelt his own foul breath, tainted with blood and bacteria. He closed his eyes, tried to *feel* the debris loosening throughout his stiff shoulder and down the length of his arm. *It's not MOVING!*

He growled in frustration and was suddenly enveloped in a red-hot, crashing rage. He was no longer gently twisting and pulling, but *yanking* his shoulder toward him, his fingers twitching in spasms at the end of his blind limb. He spat and cursed as tears fell from his eyes and he yanked harder, then *harder.* He was panting too quickly, could feel saliva mixed with old blood leak down his chin. His nose throbbed and his eyes were squeezed shut as he *pulled* with everything he had.

He felt the seam of his suit coat rip above his shoulder blade, and his arm, miraculously, felt a little less restricted. With renewed hope and vigor, he began to try and yank his bare arm *through* his coat, letting the fabric catch on whatever rock and metal were restricting him. Two of his fingers were moving now, then three. He could rotate his wrist and he felt that if he could slide it backward, into the coat sleeve, he might be able to slip it through.

"C'mon, c'mon!" he snarled through gritted teeth, because his arm felt just as stuck, as wedged, as it had been only moments before.

He stopped, breathing heavily, the frustration boiling over him like a heat rash.

"No... no... NO!" he yelled. "NO! NO! NO!"

Then he tugged, just as hard as he could.

The jacket ripped at the shoulder. There was a sharp *crack* and something slid, and something broke, like a pane of glass smashed with a hammer. Scared, he jerked frantically and, to his surprise, his arm slid free. Hysterical, he pulled it toward him as if bitten. In his quick jerking movement, his hand caught on a thick dagger of protruding glass, sharp as a razor, that caught the crease of his hand just beneath his wedding ring and punched through the finger, tearing it halfway through, just above the knuckle. Shocked, he froze. He could feel the finger dangling, the blood pulsing from the wound like a garden hose that had been stopped up by a crick, then suddenly loosened.

A second later the pain caught up, ripping through his cushion of shock like a flamethrower, shredding his mind with the stabbing thrusts of a thousand knives. He screamed, and the echo of his scream died in front of him, absorbed by the indifferent dark. His mind raced with pain and panic, terrified he was losing too much blood. He knew he *had* to free his arm, to somehow stop the pulsing blood from emptying through his torn finger. The glass was still caught in the webbing of his hand, part of his finger still hung by a tendon to his body. He could hear the dangling *clink* of his wedding band tapping the glass shard as his finger swung dumbly.

He screamed again and, with a last violent burst – eyes bugged out and wet lips curled in preparation of doing what no man should ever have to do – he let his mind slip into momentary madness, and *pulled*.

The finger caught, stretched... then ripped away.

His hand was free.

Sobbing through screams, he pulled his arm, gingerly now, though the ripped sleeve. He rolled his body as much as he could, desperately trying to get his arm out of the coat, the remainder of it thumb-tacked into his back, like a pin in a cushion, by the weight on top of him.

Feeling slightly dizzy and severely nauseous as more and more blood pulsed out of his body with every passing second, Matthew slid his arm from the torn sleeve.

He brought the mangled hand to his face, as if hoping to see the damage. He could see nothing, not even a shadow. He moved the hand even closer, hoping to get at least a sense of how bad it was, when a squirt of warm fluid shot from the jagged hole at the base of his non-existent finger and sprayed his lips.

Spitting and crying, he reached around with his other hand, managed to pull the white square-folded handkerchief from his breast pocket. He flapped it open and pressed it against the wound where his gold wedding band had once rested. He lowered his head to the blood-drenched concrete and wailed, the pain nearly unbearable. The blood had soaked through the cloth and he knew it wasn't nearly tight enough. He removed it, felt the chilled air coating the wound, and then re-wrapped the blood-soaked handkerchief around his hand again. He couldn't tie a knot, but managed to tuck the loose end into the cloth to keep it tight.

His hand pulsed and twitched, but he thought, perhaps, the flow was slowing. He pressed the wound hard against his chest, trying to apply as much pressure as he could.

"Don't let me die, please don't let me die," he whimpered, and saw twinkling lights frying at the edges of his vision. *God, don't let me die*, he prayed, and then closed his eyes and dropped his forehead to the cool, slick concrete. With his injured hand clamped beneath him, his eyelids fluttered, and he passed out.

"SIR? SIR? YOU there?" An insistent voice.

Matthew stirred. His head felt like an anvil that had been well-used. Recently.

His eyelids were gummy. His mouth a thick, rough hollow in the bottom of his face that inhaled the oxygen his brain needed to let his body know how good and truly fucked it was.

"Matthew?" the voice came again, more apologetic, questioning.

Matthew groaned, turned his head, opened his useless eyes.

"Dee?" he said, his voice a croak.

"Yes, yes," she said, sounding relieved. "I thought, well, I heard you screaming, and then you were quiet for so long, and you weren't answering. I'm sorry, I thought..."

"It's okay," he said, remembering the lost finger, the bleeding hand. He felt the clenched fist balled up beneath him, but had no desire to move it away from his body. There would be no way to inspect the damage, anyway. No way for him to know whether he would live or die.

As he woke, he thought he could feel something down by his feet. Was something pulling at him? He wasn't sure... but there was no pain. His legs were completely numb, the weight settled into his spine making sure they'd received none of the blood needed to fill their veins, feed their many nerve endings. He dismissed the loss of feeling as something currently out of his control and put it out of his mind.

"Hey Dee," he said. "I think I screwed up pretty bad here." He laughed, or thought about laughing. What came out was a soft hack followed by a groan. "It seems," he continued, "I've lost a few bits of myself along the way."

"But you're *alive*," Dee said, strongly, confidently. Almost a rebuke. Matthew marveled that the woman could have so much energy. She sounded so close. So close.

He reached his good hand toward the sound of her voice, started fingering the rubble.

"What are you doing?" Dee said, the slightest tinge of fear in her voice once more.

"Please," he begged, holding back sobs as he picked apart the pieces of glass and concrete that formed a barrier between them. "Please, Dee," he continued, "I think I'm going to die."

There was no further protest from her, no commands for him to cease and desist from his tunneling. So he went on. A lumpy chunk of brick tossed aside, the light tinkling of falling glass. He continued to pull away bits and pieces.

He paused, listening. He could hear that she was also digging now. She was helping! He almost wept with relief and doubled his efforts, the tunnel he'd created now deep enough for him to reach in up to his elbow. There was a light scratching from a few feet away, as if Dee were doing the same.

"Thank you, Dee, thank you," he said.

"I can't move much," she said, almost shyly. Again with that tone of apology.

"Can you reach your hand toward my voice?" he said, his arm now nearly fully extended toward her.

"Yes, I'm trying," she said.

And then, *then*, as his fingers burrowed, he could sense an opening. A whisper of cool air brushed his fingertips, and then he had her. His fingers touched hers and they twined, groped for each other like horny teenagers in the backseat of a borrowed car. *The coast is clear*, he thought of saying, and gripped her fingers so tightly he had to make sure not to hurt her.

Her hand was warm, and dry. Her skin felt like dust.

"Matthew," was all she said, as he sobbed and held her hand in a fevered grip.

"I'm dying, Dee," he repeated, and the contact, that connection with another living being, opened a dam inside him and released all the fear and anxiety he had been holding back. "There's a, a very large piece of concrete on top of me. It's on my back. I think my back is broken, and I can't feel my legs. I've bitten off a part of my tongue, and, please don't ask me how, I've managed to lose a finger. And now I'm bleeding pretty bad here, yeah... and I've pissed myself, Dee. I'm sorry but I have and I think maybe I shit myself. I can't feel anything but it's pressing on me and it's slowly crushing me to death."

"Matthew, please," she pleaded, begging him to silence. "Please, Matthew, please..." was all she said, until his words slowed, then stopped. He was so tired. So thirsty.

He wanted to die now. It was a horrible, empty feeling. He wanted to die.

"Matthew," her voice came, sharp once more. Her hand squeezed his own hard, causing him to wince despite everything. "You need to stop, you hear me? You need to correct your thinking."

Matthew, stunned at the scolding, like a slap in the face of someone hysterical, simply nodded in the darkness.

"I..."

"No," she said, her words bullets to his brain. "You *listen* now. You're going to get through this. You're going to live. You're going to be saved. Those are the words I want running through your head, you got that?"

Matthew nodded again.

"Say it."

Matthew thought for a moment, then mumbled, "I'm going to get through this. I'm going to live. I'm going to be saved."

"Good, good," Dee cooed. "You just hold my hand, and you remember those words. You keep them running through your head like a cool river, understand? A bright blue stream of positive thoughts running right through you, refreshing you from the inside, okay?"

"Yeah, Dee," he said, trying his best. *I'm going to get through this. I'm going to live. I'm going to be saved.*

He closed his eyes, imagined the words were soft water, running through him. He calmed, and, astonishingly, felt a little less thirsty.

"Dee?" he said, after a few minutes of silence. "Tell me something. Tell me about yourself."

Dee's fingers twitched within his, as if panicked, but then she gripped him tightly once more. "Okaaay," she said, drawing the word out with what sounded like an amused tone. "What do you want to know?"

"Well," he said, thinking. "What do you look like? How old are you? Do you have a family?"

She chuckled at his eagerness, and he smiled, relieved beyond measure. "Let's see. I'm thirty-seven. I'm married. I have a husband, Frank, and two kids. Ten and twelve. Margret is the older, and Betsy, who was named after my great-grandmother."

Matthew heard her stop, choking up a bit at the end. He didn't want to make her sad, but he wanted her to keep talking. *Needed* her to keep talking.

"And what do you look like?"

She chuckled again.

"I imagine right now I don't look like much of anything, I..." she stopped, as if distracted. There was a silence. Then, after a few more moments, she said, "I'm so scared."

He gripped her fingers. "Me too," he said quietly. Then, more loudly, playfully, "Now tell me what you look like."

"Okay, okay," she said. "I'm five-five, so I wear heels a lot to work. Don't like always looking up at people."

He choked a laugh, pressed her fingers to urge her on.

"I suppose most people think I'm pretty, but I'm very conservative. Frank and I don't go out much, homebodies, I guess. And now with the kids, forget it."

"And," he started, unsure how to continue, "you're okay? You're not... you're not hurt too badly?"

There was another pause. When she continued, it was not in answer to his question. It came out of her as if spoken from a trance. "I work on the second floor. I'm a paralegal with MacKenzie Douglas. When I left the house, Frank was getting the girls ready for school. He leaves later than I do for work. He's the day manager of RJ's Grill."

"Hey, I've been there," Matthew interjected, more to cut off Dee's eerie monotone than true enthusiasm. "I've eaten lunch there. You know, I probably met your husband, or at least saw him."

"Today I wore my favorite work dress. It's cauliflower blue with tiny white daisies. I think I've ruined it. Ruined..." And then Dee was quiet, as if she'd run out of things to say. Matthew waited for her to continue, but she said nothing.

"Dee? You okay?"

Her hand felt suddenly lifeless in his own, and he wondered with a small degree of alarm if she'd passed out. He wanted to tug at her fingers, pinch her, *shake her awake*. But he resisted those urges, simply held her still hand in his.

"I'm twenty-eight," he said, quietly. "I have black hair, blue eyes, pale skin. Too pale for California, I'm always told. But I was born here. A native. Right here in Burbank. Weird, right?"

Dee's fingers didn't respond and she said nothing.

"My wife's name is Diane. We have a two-year old son. Kelly. We named him after a friend of mine."

Dee hand remained still.

"He died in a car accident. I'd known him forever. We grew up together. He was going to move to New York, become a writer. He was so talented. I know he would have made it, you know? You can just tell with some people." He let the irony of his mistaken prescience slide away into the dark, ignored its withering tail. "Anyway, things happen. You can't control fate." He paused, gathered his thoughts. "I think we're going to die, Dee. I don't know how long we've been down here, but if feels like days, doesn't it? Probably not, but it's always so damned dark, and I've been going in and out a bit. I'm a little confused, to be honest."

Matthew stopped talking, released Dee's fingers.

He lay there, reciting the words Dee had given him. *I'm going to get through this. I'm going to live. I'm going to be saved.*

His damaged hand throbbed, trapped like a dying animal between his chest and the ground beneath. He let it throb. It was distant, no longer part of his body. He settled his head down again, thought about trying to sleep. Thought about his family.

Something large moved in the dark.

Matthew looked up and around, blind eyes jerking from point to point. "Dee?" he said, loudly. "Dee!"

She didn't respond.

He reached out his hand, found hers, groped her fingers, pressed them, tried to elicit a response. The sound came from below, a few feet from his head. It was not Dee he heard. It was something else. *How could something be moving beneath me? It's all rubble... it's impossible.*

He looked in the direction of the sound as it rose, squinting desperately to see something amongst the black. There! There, the air wavered. He left Dee's hand and reached toward it. A ripple in the air, something was coming through, right toward him. He reached for it, moaning with some mad hope, a grimace of desire on his face below wide dilated eyes.

Bright white light erupted from the ripple in the dark. Matthew screamed and withdrew his hand, the pain in his head like two ice picks rammed through his eyes. He slammed his eyelids shut, covered his face and moaned.

Somewhere, deep inside him, beyond the thick veil of pain, he realized. *My god, there's light. There is LIGHT. I'm saved. I'm saved, yes, they've found us!* He pawed at his eyes, not daring to open them but wanting so badly to see.

The blinding flash had set off an explosion of colors behind his eyelids, swirling rainbows and flickering pinpricks of hot white flashing amidst it all. He opened his eyes *oh so slightly.*

The area surrounding his trapped body had turned into the black cold of space. A field of stars dense as a glittering black blanket. Blazing specks of a billion bone-white lights flew toward him, eclipsed him. Colorful galaxies spun, pink, green and blue behemoths wallowing in their own ether. His mind expanded, cold and bright and impossibly vast, his jaw dropped in awe as the millions of worlds barraged his fragmented consciousness.

There was a tumultuous rumbling as his body shook and flailed like a rag doll caught in a meat grinder. A thousand miles away he heard Dee's voice calling to him, but his mind was bursting with kaleidoscopic colors. She was pleading for him to keep his eyes closed, to turn away, to hold her hand. He tried to look away. His head was on fire, his ears buzzed as if a thousand black flies had erupted inside his brain, whispering comforting instructions he could not resist. *Look*, they said, their voices a mountain of flickering, buzzing wings, countless eyes, twitching, spindly legs. *You are saved, Matthew. Just LOOK AT US.*

He moaned and reluctantly, slowly, turned his head to stare directly into the eternal light. He stretched open his mouth and watering eyes as widely as he could, welcoming the abyss of death as it flooded into him like a thick black river, filling him with sparkling white-hot worlds, bursting and snapping into fire like synapses, a god's mind absorbing him from the inside out.

7

THE GREEN TURTLE nightlight appeared to be crawling up the wall. Betsy watched it, waiting for it to move one of its flippers, to inch its glowing body away from the power socket where it was fastened by steel and electricity.

She looked across the room at Margret, who was asleep, breathing easily. She fought the urge to slink out of bed, run to her parent's room, crawl between them, safe and warm. But they weren't home yet. They were out, and she could never sleep when they were out at bedtime.

Betsy sighed. Her eyes left the turtle, trailed along the wall to the open closet and the black chasm within. She swore she heard noises from deep within that dark abyss, scratches and grunting. Something coming.

She shuddered, flopped over, tried to close her eyes and escape the world through sleep.

The bedroom door opened, light spilled across her face. She looked up, saw her mother silhouetted against the pale yellow glow of the hallway.

"Mom," she said, and held out her hands toward the shadow. "Come here, I need a hug."

Her mother moved to the bed, sat down and embraced her. Betsy breathed in her mother's warmth, caressed her hand against the fabric of her scratchy black dress.

"How..." she started, but her mother shushed her, released her from her hug. She started again, whispering now. "How was the party?"

"It was fine," her mother said, her face a dark void. The yellow light glowing behind her made her look like the angels Betsy had seen on posters at Sunday School. She said so, and her mother chuckled, kissed her forehead.

215

"It's time for you to go to sleep now," she said, caressing Betsy's hair.

Frank came to stand in the doorway. His body was a bright white light, illuminating the entire room.

"Time to sleep now," he said, too loudly.

Across the room, Margret woke, sat up. She looked at her dad groggily, rubbed her eyes.

Betsy blinked, then pushed away her mother's hand.

"What happens to us when we die?" she asked, looking skyward.

"Worms," her mother said. "The worms crawl in, the worms crawl out," she said, singsong. Like a nursery rhyme, something from an old book of fables long gone to dust, only remembered by ancient gods and men of magic.

Her mother brought her hand to Betsy's face once more, but it was not a hand. Never was. It was slick and black and tapered to a pointed end. It pressed into her forehead, then slid across her face, leaving a searing mark, and pushed into her mouth, gagging her.

"I love you," her mother said.

Margret yelled "Stop!" and jumped from her bed. She ran toward the bright light of her father, but her mother was too fast. Another limb shot out, ripping the fabric of her party dress. It shot impossibly across the room and speared the girl in the stomach, nailed her to the ground.

The girls wiggled, then belched what was inside them. Their mother stood and waited while their souls tore apart, in slow increments, *it was always slower in the young,* and separated.

"There are a million ways to suffer," Dee said.

The room was suddenly too small and so it expanded, and their mother with it, swallowing the light. Frank blistered and became a star. The thing's onyx trunk of a throat worked hard to take it all in, to swallow it all down, until it shone most brightly in the expanse, until it became the sky. A creator.

8

MATTHEW JOLTED AWAKE. His eyes were crusted closed, his ears ringing, canceling any sound from the outside world. He listened to the constant soundtrack of his time in the dark: the blood flowing through his body, the pulsing throb in his temple, the discordant thuds of his pissed-off heart.

An odd verse sprang unbidden to his mind. A prayer he had no memory of learning.

Blood will let blood, on my lips, on my tongue. The spark inside me is yours, the lift of my soul, that energy, yours to feast upon. My flesh is yours. I am without hope. I am without love. My humanity has been stripped from me and hangs in tatters before you, ready to accept your gift, my sacrifice. Your paradise awaits me, because all I am is gone.

He opened his eyes to slits, careful to keep his head down.

A tiny, soft hand patted his brow. "Da-da," his son's voice said. "Da-da, love you."

Tears sprang from Matthew's eyes, but he did not move. Did not dare to. His nose, though broken and clogged with cartilage and dried blood, could still catch the faintest trace of his son's smell. Baby powder and purity. Matthew wanted more than anything to bury his face in the child's soft hair, hear him laugh one last time.

The tiny soft hand rubbed Matthew's head absently while he wept and wished. When he could stand it no longer, he reached his fingers outward, hoping to touch his baby boy one last time.

There was nothing, nothing but the emptiness.

Matthew breathed in harshly, sucking large gulps of air, trying to right his mind. *The digging. The light.* He raised his chin, the effort causing his head to tremor, his neck to stiffen. He looked where the light had burst through the dark.

He heard more digging. Urgent, rhythmic. Desperate. Someone, or something, was pushing through the debris a few yards away. "Hello!" he yelled, his voice slurred wet gravel. He waved a hand in the dark. "Hello! I'm here! I'm here!"

There was no sound of rescue, no movement. Desperate for reassurance, he turned his strained neck to look toward the area where Dee lay. He reached out his hand, and after a few brief moments of scrambling panic, he found her own, still warm. "Dee! I think, maybe, we've been found." He waited, but was met by silence. "Dee?"

Then, "Yes, Matthew. I hear you, I'm sorry, I hear you."

Matthew was so relieved he nearly sobbed again, but kept himself together, kept himself hoping. "Did you see the light? Did you hear?"

There was a pause, and then Dee spoke. "I heard it."

Matthew was very still, clutched furiously to Dee's fingers. Something was tugging insistently on his exposed foot, but he felt no pain, so he ignored it.

His shirt was soggy with blood. He rolled his body, tried to slowly release his injured hand. He could feel it squelching beneath his stomach, as if he were lying face-down in a puddle in the middle of a muddy, beaten road. "Dee? Do you think they've come for us?"

"How is that possible, Matthew?" she said, her voice toneless. "You're not thinking clearly." He heard a rustling. "Here, boy. Don't let go of my hand now. It's coming to get you."

Matthew gripped her hand greedily. "Dee, we'll be saved soon. C'mon, I believe now. You should be thrilled. I believe." He waited for a chuckle, or a chiding. He received neither. He swallowed. "They must be digging toward us. Yes, yes. They're coming."

The movement seemed to come from all around. Something was tunneling through the spilled guts of the building, straight toward them. Matthew laid his ear to the vibrating concrete. In the pitch black of his world, Matthew heard *something* break through the rubble just in front of him, palm-slapping sounds smacked the ground, glass broke and iron twisted with a high-pitched groan. There was a shifting sound as the thing filled the space directly before him.

Matthew pulled his hand away from Dee and reached for what had come. His hand plunged deep into a writhing, jelly-like substance, which immediately shot up his arm and sprayed itself onto his face. He gasped and felt something wiggle down his throat.

He gagged, clawed at his lips, but felt nothing. He threw up, the stinging tang of vomit somehow bracing him.

There was an upward swell, and although he felt no pain it seemed as if his eyes were melting down his face, cold and slick. He felt his body lift then spin in a barrel-roll to one side, although he knew, somewhere in his subconscious mind, he had not physically moved. It was dizzying and he clawed at the chunks of destruction around him for purchase. But the pieces of the structure were gone, the whole of the physical world had fallen away. A blast of warm stale air gusted upward.

Was he falling? No, that familiar, constant pain was still in his back, a part of him now. *Would I miss it, my murdering lover?* he thought. But it wasn't gone. It was there. Solid and heavy. He was still trapped, but there was a gulf beneath him now, a space wider than a canyon blown open where there should be bricks and glass and dirt. A giant's dark heart beat somewhere in the abyss and he found himself staring down into it, searching. There was a flare of color, and another, erupting from the sides of his vision. The world came into focus.

There were trees, sweating slime-covered smooth black monsters that rose a thousand feet into the air, reaching for him, their sappy perspiration running freely down their sides, tracing through faint veins of stone-hard bark, splashing into a snake's nest of gray roots. They plunged upward from an impossible distance, their bases surrounded by a fetid swamp that went as far as he could see, a black horizon. The sky was pale and dead, but he knew that it was eternal, like space. An eternal emptiness. Home.

"IT'S A LETTER," his grandfather said, dropping the thick envelope on his bed.

He left and Matthew swiveled away from his desk, watched the door close. He walked to his neatly made bed, studied the envelope; it was dingy brown, soiled, old-looking. The handwriting on it was scrawled in an imprecise manner, jagged and spearing, peaks and valleys of black ink thin as an old man's hair. There were stamps, bearing language and currency symbols he did not recognize, slapped across its surface.

He picked it up, studied the front. It bore no return address, no name of sender. Turning it over he saw the envelope had been previously used. It was frayed and torn, spotted with something dark. Dreary tape held the flap closed, as dingy and browned as if its contents had been sealed for hundreds of years.

He ripped it open, pulled out two hand-written pages of scribble. Many of the words were hard to make out, but once he got a feel for the author's form, the words cleared, came into focus:

I WRITE THIS in the hopes of finding you well.
This night is a terrible night, one that will be remembered only for its

misery. Nothing of consequence has taken place and nothing of note has been accomplished. The price I ask for living is a harmonious sequence of knowledge that turns the wheels of the clock to tomorrow, diversion that makes daytime turn to night and allows me once more to close my eyes on the world which has deceived me until such time as I am forced to open them.

War is rampant and civilization is holding firm on sandy beaches of past moralities as wave upon wave of hatred, corruption and bloodshed splash against the shore. I fear I don't know of anything but what is before my very eyes. The people I think I love are deceivers, those who follow me whisper corruption behind my back and friends are true only as it suits them. I've lost the willpower to pick myself up time after time, exhausted from being knocked down by indifference, selfishness and lack of honor. We chase gods and act like children. It's pathetic.

Old friends are shadowy memories, ghosts that talk to me in the night and conjure distorted images of the way things once were. The way things could have, should have, been. They exist as passersby, breathing shallow confidence of the boy's life, of the boy's happiness. I tell them to fuck away, to leave the past buried. But it returns in my sleep. It haunts me.

I believe that love is a bauble held only by poets. It exists only in words, on paper, in songs and through acting of all kinds including the most devious. It doesn't exist any more than hope, trust, conviction, honesty or faith. Lost ideals of a racist generation, mistaken concepts taken to heart by the weak and overly sensitive, tossed aside by the strong, the survivors, the leaders. Strength lies in appearance. Appearance of person, of religion, of stature, of wealth. Gone are souls intertwining, coupling energy. Gone is romantic ambush.

We are ravaged. We are followed. We are dying.

I write you because there is no one else to write and I'm alone with these thoughts. It is haunting.

I write you though I know you won't understand it any more than the rest, any more than I. I know you don't want it. I put my heart into words because I have not the strength to put it back into the world. I'm weak. I'm a coward. I'm ashamed of myself and everything around me.

Do with my thoughts what you will, what you want. Send my prayers back to the Christian God.

No one is left to wonder what will become of us when we're gone. Not you I, nor I you. I wonder if it would help if I told you I missed you.

Okay then, I miss you.

I miss you like I would miss a pleasant daydream I cannot fully remember. Was there sunshine? Was I happy?

You are just that to me. A wonderful idea I had upon waking. An idea, I will realize fully once aware, best left to a dream.

What we follow will surface and you will know all truth. It is what we seek, what we have given everything to seek. And now we have failed, and that means nothing to you. But know that our failure is complete, with you and with the chase.

You will never hear from me again. That is my gift. That, my son, is love.

MATTHEW READ IT twice, then burned the pages in the fireplace. His grandfather never spoke of it. Matthew never forgot the words, the decipherability of which a task he ignored.

Within the year his grandfather told him of his parents' death. His parents who were not. His parents who lived a haunted life, who haunted his own.

THIS CITY IS a fairy tale. This city is a skeleton, chipped away and faded to gray.

Matthew knew he would never stop falling *fallingfallingfallingfalling falling* through the abyss. He did not know how long he'd been asleep. His consciousness was frayed, slippery. *Dying,* he thought.

Dying now. Dying.

"No... uh, no..." he stammered, shaking his head, seeking will, seeking a spark. "Dee!" he yelled out, panic boiling inside him, the last torn threads of panic that comes with death. "Dee... Dee, please..."

He heard her murmur, he heard her trying to dig through the rubble to find him, she was looking for him and her mouth was making a clicking sound that infected his thoughts with a fear so deep that he thought his heart would burst, his brain melt into syrup and drain away through his nose and ears.

"DAMN IT, ANSWER ME!"

And like that, it was all gone. The sounds of scraping, of something approaching him in the dark, of the visions of the morose landscape and empty sky. All gone.

Just black.

He touched his eyes with his fingers and felt their *I'mreal* solidity. He exhaled rattily, grateful for his broken nose because the smell of him was becoming rotten, and he was glad not to fully inhale the stench.

He reached, tentatively, for Dee's hand once more, if for no other reason than to prove he could return to sanity, and to a world – albeit painful – that was *real*.

"I'd leave her alone, boy-o. You want nothing to do with that, believe me."

The voice sounded inches away. Matthew jerked his head around, wide-eyed, and stared at the blank expanse. "Who's there?"

A hand rested on his shoulder. "Who do you think? That hot receptionist?" A pause, a frown in the dark. "Nah, she's... well, she's elsewhere. And trust me, she's not so hot anymore."

Matthew's mind spun. He rotated his shoulder as best he could and reached his hand slowly toward the sound of the voice. He touched flesh. A face, an unshaven cheek. He felt the cheek muscle flex – the face was smiling.

"Don't get fresh."

Matthew smiled, then laughed. He knew the voice now, somehow could see the features of its face through his fingertips. "Kelly?"

"You are in a bad spot, my friend," Kelly said, his hand caressing Matthew's shoulder, then moving inexplicably to his side, where he was poking. He lifted the sport coat, slid his hand beneath, began feeling Matthew's side through his dress shirt. He pinched his flesh.

"Ow," Matthew said, chuckling. "Jesus, dude."

"Sorry," Kelly said, but he kept pinching, more lightly now.

Matthew's mind quieted, it was so very dark, but he thought he could, just barely, make out Kelly's features. His skin had a slight glow to it. A silvery luminescence that reflected, repelled the dark. He *was* smiling, Matthew saw, and rested his fingertips on Kelly's face.

"God, I miss you, man," he said, tears falling from his eyes. "I really miss you."

Kelly grabbed Matthew's hand *but his hand is under your coat* and squeezed it. He leaned his head closer to Matthew's, their foreheads almost touching. He smiled, and then whispered, as if it were a secret between them, as if he were avoiding a thousand nearby ears, straining to overhear them.

"I can get you out of here, Matthew," Kelly said, his eyes bright and alive with mischievous joy. "I can *save* you."

Matthew shifted, brushed something away from his face, focused on Kelly's eyes. "How?"

Kelly smiled more broadly, laughing with secret knowledge. "Do you want to come with me? I'm only going to ask once."

Matthew's smile faltered. Reason, or sanity, tried to break through the thick webbing that had spun itself around his mind. *Kelly is dead,* he said to himself, but the words carried no weight, no practical application.

"Am I dead?" he said, genuinely curious. "Are you a ghost? A shadow of memory?"

Kelly laughed mirthlessly. "No, man!" He gave Matthew a side-long glance. "You know, you're acting a little weird."

"Yeah, well," Matthew said, rubbing his swollen, stubby tongue with his fingers. "It's been a rough week."

Kelly laughed again, sounding just like he did in the old days. Matthew wanted it to *be* the old days. He wanted to be back in college, sorting through their clothes in the communal laundry room, heading out to a party at an off-campus apartment they'd heard about through a friend or a neon-colored flyer.

"I'm married now," Matthew said, realizing his dead friend probably wasn't aware.

"I know," Kelly said, "and I'm happy for you. I always knew you and Diane were going to go the distance."

Matthew waited, debating how much Kelly would want to know about his life. His mind drifted to his family. He tried to remember them. Diane. Little Kelly, the baby. His child. *They're lost,* he thought. He drifted, his scalp tingling. White spots beat against his eyes like falling stars crashing silently by the hundreds, thousands... blinding light.

Kelly pinched him again – harder this time - and it brought him back.

"I have a son" he said, trying to swallow, his throat too swollen, too dry. "We named him after you. I think I'm dying, buddy. I feel like glass. Like really thin glass..."

Kelly's smile faltered. He caressed the side of Matthew's face.

"They're all with me now, Matthew," he said quietly, his eyes wide and watery as black lakes. "I can take you to them."

Matthew's mind began to buzz loudly, his skin began to itch, his blood cold as ice. He thought the thumping of his heart was slowing down, an erratic drum beating his blood out and away into the sacrificial earth, which drank greedily.

"Your mom and dad, they're here, too." Kelly shuffled closer. "They want to meet you. They're really sorry, Matthew, and they said they love you. How great is that?"

Matthew couldn't process, he tried to understand but nothing was coming to the surface. "You can save me," was all he could think to say, his eyes leaking.

Kelly nodded. "Say the word, Matthew. Say the word and I'll take you away from all this. I'll bring you to Diane, to your son, your folks." He paused. "I'm there too, bud. I'm there, too. God, even Stanley is there."

"That old man?" Matthew said, and they both laughed. Laughed like they had as kids, when they'd lain in a backyard tent and talked all night, trading handheld video games, looking at comic books with flashlights. *Carefree,* Matthew thought. *Nothing in the world but us. It was heaven.*

Kelly broke through his memories. "They're coming, Matthew. We're almost out of time."

Matthew was startled, shaken by the urgency in Kelly's voice. He barely noticed that Kelly had slid a heavy hand beneath his shirt, was burrowing into his belly with wiggling fingers. "Who... who's coming?" he asked.

Dee. *What about Dee?* he thought, but didn't know if Kelly could save her. "There's a woman here..." he said.

Kelly's face fell. He heard movement from where Dee lay. A wild, scrambling sound, like she was suddenly fighting through the rubble to reach him. Matthew debated reaching out for her.

"Matthew," Kelly hissed.

Dee was speaking, saying something in haughty, choked sounds, a language Matthew did not recognize. He heard her grunting, cursing, writhing. She was breaking through.

Matthew turned away, reached out and found Kelly's warm hand waiting for him.

Something heavy crawled up his legs. He shifted his weight, tried to turn and see, but he'd lost control of his muscles, and could only lie there, flipping his head side to side. "What the fuck is that!" he screamed, bile surging to his throat.

"Relax, relax," Kelly said, caressing his head. "It's your son. It's little Kelly. He's here." Kelly looked down where Matthew could not see, where it felt like a hundred small hands were pawing at his legs and back, reaching for him, tugging at him incessantly. A thousand desperate fingers ripping him away.

"He wants to be with you," Kelly said. "It's really quite adorable."

Matthew smiled at this, relieved. His *son*. He was here. Little Kelly was here. A miracle.

Kelly moved his face closer, tilting Matthew's chin to look at him. Matthew looked.

"Kelly?" Matthew croaked, his head flat against the concrete block that served as his death-bed pillow.

Kelly's eyes were bursting supernovas.

Something long, cold and wet slithered around Matthew's neck and squeezed, the tail of the thing flicking against his dry lips and crusted facial hair.

"Yeah, buddy?" the thing called Kelly said, his face exploding into light.

The hands raced across his body, patting him, pinching him, slipping inside his clothes to reach flesh. His throat was being squeezed more and more tightly. A second cold scaly tendril slid down his collar and moved across his chest like wet midnight. His guts were a flurry of movement, a voracious bubbling dance of tiny bodies fighting to be inside him. He wanted to reach for Dee's hand one last time, devoured by an incredible regret that he could not help her. But his hand would not move, the control of his body snipped from the commands of his mind as neatly as a cut string. "Kelly," he breathed, followed by a drooled trickle of ashen blood.

"Save me."

9

JIM WAS THE first one to see the hand.

The search dogs had been barking like it was the end of the world, but the team knew at this point they weren't looking for survivors. They were looking for bodies. Still, it was important to keep protocol and not rush things. No point in anyone getting hurt trying to free a corpse. *That, and if anyone was still breathing in all that mess,* Jim thought, dropping his cigarette as he watched the crane wheel into position, its bent metal arm swinging a hook the size of a small child, *they'd likely prefer it the other way 'round.*

The engineers had found an especially ugly slab of concrete – a structural pillar, one of them had announced with a grimace – lying atop a pile of what used to be a small office building. The building had stood two doors down from the bank Jim went to when cashing his checks on a Friday. He'd walked by the building at least once a week for the last three years and never took notice of it, not until it was reduced to a pile of ruins by the second-worst earthquake in California history.

Thousands dead, all across Los Angeles and the Valley region. Highways had twisted and collapsed, buildings fallen in on themselves, explosions, fires, death everywhere. Jim and his team had been told to focus on assisting Burbank Police and Fire with the clearing and salvaging, and they'd been doing it around the clock going on almost four days straight. Jim hadn't seen his family in all that time, sleeping on work sites, the giant sulfur work lights replacing the moon outside the smeared windows of run-down construction trailers. The purr of diesel generators were a constant white noise that had an effect similar to ocean waves when you were tired enough, at least that's what he told himself.

The dogs, however, did not get much chance to sleep.

They were walked in four teams of six-hour shifts, around the clock, twenty-four hours a day, trained to sniff out flesh, bark when they sensed a body. They barked plenty.

Over the last few days, Jim's team had found a total of thirty-seven souls at six separate sites. Of those thirty-seven, Jim figured around ten would live to see their next birthday. And half of those would be forever disfigured, a few horribly so. That's what was under all this destruction, all the crushing weight of concrete versus flesh and bone, the remains of a lost battle in which the frail bodies of man stood no chance.

When the dogs began their morbid barking, Jim had been smoking and studying the pink and blue peaks of the Verdugo mountains, praying for a night of quiet as the red sun blazed in the west. But damn them, they had called for him again. *Didn't even get to Amen,* he'd thought sourly.

Jim walked over as the engineer grappled the giant crane's hook to the eye nut and cable they'd so gingerly drilled into the slab. The men all stood back and the dogs snarled and Jim yelled for them to be pulled back. The hoist creaked as the chain ratcheted slowly upward, servos straining against the immense weight. The slab lifted, and the first thing Jim noticed is that it wasn't a flat slab, or a pillar, but a bearing pad with three feet of column still hinged to it. No, it wasn't flat under there at all. It had a fat projecting middle, which greatly decreased the odds for whoever was down there rather significantly.

Jim stepped forward first, as was protocol.

That's when he saw the hand, followed by the man it was attached to. Based on where that man's body lay, the protrusion of the concrete pad must have been settled quite neatly into the square of his back.

Likely crushed him on impact, Jim thought, and spat.

"MEDICS IN NOW! Swing that slab, Tom," he yelled, pointing at the large chunk of concrete hovering over their heads. "Swing it the fuck out of here." When it was safely rotated away from the rescue crew, Jim took two steps closer to look at the man's body, and knew he was long gone.

As the medics ran up behind him, Jim studied the surrounding debris and saw a flash of something else.

"We got two of 'em," he barked, yelling for the ambulance to drive up. One of the men asked if he'd need two ambulances, and Jim shook his head. He looked back toward the site, where the medics were rushing up the side of a wall of debris to inspect the man.

"There's a dress," he yelled at them. "A blue dress, right there. You see?"

One of the medics nodded and Jim turned, not wanting to see this part, his job done for now.

Two women in yellow jumpsuits ran by carrying a long wooden backboard painted bright yellow but stained and scuffed with blood and death.

More goddamn corpses, he thought, sad and tired. How many more days, he wondered, how many more hands would he see lifting themselves from the twisted skeleton of their newly broken world?

He turned to stare once more at the jagged, pastel-stained peaks and grimaced, hating their solidity.

MATTHEW'S FIRST SENSATION when being pulled back to consciousness was that the horrible weight on his back was gone. The second thing he noticed was the *noise*.

Was that... dogs? he wondered, somewhere in the soft fuzzy nowhere of his working mind. *And machines?*

Then: *VOICES!*

Matthew felt the sun's warmth on his face, and his eyelids glowed so fiercely he was terrified to open them, fearing the severity of the open sky would blind him forever. Then, as if by some miracle he was too far gone to fully appreciate, there was someone there, squatting next to him, talking to him, asking him questions.

Matthew didn't open his eyes, but he turned his head toward the voice. He opened his mouth and tried to say that *Yes*, he could hear them, and *Yes*, he was very much able to acknowledge that he was alive, if they could only help him up and perhaps get him some water.

Oh, and for the record, he thought numbly, *I'm, uh, pretty badly hurt*. He wasn't sure how bad, but it was *bad*, and he preferred not to dwell on it. He also wanted to apologize for the vomit and shit and piss and blood that had been spat from his body in different ways, at different times.

What came from his mouth was more of a groan, and a breathy hiss.

"Jesus Christ, this guy's alive!" a man yelled, a young man's voice. He sounded thrilled, and Matthew felt so good that hear that he was truly alive. *Hallelujah, boy-o!*

"Listen, mister, we're gonna get you help, okay?"

Matthew heard another voice, this one from a little further away, as if he were standing over his body, looking down at him.

"Gary, his foot! Christ."

There was a scramble of activity. Cases were being unclasped and something pinched into the inside of his arm. Hands were on him now, and he could hear the snipping sounds of his suit being cut off his body.

"Hey sir, my name is Gary, and I'm here to help you," the young man said, his voice breathless and excited. "We've given you an IV which will get you fluid, okay?"

The voice was so assured, so positive, Matthew felt instantly better, safer. He wished he could have nodded in agreement, but that didn't seem possible at the moment.

"Now listen close, okay sir? We're gonna roll you onto your back. Just to be safe, we're gonna do it nice and slow. We don't want to move you too much but we've got to get you onto the board so we can carry you, all right? Does that sound okay to you?"

Matthew said nothing but did open his eyes. The light was very bright, and it did hurt, but it wasn't so bad. He could make out shapes, blurry legs and a blue sky.

"There you are. Stay with me, okay? Stay with me. You're gonna be fine. We're gonna roll you... Bob, you ready? Yeah? Okay, we're gonna roll you now. Just let us do everything, you lie still and try to relax."

Gary felt his body roll, and the relief was trumped only by the intense pain. He opened his mouth to scream, but could only gag.

"You're shittin' me," the second man said, and Matthew wondered what he was so upset about.

"Uh, okay, Jenny, strap him down, yeah? Uh, okay, let's cut the rest of this off."

Matthew thought he heard someone gagging.

"Jenny, stay with me. Carla, you got this? Okay, let her go. We'll do it. Someone get that fucking thing off him."

Matthew felt something lifted off his skin, and a soft thump from where it must have been thrown. He wondered what it was. *My wallet?* he thought, then forgot about it as a mask was placed over his nose and mouth, and clean fresh oxygen was pumped into his lungs.

"Gary..."

"I know! Keep it together. We've got to bandage this. And the foot. Christ."

Matthew opened his eyes, looked around. He could see better now. He saw the young man's face bent over him, staring at his now very naked body.

The young man was wearing a white shirt and pants. *Like an angel.*

He looked right at Matthew, met his eyes, smiled. His eyes were brown and wide. He had a crew-cut and he looked young and strong, clean and whole.

"You're awake, that's great," Gary said. "We're just gonna bandage up some areas where you're, uh, bleeding. Looks like you've been through hell, my man. But we got you now."

Lying on the smooth, hard board, Matthew felt layers of bandages going firmly around his midsection, a cold pack of something resting on top of his stomach. Someone bound up his hand and was now wrapping down by his foot.

"What am I wrapping here..." the second man said.

"Just do it, he's awake."

Gary turned and looked into Matthew's eyes.

"We got you now, we got you. We're gonna get you to a hospital and they'll fix you right up."

Matthew nodded, feeling a little strength returning to him with the sun on his skin and the IV doing its work. He could *feel* the fluid racing to all points inside him, cleansing him, filling him with vital moisture.

After a few more moments, they strapped him firmly to the board. He was wrapped like a mummy in blankets, but felt a chill run through him despite the warmth.

"Okay, here we go, sir. On three, guys. Yeah? One, two..." and then Matthew was lifted into the air. They were taking him away. He was saved.

As they walked him carefully down the hill of broken concrete, Matthew had a moment to reflect on his last hours buried in the dark. There was something nagging him, something he was forgetting.

Dee.

Matthew's eyes sprang open, and Gary noticed right away. Matthew searched left to right, almost in a panic. He saw the other medics, and they looked back at him with sickening glances, as if he were too horrible, too monstrous for them to look at for more than a second. He turned back to Gary, tried to move his good hand but was strapped down. He tried to talk, but the mask was in the way. He began to convulse, shaking his body, pleading at Gary with his eyes.

"Hold on, damn it," Gary said, but looked at Matthew calmly, with the patience and fortitude of a saint. "What is it?"

Matthew pointed with one finger, and Gary turned to look.

Someone said, "The woman."

Gary looked back to where Matthew was pointing. Matthew used his new-found strength to lift his head and see the spot where he had lain dying. With Gary turned, he had a clear view of three other rescue workers lifting a frail woman from the rubble.

Her head, Matthew saw, was caved inward. Almost flattened. The way her legs hung he knew they were shattered. The cornflower blue dress that clung stickily to her body was entirely saturated with blood. One of the workers tried for a better grip and her head lilted backward limply, and he saw what was left of her face as long black hair fell downward off her sagging skull, the neck nothing but stripped muscles as the head rolled and dangled in an impossible position.

Then Gary stepped back in front of Matthew, blocking his vision. "You can't help her, sir. She's been gone a while. I'm sorry."

Matthew settled back and let his eyes travel to Gary's face. His mind went numb.

He tried to find answers in the faces of the medics, but they were looking away from him, toward the oncoming ambulance he heard backing toward them, a steady beeping alarm coming as it moved closer.

Gary was talking to another medic who had just approached, and they were using hushed tones so Matthew couldn't hear what they were saying.

While the two medics exchanged notes, a tall, haggard man walked into Matthew's field of vision. He looked directly at Matthew, expressionless, then nodded. He patted him on the shoulder. "Atta boy. It's all over, you hear? You take care now. You take care."

And then the tall man turned away.

As Matthew waited to be loaded into the ambulance, he lifted his head once more, trying to see the ruined building that had been his prison.

Standing at the foot of the board, just past his feet, was Diane. Her face was just visible over the shoulder of one of the medics helping to carry him. She was holding a wrapped bundle in her arms. He saw gray skin, a sagging weight dangling from her. She was smiling.

Matthew wanted to smile back, but as his brain started to kick into higher gears, and reality infiltrated his senses, his desire to smile fell away, replaced with something close to dread.

Why was she here? Was she a hallucination?

None of them are real. Kelly was dead. Diane was... Diane was...

Sullen, he forced himself to stop thinking. He wished he could hold Dee's hand again, but knew that was impossible. *That hand wasn't warm at all, was it boy-o?*

He let his head rest back against the board, and the voices surrounding him faded away, the world slipping into a cone of muffled quiet. A firm, cold hand rested on his forehead, and he knew it was his dead friend back to save him. His guide.

Matthew closed his eyes, breathed in the fresh oxygen, his brain sparking to higher plateaus of life with every inhalation.

It's not real.

Breathe.

Nothing is real.

You're badly hurt.

Everything is going to be alright.

Just breathe.

Something clicked loudly deep inside his brain, like a metal switch being flipped. His ears flooded with a rushing sound, as if he had been plunged underwater.

He forced his eyes open. The medics were gone. Diane was gone. He was no longer being carried toward the waiting ambulance. As he breathed into the mask, the sound of his pumping heart throbbing in his ears, he focused his eyes upward.

Impossibly long, spiraling black serpents filled an endless pale white sky, a massive host of creatures, a writhing plague corroding every inch of the expanse.

Shuddering, panicked, he pinched his eyes closed. His breathing quickened, his heart raced. Both eyes spilled a rush of tears, as if he had looked directly into the sun. *But there was no sun. No clouds. Just that pale sky and the beasts...*

After a few moments, his heartbeat slowed, his breathing steadied. His body felt light, so light. He waited, then heard the lapping of dark waves as they slapped rhythmically against the sticky bark of impossibly tall trees.

Did my parents really say they loved me?

And, one last wish, if his wife and son was truly there, he hoped, against all hope, that his boy could meet his namesake. Or perhaps that was just a sweet fragile dream, like everything else in this shattered world.

He felt movement. Heard muffled, faraway screams. He shook his head, clenched his good hand into a fist of prayer.

He prayed that when he once more dared open his eyes, the sky above him would be blue.

DEATH,
MY OLD FRIEND

I won't lie to you. It's strange growing up with Death as your best mate. Lots of explaining to do, hard to keep friends and all that. Tough all around, I'd say. One exception. No bullies. Free and clear are the close friends of Death. No one wants to be on his bad side, do they?

Still, wasn't all fun and games. I mean, he had a job to do and he did it with vigor and more than a little relish. In school – the both of us just wee and still figuring out the what's and who's of life – we'd sit beside each other in the classroom, as usual the last row, desks parallel, trainers kicking air.

"Took Mrs. Haberdash last night," he'd say, whispering it to me so Mr. Blackburn wouldn't hear it over his lecture on the highlights of the Peloponnesian War. "Heart disease, you know," he'd say, and I'd just nod and look forward, staring hard at the blurry saturated image of ancient Greece the projector had splattered over the room's white concrete wall. "She was nice, eh?" he said lamely, quietly, as if to himself. "I mean, never a bad word."

Mrs. Haberdash was piano tutor to both myself and Death, along with many other kids whose parents were keen on promoting the finer arts in their dullard children. I'd gotten no further than "Chopsticks" before quitting, spending the time I was supposed to be in Haberdash's parlor exploring the creek out by Westford Park for minnows and tadpoles. I had dreams of a frog farm then.

But Death always enjoyed the lessons, said they "rounded him out," for whatever that's worth. He'd brag about his knowledge of Chopin and Bach, how he'd all but mastered "Moonlight Sonata."

"So then why'd you kill her?" I asked, not for the first time. It was a question that tended to rise whenever a similar set of circumstances presented themselves.

The conversation had leaked on into break. We were on the swings by then, shooting skyward parallel to one another, stomachs lurching on the backswing, feet thrusting forward on the return, trying, without making a show of it, to stay in rhythm.

"I didn't kill her, dolt," he returned, focused on propelling himself upward, shooting toward the sky, kicking his heels at the clouds, then bending the knees sharp, dropping away. "I don't kill anyone, you know that. Don't make a fuss. Is what it is, init?"

I nodded, felt bad for vexing him. We all had our tasks. We were all just getting along. My folks, for instance, wanted me to be an athlete. Pushed me to sports every chance they could get, but it never took, primarily because I was small and weak and uncoordinated. Poor hand-to-eye contact and all that. Tried joining a couple teams after grammar school, never caught on with it. Lot of hassle over similar games you could play in the park with mates you liked versus the assholes they teamed you with at school. Still, wanted to succeed for mum and da. Failed, of course, but A+ for effort.

Death tried football but quit when a kid died during a match. Just dropped mid-field from an aneurysm. Fate, of course, everyone knew it. But Death was still there, on the pitch, in the forward position actually, and had to go over there and send the boy's soul on his way, right in front of his teammates and a bandstand full of onlookers. Not a pleasant task. Most of the opposing fans were jeering as it was their player. Parents crying, of course.

Death quit the team after that, told me it was for the best as the fellas tended to pace themselves during practice and warm-ups, keeper even taking on a helmet. Coach said it was affecting the intensity, overall effort was waning, etc. So Death acquiesced and bowed off but was distraught, to tell the truth.

What folks don't understand is that Death doesn't *cause* the inevitable, he simply handles the transaction, dresses it up, like. He manages, how do you say, the exchange, as it were, between this life and the next. His proximity to the killing itself has nothing at all to do with it. Hell, I'd had multiple sleepovers with the bloke, and I'm still right as rain. We even shared a cigarette once. Talk about tempting fate!

At least, that's what I thought at the time.

Still, he made folks edgy and no lie. He was good about it for the most part, only at certain times becoming vexed, irritated or, on more than one occasion, severely depressed by the stigma which surrounded him. But we all had our problems at that age, teenage years being what they are, so his issues were no more dramatic than my own or anyone else's. At least he knew what he was going to be when he grew up. Advantage, that.

For the most part, Death and I got along famously. We hit speed bumps, like most best friends will, but all-in-all we were great mates. Highs and lows, sure, but I was always there for him if needed and, to the best of his ability, he was always there for me.

Our biggest fight stemmed from what you could call a misunderstanding. It was our junior year of high school, and I had a major World History test the following day, first period. It was late at night and I was fast asleep, having gone to bed later than I'd wanted because of a rugby match on television I just had to watch the end of (good guys lost, btw). Anyway, it was late, and I was brought awake from what I guess was a nasty nightmare, or maybe I just heard him sneaking about. Impossible to say.

But when I woke up he was standing near the foot of my bed, heading toward an open window. We kept them open all that autumn because of the late heat, and mum and da couldn't afford air, so windows and fans it was on those hot nights. When I saw him, I didn't know what to do, what to say. Yeah, we were best mates, but we certainly didn't sneak around the other's room at night. Don't get that idea.

So it was startling, to say the least. "Hey!" I said to him, whispering loudly as I could, not wanting to wake the folks. "What are you about?"

He froze, didn't look at me at first, just stared at that open window, like he was gonna will himself through it without having to take another step. Finally, he did turn, his face caught the moonlight, and I could see he was shaken up. "I'm sorry, John," was all he said, then he took three quick steps and slid out the window easy as pie.

"Sorry for what?" I said from the bed, talking now to an empty room, asking questions of shadows.

I got up, went to the window and looked out. He was my friend, yeah, but I closed the window after him nonetheless. I liked him, Death. Not sure I trusted him, though. Besides, everything seems creepier in the middle of the night, am I right?

Back to sleep and the next thing I remember is waking up to my Da screaming. I jumped out of bed like it was on fire and ran down the hall to my folks' room, saw the old man bent over the bed, hysterical.

Mum had died in the night.

Heart failure, just like Mrs. Haberdash, the piano tutor. Very rare, apparently. Unusual, they said after, when the doctors got to her. I thought but didn't say, *Yeah, tell that to Haberdash*. It was becoming his specialty for those more sudden rug pulls, I suppose.

Obviously, I was pissed off. I tried to confront him about it, ask him why he didn't at least warn me. Told him I thought we were mates. Told him what's the point of being best friends with someone if they can't pull you a solid every now and then? Ain't that what friends are for? Jesus, would it have killed him to do me one favor, and let my ma be alive? I missed her. Cried and cried for days, for fuck sake.

He showed at the funeral, and I couldn't stay upset. It was big of him, and if I'm being honest, I was glad he was there. So I let it slide, and we came to an understanding about certain things.

"We all go alone, John," he said during the viewing, when we were sitting in the car park tossing pebbles at the hearse's hubcaps. "Ain't nothing changing that."

"Not you, eh?" I said, not even sure if I was right about that one. "Immortal, et cetera."

He didn't say anything.

"And besides," I continued, "we don't go alone, do we? You're there."

He shook his head, whispered to me quietly as if we were talking during a eulogy. "No one ever sees me, mate. See, I step in right after. Well, sort of. I mean, I'm there when they, you know…"

I nodded, not saying it aloud on account of it'd be bad taste, being Mum's funeral.

"Anyway, we all go alone. Even me. My job is more along the lines of guidance, see? If it weren't for me, fuckin' souls would be stuck in a dead body for eternity, and who'd want that?"

I shook my head, frowned. "Not me, that's for fuckin sure."

"Exactly," he said, and patted my hand with his cold one. I looked at him and he was smiling. I didn't trust that smile, and I can't say I rightly believed him about that "not being part of the dying" bit, but what was I gonna do? Call him a liar? He was my best mate. And besides, we all got jobs to do, and not one of us likes 'em. So I let it drop.

A YEAR LATER he took cousin Bernie, who I used to play lawn darts with, and who'd once put one right through my foot after an argument about whether I had or had not seen his girlfriend naked when she and I played doctor a few years back (I had). When Bernie was killed, I was better about not holding it against Death. Helped that he didn't need to climb through my room for access, but I also like to feel I'd grown a bit wiser.

Besides, Bernie died in a wreck. Where I come from that's pretty much natural causes. The roads are shite.

DEATH AND I decided to attend university together, neither of us much liking the idea of having to go it alone, at least that first year. We were both outcasts, see. Me because I was skinny and tall and had a dead tooth I refused to have pulled. He because, well, the obvious I suppose. Although his job never really bothered me (outside of his killing my ma), so our not being all that liked, or popular, certainly aided the strength of our friendship.

At university things went along as they did for anyone. We each made new friends, but stayed close nonetheless. When one of the guys in Death's new circle hung himself over a girl, some of the others held him accountable, or at least culpable, and he fell out a bit with that group. So it was important to him that he and I stayed tight, as sort of a fall back I imagine, but I had no problem with it. He was my fall back, as well. That's what best friends are for, init?

It was near the end of our second year that he came to me one morning, head bowed, and asked to speak with me in private. It gave me a bad feeling, and my guts were found to be right a few minutes later when he told me.

Turned out my da was to be taken later that day.

"He's gonna choke on a lambchop bit," Death said. "At dinner, alone. I'm sorry. But," he continued, almost excitedly, "I wanted to give you a heads up, you know? So that you wouldn't be sore, like last time."

I nodded and took it all in. I loved my da, and would miss him horribly. I wasn't sure what the world was going to look like without my parents, both dying so young, so tragically. Still, it was aces of him to tell me ahead of time.

"Can I call him? Just... say hello one last time?"

Death looked at me, met my eyes kinda funny, very serious like. "You can't warn him," he said. "It won't matter, anyway."

"I know," I said. "I won't."

He kept looking at me a minute, and just as I was getting a creepy-crawly sensation up my spine, he smiled and nodded, put a hand on my shoulder and squeezed. "Sure, mate. I'll step out, give you some privacy. I got a thing to do, anyway."

So I called Da, and just asked him how he was doing. If he was holding up all right. It was a nice talk, one of the nicer we'd ever had. We each told the other that we loved them, and part of me wondered if maybe he knew, if maybe... well, he knew who my friends were, didn't he?

I did inquire, albeit seamlessly into the rest of the conversation, if his insurance was paid up (it was).

I hung up and started packing. A few days later, I was at his funeral, Death at my side.

AFTER A FEW awkward encounters with the opposite sex, and after much comparing of notes, Death and I both found girls to mess with at school. He more than I, however.

Death didn't have as much trouble with the ladies as I did (dead tooth, etc.). He had the goth girls pretty much wrapped around his finger, and no one ever dared mess with him at parties, and he often had his drinks bought for him at the pub by some bloke attempting to bribe his good graces. But the girls he attracted were thrill-seekers for the most part, and never stuck. He was just another cock, after all, and whenever he'd be dumped we'd get a pint and laugh about it. Still, I knew it made him sad, and that he'd genuinely liked one or two of the girls, so I did my best to cheer him up if I could.

"Don't matter," he'd say, after three or four drinks. "Like I always tell you, we all die alone in the end, I can fucking guarantee you that, my friend."

It made me sad when he talked about death, which I know is stupid, or ironic, but he had a way of speaking on the subject with such authority that it never came off as small talk as it might with other folks. When he spoke on it, he knew of what he was talking about, that's for damn sure. So it gave some weight, you know? Like a weatherman on about global warming. Just rings more true, yeah? Authorities and such.

As for my love life, it's pretty simple.

Sophie.

Just Sophie, my one and only. I fell for her like a ton of bricks in our third year. We were both studying astronomy, both fascinated with the stars, and we became study partners after being forced into it our first week of class when random lots were drawn. Teacher's way of getting folks to know one another, I guess. Still, we did, and we are, if you know my meaning.

Sophie and I married at the clerk's office, with only her sister and mother present on her side (her dad being estranged), and just Death next to me, handing me the ring, being my best man. After, we all went for drinks, and had a time of it. Death danced with Sophie, her sister and her mum, which was sweet, and the small band played a waltz for our wedding dance.

TIME MARCHES ON, though, and as the years passed Death and I grew apart.

Sophie and I took a place in the city, and Death travelled quite a bit on business, so it was a matter of stationary versus motion. Still, we saw each other on holidays, and he always had some pale-faced, black-haired lass on his arm, so I suppose he was happy in a way. I certainly was.

Sophie and I got on even better in marriage than we had as lovers. We were soulmates, Sophie and I. It's true. I took a job at an insurance firm (selling life, primarily), and Sophie wanted to teach, being a lover of children. We couldn't have any of our own, but that's a story for another day.

But life goes on, grows complex, grows… well, just grows, doesn't it?

Didn't see Death much, often a year would go by and we wouldn't even speak. When I did see him, he always seemed a bit down, a bit peevish. Complained about the job and all that. It was hard, I guess. Lots of travel. Tough work, I'd think. Certainly not the most uplifting of professions. I worried about him quite a bit, being lonely, a cast-off. It's a hard life, being Death.

"And how's Sophie?" he asked one evening over pints, having met me during a layover on his way to the States.

"Oh, fine, fine," I answered. "Still teaching. Loves it, though, just loves it."

"And how's her darling sister? Fanny."

And so it went. Small talk and catching up. He still single, me still married and living the nine-to-five. Layovers and holidays. Occasional dinners and phone calls. E-mails. He'd tell me of exotic places, of strange adventures.

Years went by, and they were happy years. All of them.

I loved her so.

He took Sophie in her 67th year.

He sat with me afterward, as she lay in the other room, skin cooling. We'd moved to a house by then. Garden out back, long drive through trees in front. She was setting to retire. I had already done so a couple years back. We had planned to travel, to see more of the world. There was *so* much we hadn't seen, so much we hadn't done. I missed her in the past, and the future, if that makes sense. Sad both ways.

We sat on my sofa, his hand on mine. He looked younger than me, by decades truth be told. He said he aged slower than most. Not me. I'd aged right on schedule. Grown a nice belly, lost most of the hair, wore spectacles to see the labels on my and Sophie's medicine.

Sophie, despite being technically a month my elder, had always looked younger than me, I can tell you. Almost as young as Death himself. She'd been so beautiful, so energetic. And now she was gone, and I was truly, desperately, alone.

"You made it quick, yeah?" was all I could say.

"Of course, mate. I do what I can," he said, and I nodded, and cried. He put his arm over my shoulder as I slobbered and despaired, hating life, hating him.

As he was leaving, I stopped him, and you could say it was pity, but it wasn't that, it was anger, and selfishness. That's the truth of it.

"Don't come," I said. "To the funeral. Don't come."

He didn't turn, didn't look at me. Just stood by the open door, head bowed. A dark figure against the pale morning light, an empty man, a lonely man. He nodded, but then said, "I'd like to. I loved her."

"No, thanks," I answered. "Don't think I want to see you again, actually." And, without another word between us, I went to say goodbye to my wife, to wet her dress with my tears.

Nearly twenty years went by after that day, and I regretted my words every one of them. I missed Sophie, and I missed my friend.

Because I never did see him again.

Until the end, that is.

"COME FOR ME, then?" I said.

I was in my late eighties, not sure which exact one because I'd stopped counting; and besides, they'd been eventless years.

I was in the garden, watching bees steal pollen from Sophie's flowers. The place was more overgrown now than when she'd tended it, but I was old, and tired, and could only do so much to keep it going.

I sensed him before I saw him, standing by the back door, watching me watch the bees.

He walked toward me without a word, sat down lightly in the garden chair neighboring my own, a small table between us with a glass of iced tea perspiring on its top. We sat in silence, watched the sun lower in the sky, watched the birds flitter about, watched the long grass lean in the breeze.

"Drink?" I said, still not looking at his face, not wanting to see what expression he'd be wearing. "Iced tea is the strongest I have these days, I'm afraid."

He said nothing a moment, and I waited, listening to the wind rustle the tall flowers. "I'm sorry, John," he said finally, and I heard the despair in his voice. It sent a chill through me.

"Nah," I said lightly, holding back my fear. "I'm ready. Have been since Sophie passed. No point, really."

"No," he said. "I'm sorry about everything. If I could... I had no choice, mate..."

I bowed my head and started to weep. Just an old man crying in his garden. Pathetic, really.

"It's okay," I said, and wiped my face with my poorly laundered shirtsleeve. "You're still my best friend, and I understand. I'm sorry I told you not to come to Sophie's funeral. That was wrong of me."

I could see him nodding in my peripheral vision and, finally, I turned to face him.

He'd aged. Not as much as I, but certainly more than I'd expected. Yes, it was a hard life, I suppose. Must take its toll like anything.

"So what's it to be then?" I asked, smiling at him, feeling warmth when he smiled back. "The old heart failure? Like our piano tutor? Not very original, that."

He laughed, and the sky lightened. "No, John, I'm not here to take you."

I must admit, for all my talk, I really wasn't ready. I was actually quite scared being honest, and so was thankful to hear him say it. "No?" I said, not sounding too relieved, lest he give me shit about it.

"No," he said, then nodded toward the edge of the garden. "Have a look, mate."

Sophie stood there, young and beautiful and vibrant as the day I'd first met her. I was astounded, and leapt to my feet in happy surprise, a surprise quickly doubled by the spryness of my upward spring, at how the knee joints hadn't creaked when I bounced up, how my back hadn't murmured a complaint, at how very detailed the flowers were.

I turned to him and almost laughed at his smile of victory, of pleasure. He held out his hand and I took it, helped him up to stand beside me.

"You said we all died alone," I said, joy and strength filling me like light.

"Not my friends, they bloody don't," he said, and put a firm hand on my shoulder. "Mind if I stay a while?"

"Not at all, mate," I replied, growing brighter by the second.

I felt Sophie's hand slip into mine, felt the soft heat of her, and together we three looked on, in wonder, at the beautiful...

ACKNOWLEDGMENTS

So many folks to thank, but I'll keep it brief, because if you're anything like me you have other books to read, am I right? Let's go:

First off, thanks to my friend Josh Malerman for the incredible introduction. I've known Josh a few years now but if you'd told me when I first picked up *Bird Box* back in 2014 that the author of that straight-up classic would, one day, not only be my good friend but also be writing the introduction to my second story collection? I'd have said you were more nuts than a squirrel's nest in high summer. I'm so very grateful for him taking the time and for his incredible support.

Secondly, want to thank my amazing support at home – to my lovely, amazing wife and my warm-hearted, fast-growing son – thank you guys. Especially to Stephanie, who puts up with all the crazy (and there's quite a bit of it to put up with).

To my Patrons – thank you all for the support. Gonna give special shout-outs to my Stalkers: Alexander Mutz, Juha Kivela, and Adrienne Silk. Thank you so very much for hanging in there with me and believing in me. Can't tell you how much I appreciate it.

He already got the dedication but what the hell, I'll thank him twice. Laird Barron, thank you brother. Also want to give some shout-outs to some authors and readers who have been amazingly supportive by reading rough, early work and helping me make it better: Thomas Joyce, John Foster, Douglass Wynne, Paul Tremblay, John McFarland, Sean O'Connor, Duane Pesice, Jake Marley and many others who I'm forgetting, I'm sure. I'll get you next time!

Random shout-outs: Alessandro Manzetti, Jose Angel De Dios García, Jakub Němeček, Justin Burnett, Richard Chizmar, Sadie Hartmann, Mike Davis, John Langan, Jon Padgett, Kelly Young, Andy Davidson, Brendan Deneen, Aaron French...man, I could go on forever.

Thanks to my agent, Elizabeth Copps, who works so hard to get my work into the right hands.

Lastly, as it pertains to the book you're holding, a huge thanks to Francois Vaillancourt for the wonderful artwork gracing the cover, and for Steve Berman, who took me on and gave these stories a home.

And, for-real-lastly, as always, to you dear reader. Without whom I do not exist.

PF

ABOUT THE AUTHOR

PHILIP FRACASSI is also the author of the award-winning story collection, *Behold the Void*, which won "Best Collection of the Year" from both *This Is Horror* and *Strange Aeons* Magazine. His novel, *Boys in the Valley*, is coming October, 2021, from Earthling Publications. His stories have been published in numerous magazines and anthologies, including *Best Horror of the Year*, *Nightmare Magazine*, *Black Static*, *Dark Discoveries*, *Cemetery Dance* and others. Philip's work has been translated into multiple languages. His books have been favorably reviewed in publications such as *The New York Times*, *LOCUS Magazine*, and *Rue Morgue*. The *New York Times* called his work "terrifically scary." As a screenwriter, his feature films have been distributed by Disney Entertainment and Lifetime Television. He currently has several stories under option for film/tv adaption. For more information on his books and screenplays, visit his website at pfracassi.com. He also has active profiles on Facebook, Instagram (pfracassi) and Twitter (@philipfracassi). He lives in Los Angeles, California, and is represented by Elizabeth Copps at Copps Literary Services (info@coppsliterary.com).

CPSIA information can be obtained
at www.ICGtesting.com
Printed in the USA
JSHW040925140521
14669JS00002B/10